TALK TO ME

TALK TO ME

PAT SIMMONS

URBAN
CHRISTIAN

www.urbanchristianonline.net

Urban Books
78 East Industry Court
Deer Park, NY 11729

ISBN 13: 978-1-60162-895-4
ISBN 10: 1-60162-895-1

First Mass Market Printing March 2011
First Trade Paperback Printing November 2008
Printed in the United States of America

10   9   8   7   6   5   4   3   2   1

This is a work of fiction. Any references or similarities to actual events, real people, living, or dead, or to real locales are intended to give the novel a sense of reality. Any similarity in other names, characters, places, and incidents is entirely coincidental.

Distributed by Kensington Corp.
Submit Wholesale Orders to:
Kensington Publishing Corp.
C/O Penguin Group (USA) Inc.
Attention: Order Processing
405 Murray Hill Parkway
East Rutherford, NJ 07073-2316
Phone: 1-800-526-0275
Fax: 1-800-227-9604

Praises for *Guilty of Love* . . .

Pat Simmons' sometimes whimsical approach to delivering the message of salvation is anchored by opportune scriptures. The author boldly tackles issues like abortion, child abuse and anger toward God, adeptly guiding readers into romance, reconciliation and restoration as this novel flows effortlessly from haunting pasts to delectable happiness.

Robin R. Pendleton for Romantic Times BOOKreviews, 4 Stars

Non-Christians could enjoy this story without feeling like they were being beat in the head about their sins and choices in life. The author really outdid herself with this novel . . . as her first novel you can be sure that her gift is of God. I would have expected this work to have come from a more experienced author. And you know that a sequel is a MUST!

Idrissa Uqdah, AALBC.com Review Team, 5 Stars

In the book, *Guilty of Love,* I was intrigued as to how Pat Simmons was able to intertwine African-American history throughout the book. I really admired how she took each character through his or her spiritual walk with God. The scriptures she chose were perfect, and you can see the religious transformation each person was going through. *Guilty of Love* is a very good read.

Reviewed by Jackie for Urban Reviews, 5 Stars

A fine example of inspirational romance; I was captured from the beginning and was well satisfied to the end.
Reviewed by Inspirational Romance Writers, 8 out of 10 Stars

I loved the fact that Pat Simmons used genealogical lines. I learned valuable information about black history. *Guilty of Love* was a very good read. So there had better be a part two in the works! It has to be! I need to know what happens with the little secret.
Reviewed by Carmen for OOSA Online Book Club "O.O.S.A," 5 Stars

DEDICATION

Talk to Me is dedicated to my brother-in-law, Ben Jeffery "Rusty" Simmons—deaf since birth. Love ya!

And to all the deaf ministries across the world, including that of Bethesda Temple Church.

ACKNOWLEDGMENTS

My help cometh from the Lord, which made heaven and earth, Psalm 121:2.

I can't take credit for my own blessings, because God has no respect of persons.

Therefore, I appreciate Him for opening the doors for me to tell a story through *Urban Christian*. Not just for me, but for all the other talented authors under the imprint, and the authors-to-be who are waiting for the call. Thank you, Jesus.

Talk to Me Cover Model: Fred "Mr. Romance Finalist" Williams.

Thanks to: The village people: Sometimes we choose friends, but the true blessings come when God chooses them for us. *A friend loveth at all times.* (Proverbs 17)

Nicole Ferweda—I thank God for sending you my way.

Angi "AJ" Jones—My story consultant and voice of creativity.

Lisa Watson—You're the butter to my popcorn.

Tina Ezell-Hull—Thanks for having the Cavalry ready at all times.

Alicia Brown—The "sister" who inspires me.

Joylynn Jossel—You have been a blessing. Thanks for falling in love with my characters!

Bishop Johnson's, January 9, 2008 Bible class, for giving me a better understanding of consequences.

Elder Ron Stephens for accepting and answering all my emails.

Brother Emeric Martin Jr. and Evang. Darlene Martin for going the extra mile to secure my blessings; the McMullenses, Crossleys, Don and Mona Whalens, who have supported me in the past without me asking. Thank you.

The Rep Theatre in St. Louis, Goodman Theatre in Chicago, and actress L'Oreal Jackson.

The National Deaf Black Advocates and Pamela Lloyd.

Felicia and Renwick at Goin' Postal—you have been an author's best friend.

Special thanks to my family:

Kerry—"The" husband and a good man who has endured my writing schedule. I can see him smiling now and saying, "Whew, I'm glad that's over!"

Jared—For the touchdown.

Simi—She just wanted me to mention her name.

My many cousins (Cole, Wades, Carters, Browns, Palmers, Wilkersons, Jamieson, Thomas, Simmons, Downers, etc.) across the country, in-laws, mother and siblings.

My friends at News-Mart. Your support and love have been not only overwhelming, but also humbling.

All my readers and new friends across the country, especially California and Florida!

PROLOGUE

On Thanksgiving Day, at nine-thirty in the morning, I fell in love. It was swift and irrevocable. In other words, I lost my common sense. Without warning or fanfare, I succumbed to Mackenzie Norton's allure. Love is such a strange emotion—never enough time to savor all the sweet moments. It's hindsight now that I've lost her.

Sometimes the memories taunt me, other times they provide comfort. When my eyes close, Mackenzie appears. Her brown eyes twinkled, causing a sexy glow to spread across her face. Her hypnotic trance released strong vibes that were undeniable. She was such a puzzle, allowing me the pleasure of seeing how her pieces fit together. Inside the church walls, she was sober. With me, her mischievous antics would issue challenges.

Mackenzie. The way she commanded her body possessed my senses. Thank you, God, for my eyes to see. With deliberate movements, Mackenzie's hands beckoned to me, sprinkling magic along the way. Long, slender arms danced with the grace of a swan.

For the initial five seconds I laid eyes on her, I dismissed her until she demanded my attention without trying. A gentle spirit tempered her powerful personality. Yes, Mackenzie's magnetism was undeniable. She became my teacher and I, her willing student. I chuckle at the memories.

Mackenzie had the most enchanting smile. Ah! Did I mention her lips? They were my worst distraction and her best asset—shapely and full, in a natural pout. They moved like a musician manipulating his instruments. Have I mentioned she was a feisty, five-foot-four-inch beauty who was committed to her convictions?

Glistening skin reminded me of wet brown sugar—my attraction. A head of messy curls was her crowning glory. On any other woman, the look would've been scary, but it was Mackenzie's trademark—stylish, sassy, and sexy.

During our quiet time, we mouthed promises to each other. We honored each word with sincerity and care, vowing not to break one. It happened anyway. Mackenzie was to blame, or maybe I was.

One evening we savored the quietness. We were being silly as we watched the sunset at a deserted playground. I spoke aloud a wish as I pushed Mackenzie on a swing. "I miss dancing. The final song I heard was Donna Summers' *Last Dance.* How prophetic. More than anything, I wish we could dance the night away," I had told her.

Mackenzie dug her heels into the ground, halting the swing. Turning around, she finger-kissed the sadness, disappointment, and pain from my eyes. "I promise, Noel, one day, we'll dance." I didn't hear her, but I knew she was sharing a secret when she touched me. Now our chance will never come. I hate broken promises.

It had nothing to do with me being one of twenty-eight million deaf Americans. It wasn't from birth. I was almost sixteen years old when the doctors delivered the tragic news to my parents that I had lost my hearing. They were in shock. My mother cried, knowing my family lacked the skills to communicate with me. I'm lucky—no, I'm blessed—to be alive, unlike my childhood buddy, Keith Morrow, who died in the freak explosion near a fireworks plant. He was an only child.

Anyway, I grew accustomed to interpreters signing at events, but it was Mackenzie's contagious enthusiasm that sucked me into a storm, whirling me into the eye of the hurricane. Never had I witnessed an interpreter wrapped up in so much pleasure and total involvement in communicating what was happening around me. Not only did I see and feel; Mackenzie made me believe I could hear the choir's rendition of *My Life is in Your Hands*, a Kirk Franklin song I had never heard.

My heart jumped at a thunderous rumble inflicted by Mackenzie's imaginary wooden drumsticks, pounding invisible drums and tapping fictitious cymbals. With confidence, her fingers stroked pretend piano keys. Her expression, most humorous, depicted the altos' deep voices and the sopranos' melodious high pitches.

Who knew that when I stepped into that church, I would enter utopia? Suddenly, I felt like praising God for what I had—my eyes to gaze, hands to enjoy her soft skin, and a heart that throbbed faster when she was close. At that moment, for some unexplained reason, I thanked God that I was deaf. Can you believe that? I thanked God for allowing the worst event to happen in my life, because it made me the happiest. How else would I've met a woman whose love was fierce and unconditional? Then months after our meeting, I, Noel Richardson, lost Mackenzie Norton.

LET ME EXPLAIN HOW IT ALL HAPPENED

CHAPTER 1

Have you ever had one of those days where, while you're driving, you decide at the last minute to change course, to go a scenic route? That's what happened to me while cruising through Richmond Heights, a St. Louis suburban neighborhood. I could blame the detour on the comfort of the car I was test driving, a platinum Cadillac CTS—the Motor Trend Car of the Year.

I'd been searching for a while. Not for God, but for a car that was sleek and roomy for my six-foot-three-inch muscular frame. At thirty-one years old, I bench press almost 300 pounds, workout five days a week, and maintain a healthy weight of 210 pounds. I'm also an educated black man with two degrees.

Church was the farthest thing from my mind when I drove past a large portable sign, flashing a message in bold, bright-red lights: *Thanksgiving morning worship service, beginning at nine. Deaf ministry is available.*

Hmmm, any excuses had expired for skipping a

service with real people and a reach-out-and-touch pastor. I'd stopped attending church a long time ago because the experience left me too frustrated. For years, my Sunday morning rituals consisted of reading several chapters in my Bible and watching two hours of televangelists. Although I read lips, I'd missed something in the translation—the excitement, the power, the inspiration—despite watching an interpreter at the bottom of my TV screen.

I hadn't known that a Holy Ghost-filled church with a Deaf Ministry was minutes away when I had recently purchased my house. It was an answer to my inconsistent prayers. The one-story brick ranch house that had recently been renovated was closer to my office. Neighbors appeared to compete for camera-ready manicured lawns and intentionally posed shrubbery. Everything was perfect except the decorum. That proved to be a first-time lab experiment gone wrong. Each picture, rug, and piece of furniture confessed that all rooms were under construction.

On Thanksgiving morning, at the designated hour, I arrived at the church's corner parking lot. I'd never attended service on a holiday. The number of cars reminded me of an auto dealership as I scrambled for a space in the strategically landscaped area. I parked, got out, and began my walk to the entrance. Large weather-bleached stones and mortar fortified the church's exterior. Once inside, my eyes widened at the modern sleek décor camouflaged by the vintage front building.

Marble pillars stood at attention between stained-glass windows that allowed anyone to peep into the sanctuary. A warm presence touched me before anyone approached, as if Jesus was beckoning me home. Glancing up, I grinned. My anointing was really the outside chill that had activated the blast of heat inside the lobby.

"Welcome, my brother." A man, maybe in his fifties, saluted me and added a huge smile.

"I'm here for the deaf ministry," I signed, hoping he understood. He didn't.

As if summoned, an elderly usher appeared dressed in a faded black suit, white gloves, and a purple bow tie. After bowing like a butler, he did an about-face and walked away. I took that as my cue to follow. Entering the sanctuary, the size overpowered me. It was spacious with purple cushions and eye-catching crystal chandeliers, sparkling like night stars.

Deep-purple carpet was so plush I felt guilty for wearing shoes. Numerous ushers patrolled the three aisles as if they were programmable toy soldiers. Others were sprinkled throughout the sanctuary.

I grimaced as my escort guided me to my seat. Why did visitors always have to be paraded to the front line? I didn't have to guess that the four roped-off pews were the designated deaf area. Thanking the usher, I shook off my black cashmere coat and draped it over my arm. Scooting inside the pew, I laid it down with my Bible.

After nodding to those already seated, I sat. Bowing my head, I prayed, asking God to tell me if this is where He wanted me. Opening my eyes, I stretched my legs and wondered if my comrades were members or fellow curious visitors.

Flexing my muscles, I crossed my arms and waited for the show to begin. I have to be honest; I wasn't easily impressed. Not everyone who called themselves interpreters were polished, nor did they enjoy the communication. It was a job and a well-paying one, too. As a first-time visitor, I made note of my surroundings. Despite the grandeur, it had a cozy feel.

The next thing that caught my eyes were the people crammed into a three-level stadium style seating—the choir stood several feet behind the podium. Then two women who appeared in a doorway stole my attention.

From a distance, neither was bad looking. The taller one was dressed to showcase her endowment and I admired her bountiful assets. Her hair was straight and poured over her shoulders as a silver-colored dress clutched her body. Her shimmering stockings were meant to catch a man's eye. They did.

The other woman, who was shorter, snatched my attention. There was something about her that challenged me to look away if I dared. Her clothes were bold, her hair wild, and the combination was stunning. I had no doubts about her endowments; although it was clear she attempted to conceal them.

What had I been missing sitting at home in front of a television? Wow, was my first thought regarding her abundance of hair. I smirked at her colorful scarf that failed to restrain rebellious curls. *Yeah, set them free*, I taunted inwardly. The way she jutted her chin and held her head showed she had confidence. Her beauty was understated.

Closing my eyes, I regulated my breathing, and then reminded myself where I sat. Yes, I was in church, but God wanted me to appreciate His handiwork. A beautiful woman was worth admiring. I inhaled a deep, measured breath and opened my eyes.

The pair chatted as they walked, throwing air kisses, shaking hands, and returning waves to church members. Eventually, they approached the roped-off pews and stopped. They made eye contact with our group for a brief moment, as if they were taking a head count. The tall sister's eyes met mine a second and then a third time.

I couldn't believe I looked away first, thinking, *I'm trying to behave. I did come for the Word, not a woman.* In sync, they sat in folding chairs and faced us. They were the interpreters. *Okay, show me what ya got.* I smirked.

Unfortunately, the showcase interpreter did. She yawned wide enough for a dental exam as her eyes darted around the sanctuary. *Was she bored already?* I wondered. That was not a good sign. The other woman's head was bowed in prayer. The choir opened their mouths and swayed to sounds that were prohibited to one of my five senses. It didn't matter as I felt the powerful vibrations under my feet. My heart pounded in harmony. Masterfully, that interpreter moved her fingers, telling me a story that defied me to blink or turn away.

A large overhead screen unraveled from the ceiling, displaying lyrics to "You Are Welcome in This Place." If this worship period was a warm-up exercise before the sermon, then maybe I was in the right place.

Ending her prayer, the understated interpreter's face glowed as she signed the song with conviction. I chanced looking around. Yep, others were spellbound. When she stood and swayed, I followed.

When the singers stilled their mouths and sat, the other interpreter, whose face was draped in boredom, took over interpreting. Again, she didn't stifle a yawn as a man came to the microphone. She signed, Psalm 69:30: *I will praise the name of God with a song, and will magnify him with thanksgiving.*

It didn't take long for my gaze to stray as I attempted to read the preacher's lips. My heart ached to hear his sermon on magnifying God. I wanted to stand like a few others with my arms crossed, pacing in place, feasting on the Word from God.

"I don't like her. She's ugly," signed a little girl, sitting on my left who I hadn't noticed.

The child wrinkled her nose, rolled her eyes, and stuck a finger in her mouth as if she was trying to induce vomiting. I toyed with my mustache in amusement. The girl was half right. The endowed interpreter definitely wasn't ugly. She just had a bad attitude. Not wanting to encourage the child, I kept a blank expression.

"Keisha Marie Campbell, you're acting ugly. See how quiet your sister, Daphne, is behaving? Stop it or we're going home," signed her mother with an intimidating game face. Twisting her mouth in defiance, Keisha bypassed the interpreter and stared at the pulpit.

Minutes later, someone introduced the pastor,

Zachary Coleman, for the sermon. The message was riveting, "Letting God Loose." Almost an hour later, his sermon ended with me questioning if I was letting God have His full reign in my life. The preacher extended his arms to the congregation for the altar call, a simple invitation for the un-saved, sick, and spiritually afflicted people to seek salvation. The enchanting interpreter relieved the other woman, and she became the evangelist call-ing sinners to repent. "*Won't you come?*" she signed.

Like a pied piper on her musical flute, she en-ticed dozens to flock to the aisle, making their way to the front for prayer and baptism. "*Won't you come?*"

"*Why won't you come?*" she signed a third time, in-terpreting for Pastor Coleman.

I stood. I didn't believe in begging for anything. On the flipside, I felt no one should have to beg me to pray, so I accepted the appeal. I joined oth-ers in the aisle. Granted, I hadn't been an on-the-church-roll member in years, but I'd visited enough services to know the difference that I felt that morning. I needed restoring, and God was faithful. If I repented of the sins, those I could re-call and those hidden, God would forgive me.

The altar call meant different things in various churches. Not only was it an invitation for disciple-ship, whether someone accepted it or not, but prayer was always available, which was exactly what I needed. Halfway in the aisle, a minister met and hugged me. Then his warm breath brushed against my ear. I cupped my ear and shook my head to let him know I couldn't hear. He shrugged and instructed me to close my eyes, bow my head, and lift my hands as he dabbed a bit of holy oil on my forehead.

During the prayer, I recalled the first time I'd read a message preached from Mark 17:32-37: *And were beyond measure astonished, saying, He hath done all things well: he maketh both the deaf to hear, and the dumb to speak.* My family believed God in that scripture, including me. Without much internal debating, we, as a family, repented and requested the burial in water in Jesus' name. In the span of a few hours, God filled us with the evidence of the Holy Ghost, experiencing the speaking in unknown tongues. Reminiscing, I admitted it had been a long time since I felt that kinship.

My heart pounded as my tongue vibrated in my mouth. The anointing had a rippling effect on my body as it shook, but I knew it was God renewing my spirit. No telling how much time had passed as the minister prayed, but I couldn't make up for all the time I had sidestepped on God's praise.

The minister tapped my shoulder, and my eyes fluttered open as he removed his hand, ending the prayer. Wiggling my fingers in praise, I turned around, found my way back to my pew, and re-took my seat. Taking a handkerchief from my back pocket, I wiped the perspiration off my face. Perhaps I was in the right church. Once I composed myself, I opened a Bible before the aroma of a turkey dinner drifted into the sanctuary and headed straight for my nose. I looked up at the two women.

"Don't forget, church," the nice interpreter signed

as Pastor Zachary Coleman grinned from the pulpit, holding up a finger. *"We have prepared a Thanksgiving feast. I'm sure I'm not the only one who can smell it. Free to anyone who wishes to stay and fellowship."*

His announcement reminded me of the traditional noon meal awaiting my brothers, Pierce, Caleb, and me at our parents' house. Gina Richardson instilled fear in us early about the repercussions of standing her up when it came to her cooking. My dad enjoyed letting her have her way, not only in the kitchen, but also in the home.

Pierce, the oldest and the most compassionate, was always inclusive when it came to his brothers. Caleb, two years younger than my thirty-one years, had little patience when I didn't digest a joke fast enough, or spoke too loudly during a televised game. A powerful voice tore through my head, pulling me away from my thoughts and commanding me to stay for the fellowship. Decision made, I was staying.

After the dismissal, I loosened the muscles in my shoulders before reaching for my coat and Bible. Joining the exodus, I lagged behind rambunctious kids, soundless chatty teenagers, and slow-stepping elders.

The crowd curved around the corner to a corridor that opened to a banquet hall. The walls were painted a once-popular cotton-candy-blue, which contrasted with the updated light fixtures and stain-glass bay windows. The size reminded me of a high school cafeteria.

The atmosphere was festive, jolly, and hectic. Preteens carried food trays to senior citizens gathered at designated tables. Toddlers played hide-and-seek, using their parents as shields. Surprisingly, some men were already dissecting a second plate.

Leisurely, I glanced around for a seat until I saw *her*, the interpreter who fascinated me during morning worship. Good manners restrained me in a grip lock from shoving others in a sprint to the buffet and introducing myself. It had nothing to do with hunger. Several women were serving food, including both interpreters. I stopped moving.

Years ago, I had mastered the skill of lip-reading, most times ignoring the insults thrown at me that were usually reserved for behind people's backs. Since I couldn't hear, most assumed it didn't make a difference to slur my character in front of my face. Zooming in on the two interpreters, I listened with my eyes as I laid my things on a nearby table.

"I can't believe the turnout for the Deaf Ministry! I'm glad we're meeting a need. I counted at least twenty new visitors. I know God is pleased."

Miss Bountiful Endowment's face still lacked any luster when she responded, "Well, I'm glad you're excited, Mack, because the only fine brother I noticed was among the dead—I mean deaf, and believe me, I looked more than once. I've been praying for God to send me a mate. I hope that wasn't it," she paused, dumping green beans in a plate before she continued complaining, "I know I heard His voice saying, 'Soon,' then in walks this deaf mute. Girl, God can have him back. How can a deaf man, and I don't care how fine he is, meet any woman's needs?"

"Valerie Preston!" Mack said, shocked.

So that's her name, Valerie. She had no idea that no woman had complained about me meeting their needs. Unfortunately, that was during some down time between when the Lord first saved me and the televangelists. Today, I was searching for a woman who could meet more than my physical needs.

"Well, I'm being honest. Why does something always have to be wrong with the fine men? What a shame, for all his good looks, it will go to waste. Ha! Brother man had some serious muscles straining under that suit," Valerie commented. "Girl, I thought the Incredible Hulk was going to bust out." She laughed, but I missed the joke.

"And I thought we came to praise the Lord, shame on me." Mack's lips twisted in disgust.

"Yeah, shame on you, Mackenzie, for not noticing Mr. Fineness and Flawness, because he had some flaws. When he wiggled his mustache, I almost fainted, but I would've missed something. A defective man has no right to look so sexy! Maybe he was sitting in the wrong section."

Valerie spared me no mercy. Her hypocrisy temporarily overshadowed the church fellowship, celebrating a day of thanksgiving. I pitied any man who had the misfortune of being the one for her.

God prohibited my anger from taking root. Instead, a genuine grin stretched across my face. *Mackenzie.* I rolled her name around in my head. She didn't look like a Mackenzie, as if a name came with a description, definition, and warning.

"Val, that is the most non-Christian, insensitive, and rudest comment to utter," Mackenzie accused, appearing appalled at the same time I registered the insults. Questions raced through my mind, including whether the two were close friends.

"Why are you even a part of this ministry? God doesn't like ugly, and girl, you're looking rather unattractive right now."

"Ben," Valerie gave the one-word answer with a shrug.

My interest peaked, I focused harder. That's when two women approached me, interrupting my newly addictive soap opera.

"Hi. I'm Sister Alexis Brown. Glad you could come out today," one of them said to me.

I gave them a genuine smile before placing both of my hands to my lips to say, *"Thank you."* To an outsider, the gesture was blowing a kiss. I finger-spelled my name and indicated I was about to eat.

Confusion marred their faces. Clearly they weren't part of the Deaf Ministry. Embarrassed, they waved goodbye before hurrying off. *Good*, I thought as I refocused on Valerie and Mackenzie. I didn't know how much I had missed.

"Benson Little, he was sooo fine, Mack."

"Excuse me, what does a man who doesn't even attend this church have to do with this?" Mackenzie asked before she greeted a small boy and served him a portion from an aluminum pan. "Take your time, Thomas, and be careful," she instructed.

With determined concentration, Thomas slowly walked away, using both hands to balance a plastic plate laden with food.

Valerie continued, "Girl, he needed an extra credit to graduate. When he signed up for American Sign Language class, so did I. You know it's considered a foreign language." She grinned as if her scheme was original. "Bingo! It was the beginning of a relationship when he selected me as his study partner."

"Well, that should explain everything, but it doesn't. By God's grace, we're not on the other side of that pew. Did you hear the message this morning? We're supposed to praise and magnify God, not tear each other down, but you probably missed that part." Mackenzie's eyes were expressive.

Folding my arms, I grinned. I liked Mackenzie's attitude. Maybe she did define her name. A sweet servant when she signed, but a spitfire when provoked. What a kindred spirit. Valerie gave a new meaning to "Don't judge a book by its cover." Physically, she was pleasing to the eye with her nutmeg skin, and shape that wasn't lacking on her tall body. Spiritually, she seemed to lack the essential spiritual fruit of love.

An usher shooed me off the wall, motioning for me to get in line. I mouthed, okay, but didn't move.

"Anyway, I loved the altar call. As always, it's the highlight for me," Mackenzie said.

Valerie squinted. "Please tell me you didn't sign with your eyes closed, again?"

"Yep." Mackenzie bit her lip almost in a tease. "People come to church seeking deliverance. Music soothes the soul, and preaching delivers it, but the baptismal washes their sins away. It's like a 'don't leave home without it' motto. How can you sign without enjoying the beauty of the language? Re-group, Valerie, re-group."

Valerie stopped serving and rolled her eyes. Her free hand rested on her hip. "I know the purpose, Mack. I am a member, too, you know."

The serving line thickened as some returned for seconds. "Glad to know." Mackenzie shrugged. "Anyway, I counted seven guests sitting in the hearing-impaired section. The two little sisters, who couldn't have been more than seven and ten, were adorable in their matching emerald-green dresses with cream collars. I wonder if meningitis, ear infections, or birth defects caused their deafness."

"Girl, you worry too much. Deaf is deaf, the cause is unimportant."

"Repent."

Contrite, Valerie huffed out her chest. "Sorry. Just being honest, I'm glad the outreach ministry is working and our church is growing, but where are the men?" she mumbled as she turned her head, breaking off my interpretation.

"They're coming, Val. Pray on it. Just don't pray amiss for your own selfish wants."

"All I want to do is put my order in for a brother whose skin reminds me of maple syrup, a mustache thick enough to tease a woman's lips, and some biceps and abs. Girl, I'm set for life."

"You're talking about that hearing-impaired brother, aren't you? No woman in this church could help but notice him, but he's still a man who wants the same thing as us—acceptance—instead of having discriminatory remarks thrown his way."

Rubbing my chin, I smirked, impressed. Although Valerie gave an accurate description of my attributes, Mackenzie also noticed.

"Well, he can't hear me, anyway."

Better. I can read your lips, I wanted to confront her. Since I wasn't interested in her, she missed out.

Mackenzie shook her head and directed her attention to the hungry people in line, never looking in my direction. Jostled by some boys horsing around, I was forced off the wall again. This time I took determined steps, approaching the food table. I wasn't hungry. I was intrigued.

With one statement, Mackenzie—a stranger—had, unbeknownst to her, fought a battle that I was equipped to do myself. As the line advanced, on autopilot, I lifted a plastic plate and snatched up a set of napkin-wrapped utensils. I inched closer until I stood face-to-face with Mackenzie. Her smile was unconditional as she reduced me to a servant in her highness' court; because whatever the pretty lady wanted, I wanted exclusive rights to provide it. Whoa, I hadn't been in church in years, and after one day, I was flirting with an interpreter.

Laying her plastic ladle in the pan, she signed, asking me if I preferred turkey or ham, and my choice of side dishes. Grinning like a schoolboy, I pointed to dishes without taking my eyes off her face. She pointed, and I glanced down. I was holding the plate upside down. I shook my head in amusement.

"I'm Noel Richardson," I introduced, signing with my right hand as I held the paper goods in my left.

Releasing the serving spoon, she signed back, *"Praise the Lord, and welcome. I'm Sister Mackenzie Norton."*

"I enjoyed the service today. You were breathtaking. I really felt like I had church, not just being at church."

As she lowered long, thin lashes, blushing, I took note of two things: Mackenzie was beautiful and she wasn't wearing a ring. Good. Honestly, I wasn't looking for it earlier.

"Then I hope you'll come back and visit again."

"Definitely," I responded, lingering at the table until a dark-skinned, wrestler-built brother jokingly tried to push me forward, only I didn't nudge. He gave me a fake apologetic grin as he carried two plates, one tilting with rolls, ham, and string beans. Nodding at Mackenzie, I walked back to where I'd laid my stuff. It also gave me an unobstructed view.

I feasted on Mackenzie while my stomach digested a Thanksgiving meal I didn't taste. I couldn't tear my eyes away from her. With patience, kindness, and attentiveness, Mackenzie continued to feed the never-ending line.

A man, whose oversized head didn't fit his body, scuffled to the buffet table. His faded black jacket with thinned elbows humbled me. My suit, a designer custom-fit, was one of many I'd never subjected to that much wear. His baggy pants hinted of a drastic weight loss. Oddly, his steel-toe shoes shined like military regulation. With two plates stacked lopsided with holiday fixings, he glimpsed suspiciously over his shoulder before leaning closer to Mackenzie.

Concerned, I stilled my fork midway to my mouth. Should I be concerned? I didn't know their relationship. When Mackenzie smiled, I chuckled. The old man was flirting.

As the crowd thinned, Mackenzie, Valerie, and three weary servers collapsed in nearby folding chairs at an abandoned table. The urge was strong for me to lift Mackenzie's feet into a chair and wait on her as if it was our routine. Chiding my foolish thoughts, I approached anyway, not knowing my own intentions.

Leaning down, I spoke close to her ear, praying that I somehow controlled the volume and tone of my voice, "Mackenzie." Turning around, her expression shifted from startled to hypnotic. Honey-brown eyes let me know I had her undivided attention. The moment was sweet until movement of her friend's lips dripped with sarcasm.

"Oh, he talks, but probably rides on a handicap bus."

The scowl Mackenzie shot Valerie was my priceless reward. "You look tired. While I'm up can I get you anything? More punch, rolls, dessert?" I refrained from saying better company.

"Something to drink, please" she didn't sign. Her eyes sparkled with fascination, her cheeks blushed, and she sucked in a deep breath. Then she remembered to hand me her cup. I bit back my own smile. The message was loud enough for even a deaf man to hear. We were attracted to each other.

CHAPTER 2

What had gotten into me to flirt with a woman in the House of God? I smirked as I drove away from my house. That wasn't the first time I asked myself that question since I walked out the church doors, but something about Mackenzie appealed to me. I didn't want to think I had bad taste in choosing dates, but the women before Mackenzie? They seemed shallow now. Without knowing much about the interpreter, I was certain Mackenzie's complexities were as understated as her beauty.

For example, there was Taylor Tillman. She was beautiful, sweet, and I later leaned she was an opportunist. Without asking for an opinion, God let me know that Taylor had no purpose in my life. She was all about appearances, and I still remember the simplicity of our final disagreement.

"What are you saying?" I braced for an argument. Usually I'm the peacemaker, but Taylor was testing me. Something had been brewing between us for a while. I was determined she was going to give me answers that would help me decide if our relationship would continue.

"It's not working, Noel. I'm not deaf. I mean, the more we're together, the more uncomfortable I've become. Every time you take me out to dinner, I have to do all the ordering because you can't hear."

Squinting, my nostrils flared. "But I sure can talk, woman. It's you who preferred to order for both of us, to drive on dates, and on and on." I jabbed a stiff finger in the air. "I was trying to please you! You won't say it to my face, but I see the boredom blooming in your eyes when we're together. You didn't seem to mind my lack of hearing when we started dating. Unless my memory is failing, you seemed to enjoy the shopping, dining, week-end getaways, the intimacy . . ." I hoped I raised my voice.

Taylor turned away from me. She knew the gesture was not only rude, but a deliberate insult to a deaf person. Basically, she was terminating our conversation whether I agreed or not. The problem was, I wasn't finished, so I reached out and touched her arm, intercepting any possible escape.

"We've been through this before, Taylor. I don't need you or anyone else speaking for me."

She paced as we strolled on the walking trail in Forest Park, a city-owned park shared with suburban dwellers, which was only blocks from Taylor's apartment. The park boasted the free admission to the St. Louis Zoo, a boat room, and a five-mile spread of golf course.

During the summers, Forest Park always reintroduced its residents to the outdoor stage at the

MUNY. Each fall, thousands descended on the park for the annual hot air balloon race. Despite the major attractions, Forest Park was intimate enough for the walking, and bike trails carved throughout it.

I stopped walking, folded my arms and faced her. "You're wasting my time and yours. I'm not very good at handling mood swings. Be hot or cold because warm doesn't work for me."

She put her hands on her hips. "Fine," she spat. "I just can't handle our different worlds anymore. You don't listen to me," Taylor said as her lips pouted.

Dropping my arms to my sides, I stepped closer, invading her space. This woman was crazy, and I was insane to be attracted to her. "News flash, I'm deaf." I guess I elevated my voice because she jumped. I rubbed my face to calm down.

"I found someone else, Noel."

"So now the truth comes out."

With big brown eyes as innocent as a five-year-old child, she said, "Sorry."

That was a defining moment for me. I dared shock to register on my face. I was furious at myself for misjudging Taylor's character. I made the decision not to date another woman from the hearing world.

As I pursued women from the Deaf culture, that proved to be a disaster, too. I thought about Sheila. She talked too much, but not with her mouth. My eyes couldn't read her hands fast enough. Plus, she was intimidated by the hearing world, which is a part of me. Once again, I had compatibility issues.

I dismissed the memories of a road that had too many side streets, forbidding my mind to continue wandering while behind the wheel. Scrutinizing the past was tiresome and distractive, and I couldn't afford that. Being a good driver meant watching for flashing emergency lights from ambulances and road rage. My eyes had to see what my ears couldn't hear.

Five minutes later, I reached my destination and drove into the bank's parking lot and turned off the ignition. Briefly, I thought back sixteen years ago. Workers at a warehouse in Jasper, a small Missouri town, were loading a mobile trailer with explosives for a fireworks display headed for St. Louis. The only problem was the men forgot to lock up the building securely—a bad combination for curious teenagers. I will forever be grateful to God for sparing my life whether I hear again or not. I'm still in awe in how I do it—assimilating between two worlds, sometimes with ease, sometimes in complete disaster.

Getting out of my car, I inhaled and released the chilled air. The past was just that; the past. I strolled into the entrance of my bank searching for Jackie, my regular teller. It was the day after Thanksgiving and the lobby was crowded with customers in line. My regular teller was helping another customer, my personal banker was absent, and staff members were waiting on their clients. After getting in line, I mentally reviewed my transactions. I needed to transfer money and purchase two certified checks.

Fifteen minutes later, a woman teller, who looked as if she graduated from high school the day before, motioned with her hand for me to approach, but her mouth never stopped talking to another worker about a guy she was dating.

To minimize miscommunication, I always wrote notes ahead of time for conducting business. After retrieving instructions from inside my suit jacket, I pushed my note in front of Miss Recent Grad. That's when my day went from a bad dream to a living nightmare.

I glanced over my shoulder and saw customers steadily backing away, some were scrambling for cover, visually shaken. Before I could wonder about their odd behavior, my body was slammed against the floor as a sting pierced my back. The discomfort was sharp and agonizing.

Grimacing in pain, I struggled to lift my head, and came face-to-face with a gun, the officer ready to pull the trigger. I strained to roll my head from right to left. Another officer had both hands wrapped around a stun gun. His flaring nostrils warned me that he controlled my pain management like a driver steering a remote-controlled car.

The bank manager, Mrs. Harris, a black version of Miss Jane from the *Beverly Hillbillies*, ran to my aid. She knelt, assessed my condition, and turned to the security officer then the police, cursing them to stop. I would've found the scene humorous on television if I wasn't the main character. As the pain subsided, I wanted to know why I, the CEO of a company, was sprawled on a bank floor.

Lowering their weapons, the men reluctantly stepped back with their eyes trained on me. With the stingray retracted from my back, I gently rolled over until I could brace myself on my elbows. The remnants of the stun gun vibrated through my body. Every movement was a struggle. Crawling to the teller's station with the aid of bystanders, I gripped the counter, and heaved myself up.

The pain's aftershocks didn't keep my jaw from dropping as I faced the unapologetic bank teller. She looked from me to my note. Her expression became angelic when her mouth formed an "o." If there was ever a time not to be saved, this was that moment. Death by strangulation would've been too good of a punishment.

"I may be deaf, but you are definitely blind." I gritted my teeth and slid back to the floor in pain. At that moment, I didn't care that I was trying to strengthen a relationship with God, an entrepreneur, or a mature adult.

My back hurt, my head hurt, and the humiliation was barely tolerable. I don't know when Mrs. Harris left my side, but she returned with a George Foreman Grill and a pad.

"I know at the time you opened your account, we gave out store gift certificates. This month, it's a toaster broiler. Please accept this as an apology. From now on if you can have a relay operator call ahead, I'll make sure me or one of the personal bankers is available to assist you. I'm so sorry, Mr. Richardson. This will never happen again."

She shoved the box in my chest seconds before

paramedics rushed in. They assisted me in sitting up. Before they examined my wound, they asked for an insurance card. Frustrated, I thought it was a good time to black out, so I did, letting them bear my weight.

CHAPTER 3

A George Foreman Grill couldn't buy my silence. I don't know which was more humiliating, being brought down by a stun gun or blacking out. However, my efforts to contact the bank's headquarters to register a complaint using the telephone relay system dwindled.

The operator—a third party representative acting on deaf clients' behalf—couldn't outwit an automated telephone message service. After the network system disconnected my call the third attempt, I opted to send them an email from my BlackBerry. If that didn't work, there was always videoconferencing, which was my preference.

Saturday afternoon, I sat slumped in a chair at Starbucks. I was still stewing over the previous day's events while I stared out the window. Propping my elbows on the table, my forehead rested on my fists.

To passersby, I was praying. I wasn't, but I should've been. That had been my problem. I hadn't had a consistent prayer life in years. Thanks to the recent church service and a very pretty interpreter, things were about to change. I smiled, thinking about my brief encounter with Mackenzie. A tap on my shoulder distracted me. Turning around, Caleb Richardson stood behind me with a concerned expression.

"You okay, bro?" He fumbled a signing that translated into *"You okay, uncle?"* I frowned in mock annoyance. After sixteen years, a person would've thought that my brother knew the difference between placing his two index fingers near his right temple, which meant uncle and two fingers poised near the forehead as if gripping a cap for brother. One thing that impressed me about the church was a few members could finger-spell their names, some could sign the phrase how are you, but the competency seemed to be with the Deaf Ministry. That alone showed an attempt at inclusion.

Before the deadly accident, Caleb and I were inseparable. We didn't have a choice. Sharing a bedroom and bath created a special bond—until I caught one of Caleb's legs sneaking into my new designer jeans. There was no way he was going to wear my brand new stuff before I had the chance. That's where I drew the line. Our sharing days were over.

Caleb, sporting a glistening bald head and the latest expensive clothes, flopped down in the chair across from me without waiting for an invitation. Stealing one of my used napkins, he smoothed it out and scribbled on it before turning the napkin around. *"You all right? Why are you sitting here alone? Want to hang out?"*

"Bro, if I wanted to read notes, I'll read my book," I replied.

He snarled. "Hey, what's with the attitude?"

I held up my hand. "I just need some quiet time, all right? I may catch up with you later."

He twisted his lips. "You can't hear, so it's always quiet." Shrugging, he stood, and with his arrogant "Do you know who I am?" walk—which, of course, nobody did—strolled away. Caleb believed in speaking his mind even if his words stung from time to time. For a period after the accident, he held his tongue. He was scared and suffered insomnia, wondering if I was going to die during the night. The accident terminated our late-night talks at bedtime that had always gotten us in trouble. That, by itself, was a constant reminder that our worlds had changed.

I lifted a cup of cold Espresso to my lips. After taking a gulp, I swallowed and let my taste buds call the shots. It wasn't bad if I liked the increasingly popular ice coffee drinks, which I didn't. I preferred coffee and tea served hot and milkshakes and Kool-Aid cold.

As more patrons crowded the café, I began to watch them, observing their facial expressions and translating their intimate conversations. An unexpected jab in my back disrupted my musing. I glanced over my shoulder and came face-to-face with Pierce. If Caleb was worried about me, he made sure to pass his anxiety to our oldest brother.

Often labeled as "My three sons," whatever features my older brother, Pierce, possessed—eyes, mouth, nose, chin, hair, and height, so did Caleb and I. My father often teased my mother that she kept Pierce's leftover genes for us. Most strangers couldn't tell us apart, but there were differences besides Caleb's fashionable shaved head look.

Caleb and Pierce preferred to go bare chest or wear muscle-man T-shirts as soon as the temperature hit sixty-five. The scar tissue, stretching from below my left nipple to inches above my navel, prevented me from that indulgence.

Years before the accident, my family and I weren't faithful Christians, but we weren't agnostics either. Lukewarm was probably the best description. If church fit into our schedules, we attended, if not—well, we would hit it next time.

All that changed the summer of 1977, when tragedy and thankfulness forced my family to turn our lives over to Christ. Out of obedience, we requested the baptismal in Jesus' name after we read about it in Acts 2:38: *Then Peter said unto them, Repent, and be baptized every one of you in the name of Jesus Christ for the remission of sins, and ye shall receive the gift of the Holy Ghost.* That applied to everybody except Caleb because he rebelled about getting baptized. To date, he still does.

When I survived, my family didn't argue with God about anything in the Bible. My father reevaluated his position as the spiritual head of our family. We always felt he was the best example any boys could have as a father. But after our conversion, he struggled spiritually, and through trial and error, he submitted to God's superior authority. During that time, the Bible also gave my mother comfort.

At sixteen, I was beyond rebellious. I felt cheated.

The honor of having obtained my driver's license and cruising in my dad's car to the popular parties was put on hold. Classmates avoided eye contact with me. So-called friends taunted me as a freak. The teasing made me wish I suffered from acne instead; but look at me now. It's ironic the appreciative stares I get from women.

For a long time, I blamed God for the explosion. I figured it was His way to pick on and punish me for stealing my dad's cigarettes, then using profanity among my buddies to prove I wasn't a sissy. Through my dad's encouragement and professional counseling, I warmed up to the idea of reading my Bible and sought out the 370 scriptures concerning death. I ceased my mind from wandering and glanced back at Pierce. I couldn't ask for a better brother. Two years older than me, Pierce was my fierce protector, confidant, and the most respectful guy I knew.

Pierce was dressed in his usual attire of a starched oxford shirt, his signature expensive tie, and discounted pressed jeans. Uninvited, he straddled a nearby chair. With fluency, he fired one question after another at me. Pierce had excelled in signing while he studied and passed the bar exam.

He was well respected and sought after for legal matters in the Deaf community. Capital 'D,' because, as a group, they compared themselves to ethnic groups such as Caucasians, African-Americans, Native Indian, Hispanics, etc. He worked hard and long hours to make junior partner in an up-and-coming law firm.

Then in a surprising move to his colleagues,

Pierce rethought his career goals. He paid back his student loans, purchased a new house, furniture, and an expensive SUV before he quit. Matured years beyond the age of eight, level-headed by nine, and more honest than most preachers were at ten, Pierce said he accepted the calling from God. He took the salary reduction and sought an unpopular position with the city's public defender's office without blinking. He wanted to represent underserved citizens.

"What's going on?" Pierce signed, staring with the intensity to make an innocent man plead guilty on a witness stand.

"I'm in a mood." I shrugged.

"Get out of it." He didn't smile or blink.

We argued back and forth, signing until heads turned and brows lifted in curiosity. Let them stare and wonder.

"Sorry" Pierce stood. *"Whenever you're ready to talk, text me."* He squeezed my shoulder and pounded his fist twice against his chest. It wasn't a deaf phrase, but one among brothers, reminding me he had my back before he hesitantly walked out, unconcerned about attracting attention. He did anyway.

If Pierce and Caleb were hanging together, that meant they were on their way to shoot a few games of pool, and were probably in one car. Chuckling, I may have moved out of the North County area, but the neighborhood zip code was still in me. I could've stopped at a Starbucks closer to my Mid-County house.

Actually, I came across town to pick up a suit from my tailor. He knew my pants had to fit without suffocating my quads, and the length after a finished hem should be no longer or shorter than thirty-four and a half inches. The man was awesome in designing stylish suit jackets to cover my broad shoulders, chest, and the arm muscles that were the result of daily push ups. There was nothing worse than to struggle to button a blazer. I had to be able to slip the button in the slot once with ease, and then free it with the snap of my thumb.

I leaned back after my two baby-sitters were gone. My coffee cup was empty, but I wasn't ready to leave. I slipped my newly purchased sci-fi book out of my bag. Bending back the cover, the first line sucked me in. *It was a matter of time before Abo died, inhaling the sour odor of* . . . My finger was posed to turn the page when a soft pat on my shoulder forced me to hold my breath and tie down my irritation.

Now what? Again I chided myself for not going to the Starbucks closer to my house. If Pierce and Caleb were back, I was definitely leaving. I blanked the annoyed expression and mechanically turned around. My eyes widened, enjoying the delightful interruption. Familiar eyes sparkled and curved lips spoke to me without moving.

"Want some company?"

If I didn't know better, I would've guessed my brothers sent Mackenzie, but they had no clue who she was. I exhaled. Smiling, I scooted back and stood, towering over her. Chivalry in high gear, I pulled out the chair Caleb had vacated and waited for Mackenzie to take the seat. The unique scent of her perfume drifted.

"*Rough day?*"

"*Rough life,*" I signed back, reflecting on the previous day's mishap.

Mackenzie reached out and touched my hand. Her long fingers were warm from the steaming coffee cup she had placed on the table. As she opened her mouth to speak, I leaned forward. She paused, smiling. I waited, grinning. She was a captivating vision with her carefree curls that bounced at the slightest move.

"*If you ever want to talk, I'll listen. Promise. God has this keen perception about when we need a friend. I had no idea you were here until I was about to leave. My cousin stays a few blocks from here. Since he wasn't home, I came here to kill time.*"

The latches on the floodgate broke. Opening my mouth, I talked. She listened. She signed. I signed back. I shared my previous disastrous day. With her elbows resting on our parlor-style table, she positioned her chin on inter-locking fingers.

When she laughed at the bank teller's stupidity, I laughed, shaking my head. Looking back, if I removed myself from the situation, it was comical.

CHAPTER 4

Mackenzie almost made me lose control—not self-control, but that of my beloved car as I steered into the church parking lot the Sunday after Thanksgiving. Mackenzie distracted me as she strutted—no, floated across the pavement. She was gloriously wrapped in a long mustard-yellow wool coat, matching hat and one gold and one purple glove that completed her ensemble. I didn't know if the purple glove was a fashion state-ment, the newest trend, or a Michael Jackson "glove thing," but whatever the reason, Mackenzie had my attention.

I tapped on my horn. Mackenzie didn't stop or glance my way. Determined to make my presence known, I pressed harder. Mackenzie and several other churchgoers whirled around, covering their ears. Oops. Sometimes I don't know my own strength. I shrugged my apologies, figuring I had gotten her attention.

Mackenzie halted. With her ears still covered, she smiled so wide, her eyes closed. I wished I could've heard the sound as her mouth moved with laughter. It didn't matter. Her face told me the story. I couldn't park fast enough, a minor technicality that I resolved. As a matter of fact, when my Cadillac began to roll, I realized I hadn't shifted the gear into park. Finally, after locking my car, I took long strides until I came face to face with Mackenzie. Her jovial expression was not of ridicule, but of amusement. She was teasing me, and I laughed, too.

"Hi."

Nodding, she curled her lips upward. *"Good morning, and praise the Lord, Noel."*

"Praise Him," I replied, wishing I could hear my voice. Was it loud, strained and annoying, or deep and mesmerizing? I had stopped trying to impress women, but after that day in Starbucks, I wanted nothing more than to dazzle Mackenzie. The woman was refreshing. *"Would you like an escort to the door?"*

Without hesitation, she nodded, despite us being only a few feet from the entrance. Once inside, I followed her to our section. Selecting a pew closer to her chair, I knelt to pray. I got off my knees, removed my coat, and sat.

Casually, I searched for Mackenzie who had disappeared into a group of parishioners as Valerie appeared, strolling toward the group. With a cat-walk strut, she carried an oversized Bible, which lay on top of a black leather coat tossed over her arm. She almost stumbled when she saw me again.

"Oh, you decided to come back." Her expression wasn't questionable, it was a statement. She shook her head in disappointment, assuming I didn't understand her so she signed. *"I wish you had some brothers. Are they all deaf? What about any hearing cousins? You know a good Christian invites others to church."*

Frowning, I studied her features. What came across as anger or rudeness seemed like a mask for a glimpse of sadness. Valerie's signing skills weren't lacking, but I dismissed her hypocrisy with a shrug. Opening my Bible, I scanned the scriptures, anything about obtaining wisdom. No matter what, I wanted to walk faithfully with God this time, regardless of the obstacles. At least I was in the right place to ask for wisdom; too bad when the church doors open, the devil parades in, too, uninvited.

I smiled at Mackenzie's return. Valerie was about to return my smile when she followed my eyes. She dismissed me when she realized Mackenzie held my fascination and appreciation.

She stopped Mackenzie. "Mack, you think you can handle the interpretation today by yourself? I've invited a guest from my job, and I'd rather sit with him."

Valerie didn't wait for Mackenzie's response as she sauntered away. Minutes later, Mackenzie settled in her seat. I sucked in air as she closed her eyes to pray. Her eyes sparkled as she opened them and met my stare. Mackenzie was tempting me with thoughts not appropriate for small children or while I was in church. How did she do it? She wasn't overly made up, her clothes weren't revealing, and she wasn't even flirting. So why did I feel seduced? She hadn't said anything overtly suggestive. She didn't know the man in me could undress her with my eyes, but God was helping me control my carnal thoughts. I glanced at the bandstand as a diversion. The musicians lifted trumpets, saxophones, and trombones to their lips. When wood sticks smacked the drums, the air stirred, vibrating around me. My chest pounded as testimony.

Mackenzie coaxed the sound into my world. Her head bobbed to "The Blood Will Never Lose Its Power." I didn't know the song or melody, but the words told the story. Before long, I stopped watching her as I closed my eyes and thought about the words from the chorus, " . . . it reaches to the highest mountain . . . it flows to the lowest valleys . . ." Without opening my eyes, I stood and stretched my arms to God, swaying to the internal rhythm God gave me.

When the energy around me stilled, I opened my eyes. The praise and worship had segued into a scripture reading, yet numerous people continued their praise. It was something to be said about a church where praise was the norm, not an interruption. As I took my seat, Mackenzie instructed us to begin at James 1:17. As the minister read, Mackenzie focused on me when she signed verse nineteen, *"Wherefore, my beloved brethren, let every man be swift to hear, slow to speak, slow to wrath . . ."* She smiled, adding, *"Hear with your heart the voice of God."*

She emitted tenderness and understanding that reduced me to taffy—banana flavored. I hated bananas, but that's what she was doing to me, making me mushy. Mackenzie presented me with a repeat performance of her one-of-a-kind signing.

Captivated by the message and not just the

woman, I leaned forward in my seat, mentally dissecting God's message. Despite the gulps of information, I remained thirsty when the sermon ended. Pastor Coleman offered the altar call as the congregation stood. In some Pentecostal churches, that part of the service could be lengthy.

The man of God pleaded for those who recognized themselves as sinners to repent. *"Start over, renew your mind, and erase your debt. The way to God is an open door. Let God cleanse you with a simple wash. He doesn't have to soak or scrub you. All you have to do is go down in water in Jesus' name. When you rise, you may look the same, but your life will be anything, but the same."* Pastor Coleman chuckled. *"Who knows . . ."*

My mind drifted. Briefly, I thought about how God protected me from dangerous situations before my eyes and the dangers that I would never see. I reflected on His unbiased love and blessing for the thieves and the faithful.

Pastor Coleman wagged a finger in the air. *"This day isn't promised nor is this minute. Why do you remain rooted in your spot when you can come down and be washed? God is on stand-by. You don't need an appointment. Come now. Don't walk out of this place with a broken heart when God can mend it. We have baptismal clothes for you to change into regardless of size. We're ready. Are you?"*

After the last candidate was submerged in the baptism, the offering was received, and the pastor gave the benediction. Youngsters ran out of the pews as if it was recess. Women scurried to friends and their men stood around, waiting for them.

As the crowd thinned, I lingered for only one woman, signing with a few deaf members. Never far away from Mackenzie, I remained until I could say goodbye to her, and judging from her subtle glances, she wasn't going to let me. Relaxing in another pew, I crossed my right ankle over my left knee. Making myself more comfortable, I flexed my muscles. With my thumb, I released the button on my jacket from its hole and stretched my arms across the back of the seat. Call me overconfident, but I wanted Mackenzie to feel my presence and come to me. She did. What I didn't expect was for her to get comfortable beside me.

"Do you want me to talk or sign?" Her smile beamed.

A choice; I liked a woman who wasn't demanding. A hearing person preferred talking. A deaf person insisted on signing. So Mackenzie caught me off guard. A few women had cursed me out for my silence. To my amusement, I was glad I was deaf. I had been called arrogant, conceited, and a jerk. Sometimes I could be arrogant or conceited, but never disrespectful.

Living in two worlds wasn't easy. Speaking versus signing was an issue that alienated the Deaf community. They demanded a distinction. Those Deaf—the ones born deaf, and not dumb—were proud, and wouldn't dare learn to speak to appease the hearing community. The profoundly deaf—those who could hear sounds through hearing aids, implants, or other procedures, intermingled between speaking and signing.

Some considered me a traitor since I was legally deaf and talked when I could've signed. I was classified as oral deaf, and became a late deafened-adult until, well I was an adult. If this is confusing to a hearing person, imagine a teenager trying to understand it.

Mackenzie sat regally, awaiting my answer. Shifting in my seat, I relaxed my arm on the back of the pew. "Talk to me. I like to watch your lips move." I leaned closer. "Am I speaking too loud?"

Giving me the universal okay sign, she said, "You're perfect."

Really? I thought, as I planned to explore her answer later. "What's so funny? Why are you smiling? Although, I think you're more fascinating when you do." Once again, I was flirting with Mackenzie in church, but she was ambushing me. Reaching out, her hands gently covered my ears. Her gesture shocked, surprised, and seduced me, because I was becoming more attracted to her and I didn't know anything about her except her name, a mystery that I would solve soon.

I gritted my teeth in temptation. *Lord, you're going to have to help me as far as Mackenzie is concerned,* I silently petitioned God before I marveled at her touch. I was curious as if she had planned to pray for a healing, something that hadn't come yet, or yank on my ears. She was taking a lot of liberty and I didn't have any qualms about letting her. Anyway, I welcomed her communication even if it was foreign to me.

"If you could hear, you'd love the sound of your voice."

I surprised myself when I thought, *If I could hear, I would listen to her voice forever.* Let someone else make that statement, I would've dismissed that person and viewed the comment as a ridicule. That smile of hers snapped my wall of resistance like a toothpick. My finger worried my mustache as my nostrils flared. "Yeah?" I encouraged her flattery.

Her smile widened as she matched my stare. "Yeah."

Embarrassed, Mackenzie quickly removed her incredibly soft hands, but the memory of her touch remained. I blocked out the activity swirling around us, ignoring parents grabbing toddlers, or deacons gathering discarded items. Mackenzie's undivided attention ignited an explosion of joy within me. I was fighting a losing battle to contain it.

An hour disappeared as splinters of sunlight peeped through large stain-glassed windows. We chatted until the last light fixtures flashed off. She was so easy to talk with. I couldn't remember the last time I had a verbal conversation and enjoyed it so much. My parents and two brothers didn't count.

"Noel, I can tell by your speech, you weren't born deaf, right?" Mackenzie asked.

I nodded. She was perceptive. I wondered what else she would guess about me. It didn't take long for her to answer my unasked question.

"Okay, that leaves you deaf or a late deafened-adult."

"I'm impressed. You've been studying or something. I'm deaf with a small 'd' since I could hear up until my sixteenth birthday. The short story version is I was visiting two friends during the Fourth of July weekend. My two buddies and I were nosing around what we thought was an abandoned building. It happened to be an unsecured explosives building. When we snuck inside, a fire cracker with mission-like speed came out of nowhere, setting off a chain of blasts.

"Two of us escaped alive. My friend didn't." I shifted in my seat. Mackenzie became a blur. I couldn't say his name without recalling the times we shared. I took a deep breath and continued, "Keith was dead before the ambulance arrived. He had burns over eighty percent of his body. My chest took the bulk of the flames." I patted my muscular chest as if to prove I had recovered. "Some sparks ate at the flesh on my back, too."

Mackenzie's alluring eyes were filled with compassion. She nodded for me to continue. It was hypnotic observing her watch me. I rubbed my mustache before stroking my chin. I smiled to let her know I was all right.

"Three days later, lying in a hospital bed in excruciating pain, I freaked out when the doctors' lips moved and I couldn't hear a thing. My dad wrote a note telling me I'd never ever be able to hear again. That's the short version, Mackenzie."

Her head tilted to the side as she digested my words. Mackenzie frowned and leaned in closer. "Give me the long version, Noel. Was that your journey toward salvation?" She touched my hand, prompting me. "When did you finally realize God was drawing you to salvation?"

My brows knitted in a frown this time. Since I wasn't signing, I didn't have to worry about holding eye contact. I scanned the sanctuary. It had been a long time since I had thought about the Dawsons, or given them credit for being a witness for the Lord. I regained eye contact with Mackenzie. "For years I believed that explosion was God's payback for the stupid stuff I did behind my parents' backs, or my family's slander of a neighbor. You know how you can make fun of things you don't understand?"

Mackenzie's eyes twinkled in understanding.

"Well, the Dawsons lived two doors down from us in the city. I have to admit, my brothers and I teased them because their family went to church every night. Seven-thirty on the dot, they loaded up the family car. I looked at it this way. Why go to church when there were other things to do?"

Mackenzie didn't interrupt. She neither agreed nor disagreed with my assessment, but her eyes reflected the gentleness in her heart. A slight smile confirmed she was listening. A quick wink said she understood.

Yes, she was flirting. God help me from this little temptress, I joked inwardly before I continued. "Then I remembered when I made fun of a boy in my kindergarten class who was deaf. I called him dumb, too. It wasn't funny after all when I became the object of what I once mocked. I learned what it meant to face life-altering events, and why God sanctified people to weather the storms that were far off."

Watching me patiently, Mackenzie listened. The other day at Starbucks, she had me laughing at a bad situation. What would she say about the most devastating moment in my life?

" 'The inquisitive trio,' as we called ourselves, went to explore what we called the forest in the woods on the other side of a picnic area. When we saw a warehouse that looked deserted, we decided to scope it out. We had just climbed inside of an unlocked window when a firecracker flew over our heads. That's when the popping started. We couldn't get out fast enough."

I bowed my head. I couldn't finish because every time I thought about this part, I saw blood and two bodies. Not a good combination. I forgot Mackenzie was there until her fingers pried apart my hands, which were locked in an involuntary clutch. She linked hers with mine. I looked up.

"You don't have to finish, Noel."

My lips curled as my right hand tapped my mouth. *"Thank you."* I was about to change the subject when she stopped me with a stroke of her hand on my arm.

"But I would like you to."

Throwing my head back, I had no idea why I started laughing as a tear leaked down my face. She joined me. Suddenly, I stopped. "What's so funny? I don't even know why we're laughing."

Touching my face, she lifted my lone tear with her thumb. The look Mackenzie gave me hinted I should've known the reason. "Would you rather cry?"

"No," I answered, wishing I could get inside her pretty little head.

"Noel, I'm sure after what you've endured, you know how much strength it took to recover. The joy of the Lord is our strength. 'Weeping may endure for a night, but joy cometh in the morning.'"

"You know I wasn't crying," I clarified.

"Right," Mackenzie said jokingly.

"What is it about you that I divulge things I usually shy away from discussing?"

She shrugged and delivered a killer grin.

I shook my head. If I weren't sitting in church, I would've believed she had cast a spell on me. "I bet you could get my social security number out of me, couldn't you?"

Teasing, she shoved out both hands flat, alternating them up and down. *"Maybe."*

Her confidence was an appealing asset. "Never mind your underhanded tactics," I quipped, shifting in my seat. "The force of the explosion ignited a domino effect, spitting us through the air. Keith was the first one in, but he was the last one out. He died almost instantly. Dre Smith lived, but stayed in the burn unit for six months. I was the lucky one, I guess. Besides some burnt patches on my body, I'd only lost my hearing."

"So, did you get baptized after that?"

"You better believe it, lady. I was the first to receive the gift of the Holy Ghost. Witnesses say they heard me speak in unknown tongues." My fist touched my chest. "I couldn't hear it, but I felt it throughout my body. God's anointing power poured over me, controlling my mouth. I couldn't stop, not even to shut it. My body felt limp before a surge of energy renewed my limbs. Yes, it was an unbelievable experience. End of long version."

"God doesn't discriminate who He saves."

"I know. I'm hoping your church's Deaf Ministry will help me grow stronger in the Lord. It's definitely better than having church service at home. To be honest with you, prior to Thanksgiving, I hadn't been inside a church in a long time."

Mackenzie's brows frowned in concern. "Why?"

"It's not just businesses and employers that fail to embrace the deaf. Churches, cultural events, and other functions also come up short. We can be isolated in the middle of a crowd. You know the saying, a five-hundred-pound gorilla in the room?"

"What about your family? Are they baptized and filled with the Holy Ghost?" Her concerned was endearing.

"Saved, sanctified, and rejoicing, all except for my youngest brother, Caleb. I guess God hasn't called him yet." I tried duplicating Mackenzie's theatrics when she signed. *"My parents worried about me finding the right church to cater to my needs."*

"Well, all that has changed. Let our Deaf Ministry be a blessing to you and others. Please pray about joining. Don't just visit. Become a member . . ." she paused as she squinted, distracted at something behind me.

Curious, I glanced over my shoulder, and sighed—Valerie. *Why wasn't she occupying her guest, or did she chase him away, too?* I wondered. A few pews away, Valerie transformed her face into ugly expressions. She abruptly stopped when I caught her. My chest tensed in annoyance.

Since the woman appeared to have a problem with me, I wanted in my deepest fantasy to become a bull, release steam through my nostrils and charge her. As long as she didn't get in the way of Mackenzie and me, we were cool; otherwise, God would have to intervene on my behalf. Somehow, I had no doubt that Mackenzie was part of the package God had for me.

Mackenzie patted my leg to regain my attention. My muscles tensed under the contact, so I really focused on her lips as she asked if I'd like to go to Applebee's with some other church members. Without thinking twice, I nodded. Out of the corner of my eye, I saw Valerie stomping her foot in a tantrum. Mackenzie's mouth twisted, suppressing a smile. I didn't and released what I hoped was a roar of laughter. Who cared if Valerie wasn't happy with Mackenzie's invitation? I was ecstatic.

CHAPTER 5

Icouldn't believe it. Not only was Mackenzie wrapping me around her finger, she was running a circle around me. Actually, I had become dizzy trailing her late nineties red Mazda. It was by the grace of God that I barely kept up as she zipped in and out of traffic lanes.

The city, motorists, and pedestrians had nothing to fear once she parked and turned off the ignition. I parked next to Mackenzie, got out, and swiftly walked to her driver's side. Her car door was stiff, but I had the upper hand and opened it, frowning, but Mackenzie's easy smile and trusting honey-brown eyes greeted me. Yep, four days and the woman had me wrapped around her finger.

"What?" Her eyes were wide and innocent.

With a stern expression, I brought my right hand to my lips as if I were kissing my fingers. I dropped my hand as if I had a nasty taste in my mouth before pretending I was gripping the steering wheel.

Mackenzie's head fell back and her lips curled.

She seemed to chuckle before defending herself. "I'm not a bad driver."

Folding my arms, I leaned against her car. "Want to bet? You're lucky the saints don't gamble because you would lose."

"You're right, Brother Noel."

"About what, gambling, or being a bad driver?"

Mackenzie winked. "I never gamble."

Raising my brow, I hoped I mumbled, "mm-hmm," as I offered her my hand. With the grace of a princess, she elegantly accepted it. I recognized a few people from the church as they hopped out of their cars and briskly walked to the entrance. Contrary to the mad dash, Mackenzie and I didn't hurry. A few times, we stopped, as she signed a question. I would answer and then I'd stop and ask her something. I enjoyed our camaraderie.

When we made it to the entrance, I held the door for her to enter, indulging in a whiff of her hair as she passed. I smirked. The fragrance subtle, I dared not take a deeper breath, but I inched closer anyway, trying to maintain an acceptable distance. Even though I sensed a mutual attraction, I didn't want to assume. I didn't have a clue whether she was interested.

My stomach vibrated, bracing for a long wait. Squeezing her shoulder, she turned around. I mouthed, "Are you okay standing?"

"Yep," she answered, unbuttoning her wool coat. She removed her cap, releasing her tamed curls into the wild. She slipped off her mismatched gloves and jammed them into her coat pockets as the line stirred. We shuffled our way through the French double doors to the lobby.

Ahead of us, a few sisters from the church turned around and waved at her. Valerie glanced over her shoulder, ignored me and acknowledged Mackenzie before resuming her conversation with another woman.

It was something about that woman that bugged me. Mackenzie seemed uncomplicated. Valerie had complication tattooed on her forehead.

Then God spoke to me, *"Moreover if thy brother shall trespass against thee, go and tell him his fault between thee and him alone: if he shall hear thee, thou hast gained thy brother."*

You've got to be kidding. I grimaced inwardly. *I can't fathom why she's hostile toward me,* I tried to reason with God. *Why, I don't even know the woman besides her name,* my soul reasoned. No further message was forthcoming. I didn't have a problem with Valerie. She was the one with issues, and I sensed she would let me know what they were sooner or later. The latter was my preference.

A big bear of a guy nudged his way to the front. I was about to confront him about jumping ahead when he and some ladies from church laughed together. Towering over them, his eyes scanned the crowd. He recognized Mackenzie. Leaving the ladies, he shuffled his way back to us. I was guarded as he hugged Mackenzie, lifting her off her feet then acknowledged me.

"How's it going, brother? Nick Dixon," he introduced himself before hugging me like a member of a family. I flexed my muscles and returned the grip.

"I'm good. I'm Noel Richardson. I've been visiting your church's Deaf Ministry."

"Oh, it's all good." Nick slapped me on my back. "Maybe, we can get together when we don't have to fight the women for our food."

I chuckled, pegging him as the church comedian. He was a Cedric the Entertainer minus ten pounds, maybe fifteen. The man was solid muscle. We had that in common. Overall, after two services, I felt comfortable at the church. The members, the preaching, and especially Mackenzie, were very appealing.

After a few minutes, Valerie left her post and intercepted. *"I noticed you didn't park in the handicap spaces."* Valerie made a big production of signing to draw unwanted attention to me.

"That's because I'm not disabled. I'm deaf." I had to catch myself. Sometimes my thoughts became words and slipped out of my mouth. Now was not the time for her to cross me. I'm not even on the church's roll.

God reminded me of His earlier scripture. Before Valerie could counter-attack, a hostess approached. "How many are in your party?"

Nick took charge of counting faces. "Ten."

"Would you prefer smoking or non-smoking?" the short young girl asked, clutching a clipboard to her chest. Her smile was genuine, her face adorable, and demeanor respectable.

"Non-smoking," Nick replied, squinting around the restaurant for some vacancies.

The hostess gritted her teeth. Her next expression revealed it wouldn't be good news. "Do you mind splitting up? Otherwise, you'll have to wait almost an hour and a half."

Nick's thick hand patted his never-missed-a-meal stomach. Squinting, he looked around then rendered a verdict. "I'm hungry. Y'all on your own. Whatever you've got to do, Miss, go for it."

I laughed, apparently loud enough that some joined me, including Mackenzie. Our group trailed the hostess to a platform loft that stretched across the back of the restaurant. She offered three choices: a corner booth, a table for two by the window, or a round bar table with four stools.

Most piled into the booth while Nick and three women opted for the bar table where smiling faces revealed that Nick had captivated them. Mackenzie and I were left with the only option—the window seats. I restrained from grinning my approval. Mackenzie Norton was fascinating so I had no qualms about sharing a table with her. There was a big tip coming. I helped Mackenzie remove her coat, again inhaling a whiff of her hair before extending my hand for her to take a seat.

While we waited for our server, I scanned Mackenzie's face, trying to find something else—a mole, a scar, a pimple—well, not that, but anything I could memorize. *Do you mind if we sign? It's easier in a public place, and I don't have to wonder if I'm shouting.*

"No." She signed, wiggling two fingers in the air like a peace sign before she rested her fingers on her thumb.

I lifted my fingers and thumb to my forehead and began signing just as a perky teenager appeared at our table. His black hair was slicked back except for three spiked sections tinted deep blue. I tried to ignore the four silver earrings in his left ear. I couldn't because they were shouting at me. This wasn't the person I wanted handling my food.

He concentrated on our hands as he gave us our menus. Then to my surprise, he began to sign, *"My name's Jason, and I'll be your waiter this evening. What would you like to drink? I suggest the strawberry lemonade or the peach tea."*

Shocked, I shrugged, recovering enough to nod at Mackenzie who smiled knowingly.

"We'll take two strawberry lemonades," Mackenzie signed.

Jason clasped his hands together, showcasing bitten, dark polished fingernails. *"Good. I'll get your drinks and give you a minute to look over our menu."* He laid them on the table before us.

Mackenzie tilted her head and stared at me. *"You can close your mouth now, Noel."*

Shaking my head, I did just that. Funny how I was quick to judge, but I didn't want to be judged.

"Looks are deceiving, aren't they?" She smirked.

Yes, they are, I thought. *"You think he's deaf?"*

"Who knows?" She turned down her lip and shrugged. *"But he knows the language. That's one more person to talk—I mean to sign with . . ."* she corrected, winking.

"At first, I thought he was trying to mock us. I'm impressed." My fingers tapped on the menus. I stared at Mackenzie. *"I have to admit, unless I'm attending a deaf event, I don't come across that many people who sign. As a matter of fact, never."*

"Many people are becoming bi-lingual. That includes signing. Embrace it, Noel, and next time, close your mouth."

I shook my head. *"Mackenzie, either I'm transparent or we've met in another life."* If it had not been for my deafness, maybe Mackenzie and I would never have met.

"Neither. I've learned to accept people the way they are. When you love Jesus, you'll look beyond their faults, fingernail polish . . ." She grinned. *"And see their needs."*

Needs? What if I made Mackenzie one of my needs? She possessed a contagious carefree personality balanced with refined mannerisms. She had an airy walk as if she had never seen a bad day or person in her life. She was a striking woman. If she said I could fly, I would leap off the cliff. I couldn't believe how fast my emotions were surfacing, and I couldn't halt them.

Jason returned and placed our glasses on the table. *"What have you two decided?"* Then for the first time since his arrival at our table, Jason spoke. "Or do you need more time?" He grinned like a Cheshire cat, clearly pleased with himself.

Mackenzie flashed a smile at Jason, displaying the whitest teeth I've seen. I had noticed them earlier, but my mind was beginning to catalogue Mackenzie's assets. She looked at me, but I nodded for her to go first. When I added a wink, her chest rose slightly. She was affected.

She jutted her chin forward with a subtle challenge as if to say, bring it on, then she lowered her eyes to her menu. I had no choice but to peruse the selections. "I'll take Applebee's seven-ounce sirloin dinner with an extra serving of steamed vegetables. Mackenzie?" I said as I refolded the menu and laid it on the table.

"Jason, I'll have the buttermilk shrimp," Mackenzie said after she looked up, putting a spell on the young server. "Instead of cocktail sauce, can you replace it with tartar sauce? Thanks."

He scribbled an order on a narrow pad then stuffed it in his apron. *"By the way, I'm not deaf, but my girlfriend is. We met when I served her group when they came here for a signing supper."* Jason gathered the menus and walked away.

I had attended a few silent or signing suppers before. Eating was just a cover. It was a social where couples, mostly deaf, met. I had met women at a few of them, but none was as tempting as Mackenzie.

Jason returned within minutes with our drinks. After he placed them in front of us, he paused before his hands became animated, recapping things I already knew about deaf culture. *"The scene was fascinating. No,"* he paused, *"Jewel is fascinating, and she's beautiful."*

I chuckled. Not as beautiful as Mackenzie, I imagined. This woman had me losing my mind. I had to stop thinking to myself around her. No telling what would slip out of my mouth. As Mackenzie scanned the restaurant, I furthered my assessments, locking in on her features—full lips, high cheekbones, and big brown clear eyes. Wild, wavy black curls framed her narrow face and continued a little down her back. A tiny mole kissed her neck below her right ear. Her five feet-something-inch height had a body built with temptation in mind.

Her subtle-sweet perfume announced her presence and lingered when she passed, but it was her open honesty and infectious energy that sucked me in. These were things I had already noted in our brief previous encounters, but every time I looked at Mackenzie, there was always one more thing I missed. I wanted to look at the world through her eyes. My mind was telling me to take things slow. My heart yelled I had wasted enough time in unproductive relationships and go for it.

I've never been attracted to interpreters. To my embarrassment, I've never dated a Christian woman. It's not as if I had been a poster child for Christ either; but now that I was on that road, I wanted to continue the journey with Mackenzie as my passenger.

"What?"

"Did I call your name?" I frowned.

"A few times," she teased.

"Will you go out with me?" My words came from nowhere, and I refused to take them back.

"Yes."

The breath I was holding, I exhaled. *"I wasn't expecting that. I was looking for a challenge, hesitation, anything, but yes."*

"I don't play games, Noel. I'm 29 years old, and I leave play time to my students. It's something about you that makes me feel comfortable, and I'm not going to question that. It is what it is." Folding her arms, she lifted a brow and twisted her lips. Her cheeks hinted of a dimple. *"Or would you prefer me to say, I'll get back to you, or . . ."*

"I may be deaf, but I'm not stupid, woman," I mouthed, afraid I would speak too loud. Covering her small hand with mine, I squinted before removing my hand. *"Tell me everything about you, Mackenzie."*

Mischief not only danced in her eyes. It was doing cartwheels. *"Everything?"*

"Don't ask me that, woman." It's not that I didn't want to know, but just like my favorite cake, I wanted to savor each piece slowly. Grinning, I shook my head. I wondered how this woman remained unattached this long. Maybe she was created just for me. A moment of wishful thinking came and went. *"Okay, about a few things you like to do?"* I took a small sip. Mackenzie was pleasing to my eyes. Ready for any revelation, I folded my arms and sat back.

Tilting her head to the side, she frowned. Finally, she smiled, not a Colgate one, but one that marvels parents when a baby grins the first time. *"Besides listening to church sermons, attending Bible classes, and other church-related events, Brother Noel?"*

I wiggled my mustache at my own mischief and nodded.

"I enjoy musicals." Mackenzie's eyes lit. *"Concerts, theatrical productions, and oh, I love attending auctions."* Her expression brightened. *"I don't care if it's an estate sale or Christy's—of course I've never attended that one, but I enjoy the sound and art of it."*

Key word—she said it—sound. Could she survive without sound? It wasn't as if the Deaf culture didn't make sounds, but at times we could be so unpredictable. One annoying habit, according to my mother, was my laugh. She called me a bull horn.

"I was a theater major in college, actually I double

majored. I have a B.A. in primary education to pay the bills, and a minor in theatre. As a matter of fact, I'm still active in stage costumes or set design for local productions. A year ago, I decided to go back for my masters. There's no rush, so I'm taking my time."

Mackenzie was more complex than a thousand-piece puzzle. She wasn't coy or arrogant, just complex. I drummed my fingers against the table, trying to figure this woman out. I considered myself a confident man, but Mackenzie scared me. She was throwing things in front of me that required more effort on my part. Yeah, bring it on.

Mackenzie waved her hand. *"Noel, you're not paying attention."*

I smirked. *"Mackenzie, I'm looking right at you, believe me."*

"But you aren't paying attention."

The woman had skills. I couldn't put anything past her. Shaking my head, I apologized. *"Sorry. What were you saying?"*

She twisted her lips in a mock victory. *"Focus, Noel. I said I'm starting to get hooked on ballroom dancing."* Mackenzie chuckled, not knowing how much my ego was deflating. *"I can't shake and twist my hips like the woman who danced with San Francisco's former wide-receiver, Jerry Rice, but after watching a few episodes of Dancing With The Stars, sign me up. I just haven't had the time."*

The woman was pouring salt into my wound. I had enough. *"Mackenzie, I can't do any of those things with you,"* the words spilled as I reached for my glass.

"Why? You can do all things through Christ. You appear to be in good condition. Valerie says you're hot."

I almost choked as I sipped on my strawberry lemonade. Maybe Valerie did have some good qualities. *"I'll take her compliment, but I'd rather it come from you."*

She leaned closer, forcing me to meet her halfway. I hoped we were about to share a secret. My nostrils flared from her perfume in anticipation. I concentrated on her full lips.

"Noel, you're like no other man I've met. Yes, you're hot, but there's more to you than abs and biceps. God sent you to my church for a reason. Explore it."

On a scale of one to ten, Mackenzie had me blushing at ten plus. Sitting back, her fingers played keyboards on the table as she awaited my response. I had no comeback.

"What's the matter? Cat got your tongue?" She didn't suppress her smirk very well.

"No, actually, you do." When she laid her hands on the table, I took the liberty of reaching across, wrapping my hand around hers. This was going to work between us. I would make sure if that. *"Something tells me it's going to take me a while to figure you out."*

"Take your time, Noel. My late mother once told me we only get one shot at the most important thing in life."

"Something tells me you're going to be very important in my life. What else . . ."

Jason chose the wrong moment to return, and I could've strangled him for interrupting. Mackenzie gave the waiter her attention as he placed our meals on the table.

Grabbing Mackenzie's soft hands for prayer and my own selfish reasons, I bowed my head and we prayed. When I opened my eyes, she watched me with amusement. *"What?"*

"I've got to save some information about me until date number two."

"You're a tease, and you know it, don't you?" I accused her as we continued to sign throughout our meal, ignoring a few stares directed our way. We exchanged email addresses and cell numbers for text messaging. When Jason placed a sizzlin' apple pie before Mackenzie, she licked her lips. *"A woman with an appetite,"* I joked.

"We'll talk later. I'm busy."

Agreeing, I laughed to myself before digging into my Triple Chocolate Meltdown—a chocolate cake filled with a fudge-center topped with dark and white chocolates. Mackenzie's eyes coveted her dessert as she ate. My eyes admired her. I didn't need to see my food to taste it. Finally, I swallowed my last bite and picked up our conversation. *"So you're a theater major, are you? What school?"*

Wiping a dip of ice cream off her lips, she swallowed. *"Emerson College in Boston. What about you?"*

I stroked my mustache, watching the pride in her eyes that had to be reflected in her voice. *"I did my undergraduate at Gallaudet University, D.C., and MPA in Public and Nonprofit Management and Policy, New York University Wagner."* I leaned back as if I just checkmated her king. The only problem was I didn't know how to play chess.

Tilting her head, she studied me. *"You're a package, Noel Richardson, especially gift wrapped by God. How old are you?"*

"Thirty-one."

"And you haven't been snatched, yet?" She frowned.

"I'm selective about who traps me." Now take that, Miss Norton, anyway you want.

Jason returned shortly with the bill. Mackenzie reached for her purse. I touched her hand to stop her.

"I invited you to come along, not to buy me dinner," she signed with an attitude.

"A man never lets a lady buy a meal." My fingers walked across the table in a mock dance to the bill again. *"You can buy me dinner when I leave my checkbook and credit cards at home."* I reached into my back pocket for my wallet.

"Something tells me you never do. She challenged.

Add stubborn to her qualities. I've never met a woman who turned down anything free, even if it was a pack of gum. *"Mackenzie, we're not getting off to a good start. We just had our first argument after church and in a restaurant."*

Our heated gestures over who should pay began to draw attention. Embarrassed, we rubbed our right fists in a circular motion against our chests, *"Sorry."*

Valerie appeared and invited herself to our table, forcing a space on the edge of Mackenzie's chair. She actually smiled at me. *"I never turn down a free meal. You want my bill?"*

The woman knew how to crash a party. Mackenzie seemed to ignore the intrusion as she combed the inside of her purse. Before she could retrieve her money, Nick scooped up a chair from a nearby just-vacated table and dragged it to ours as if he was the final partner to a card game.

Nick plucked our ticket from my fingers and grinned. "Got it, brother. Consider it my treat."

"What about me?" Valerie said, pouting.

"You, Sister Preston, are a regular. Everybody knows you."

Nick and Valerie exchanged words about her bill until other church members began to referee. Jason elbowed his way through the gathering and offered to pay for our meal. Realizing our disagreement had gotten out of hand, we called a truce. Mackenzie and I left Jason a tip that was more than half our meal.

Standing, I helped Mackenzie with her coat before putting on mine. I slid my hands into black leather gloves, not commenting about the mismatched gloves pulled from her coat pocket. I smirked at the contrast colors. The woman and her fashion statement. Once outside in the restaurant's parking lot, I looked up into the winter sky. "Still mad at me?" I asked as I escorted Mackenzie to her car.

She stopped and issued her challenge. "Should I be?"

"Listen, Mackenzie, I apologize for making a scene, but not for being a gentleman."

She resumed walking as if she didn't hear me. Pointing her remote at her car, the headlights blinked. She turned and faced me, mischief danced in her eyes. "Next time, I'll order more."

So the teasing interpreter returned. I was geared for another round, so I leaned close to her ear. "Should I follow you home and make sure you don't hurt anybody?"

Mackenzie pulled her wool coat tighter around her neck. *"Nope. Prayer will protect any motorist. I'm a strategic driver. Someone sways to the right. I'll pivot to the left. They stop, I swerve. They jump out, I speed away. Plus, for the time being, I still live at home with my dad. He generally doesn't go to sleep at night until he knows his little girl is safely in the house. If I don't move out soon, I'll be fifty years old and still his little girl, but it's okay. Without my mom, we check on each other."*

Taking off my gloves, I wrapped my hand around Mackenzie's cold fingers that still clutched her gloves. Closing my eyes, I bowed my head. "Father God, in the name of Jesus, I stand before you with a woman so precious, so special. I ask that you guide her over the highways and the byways. Please keep her and everybody in her direction safe. Amen."

CHAPTER 6

A week later, I admitted I was ready for love, wanted to be in love, and wanted Mackenzie to be the recipient. Stretching, I folded my arms behind my head. Pleased with my assessment, there was nothing I wanted to do about it. That didn't mean that I would say or sign those words to Mackenzie next week, but I was willing to explore the possibility. She had everything I desired in a woman: knockout looks, a sweet spirit, and a one-of-a kind sense of humor.

Midweek Bible class didn't satisfy my craving for Mackenzie. We had exchanged a few emails, but it wasn't the same. I didn't have the privilege of walking her to her car. Valerie was at Mackenzie's side, pleading for a ride home. Nick offered, but Valerie declined, insisting she had something to talk over with Mackenzie. I had no other option than to bid Mackenzie goodnight as she walked away.

Friday morning, while on my home computer, my older brother Pierce's instant message request flashed at the bottom of my screen. He was more regular than prune juice. We communicated daily. If he didn't email me, I text messaged him.

Pierce typed: *"What's up, Noel? How did your week go and any plans for this weekend?"*

My hand trailed the waves in my hair. Then I twisted the hair in my mustache before replying. *"Don't think I'm crazy, but I feel like I've lived a lifetime in a week."*

Pierce: *"Explain."*

"Going back to church was one of the best decisions I've made in a long time, and an unexpected blessing was waiting for me, I think. I'll tell you all of the reasons why I was late getting to Mom and Dad's house on Thanksgiving," I tapped on the keyboard.

Pierce: *"Okay, Noel, I'm waiting. You're typing slower than Caleb signs."*

"God drew me to the church, but Mackenzie Norton is keeping me rooted there. From the moment I sat in that pew, it was like a build up of attraction—her somewhat tamed curls, her convictions, and her honesty. That woman had me tangled up in a net before I knew I was captured."

Pierce: *"You told me the focus of going back to a physical church was to strengthen your relationship with God. When did your mission change to include a woman?"*

Did I mention there were no secrets between us? I wanted Pierce's opinion on Mackenzie. *"Don't jump to any conclusions. The church more than meets my spiritual needs. It's the answer to the family's prayers . . ."* I paused. Mackenzie was a full-length novel that I couldn't write about in a sentence or two.

As I rubbed my face, Pierce prompted me: *"Well?"*

I finished typing, *"Maybe mine, too. She's one of the church's interpreters. I can't believe I asked her out days after I met her, and without any hesitation, she said yes."* I bit my lip to hold in a laugh. Pierce would deduce the same thing I thought. A few seconds later, he typed in the words.

Pierce: *"Noel, I know you're not desperate, so what was it that made you lose your mind? It's as if you went to the supermarket to purchase toiletries and came out with a year's supply of canned goods. What gives? Is she pretty? Is she spiritual?"*

I did release my laugh. *"Yes, she's incredibly pretty. Her walk with God excites me. Her attitude fascinates me."* I hit send and waited. *"Pierce, are you there? What are you thinking? Talk to me . . ."*

His message interrupted my thinking. *"A week, huh?"*

"Actually, nine days, but it seems like nine weeks," I corrected.

Pierce: *"Noel, if you start picking out an engagement ring, I may have to step in, and you know I will."*

"I don't expect anything less. I'll keep you posted, within reason. So, no bowling for me this weekend, I'm booked. We're going out for a quick dinner this evening because it's the last night of some theater production at the Uppity Theater." I didn't care if Mackenzie had five minutes to spare, I planned to steal six. *"We're also going to the Chris Botti concert tomorrow at the Blanche Touhill Performing Arts Center."*

Pierce: *Not only have you lost your hearing, you've lost your mind. Chris Botti? You can't hear, Noel. You're way over your head, way over your head."*

"Thanks for reminding me, Pierce."

"Now, I know it's time for me to start praying. I may

have to throw a little fasting in there, too. I'm interested in how this will turn out. Gotta run. Stay focused on Jesus." And with Pierce's signature line, *poof,* he was gone.

Unconcerned about my unopened emails, I logged off the computer. Pierce was my voice of reason, or my conscience, and he kept me grounded. I also believed blessings came unexpectedly. Without him mentioning anything, I had the same concerns about my immediate attraction to Mackenzie.

I stood from behind the desk in my makeshift office in the second bedroom and strained my brain to remember the noise of a trumpet. I couldn't. Strolling across the hardwood floor to my closet, I didn't feel like a suit today, so I chose casual attire. As the founder and chief executive officer of PRE-SERVE-St. Louis, I gave myself permission to work half a day.

My company, a non-profit organization, was my brain-child after attending grad school at NYU-Wagner four years ago. Its MPA curriculum with a concentration in Public and Nonprofit Management and Policy ignited my hunger for community involvement. After volunteering at Brooklyn's Catholic Charities office, I was hooked. Although it was a national private organization, I wanted to concentrate solely on the community where I lived—the displaced, underpaid, and uninsured.

I'm thankful God gave me the desire to continue my education after I received my business degree in Economics from Gallaudet University in D.C. Created by an Act of Congress for the Deaf Culture, it was the premier school that offered an elite education. How many other colleges and universities could boast that President Abraham Lincoln signed their charters?

Then in 1961, President Kennedy introduced affirmative action. Later, President Johnson enforced it. Gallaudet University, segregated Southern Black colleges, and predominately white schools/universities were changed. If schools wanted government funding, they had to offer equal access, which also gave the Deaf culture more opportunities in a hearing world by schools providing necessary tools for us to succeed. We had choices, and for some, that did not include a Gallaudet education.

My professional memberships weren't limited to the National Association for Speech Language and Hearing, the National Black Deaf Association, but also the National Association of Black MBAs and the Association for Public Policy Analysis and Management (APPAM). Not bad for a deaf man, but I had a lot of inspiration. The accomplishments of African Americans like Martin Luther King, Rosa Parks, James Hubert Blake, Jackie Robinson, Dr. Mae Jemison, and countless others are instilled into every black child.

When I lost my hearing, my family indoctrinated me to the famous deaf pioneers like bodybuilder, Lou Ferrigno, actress, Amy Ecklund, Miss America talk show host, Heather Whitestone, and even Rush Limbaugh. How many people knew Rush wore a cochlear implant because he had experienced sudden deafness?

I was preaching to the choir again. At PRESERVE-St. Louis, we organized weekly forums and workshops, sometimes we facilitated more than two a week. Occasionally, we hosted evening fundraisers that required our presence until ten at night. If there were hot-button topics, our role was to act as the mediator between the rich and poor, communities and corporations, Jews and Muslims, or black and white.

With the end of the year approaching, our main focus was choosing the hundred neediest families in St. Louis and assisting them. The one hundred neediest families program was designed to match corporate donations with families that would miss out on the holiday without the help from others. We had been working on that project since October.

At nine-thirty, I walked through the glass doors at PRESERVE-St. Louis. Waving at my receptionist, I continued to my office where I booted up my computer and scanned the scribbled messages on my desk. Opening the file, listing the families still waiting for assistance, I wrote a note to have my assistant make additional phone calls and to follow up on correspondence about donation pledges.

Despite my financial and educational achievement, it was my spiritual tank that was empty. Was I baptized in Jesus' name? Yes. Did I receive the Holy Ghost with the evidence of speaking in unknown tongues? Yes. Have I been faithful in reading my Word? No. In praying? No. In witnessing? No. Was I ready to embrace the forthcoming changes to my life, which would include Mackenzie? No question about it, yes.

* * *

At one-thirty, I turned off the overhead lights in my office. Minutes later, I slid behind the wheel of my car. Before driving off, I paused for a short prayer. For some reason I wanted God pulling for us for this thing to work out.

Taking a deep breath, I opened my eyes as I lifted my head. I stared through the windshield. I've never prayed so much as since I started going back to church. Still, I wanted to be more than a visitor, I wanted to join, be part of the flock. With that thought, I took off and drove west on Forest Park Parkway.

Thirty minutes later, I entered a ten-acre school campus, which seemed to divide the east from the west and the poor from the up-and-coming middle class. Landscaped lawns, manicured flowers skipped up man-made mounds. The Watkins School was a transplant in the worst part of the city of St. Louis.

The only remnant of the original structure was the etching on the front of the building—erected in 1920. Otherwise the building could be the winner of an architectural competition. Mackenzie seemed to fit the profile of an instructor, charming her way into an adult or child's heart and making them believe the impossible.

A black wrought-iron fence rode the perimeters of the property. A winding path took me to a large rear parking lot. Every type of playground equipment designed by man was sprinkled throughout the backyard.

Entering at the front of the building, a sign directed all visitors to the office. I spotted it immediately through a glass wall. Opening the door, heads popped up. I had everyone's attention, especially three women on the other side of a counter. That I expected. One stood from behind her desk, smiled, and approached the counter. She straightened her shoulders and angled her breasts. "May I help you ?" Her eyes darted to my ring finger. "Are you a . . ." her words were lost as she looked down, fumbling for a pad. She grabbed a pencil as she continued to speak.

"Pardon me. I need to see your lips." It was interesting to watch her response. I knew exactly what I was doing.

"Oh, okay," she said, flattered. Puckering, she presented me with different angles.

"I need to read lips because I can't hear."

"Oh." She frowned as her shoulders slumped.

"I'm here to see Mackenzie Norton."

Tossing her pad and pencil a few feet to a desk, she looked back at me. "Well, she's still in class for at least another twenty minutes. You can take a seat over there."

I glanced at the unappealing chairs that lined the wall. "Is there a school policy against sitting in on a class?"

She shrugged. "No, not really. Sign in here, put on this badge and I'll escort you to her classroom."

I did as instructed and accepted the peel off white badge label then followed her down a multi-color carpeted hall. I sniffed the fresh paint on the walls. After passing three classrooms, we finally stopped. Thanking her before she left, I peeped inside the closed half glass-and-wood door.

Mackenzie held the classroom of small, inquisitive eyes spellbound. She also had pulled my hazel eyes in with them. One student, a girl whose skin reminded me of sand, wore precision parted corn-rows that raced down her head. Her white blouse and tan pants uniform was crisp. When she raised her hand, she flashed yellow fingernail polish. Her arm continued to jab the air, pointing at me to get Mackenzie's attention.

Glancing over her shoulder, Mackenzie's face brightened and her ready smile blossomed. She beckoned for me to come inside. Every scrutinizing eye followed my entrance as Mackenzie motioned me to the back of the class. I scanned the large classroom for adult-size furniture. Only Mackenzie's desk and chair would fit the bill, and those were in the front of the class. Suddenly, I felt like a super-size kid in a doll house.

After trying two chairs, I squeezed into one that I was convinced wouldn't release my behind once I stood. Folding my arms, I stretched out my legs as Mackenzie turned back to the chalkboard. Every student followed her lead except a dark-skinned boy whose locks were longer than some women's hair. He threw a miniature eraser at me. Shocked, I frowned at him. Is this what students did inside the classrooms now? Ignoring him, I focused on Mackenzie, hinting for him to follow.

Not to be deterred, he began a slow scoot back in his desk. The authoritarian look I shot his way didn't faze him. His desk was on the verge of tilting over when Mackenzie caught him. His neck whipped around.

"Moses, what do you think you're doing, young man?"

He mumbled a reply. From the look on Mackenzie's face, his answer was unsatisfactory. She glanced at the wall clock and motioned for Moses to come to the front of the class. The boy hesitantly stood, and with one final moment of defiance, glared back at me. "Are you Miss Norton's boyfriend?"

In one synchronized move, the heads of about twenty students turned to me. They waited, including Mackenzie. Leave it to an eight-year-old to put me on the spot. My eyes bounced off faces as if I was in the Bermuda triangle. "Yep. You wanna step outside?" Where did that taunt come from? Evidently, Mackenzie enforced zero tolerance in her classroom. She sent us both to the office.

Once school was dismissed, I escorted a fuming Mackenzie to her car. She had every reason to be upset. My behavior was so out of character. Yet, I couldn't explain why being around Mackenzie, I dropped defenses as a CEO or a man trying to impress a very desirable woman.

As she walked faster, my long strides matched hers. "Listen, Mackenzie, okay, I blew it and I'm sorry I disrupted your class. My sole intention was to share a quick bite with you. I did apologize to a smug Moses Hilton."

She was almost to her car when she whirled around. Instead of lashing out, she laughed.

I didn't get the joke. I stepped closer, confused. "What? Mackenzie, what's so funny?" I rested my elbow on the hood of her car and waited. I stifled my own amusement. When she gulped pockets of air, I hoped an explanation was forthcoming.

She stopped abruptly and faced me, lifting her chin. Her eyes still glistened and her smile was mesmerizing.

"I don't know why or how, but I have a suspicion you set me up, didn't you?" I snarled.

She shook her head. "Nope, that was all Moses. He's the troublemaker. Why do you think I have his desk at the back of my class? He's the one who set you up. Noel, admit it. The CEO isn't smarter than a fifth grader or a second grader."

I grabbed her before she could register she was wrapped in a web of my arms. "Grade me on this." She struggled as I kissed her. I didn't stop until I needed air.

CHAPTER 7

Mackenzie was hot! Things spiraled out of control when I was around Mackenzie. I lost control with Moses, but I was in complete control when we kissed. When I released her, three expressions played on her face: dazed, pleased, and indignant. "I can't believe you did that on my job and at school where children could see!" She got in her car and drove off. Shrugging, I got behind my wheel and trailed her. She had a point, but I wasn't thinking, which was becoming the norm.

Mackenzie's driving hadn't changed from the first time I followed her. She still endangered my life and made me dizzy. Once we parked, I exhaled. Climbing out my car, Mackenzie didn't wait for me to open her car door. I was there anyway.

"Still mad at me?"

"Should I be?" With her face upturned, she issued the challenge.

"If I kiss you again, you might." I didn't blink.

"Noel, although I enjoyed your kiss, don't let it happen again on school property. I am a teacher and I'm a saint of God, not some hussy. My dad gave me a good name and I plan to keep it. Treat me with respect, Noel. Take note." She turned and marched into O'Charley's without giving me a backward glance. I don't think she cared if I followed.

Inside, she allowed me to catch her coat as she took it off while a hostess greeted us and showed us to a table. After waiting for her to sit, I slid into the booth seat across from her. "Can we start over?"

"Yes."

As she initiated a stare, I cataloged more of her features. In class, I admired her outfit, a two-piece sweater set with a faux-fur collar in the deepest purple I'd ever seen. I reached across the table and caressed her hand before signing. *Why is a beautiful sister who truly loves the Lord unmarried?*

Without contemplating, she shrugged. *The Lord hasn't sent husband material yet.*

As I mulled over her comment, our waiter appeared. I wondered how much material she had rejected.

"Would you like me to order for you?" Mackenzie signed.

Not again, I didn't need another woman feeling she had to order for me. I shook my head. If God revealed to me that Mackenzie was my Proverbs 31 Woman—filled with wisdom and charity and strength—then now was the time for me to strive for the 1 Peter 3 Man—who understood his woman, his wife, and accepted that the husband, by God's standards, is weak. His wife is weaker and together their prayers would please God. That's

one sermon I had remembered from a televangelist's program.

"Then order," she stated, instead of signing, ignoring the bewildered expression from our hostess.

The poor girl looked young enough for this to
be her first job. I had compassion when I spoke
and signed our selections. "The California Chicken
salad for the lady, the Chipotle Chicken for me,
and a glass of water." I paused, looking to Mackenzie for her choice of drink. She tapped her three
middle fingers on the right side of her mouth a
few times. Nodding, I turned back to the hostess.
"And water for the lady."

Mackenzie reached across the table and placed
an incredibly soft, moist hand on top of mine.
"Noel, did you see that stricken look on that girl's
face? You would've thought a monster was about
to attack her. I could have ordered for both of us."

*"I asked you out to dinner, not to be my personal in-
terpreter, Mackenzie. You're my interpreter at church
only."* Being with Mackenzie was like enjoying cake
and ice cream—both tasted better together. *"How
much time do we have?"*

Mackenzie lifted a slender wrist wrapped in a
colorful rhinestone bracelet. She toyed with the
jewelry until she tapped the face of her watch.
*"Two hours max. Now, back to that stunt you pulled
back at my school?"*

"We don't have time to revisit that."

One brow lifted, her lips squeezed in an unflat-
tering pucker, her nostrils flared as she leaned in
to me.

"Pucker again, and I'll kiss you again," I mouthed,

waiting for Mackenzie's Category 4 storm to be un-leashed.

For a moment, Mackenzie debated. She opened her mouth to speak then changed her mind, slumping back in her seat. I didn't blink as I reigned victorious.

"Listen, Noel," Mackenzie signed as a waitress appeared, wearing a haggard expression that matched her uniform. She placed tall glasses of ice water on our table without acknowledging Mackenzie's glistening smile. Once the woman left, Mackenzie's charming smile evaporated as she focused on me again.

To push her button, I held up my right finger and signed, *"Technically, Mackenzie, I can't hear."*

"You're nuts." Reaching for her glass, she gulped a mouthful of water. When Mackenzie removed the glass, her cheeks were expanded. Granted, I didn't know her well enough to predict her next move. It was a toss up between releasing a flood-gate, or swallowing. She must have learned this trick from one of her students. *"Got you wondering, don't I?"*

Nodding, I wondered if I should duck. Then she swallowed. The woman was a prankster, and she was ready to scold me about the theatrics in her class room?

She leaned forward. "That's payback for cutting up in my class."

"Okay, truce." I extended my hand as our wait-ress slid our meals in front of us, and stood at attention. I didn't break eye contact with Mackenzie until she tapped me on my hand and pointed to the intruder, talking to me.

The waitress frowned in irritation. "Would there be anything else, sir."

"No, thank you." I waved her away. "Now, where were we?" I asked, wiggling my mustache.

"You're about to bless our food."

Wrapping my hands around hers, we bowed our heads, and prayed. As our hands separated, I checked my watch before forking off a piece of chicken and lifting it to my mouth. I admired that Mackenzie maintained a busy lifestyle with work, school, church, and the theatre, but she had to make an adjustment. *"Can you see yourself spending more time with me?"*

"Yes, Noel, I can."

I liked her straight-forward answers. *"Tell me about your mother."*

"Katherine Norton passed away when I was ten years old. She always said we have to face the good and bad in life. One day, she reminisced how she and my dad fell in love. More than once, she talked about the one chance or blessing we get in life. When she gave birth to me, my dad named me Mackenzie which means daughter of wise leader. It has an Irish origin. I hoped and prayed she imparted some of her wisdom on me. I'll never forget her words, all things are important in life, but there's always something most important."

Picking up her fork, she resumed eating. I slowed my pace to match hers. With Mackenzie, I wanted to eat up her presence and chew on her every word. The only drawback was our time was limited. I dabbed my mouth with a napkin and pushed away my plate.

"Tell me a secret. Tell me something that you hold so

dear that you wouldn't share with your best friend." I paused and brushed my hand against her fingers.

Her eyes sparkled in merriment. *"After a week, what could I possibly want to bare about my soul to you?"* Her fingers danced with mine in a tease.

"You could say I'm like no other man you've ever met."

She tilted her head. *"I could."*

"Whatever you say, don't say you regret getting to know me, because Mackenzie, I'm not feeling that." Just as Mackenzie was about to lean across the table, the waitress returned to remove our plates. She didn't interrupt us as she tore our ticket off her pad and allowed it to drift between us on the table.

"Noel, one thing I would definitely share with you is how crazy I am about your voice. When you whisper to me, the sound is strong, deep, confident, and perfect. That's the only compliment you're getting from me today."

My heart pumped faster with her admission and fell in love. Somehow I predicted a relationship between us wouldn't be that simple. Maybe that's why I thought about the word wife earlier. I was willing to learn everything about her. It had to be an even exchange. *"Are you a lot like your mother?"*

Shrugging, she gave me a childish grin. I imagined she used it when she wanted a double scoop of ice cream when she knew she could only have one. "It all depends."

"On?" I enjoyed her tease.

"Oh, that depends on what day you ask my father. When I'm making him the proud papa, I'm just like him. When I'm stubborn, defiant, and free-spirited, he says I'm my mother reincarnated."

The laugh rumbled from my stomach and climbed up my throat. By the time it escaped, I couldn't snap my mouth shut. I didn't care how it came out, but I delivered it to the stares of some patrons. Mackenzie's eyes sparkled as she joined me. She slammed money on the table and yanked me out my seat. With her arm tangled in mine, she dragged me from O'Charley's. The little vixen had paid the tab before I realized it and without even blinking an eye.

Opening the door to her car, I refrained from another kiss although she was alluring.

"So, Noel is this our first date?

"It's only a prelude."

CHAPTER 8

The following night, I was Mackenzie's chauffeur as she reclined in my passenger seat after she inspected the features of my new CTS model. "Is it to your liking?"

"It's very nice. I thought about getting a new car. I love the smell."

"Then why don't you?"

Mackenzie shrugged. "My friend calls me cheap. I consider myself frugal. I'm just particular on how I spend my money. Cars are not a priority." She paused to connect her seat belt before regaining my attention. "The concert is smooth jazz, and sometimes they play inspirational instrumentals."

"I know." That's because I Googled the artist. Driving like a drunken man under the influence of Mackenzie's perfume, I glanced as she fumbled with knobs on my radio panel.

Steering my Cadillac through the winding road on the campus of the University of Missouri at St. Louis—dubbed UMSL by Missourians—my strong black man, black deaf man exterior was shaken with nervousness. This was our first official date. I wanted to give Mackenzie memories of a fantastic evening.

From the moment I stood outside her front door, I had to rebuke the devil for taunting me that a disastrous night was forthcoming. I had hoped to formally introduce myself to Mackenzie's father, but he wasn't home.

Over dinner, my anxieties ceased as we ate. Several times, she leaned closer to me. I assumed she was sharing a secret. It had become an endearing act that I had come to expect throughout the night.

I inched into a parking space and removed my key from the ignition. Glancing at Mackenzie, she rewarded me with a one-dimple smile. Reaching for my hand, she blessed it with a soft squeeze.

"Thank you, Noel. You're really going to enjoy this."

Somewhere deep inside me I found a grin to give her. If I ever needed a Tums for an upset stomach, tonight was it. I should've driven downtown to Tums's headquarters and asked for samples. A bad feeling settled in my stomach. Was this a test to see if I passed? Our dating experience was already starting out lopsided. A few former hearing girlfriends had used this technique as a measuring stick.

In my mind, I was already devising a payback. Mackenzie had a test she would have to pass for me. My scheme was deflated with one peek at Mackenzie. She had her head bowed. I hope she was praying for me.

Gripping my steering wheel, I closed my eyes and said my own silent prayer. When my lids fluttered, hazel eyes met brown ones. I couldn't back out of this date if I wanted to.

"Ready?"

She nodded.

Forcing myself to break Mackenzie's trance, I turned and slipped out of my car then opened the back door. Reaching for my hat, I placed it on my head and positioned it to my liking before I retrieved my coat. My mother often teased that my Fedora and wool trench coat painted me as a mysterious man. What do mothers know? Walking around the car, I helped Mackenzie get out.

With her hand—ungloved tonight—in mine, we synchronized our steps. Seconds later, we harmonized our breathing as we inhaled and exhaled the crisp December air. Once inside the Touhill Performing Arts Center, we maneuvered through the crowd, which was a mixture of well-dressed couples, seniors, and jean-wearing college students of every ethnicity, to the coat room. I stopped counting the number of times I stared at her hair. I had to ask, *"Do you sleep with curlers?"*

She gave me the oddest expression before shaking her head, which further added to her carefree persona. *"Why?"*

With a slight tug, I twisted my finger around one spiral curl like a rope. As she waited for an answer, I stood in the middle of the lobby, playing in her hair. Playfully, she slapped my hand away. Amused, I reached for another lock.

She leaned into me so that I had a clear view of

her mouth. *"What are you doing, Noel? You think I wake up looking like this? It takes me almost an hour every morning to do my hair."*

I didn't care about her explanation as I scanned her face, making sure I didn't overlook any spot. If she wore makeup, it was entrenched in her skin because there wasn't a hint of it. My eyes locked in on her untouchable glossy lips. *"What does it look like I'm doing, Mackenzie? I'm playing in your hair, and of course, I think you wake up looking beautiful."*

Under the guise of looking down, I appraised Mackenzie's attire. Through hooded lashes, I got an eyeful. Mackenzie's simmering silver two-piece suit was a mixture of satin ruffles and dazzling beadwork. I was forced to do a double take at her feet. The see-through material gave the illusion that she was shoeless. The tell-tale sign was the glistening rhinestones. Like a Rolodex, I recalled every scripture about temptation. When my eyes ascended, Mackenzie's lips were curled in amusement.

"Enjoy the view?"

"Yeah, I did and still do," I flirted.

"I was checking you out, too. You look very nice in your peanut-color suit and chocolate tie. It matches your hazelnut eyes. I wouldn't be surprised if your socks were coffee-colored to go with your hot cocoa-shaded shoes," she teased, wrinkling her nose.

"Woman, how could you lump me on a menu in sixty seconds? If you were hungry, I would've fed you before the concert."

We linked hands as her face lit up with laughter. She didn't answer, pulling me toward a theater usher. Without any resistance, I let her. A plump elderly woman wearing an over-sized blazer read our tickets and mumbled. She flagged another usher at auditorium's entrance. Mackenzie nodded and tugged me along.

A gentleman greeted us, guided us to the designated row, and pointed to our seats. I offered Mackenzie entrance first. After we settled into thick, dark velvet-covered seats, we accepted programs. The words blurred as I thought about the long concert ahead. It would make Mackenzie happy and me miserable. Just like church, I would have to depend on the vibrations in my chest and under my feet to stay in sync. We were too far away to read lips since I was lucky to get any tickets on short notice and I didn't have an interpreter.

Minutes later, the lights dimmed and a heavyset gentleman, stuffed into a tuxedo, teetered on the stage and faced the audience. Mackenzie turned and nudged me. "You want me to sign for you?"

I shook my head. "I'll let you know when I need an interpreter, Sister Mackenzie Norton. Right now, I need you to be my woman on a date."

Mackenzie's mouth formed an "o."

"After all, I did tell your class you're my girlfriend." I winked right before darkness blanketed the auditorium that was filled to capacity. A preppy-dressed white guy in faded designer jeans and a worn corduroy blazer strolled onto the stage. When he lifted a trumpet to his lips, I assumed he was the musician, Chris Botti. I stretched my arm across the back of Mackenzie's seat and urged her closer.

A young black guy walked out of the shadows onto the stage. Gripping sticks, he made a beeline to the drums. From where I sat, he didn't appear to be someone who would stand out from a crowd. Then the drummer proved me wrong. His body language let me know he was setting the pace. Drumsticks twirled in the air like an ice skater, slowing down just enough to fake a baton.

Without realizing it, my head bobbed from side to side as I mimicked him. I had to force my concentration from the stage to look around. Heads moved, but in a different rhythm. I figured they were off beat.

The guitarist took the spotlight after the drummer. I was riveted as his fingers stroked the strings, manipulating my internal tempo. The silent serenade lulled me to sleep before the vibration of the drummer's thump alerted me he was back in his groove.

When I snuck a peek at Mackenzie, her eyes spoke to me with an I-told-you-so expression. Two hours later, Mackenzie distracted me when she shook my shoulder. Swaying, my lids fluttered open at the interruption. I frowned. "What?"

"It's over, Noel."

Frowning, I jerked my head in all directions. People were spilling into the aisle toward the exit. When Mackenzie stood, I did the same, stretching.

"Did you enjoy yourself?" She knew the answer without asking.

Taking her hand, I lifted it to my mouth and brushed my lips against it. "Every minute."

CHAPTER 9

Sunday morning, church was the first thing on my mind. Mackenzie was the second. Mackenzie was going to be my strength and temptation.

This was the only day I didn't jog. My routine was usually fifty pushups and weight lifting from my bedroom. After that, I prayed and showered. I was about to select my shirt and tie when I stopped for a moment of praise. I recited Psalm 150. I praised God for His sanctuary, I praised the Lord for His mighty acts; I praised Him with my soundless sound of the trumpet, the timbrel, and the vibrating cymbals. I made my own sound, shouting verse six. "*Let everything that hath breath praise the Lord.*' Praise ye the Lord!"

My flashing strobe light alerted me that someone was at my front door, ringing a bell. It was Sunday morning and I was in no hurry to answer it for a solicitor, neighborhood kid, or someone else. Neither was I concerned about being shirtless and barefooted.

Annoyed at the interruption, I checked the

peephole to find Caleb's teeth blocking my view. Opening the door, I nodded at Caleb, then Pierce who stood behind him. They were dressed in dark suits and ties. I summarized it was Caleb's monthly church visit. Otherwise, he would've been in bed, recovering from a hangover. That was one promise he kept to our mother, an occasional visit to church. Both wore frowns that marred their identical faces.

"You all right?" Pierce asked, poised for action.

Caleb snapped his cell phone shut, barging in without an invitation with Pierce trailing. Leaving me no choice, I closed the door and followed them as they searched my rooms like crime scene investigators.

"Okay, what's going on? Why are you two here, and what are you looking for? " I directed my questions at Pierce. I'd never get a straight answer from Caleb on the first try.

"I came to see how everything went last night."

Realizing my fly was open, I zipped up my pants. "And you came twenty minutes out of your way to ask me when texting or emailing me would've worked, Pierce?"

Pierce unbuttoned his suit jacket and didn't back down. *"You're my brother and I can communicate with you in whatever manner I want. This morning, I chose to talk to you in person, and I wanted to do it before service, so that I would know what to pray for at church,"* he signed and then for Caleb's benefit he stopped. "When you didn't answer the door and we heard voices, Caleb was one minute into talking to the relay call operator. I was thirty seconds away from breaking into the joint."

I started to sign, but reconsidered. Folding my arms against my bare chest, I was no longer self-conscious about the disfigured skin tattooed on it. "I'm alive. I'm fine, and you two are making me late for church. Goodbye. I was praying."

Instead of heading to my front door, Pierce walked into my living room and made himself comfortable in my reclining chair. Caleb went into my kitchen, triggering the sensor on a floor mat that let me know his whereabouts. He was raiding an overhead cabinet for breakfast food, again. Many deaf parents used the sensor to monitor small children. I did it just to stay one step ahead of my younger brother.

"I'm out of milk, Caleb. Don't you have cereal at home?" I shouted over my shoulder as I watched Pierce.

Anchoring his elbows on his knees, Pierce bowed his head before looking up. "I'm sorry, Noel, things didn't work out last night. Don't be discouraged. That woman should've never suggested you go. It was a mockery. I know God heard your cries and will give you the woman who is right for you."

"Mackenzie could be that woman..." It took three tries before Pierce registered my time-out signal, and stopped his rambling. "Pierce, you and Caleb need to leave now."

Caleb walked in to my living room, his jaw bulging with grapes. "We're not going anywhere. We're here to support you." I interpreted his words between chews.

"Don't forget the free meal." I shook my head in amusement while I planted my hands on my hips.

"Listen, Richardson one and three. For the record, I never enjoyed myself more. Believe me when I say that the few times I've spent with Mackenzie, I hear things I'd never thought possible. That's all I'm saying for now. You two can see your way out. I've got to get dressed for church service."

I retraced my steps and almost squashed a grape rolling under my foot. When I turned and yelled at Caleb as another grape shot from his mouth. I laughed until he began to choke. Instantly Pierce and I were at his side, pounding on his back as he gulped for air.

"Hey, you all right?" I asked, straightening his tie.

Caleb stood. "Yeah, yeah, man." He waved us away. "Noel, what I was trying to say is the last we checked, you're still deaf. Now if that changes, I want to know. She has you hear-cinating, not hallucinating."

Pierce eyed me carefully. *There's no need for you to get so caught up in this woman yet, Noel. If you start losing your mind, then I'll be praying for you.*

"Although I'd never turn down prayer, your concerns are unwarranted." After my date last night, I was confident that my relationship with Mackenzie was moving in a positive Holy Ghost-filled direction. Checking my watch, I practically trotted down the hall to my bedroom. On a mission, I put on a T-shirt. I splashed on my aftershave, brushed my hair, and scrutinized my mustache to see if a trim was necessary. Passing inspection, I slipped on a shirt. After snaking my belt through my pants' loops, I finished dressing.

With my Bible in hand, I stopped by the hall closet for my coat. Surprisingly, my brothers hadn't moved. As a matter of fact, they seemed comfortable. Waving, I walked out of my own door. They were free to stay. I knew they wouldn't. As I drove off, they were closing my front door as if they owned the place.

Ten minutes later, my soul rejoiced once I stepped inside the church's vestibule. My heart pounded excitedly in anticipation of being in God's presence and seeing Mackenzie. As I reached the door to the sanctuary, I caught a glimpse of her to my left in a far corner. She was gorgeous in her off-white ankle-length dress that hid too much. I sighed in disappointment.

Grinning, I thought about our date at the concert last night. Swaggering in her direction, I stopped when I saw Valerie who seemed upset, judging from her body language. I should've walked away, but I didn't. I didn't want to intrude, but I was about to.

"And here, I thought we were prayer partners, making intercessory prayers on behalf of each other. What happened, Mackenzie?" Valerie's lips dripped with venom. "You sure you didn't slip in your request first and just so happened to remember mine later?" Valerie wagged her finger so close to Mackenzie's face, Mackenzie should've taken a bite.

"How could you steal Noel from me? I'm the one who wanted a husband. You wanted God to open a door for you in Chicago."

How ridiculous? God wouldn't be that cruel to

bind me to Valerie till death do us part. Exactly what did Valerie mean about Chicago? I stepped back, but I didn't go away.

"Girl, I'm going to be praying night and day for you to leave permanently. You're nothing more than a husband stealer. You took what God sent for me!" Valerie's lips were so tight with emotion. I misinterpreted Valerie saying, God had sent me for her. I chuckled, yeah, right. If it wasn't for Mackenzie, I would leave now and return to televangelist sermons.

It was getting a little warm, so I loosened the knot on the tie that took me three tries to manipulate to perfection. I processed Mackenzie, husband, and Chicago. Neither would be happening if I wasn't involved.

Pierce's words of caution haunted me. I might be deaf, but I was no fool. Fuming, my nostrils flared. Maybe I had acted too soon and assumed too much. She doesn't play games, huh? Well, Valerie wouldn't be the only one confronting Mackenzie.

Mackenzie scratched her head in annoyance, a habit I noticed once when I criticized her driving. "Listen, Valerie, I sincerely and earnestly petitioned God on your behalf for a mate. How could I get blessed if my prayer was about me, me, me? I wasn't looking for or asking God for a boyfriend and you're accusing me of stealing Noel from you? And any relationship I have with Noel is not your concern. Oh, and guess what, my sister? Don't stop praying about Chicago." She turned to walk away, but paused. "Valerie, let's suppose God did send you a wonderful package like Noel. You would miss every blessing that Noel has to offer because you can't get past his deafness. I like Noel and enjoy his company. He's not only nice-looking, but he's also sincere. And there's one other thing, Noel could fit into your world only if you let him. If God has him for you, then he wasn't mine to take."

Naw, you want to bet? I thought about interrupting, but I had to process Valerie's moment of insanity. If her twisted mind really believed that, why her hostility? I grimaced. *God, I came to this church for you. Lord, I know I have to talk to this woman soon, but God, grant me favor to hold off a little longer.* Then there was Mackenzie. Yes, we spoke briefly about her aspirations in theater but I'm positive Chicago wasn't mentioned in the same sentence. As Valerie balled her fists, I was ready to intervene, but Mackenzie attempted to diffuse the volatile situation as she covered Valerie's hand, bowed her head, and prayed.

Squinting, I recognized words from Romans 13. After Mackenzie finished praying for Valerie, she'd better pray for herself. There would be a change of plans about this Chicago nonsense. As I turned around to head to the sanctuary, Keisha and Daphne ran into me, signing with animated faces. With them in tow, I continued on to the sanctuary.

Just like little women, the pair selected a pew for all three of us. I bent to pray and the Campbell sisters followed. I closed my eyes and prayed. When I opened them, they were still beside me like guards.

While still on my knees, I searched for their mother. Finding her sitting two rows away, she shrugged her apology for their pestering.

I sat and faced the interpreters. Valerie squirmed in her chair, shooting me expressions that shifted between murderous and longing. Mackenzie made eye contact with everyone else in the group, but me.

CHAPTER 10

Mackenzie signed as Pastor Coleman began his morning sermon asking questions. *"Has anyone wondered what to pray, how to pray, or what is God's will in your life? If you want to build something, you've got to have a model. If you cook a dish, you have a recipe. If you become ill, you follow instructions from your prescription to get better. I'm going somewhere with this, so stay with me."*

I briefly glanced at Valerie who sat next to Mackenzie and appeared tortured. As Pastor Coleman dissected each verse in Luke 11, Valerie relieved Mackenzie and continued the interpretation. *"Remember, saints, prayer is all about God, recognizing Him as the Supreme Being, praising Him for the name Jesus Christ, requesting His will, thanking Him for being our Provider, and accepting His forgiveness. This is the formula for prayer. Before you get up from your knees, go through the checklist, then God will bless you . . ."*

Mackenzie resumed signing during the altar call. I wondered about my checklist. A finger poked my leg, distracting me.

"*She's still ugly,*" Keisha signed.

Daphne nudged her. "*Momma told you about say-ing that. I want candy after church and you're going to get us in trouble.*"

I chuckled at their antics. Ten minutes later, be-hind the pulpit, water shifted in the glass tub as three men, redressed in white clothing, descended into the baptismal pool. I didn't need to read Mackenzie's hands as they stroked the air to know what the ministers in the pool recited once they lifted their hands. "*My dear brothers, by the confession of your faith, we now indeed baptize you in the name of Jesus for the remission of your sins, and ye shall receive the gift of the Holy Ghost with speaking in tongues.*"

The men were submerged then raised up out the water, standing they walked up a few steps out the pool. The baptismal always fascinated me. Yes, I had been baptized, and yes, I experienced the fire of the Holy Ghost. After we were dismissed, Va-lerie stomped away. I sought Mackenzie, which wasn't easy either as I tugged her away from Nick, the church comedian from Applebee's. At first, she resisted; but with her hand securely in mine, I led her to a nearby pew.

Her behind hadn't touched the cushion before she started in on me. "You have a lot of nerve, Noel Richardson, eavesdropping on a personal conversation."

Cupping my ear, I feigned innocence. "What?"

Mackenzie slapped my hand away. She was fum-ing. "You heard us. I mean," she paused, searching for words.

Jokes aside, I engulfed her small hand in mine.

Our disagreements were outnumbering our kisses. "Yes, Mackenzie I know what you mean. Why didn't you tell me about Chicago? I thought we were sharing things. Secrets."

Sarcasm twisted her lips. "Because, silly me, that's a dream I only shared with Valerie. Now, I wish I had kept that to myself." She stared at me longer than I felt comfortable. *"I didn't pray for you, Noel."*

If her words were a sledgehammer, I would've been crushed. Instead, I focused on her face. I didn't blink, breathe, or move. I waited for her to continue.

"My life changed on Thanksgiving Day when you spoke into my ears. Ever since that moment, it seems like you have always been in my life. The teasing, the holding hands, the kiss . . . God, Noel, I didn't feel like I had to question things, wondering if you were here for Valerie."

"You don't. Valerie has nothing I want, including friendship, and let me tell you, I'm struggling with my attitude on that."

"When you asked me out, I didn't hesitate. When you kissed me, I didn't slap you. Noel, here's another note for you to take. My private conversations are just that. Don't violate my privacy."

"Noted." I adored her stormy spirit and honesty. Properly chastened, my hand trailed the wave of my hair down to my neck. Briefly, I broke eye contact before meeting her eyes again. "Mackenzie, there's a relationship out there waiting to blossom between us. I know you feel that. I'm willing to pull

out all the stops for you, but that doesn't include a long distance relationship. Plus, I don't live in Chicago." I had no right to make demands on her, but I had every right to pursue her until she made a decision that was favorable to us—to me.

"No, but Goodman Theatre is there. Its reputation is legendary for hiring the best of the best directors who conceive authentic plays that many playhouses couldn't duplicate. A lot of theatres lack the funds to construct elaborate stage sets and hire highly trained talent."

I lifted a brow. "Aren't you already busy with theatre companies here?"

"Yes, I am. During the school year it's worth it to me to keep up with eighteen second-graders, jump from theater projects to the next play, be active in church, sometimes taking a graduate class. I'm single and living with my father who keeps me from getting lonely. The exhausting schedule serves two purposes. One to amass the prerequisite for acceptance into Goodman Theatre, and . . ."

"Two?" My nostrils flared in frustration, so I regulated my breathing.

"I'm single. Busyness conquers loneliness."

I wanted to make sure I spoke clearly so she wouldn't miss a word, be it a misunderstanding, or a misinterpretation. "Mackenzie, you may not have prayed for me, but I'm here now. I think there needs to be a change of plans."

A smile spread across her face, giving me a peek of her dimple. "Then I guess it's up to you to make sure that happens."

Shaking my head, I folded my arms and smirked.

She was unbelievable, unpredictable, and unquestionably the most fascinating woman God had formed. This is when seeking the Lord was the only option. Mackenzie wanted Chicago, Valerie wanted me, and I wanted Mackenzie. I didn't blink as I accepted the challenge. "Consider it done."

CHAPTER 11

Mmm, wrapped in a blissful cocoon, I cupped Mackenzie's mesmerizing face between my hands, convincing her that Chicago was not in my plans. "Don't make me have to move up there, because there's no way I'm not going to finish what you started the day I entered that church."

She teased me, chuckling. With mock innocence, she asked. "What did I start?"

"You, Miss Norton, started my heart beating faster. You created a desire in me so strong that I planned to ask you out as many times as it would take for you to say yes. And," I held up a finger and jabbed my thumb into my chest, "you're this man's temptation. I believe in giving warnings when I'm serious. I will pursue you until you say yes, you'll marry me."

Mackenzie closed her eyes as she digested my words. She inched closer to my lips, leaving just enough space for me to read her. "Then I guess we better keep our eyes open and pray. Matthew 26 says, the spirit is willing, but the flesh is weak. I don't want to tempt you, Noel."

"It's too late. You do, Mackenzie, and that's what drives me crazy; you don't try."

"Sometimes, I'm barely holding it together."

I was a breath away from smothering the rest of her words when I was snatched away from her presence. It wasn't God's wrath, but my bed that rocked and angrily tossed me overboard onto the floor. Drowsily, I woke and rubbed my head. It had been a dream. "Man," I huffed. "Too bad."

My king-size bed was the real temptress in my bedroom. Many a night, I had collapsed squarely in the middle of the mattress, expecting hours of peaceful slumber. Somehow by morning, I had been lured to the edge in the right position ready to be thrown over the edge. Every morning at a designated time, the alarm on my sonic boom clock clicked. Annoying flashing lights and the powerful bed shaker took me for a rodeo ride until I was completely awake.

After a quick prayer, I staggered to the bathroom. When I came out, I donned a sweat suit, grabbed my keys and wallet, and left my house for a quick forty-minute five-mile jog, finishing with pumping some iron at home. Lately, I've been trying to quote scriptures. This particular day, I had a desire to exercise my mind with the oddest Bible trivia.

Racking my brain, I tried recalling every man who was troubled by a woman: Adam and Eve—she was weak, he was weaker; Abraham and Sarah—she didn't believe God and persuaded

Abraham to help God's plan along; David and Bathsheba—drama from the beginning; Isaac and Rebekah—deceit in the end; Samson and Delilah—bad combination; Jacob and Rachel; Ahasuerus and Esther—she wasn't his first choice; Moses and Zipporah; Joseph and Mary; Hosea and Gomer—I didn't want to go there; Ahab and Jezebel—both were bad news and she was eaten by dogs? I shuddered at the thought of dogs licking my blood. "C'mon, God, I need to know if Mackenzie is the one, my destiny." I raced harder, frustration building.

Then I heard God's voice. "Have you considered Boaz and Ruth, and Aquila and Priscilla? They worked side by side for the good of my Word."

I accepted the hint. Energized, I completed my jog. Minutes later, I turned the corner to my block, determined to revisit those passages. When I barged through my door, I was famished. I consumed my routine breakfast: a soup-size bowl of Cinnamon Toast Crunch, three pieces of bacon, and a twenty-two-ounce glass of orange juice. To minimize my caffeine intake, I limited myself to a small cup of coffee.

I showered, shaved, and by eight o'clock, I was unlocking the double doors to the PRESERVE-St. Louis office. Within the hour, I reclined in the leather chair at the head of the table in the conference room, ready to oversee our Monday meeting. Draping my black suit jacket over my chair, I smoothed down my multicolored tie. Briefly, I checked my attire, making sure what I saw in the mirror at home had made it to the office without a wrinkle. Satisfied my navy slacks were still military straight, I annoyed one of my blue suspenders.

As my staff filed into the room, I nodded good morning to my hearing employees and signed at the deaf ones. I winked at my close friend and a recent new employee Lana Dawson. She didn't need much coaxing to lure her away from a shipping company. A hefty salary increase and a generous health insurance package have that influence on people. Plus, Lana had concerns about work conditions. Deaf employees had accused the company of excluding them for promotions and possibly exposing them to anthrax.

Lana was beautiful on the inside and gorgeous on the outside. Strong Italian features enhanced her loveliness. She was so pretty, she was crowned Miss Deaf America, and served as a spokeswoman for the National Association of the Deaf.

Deaf from birth, she was a card-carrying member of the Deaf culture. Her looks drew all types of men until she spoke. That's when they were tested. Once Lana began talking, I guess she was too loud or didn't sound right. The potential suitors retreated, thinking she was mentally disabled. The losers had no idea of Lana's intelligence or their roles as being major discriminators.

Despite our diverse ethnic backgrounds, we shared a kindred spirit. Our friendship was solid, and our loyalty to each other was never questioned. More than once we contemplated a serious relationship. The last attempt was earlier in the year. Our evening had started off nice until I drove her home.

"I loved that movie," Lana had signed after leav-

ing AMC Theatres in Creve Coeur, a middle ground for city dwellers and recent urban flight residents. The theatre was hosting Deaf Movies Night, showing *The Pursuit of Happyness* in open caption where every word, sigh, and emotion is flashed on the bottom of the screen.

"Me, too." Linking her arm through mine, we strolled to my Impala back then. We were blocks away from her downtown apartment when an officer pulled up behind my car, flashing his lights.

Turning on my signal, I obeyed and pulled over. My brothers complained about "driving while black," which I equated to "driving while deaf." African-Americans or Caucasians, we had to be more alert than the hearing drivers were.

Peering through my rear view window, I saw a stocky officer struggle to extract himself from his patrol car. Once he was freed, he took deliberate steps to my car, adjusting his belt. I couldn't decipher his body language, which worried me. As he got closer, I activated the power button down on my window. I placed my hands on top of my steering wheel. When he bent and scanned inside my car, I focused on his lips.

Bad move. He considered my stare suspicious. His lips twisted and turned faster than a race car on a track. "Get out of the vehicle," he demanded without asking for my driver's license, which would have indicated I was hearing impaired.

"I'm deaf, officer." I remained calm as I towered over him. My height could be intimidating to a man less than six feet, and he was inches below that measuring line. Still I scanned his name badge.

"Let me see your driver's license," Officer Boxer demanded.

Slowly, I slid my wallet from my back pocket. He scrutinized my license, verifying the J88 code that signified that I was indeed hearing impaired.

Tilting his head to the left, he mouthed if the young lady in my car was also deaf. I nodded. Stooping, he eyed Lana then back at me, keeping a hand on his holster. I don't think I breathed.

Coming to a decision, he stepped closer to my face and enunciated each word. "You may be deaf, but you were four miles over the speed limit. Slow down," his lips bit out, giving me a warning only. Thanking him, I steadied my anger and got back behind the wheel, fastening my seat belt. After I pulled away, I made sure I drove four miles under the speed limit.

Lana watched me until I acknowledged her. Her slight smile said it was okay, but her watery eyes betrayed her. The scenario was unsettling. *"I was afraid for you, Noel."*

I never would admit it, but I was scared, too. A man with a gun was dangerous, with or without a badge. That's why trailing Mackenzie had been a dangerous task for me.

The Officer Boxer episode changed my and Lana's relationship. She felt the need to protect me. I appreciated the concern, but that's where our compatibility ended. I was one-hundred percent man; I already had a mother. I needed a woman who had confidence in my ability to make the right decisions and endure the consequences of bad ones. I didn't need or want anyone's pity.

That's why Mackenzie appealed to me. She seemed to always meet me on any level.

My hesitation about pursuing a romantic involvement with Lana wasn't race-based. I wasn't near the spiritual commitment level I needed, and Lana wasn't interested in trying to build a bridge to God. Churches without a Deaf Ministry were meaningless to Lana, and I concurred.

That was months ago. Blinking the past away and in Lana's presence now, I made a mental note to invite her to come with me where the Deaf Ministry had made a difference. An addendum to that note was for me to talk to Pastor Coleman about joining the membership. It was important for me to be on the church roll, not as a permanent visitor every Sunday.

With my conscientious staff seated in the board room, I forced my mind to stop drifting and to return to a business mode. Taking a deep breath, I opened the first page of our agenda. PRESERVE-St. Louis had an annual budget of $1.5 million, and we had to give account of how we used every penny. I created my own rainbow coalition staff—black, white, Asian, Hispanic, deaf, hearing, one wheel-chair bound, and no non-profit organization could be effective without dedicated volunteers.

I looked up from my file. "Okay," I said, knowing that those who could hear would tap the deaf co-workers.

"Lana, before we take a look at any new issues, give us an update on Triple A." In addition to my staff, I employed the services of an interpreter through an agency for my employees who weren't as efficient in lip reading as Lana or me. I didn't need the service since I usually signed and talked during our meetings, but I used the interpreter as backup, and I didn't balk at the hourly rate no matter the length of our meetings.

This was one expense most companies monitored to the penny since the law required them to provide interpreters for their deaf workers. Oftentimes, they requested the minimum hours and not a minute more. Of course, my philosophy was different. Interpreters were a large portion of my budget for meetings. I didn't want my staff acting as interpreters when information was being disseminated.

Lana gave the latest. "I told Mrs. Allen, Mrs. Anderson, and Mrs. Albert that they'd have to give up the forty baby chicks and ten baby pigs they just bought, plus the chicken house in the front yard," she spoke as an interpreter signed for the other deaf employees.

"What?" I shook my head as faces around the table showed amusement. The eighty-plus-year-old neighbors defied county officials and developers who wanted to insult them—their words, not mine—by offering them a couple hundred dollars for the homes their late husbands had purchased for them. They were three tough ladies who didn't scare easily and insisted on labeling their remaining three houses on the block a neighborhood.

For the benefit of her hearing coworkers, Lana continued to speak although she preferred signing. "They were under the uneducated impression that if their property was considered farmland, it wouldn't be subjected to seizure under the condemnation or eminent domain law."

I jotted down my notes before turning the page. "Okay, it's time we secure some type of transportation to get them to the next public forum on eminent domain. We need to suggest they get legal representation. This is way out of their league."

"It had better be fast because I saw some contractors breaking ground on the far corner this morning. That new proposed shopping center is coming up whether the Triple A's like it or not," advised Carl, my executive assistant. Then he added, "Berkeley Police have already confiscated Mrs. Allen's loaded shotgun last month. Of course, it wasn't registered. No telling where she got that."

Everyone laughed, including Sharon, my paid interpreter, who continued to sign. Suddenly, the interpreter's hands faded and Mackenzie's hand beckoned to me. She was becoming a distraction even when she wasn't physically around. She dared to challenge me to persuade her to stay in St. Louis. That's what I intended to do.

Fingers danced before my eyes. They were not Mackenzie's or Sharon's. Jerking my head, I frowned. A staffer grinned. "Stay with us, boss, or we're likely to go to lunch at the company's expense."

I slapped my hands on the table. "Okay everybody, year end reports are due in two weeks." I waved two fingers in front of them. "No excuses. It's going to take all of us to achieve next year's fundraising goals. That's it." I stood, adjourning the meeting and headed down the hall. I had almost reached my office when Lana elbowed me.

"Noel, are you okay? You seemed to zone out at times."

"I'm fine; better than fine." I chuckled. *"I'm back in church, one that has a great Deaf Ministry. I was thinking about inviting you since you have no reason now to say no."* Folding my arms, I waited.

Displaying a seductive smile, she slanted her head, thinking. Finally, her eyes sparkled as if a light bulb turned on. She signed yes, moving her fist up and down.

Ecstatic, I wanted to squeeze her in a hug, but she often complained that I didn't know my own strength, so I refrained. *"I met a woman who I would consider special. Well, it's hard to describe her. Mackenzie epitomizes so much."*

"No." Her angelic look faded.

I frowned. *"No? What do you mean no?"*

Lana's hands moved rapidly. *"Noel, what do you know about her? You haven't hidden your deafness from her, have you?"* Her expression was one of concern.

"I don't see how that's possible." Reaching out, I patted her shoulder. *"Relax, Lana. Mackenzie is an interpreter at the church."*

Her lips formed an "o" as she signed. *"You sure it's not a student fascinated with his teacher? This sounds like a one-sided setup. She can hear, right, so don't you think you've gotten plenty of competition?"* The light dimmed in her eyes as a coworker pulled Lana away, needing her immediate attention about payroll.

"Go ahead. We'll talk later."

I continued to my office, piqued about Lana's

odd behavior. I dropped my folder on my desk, and pulled out my bottom desk drawer. Sitting behind my desk, I grabbed the phone book and flipped through the pages until I found the church's number.

Next, I lifted my remote and pointed it at my wall plasma TV with high-def and high-speed internet. I was channel surfing when Tom appeared at my door. As soon as I beckoned him in my office, a grin swept across his face.

"Cool." He dragged a chair and angled it with an unobstructed view of the TV. When I bypassed *ESPN*, airing the previous days' highlights, I thought he was going to faint. "Man, why did you change the channel? Terrell Owens—"

I held up my hands to calm him down. "Tom, I'm about to make a video conference call."

His shoulders slumped. "Oh, that was the play, boss. You should've seen it." Tom became animated.

I laughed at his antics. "I did." I returned to *ESPN* and for a few minutes, we watched the playbacks. Tom folded his arms and relaxed in the chair. That's when I switched to channel 34 and Tom whirled around in a panic.

"Out." I pointed without asking him what he wanted. I laughed because I had already watched the highlights twice this morning.

Turning on my TTY or my text telephone device, often mistaken for an older model calculator by its keyboard and display window, it auto dialed my video relay service provider. When a representative answered and typed in 'GA' for go ahead, I typed back a phone number and name.

A young white woman appeared on the screen, signing to me that the phone was ringing. Video conferencing was a free service to deaf persons, allowing them to call anywhere in the world. Unfortunately, con artists, especially across the world, saw our advantages as theirs. They could use the replay service free of charge and hide their foreign accents under the guise of using the replay operator as the middle man who is sworn to secrecy of any conversation they interpret. Criminals used stolen credit cards to steal thousands of dollars in merchandise.

"I have Mr. Coleman on the line. Go ahead, Mr. Richardson," the operator signed.

Pastor Coleman, this is Noel Richardson, and I would like to set up a meeting before Bible class tomorrow, I typed into the keyboard and waited for my interpreter to read it on his TTY then relay my message through his headset.

I have six-thirty, young man, my video conference interpreter signed, translating the minister's message. *Should I have an interpreter present?*

I wanted to say, yeah, Mackenzie Norton, but this was something that had nothing to do with her. A man had to take care of his own business. *Oh, no sir. I can read lips.*

CHAPTER 12

Mackenzie was a tease. She knew it, and I knew it, but we seemed to enjoy every minute of it. For the past three days, we were in a contest on who could type faster text messages. My Black-Berry vibrated so much on my waist belt; I thought I was a cowboy, grabbing my gun from my holster. I smiled more. It became a game to us, and I played to win. Mackenzie didn't know that, but I was confident she would learn the rules real soon.

Mackenzie: *Have u come up with a scheme 2 convince me 2 stay away frm Chicago? LOL*

Mmm, maybe, but I ain't talkin, I typed back. When I became frustrated with these snacks of conversations and wanted a whole meal with Mackenzie, I'd let her know. *I c that ur pretty little fingers r smarting off again. Maybe when I c u, I'll make u close ur eyes, and kiss each finger.*

Mackenzie: *Why do I need 2 close my eyes? U scared 4 me 2 watch u kiss my hands? Maybe I'll cook a dish with plenty of onions. LOL*

See what I mean? She was a beautiful, curly haired tease. *I'll email when I'm home.*

To show me she was in control, Mackenzie always had to get the last word. *Maybe.*

I never appreciated Instant Messaging until Mackenzie. It seems like nothing was better in my life until Mackenzie. Even my bowl of cereal in the mornings tasted better. One night, I had to attend a PRESERVE-St. Louis soiree. The event was a big deal for fundraising, and without my presence, the donations would suffer. I was no fool. I wasn't about to miss a fundraising event my staff had worked so diligently on over a woman, but I thought about Mackenzie—often—who was doing something with a theatre.

It was after eleven Tuesday night when I walked in my house, shook off my overcoat, and kicked off my shoes after I locked the door. Nothing was keeping me away from my computer even as I almost slid into a wall as my silk socks skated on my wood floor. Usually a neat person, I flung my clothes and let them land wherever as I booted my computer. I was hopeful Mackenzie was still awake when I signed on. She didn't disappoint me when a message flashed at the bottom of the screen. I opened the window.

Mackenzie: *Hi*

I was hoping you'd wait up for me. I'm sorry I'm late. I know you're probably tired.

Mackenzie: *I am tired, but reading your words is like hearing your voice. Plus, I wanted to tell you about my day.*

I want to know about it, too. I'm sure that made

her smile. Just typing the words brought a smirk to my mouth.

Mackenzie: *I've only been home for about an hour. After school, a few of us went downtown to this historic home that was about to be demolished. The owner said we can take anything we found.*

My eyes were strained and my body demanded rest as I rubbed my face and rotated my neck, but reading the excitement behind Mackenzie's words rejuvenated me. *What could you find in a vacant house?*

Mackenzie: *We removed a door off a bedroom. A few ceiling lights, a few panel sections of a wall, and other stuff.*

I shook my head. *Woman, you are amazing. I had no idea such treasures were hidden in a house that had nothing in it.*

Mackenzie: *Actually, an empty house can be a gold mine for theater set designers. Since this house was built in the early 1900s, we'll have authentic pieces for plays from that era. We could've used it for "Guys and Dolls" that's currently playing. We did our best.*

After her words slowed and my eyes blurred, I was too tired to tell her about my evening. *Maybe, I'll invite myself to one of your plays.*

Mackenzie: *Is that a hint?*

When have you known me to hint at anything? LOL Mackenzie, get some rest. We'll see each other tomorrow at Bible class. If we were on a date, could I kiss you?

Mackenzie: *Nite, Noel.*

I took that as a yes.

An hour before Bible class, I sat in Pastor Coleman's office. The wood was dark and books lined the shelves. The man had a library. I wondered if he had read each book.

Pictures hung neatly on two walls, depicting church events. Stacks of programs and booklets rested in several piles. Surprisingly, his massive L-shaped wood veneer desk was clutter free.

Pastor Coleman didn't frown, nor did he smile. He rocked back in his massive cushioned chair behind his desk as he grabbed a note pad. With his pen poised in the air, he asked. "What can I do for you, Mr. Richardson? You have visited us a few times."

Leaning back, I crossed my ankle over my knee. "I have, and I want to join God's Grace Apostolic Church."

"I see. Have you been baptized in Jesus' name?" he asked with an exaggerated slowness.

"Yes. It was about fourteen or fifteen years ago."

Folding his hands, the pastor asked, "Where?"

I bit my lip, racking my brain to recall the exact name of the storefront church. "I believe it was The Last Days Church of God."

Assessing his features, I waited for his response. Thick graying hairs matched patches springing up in his short afro. The wrinkles on his forehead and between his brows aged him.

"I recall Elder Quinn. I believe he passed away some time ago. Did you receive the gift of the Holy Ghost?"

"Yes, I didn't hear the tongues, but nothing could've moved my mouth like that unless it was God," I said with conviction.

Pastor Coleman released the ink pen and clasped

his hands on top of his desk. "A letter from The Last Days Church of God should confirm there were witnesses that the Lord had poured His Spirit upon you. After I receive it, then we can talk about membership. You don't need to be baptized again once you have been in the name of Jesus." A red light flashed on his phone, but Pastor Coleman ignored it.

"I haven't been back to that church or any church in years. Honestly," I admitted, "I didn't know I needed such a thing."

"That's understandable. In the Pentecostal Assemblies of the World organization, all of our churches require the letter as a precaution."

He wasn't making sense, and my face must've reflected my bewilderment.

Flipping through the pages of his Bible and locating the desired scripture, he turned it around and pointed to Jude: *For there are certain men crept in unawares, who were before of old ordained to this condemnation, ungodly men, turning the grace of our God into lasciviousness, and denying the only Lord God, and our Lord Jesus Christ.*

I shifted in my seat. Now wait a minute. What was Pastor trying to say? I looked up, squinting. He met my stare with equal concentration.

"Noel, as saints of God, we can't take any chances and assume every person who walks through those doors is saved. The proof is in the baptism and filling of the Holy Ghost. I'm just following orders from the Master. Please don't take that as a personal offense."

He folded his hands again. "It's a simple letter, but we read between the lines for any warning of a person who has stirred up mischief. This is what I'm going to do. I'll have my secretary call and see if their secretary can locate a record."

I nodded a thank you.

Closing his Bible, he stood and I followed. "Until then, I recommend you go to the prayer room with some of our ministers as soon as your schedule permits. One thing about the Holy Ghost: He never leaves us. We leave Him. If God spoke through you once, He'll speak again and someone from our congregation will have witnessed it." After shaking hands, I left his office.

The foyer was busy with people scrambling to the sanctuary for prayer before Bible class. As I opened the door to the sanctuary, I reflected on what Pastor Coleman had said. Two questions remained. Did he really think I was ungodly, and would I speak again in tongues? Choosing a pew, I knelt, and prayed.

As I got up and made myself comfortable, a soft tap on my shoulder preceded mysterious sticky fingers, covering my eyes. *Mackenzie,* I thought, smiling, praying it wasn't the onions she promised. When juicy lips smashed into my face, my heart pounded. Mackenzie was becoming bold with her affections, and in church. She was really trying to get me put out. I reached behind me to wrap my fingers around her hands; instead I clinched two tiny wrists. They weren't Mackenzie's.

Surprise! Keisha, the younger of the two sisters, signed, giggling. I tickled her ear as Mrs. Campbell put a finger to her lips, hushing the child, offering me an apologetic smile.

Minutes later, with Keisha on my left and Daphne

on my right, their mother sat directly across the aisle from us in the hearing section. Mrs. Campbell had apologized about her girls pestering me, but I explained I welcomed their attention. Thank God she didn't suspect me as a child molester. The sisters sensed Mackenzie's presence. Turning, I looked over my shoulder. *Wow.* Tonight a brown cap held back her curls, highlighting her cheekbones. A brown turtleneck sweater and a long velvet skirt covered her curves. Brown boots added height. Casual for her was sophistication to me.

She stepped into the row in front of me and knelt to pray before sitting in the designated interpreter's chair. The sisters signed excitedly at Mackenzie. She gave them her undivided attention. After a few minutes, she gave me her undivided attention.

"You haven't been at this church a month, and already you've got two girlfriends," she scolded.

After appraising her beauty, I smirked. *"I thought I settled that."*

"That's still in negotiation," she teased as her eyes twinkled with mischief.

"It's just a matter of time before I seal the deal."

CHAPTER 13

Our attraction was growing with every look, touch, email, and text message. I waited all day to smell her fragrance, to hold her slender fingers, and brush my lips against hers when Lord knows I wanted more. The scripture in Jude came back to nag me. Since I was convinced that wasn't me, I dismissed it.

Just as I had felt Mackenzie's closeness, I could sniff out Valerie as she strutted into the sanctuary. She darted her eyes in my direction. I sighed. She needed to let it go. I was not to be her husband. As she approached the section, I assumed she was about to take her seat.

She didn't. Valerie stood in front of Mackenzie and blocked my view. She might as well have been standing in front of a TV right before the quarterback scored his touchdown. Man, Valerie was really beginning to annoy me.

If Valerie wanted to feud with Mackenzie over me, it was too late. She had already lost. However, that didn't keep Valerie's presence from making my life miserable. My nostrils curled as I tried to control my breathing. *Lord, there's got to be someone else who can talk to Valerie, because I'm not feeling it,* I thought.

As the class started, Valerie signed, shooting daggers at me and everyone else. She even rolled her eyes at Pastor Coleman. I mentally fought to concentrate on the pastor's teaching from Romans 8, which seemed to be timely: flesh versus spirit, sin and death versus holy and life, and fear versus faith.

I was relieved when Mackenzie took over, but her interpreting flair seemed downgraded from astounding to mediocre. What was going on? Valerie's skills went from mediocre to awful. Even the Campbell girls became fidgety, drawing cartoons on their Bible covers. No one seemed to be interested. More than a few heads bobbed from dozing.

When the class ended, suddenly everyone became alert. Many dumped their offerings in the plate and bolted for the door. I lingered for Mackenzie to walk her to her car. I was interested in finding out if she felt the distraction. One minute we were flirting with each other, the next we barely made eye contact as she haphazardly signed. A heavy pound to my back caused my back muscle to tense and prepared for retaliation. Whirling around, Nick stood, grinning.

"What's up, man?" I reluctantly shook his hand, agitated with the entire night. I got very little out of the class and it wasn't because Mackenzie distracted me.

"I don't know about you, Noel, but I had a hard

time getting into the message tonight." Nick scratched his hair, perplexed.

"Yeah," I had to agree.

"Hey, you want to grab a bite to eat?"

"Don't take this wrong, but if I eat, it's going to be with Mackenzie."

Nick smirked. "So you and Mackenzie are getting that close, huh? You work fast." He wiggled his brows.

"That's where you're wrong. If I move too fast with Mackenzie, I'll miss something, and that's not going to happen." I glanced over my shoulder to the spot where Mackenzie last stood, and it was bare. I scanned the sanctuary to see Mackenzie walking swiftly out the door. I didn't tell Nick goodbye as I snatched up my things and stormed after Mackenzie. If I caught her, I caught her, if I didn't, so be it, but I wasn't about to chase her. An elderly mother intercepted.

"Glad to see you, young man," she greeted before wobbling away on her cane.

Nodding, I patiently returned her greeting as I watched Mackenzie's retreat without a word. What was wrong with her? Once outside, I scanned the parking lot for her coat.

Then I withdrew my earlier statement. I was about to hunt her down for some answers. "Mackenzie," I yelled, not caring if I drew attention. She never stopped or slowed her steps. I took off, dodging between church traffic. "Mackenzie!"

She twirled around, irritated. *"Why are you yelling?"*

"Considering that you kept walking, it's because you didn't hear me."

"I heard you, people inside and outside the church heard, and I wouldn't be surprised if Pastor Coleman didn't hear you."

"Excuse me?" My anger began to rise as Mackenzie resumed her trek to her car.

I easily caught up with her steps. "Mackenzie, I can't say that I know what's going on in that head of yours, but since we're building a relationship, let's set up some perimeters. The first is when you're talking to me, I suggest that you don't turn your back on me again." My words made her freeze. She turned around and faced me. In the darkness, I could see her deep breathing by the cold air evaporating near her.

"I'm glad I finally have your attention. Mackenzie, you have a slight advantage over me." I slowly walked to her. We were so close that our breaths mingled. Her apologetic eyes searched my no nonsense expression. "That small advantage is you can hear. It's your turn not to disrespect me. Now," I paused, sighing. Reaching out, I brushed my hand against her cheek before lifting her chin. "What's the matter, baby?"

Sniffing, she relaxed and wrapped her arms around me. I embraced her, completing the hug. Rubbing her back, I tried to comfort her. Somewhat composed, she stepped back.

"I'm sorry, Noel. When I'm upset, I don't think. I do want your respect and I'll never violate yours again."

When her eyes watered, I grew concerned. What happened between our last text and church service? "Hey. Talk to me, Mackenzie."

"I almost lost a friend tonight."

"What your friend's prognosis?"

Her eyes widened in confusion. "I don't mean health wise. I'm talking about Valerie."

I nodded, without responding. *That wouldn't be a loss, but a blessing,* I thought.

"I know Valerie doesn't come across as the most likeable person, but we're still friends. Sometimes, we don't pick our friends, God does, and when she's hurting, so am I. I have the habit of saying the wrong thing when I'm upset, so I thought it was best if I left without facing you."

"Listen, for the past few weeks, we've always waited for each other after church. I have two brothers, so I can't say I'm very good at handling mood swings. But for you, I'll try. It's getting late, but I'm hungry. Do you want a salad or sandwich?"

She shook her head. "I really can't. I have a long day tomorrow between school and working on the set of *Guys and Dolls.*"

"Okay, email me when you get home?" I warmed her cold cheeks by cupping them with my hands.

"I will." When she wrinkled her nose and smiled, I knew the real Mackenzie was coming out. "Do I have permission to leave now?" she teased.

As I twisted my lips, thinking, she swatted my chest.

"Good, I'm leaving." She spun around without waiting for my answer then looked over her shoulder and laughed. "Noel, you may think you run this show, but you forget I'm the executive producer. You may set up perimeters, but I have to approve them." She resumed her walk, knowing I wasn't about to let her have the last word.

I stayed rooted in my spot, enjoying her strut to her car. As her headlights flashed, I closed the final distance between us, blocking her access to her car door. "One more thing."

"And that is?" Mackenzie lifted a brow.

"I want us to pray because about now, God's the only person keeping me from hugging and kissing you like I want to."

Her expression changed to admiration. "I like your honesty."

"Good, because I expect the same from you."

With the cascading light from the light pole, I watched as Mackenzie's hands led us in prayer. Her slow soft strokes built to forceful movements as her lips trembled. Realization hit. God was interceding for us and took over our prayer, speaking through Mackenzie in an unknown tongue.

That's when I bowed my head and prayed, but she touched me. When I looked up again, tears crept from her eyes and slid down her cheeks. "Thank you. I needed that."

I gently brushed the tears from her cheeks. "You were the one praying," I reminded her.

"You didn't let me pray alone. Something just wasn't right tonight. Spirits of confusion were fighting against us within the church walls."

Yeah. And one spirit was sitting right next to you, I thought.

CHAPTER 14

"Wait for me? This won't take long. Our church puts on the Night of Miracles every year," Mackenzie asked after Pastor Coleman dismissed the following week's Bible class.

"You never have to ask." Retaking my seat, I prepared for a long meeting. Surprisingly, Mackenzie returned fifteen minutes later. When she took her coat off the pew, I plucked it out of her arms and held it open for her.

Twirling around, she buttoned it up while thanking me. "I've been invited to a Christmas party on Saturday night. It's given by some of my friends from the theatre, and it doesn't start until 10:30. I know this is short notice, and it's late, but honestly, I forgot. I would love for you to escort me. If you can't, I'll still go."

"If I don't escort you, no other man will. That's my honor. I don't care about short notice or the lateness of the event." I accepted with a counter-invitation to attend a Deaf Movie Night and a holiday party with me. Since meeting Mackenzie, I hadn't thought about activities I enjoyed within the Deaf culture.

Lifting her brow, she shrugged so nonchalantly. "Name the date and time and I'll be there. My only commitment to the church musical is to tweak the set from last year. Then it's all about you, Mr. Richardson."

"That's good to know." Afterward, I walked her to her car, prayed, and stole a kiss.

On Saturday night, I drove to the Central West End, a pricey area within the city limits. Three-story mansions were a staple in the neighborhood, peeking through century-old trees and front doors several yards from the curb. We parked in a spot houses away down the block, got out, and started walking until we were at the correct address.

Facing the titanic structure, we stared at the innumerable colored bulbs weighing down the house like a sagging Christmas tree. Mackenzie looked from the "small palace" to me as if going inside may require a second thought. Her expression was amusing. She pressed her high-glossed lips together in dread.

On cue, God beamed a stream of light from the moon, casting a spotlight on Mackenzie's face. Or maybe it was the lights radiating from the home's large double windows—same effect. Tonight, Mackenzie was irresistible festively dressed. The globe-shaped faux-fur hat softened her already sensuous face. *Gorgeous.*

I guided Mackenzie up three brick-covered stairs to a front porch the size of a back patio. A large, intimidating stained-glass door made us freeze in our steps and admire meticulous placement of holiday ornaments. A glowing cluster above our heads held us spellbound as the overhead chandelier shook and my chest vibrated from the pulsating sounds coming from the other side of the door. The crystal teardrops teased us as they jiggled to a steady beat. Mackenzie stepped closer to me, possibly afraid the chandelier would crash any minute.

The door swung open and a crowd dragged us inside. The small get together was a full-scale club-style party. Mackenzie warned me that theatre people were passionate about everything, including celebrating. Mouths moved all at once. This would've been an ideal situation for an interpreter, but not Mackenzie. She ceased being my interpreter after our first date.

I went into defense mode when two body-builders tugged at Mackenzie's arm before crushing her in a group hug. When she was released, another guy whirled her around for his hug. That was one hug too many as I stepped forward. Two women, with drinks in one unsteady hand and forgotten cigarettes in the other, blocked my rescue. Taking turns, they brushed kisses against my cheeks.

"Noel, we won't stay long," Mackenzie mouthed. "I've been trying to sign to a few people that you're deaf, but they're so drunk, they thought I was playing a game."

"C'mon." I grabbed her hand, mumbling, "There has to be someone here celebrating some type of a Christian Christmas." She squeezed as strong vibrations shook the soles of my shoes.

The place resembled a museum as we strolled into one lavish room after another, designed as a maze. Fed up with the crowd, we drifted up a wide marble-covered stairwell, following other somber-looking guests. Evidently, others were fleeing the subway of party extremists. Upstairs, we chose a door where another party was underway. The atmosphere didn't compare to the one downstairs. About thirty people, mostly couples, were bunched on the floor, cushioned by expensive Persian rugs. A fire raged in a towering floor-to-ceiling stone-and-brick fireplace.

Some guests lounged in overstuffed chairs. Few eyes betrayed the center of attention—a trio of women, all dressed in gold. They stood between a table-sized machine and large screen, scrolling with words to "O Come All Ye Faithful."

Enthusiasm beamed from many faces. I looked to Mackenzie, and she shrugged, so we decided to stay for a while. At that moment, she leaned into me, wrapping her arms around me in a hug. I didn't know the cause, but I enjoyed the effect.

Then all eyes turned to us. Mackenzie mouthed, "They want us to sing 'Joy to the World.'"

"I can't sing."

"Neither can I." She grinned. "C'mon, let's have some fun. You're not scared, are you?" she challenged.

I tugged her to the front. When the words started, I opened my mouth when the words began to scroll. I somewhat remembered the melody from childhood. I winked at Mackenzie who laughed and seemed to stumble over her words.

Many stood and joined us. As the words to "Joy to the World" disappeared from the screen, people clapped. Grabbing Mackenzie's hand, we bowed.

Afterward, she turned to me, clapping as others followed. I lifted my brow in suspicion and I turned back to the screen. Sure enough, "The First Noel" began to roll. We finished as the door opened and in walked a fresh batch of guinea pigs. We had our escape from that room and stayed at the party long enough to gorge on delicacies I doubted chefs from the Food Channel would recognize. After failed attempts to find the hosts so that we could say goodbye, we gave up, retrieved our coats, and left.

CHAPTER 15

I almost ran a red light reading one of Mackenzie's text messages. It had become routine. I had come to expect them every evening on my way home from work.

They were one-liners until we could email each other later, but they were meant to tease. Today's message read: *Noel, did you know your hazel eyes change colors?* Yesterday's text: *My coat smells like your cologne.* The day before that: *I can't sign when you wink at me at church,* and on and on. When we were together her feigned innocence provoked my hormones.

Mackenzie had become my focus. I didn't pray in the morning without including her name. I didn't jog or lift weights without wondering what she was doing. I logged onto my computer to check my inbox for messages. Realizing we hadn't shared a morning scripture, I pulled a pocket Bible out of my desk drawer and fumbled through the pages. Pausing in Ephesians, I perused chapters and decided on one that I hoped would be inspiring:

Good morning, my favorite and only interpreter of my heart. My brethren, be strong in the Lord, and in the power of His might. Put on the whole armour of God that ye may be able to stand against the wiles of the devil. Ephesians 6:10-11. Whatever you face today, you'll make it because you're wearing God's protective gear on your feet, chest, loins, and head. Watch out, devil, Mackenzie is armed and dangerous.

Mackenzie replied with another one-liner tease: *LOL. Do I look dangerous?*

Yeah, I thought, smirking. I imagined her quirky facial expression when she laughed, or smelled the subtle, but sweet perfume when she touched my face.

My reply: *You have no idea, woman. Hey, I know it's Thursday, but if you don't have plans after work today that don't already include me, how about dinner? Regardless of a response, I'll take that as a 'yes, Noel.'* I touched SEND.

Standing, I dressed for work. Before I left my house, I splashed new cologne on my neck, tickling my nose. I couldn't resist the purchase after sniffing from a vial that was shoved in my face as I walked through Macy's a few days ago. The right blends of spices enticed me to head to the fragrance counter. Without a sales pitch, I purchased a bottle with Mackenzie on my mind, wondering whether she would notice.

Less than an hour later, I hung up my coat in my office. I sat at my desk, and extended my legs as I booted my computer for work purposes. The first task was to check my agency's email accounts. A major donor, Henry Livingston, was requesting PRESERVE-St. Louis's assistance about a proposed

eminent domain takeover in one of the most afflu-
ent suburbs of St. Louis. It would be the third
incident we had played a role in within a year. Personally, I didn't see the Livingston & Kindle Co.
winning this battle; but since private donations
made up to twenty percent of our budget, when a
request was made that we intervene —even for the
ridiculous—I paid attention. After all, we remained
a neutral party.

I had my assistant pull every newspaper article
on the controversy to see who made up the oppo-
sition team, and place calls to track them down
about a possible negotiation. Soon, I had a pulse
on their concerns. The light flashed on my TDD,
alerting me to a conference with the CEO and his
director of public relations. I typed, *Hello* and
waited for their response.

After their greetings, I explained my position.
*Mr. Henry and Ms. Overton, as you know, the city of
Clayton's tax base is self-sufficient with major staples of at-
torneys, doctors' businesses, and residences. Their quaint
shops and tasty outdoor eateries highlight the city within a
city.* I waited for the interpreter to translate my
message to my parties over the phone.

Our messages bounced back and forth for thirty
minutes. *Mr. Henry advised he would get back with you
about a date and time that would work into his schedule.
He really needs PRESERVE-St. Louis to be the liaison to
at least get the citizens of Clayton to listen to his lucrative
proposal,* was his last communication.

I shrugged. The man was facing a losing battle.
*All right, Mr. Henry and Ms. Overton. In the meantime,
I'll search for a place that will accommodate a large
crowd. Goodbye.*

When the call ended, my stomach shook with hunger. Once Mackenzie confirmed our dinner date, then I'd run around the corner for a small snack, perhaps a couple of sandwiches and a side salad that was heavy on meat strips. I signed into my AOL account. I grinned. Four emails were in my box, three from Mackenzie. They were five minutes apart.

Noel, I think I can allow you to buy me dinner. Mackenzie.

Hmmm, I was starting to like my women sassy. Closing that one, I moved to the second.

I've got a taste for the Cheesecake Factory at the Galleria. I'll pay for dessert. Mackenzie.

Of course, she had to show independence. Maybe for the fun of it, I should order three cakes to take home. I clicked on the final one.

Meet me at the mall entrance, four-thirty sharp! :) Mackenzie

I smiled. There was still so much I didn't know about Mackenzie: her passion for the theater stuff, her delusion about going to Chicago, her odd friendship with Valerie, and anything else that described the woman who enchanted me. I replied, *See you later, baby.*

After signing off, I looked up. Lana was standing in my doorway. I waved her in. She approached and angled a cushioned chair in front of me. When her fingers started, I gave Lana my undivided attention. *"Noel, we finally have commitments from three major insurance companies that are willing to participate in the forum on underinsured workers."*

This project was Lana's baby from the beginning. Grinning, I shared in her jubilation. Besides her other responsibilities, Lana was passionate about seeing that everyone have adequate health coverage. *"You are amazing, Lana. You have so much passion."*

"I know." She returned my smile. *"See, I'm not a bad person."*

I reclined in my chair. *"Never said you were."*

Tilting her head, Lana stared. *"Noel, your eyes are smiling."*

We were volleying compliments. We did this thing from time to time more as a stress reliever. Now, Mackenzie was becoming my stress regulator. *"Yeah, well your hands smile."*

"Noel, you're talking to me, but it's not about me, is it?"

I took a deep breath, stalling. I wished I had a stack of folders that beckoned for my attention, then I could stall. I shook my head. *"No."*

"Is it that interpreter from that church?" She frowned, accusatory.

I nodded. *"Yes, and I don't regret going to that church. I acknowledged that I needed Christ, but she was a treasure waiting for me when I got there."*

She frowned. *"We've been friends for a long time, Noel. If I recall, you're the one who told me Christ is the same today, tomorrow, and forever. It was something like that, so you already have Christ. You know I'm a good person."* Lana jumped to her feet, upset. She stabbed her fist in her side and waited for my comeback.

"Lana, there is nothing wrong with you."

"Are you sure?" She squinted.

"Of course, I'm sure, but don't you wonder sometimes if our good is good enough? I remember hearing our righteousness is like filth."

Indignant, Lana crossed her arms then uncrossed them and signed, *"There is nothing filthy about me. I love people."*

"Then you're a better person than I am, because I can still think of some people I wouldn't mind meeting up in an alley."

"And church is going to keep you from a brawl?"

"For the other person's sake, you better hope so."

"Well, I guess I better watch you first to make sure you don't slip." Lana dismissed herself.

Lifting my brow, I wondered if that was her reason for coming to my office. Suddenly, she whirled around. *"The forum starts at seven at the Bridgeton Community Center. I'll be there at sixty-thirty to set up the brochures. Are you coming?"*

I shook my head. There was no way I'd cancel a dinner date with Mackenzie—no way. I could count on one hand how many community forums I had missed—two. PRESERVE-St. Louis had been my passion. Now, Mackenzie was. My staff was well informed on all issues we participated in, and they could carry out their duties, which I paid them well to do.

"Then I guess I'll facilitate the meeting all by my sinful self."

"Okay."

Pacing the sidewalk outside the Galleria, I checked my wristwatch again. No sign of my 4:30 sharp woman. Mackenzie was more than twenty minutes late. That woman! Two things I had noted about her. She was punctual for church, on time for school, but the few times that we had met after work because she had banned me from her class-room, she was always late.

When my BlackBerry vibrated, I snatched it off my belt. The message added to my frustration. *Sorry I'm running late. I'm right around the corner. C u in a few.* That woman! Gritting my teeth, I resumed pacing as I scanned the parking lot. When I turned around, brown eyes blocked my view. They weren't Mackenzie's.

"Excuse me." I moved to the side and she matched my step. Was the woman flirting? She was attractive, but so were so many women. I didn't focus on her mouth as she spoke. My mind was on another woman. Where was Mackenzie? Then peering over this bold woman's head, I spotted Mackenzie strutting across the lot in a manner portrayed by models on a runway. She was stop-ping traffic, literally, because she wasn't watching where she was going. Thank God the drivers were, especially one man behind the wheel of an SUV.

Half-relieved, half-annoyed, I smiled anyway. Fo-cusing on Mackenzie, the woman was forgotten as I walked toward my date. She beamed when she saw me coming. Face-to-face, she grinned. I frowned. She pouted. I laughed.

Tugging her hand, I pulled her closer to me. "You're late. The next time I invite you to dinner, I'm coming to get you. If you have a problem with that, put your complaint in writing," I said, tower-ing over her.

"Would you like that sent priority or FedEx?" she shot back with a smirk, looping an arm through mine as we walked back to the mall entrance.

"It's a good thing you're here. I needed a bodyguard earlier. A stranger tried to pick me up," I said, rubbing a kiss into her hair.

Swatting my arm, she faced me. She squinted as her lips curled in amusement. *"Really? I thought it was normal for a handsome brother to get hit on all the time. Are you telling me this is your first time?"* Folding her arms, she waited for my reply.

I laughed. There was no way I was answering that. *"Come on, woman."*

"FYI, Noel, I won't fight over a man."

"You'll never have to."

"Let's go shopping," she said as soon as we stepped up on the sidewalk in front of the Cheesecake Factory.

"Can't. We're on a waiting list to be seated. That was twenty minutes ago when you were just around the corner. My stomach is drained from worrying about you. Can I ask why you're so late?"

Unbuttoning her coat, she shrugged. "I had to pick up your gift."

"Mackenzie!" Granted, Christmas was days away, but we hadn't talked about exchanging gifts, and if we had, I would've forbade her from getting me something. She was so unpredictable, and I loved it. I loved her. I held my breath. I said it, didn't I? Hopefully, not out loud.

Years ago, my brother had broken up with a woman he really cared about, but she dogged him out. That's when Pierce had warned me, "Noel, love should only be spoken to one woman. When professing it, you had better make sure she is the one."

Recently, I had been toying with that emotion. I briefly thought about being a husband and having a wife. After just a few weeks, could this be the real deal? Once I said it, I couldn't take it back. There seemed to be no barriers between Mackenzie and me, but was it love? Did my heart swell? Yes. Mackenzie made me lonely when we weren't together. I hadn't realized I was frowning until she pinched my side.

"Did I tell you how handsome you look tonight? Turtlenecks were made for you. Yes, very, very nice, and your hazel eyes were made to fall in love with. Are my compliments working?"

Working? Mackenzie had no idea.

"Do you want them to work?" I asked through hooded lashes that allowed me to feast on everything about her.

"Yes."

"Nope, stop trying to distract me." She was working a number on me all right, but I wasn't going to let her know it. "Mackenzie, I didn't want you buying me anything."

"What?" She cupped her ear. *"I can't hear you."*

The innocence draping her face could convince me of anything, almost. I had news for her. She wouldn't win this battle with her buying me gifts. It would be the other way around. I was a man, not some freeloader. As I moved my hands, she grabbed them.

"My name is on my bank account and the checkbook. You were on my mind when I saw it."

She had the last word as the restaurant pager trembled in my hand, signaling a table was ready. Navigating through the crowd, we approached the greeting station and turned in our pager. A petite hostess led us to a dimly lit section, cozy for two, but too crowded for any more. Scooting back Mackenzie's chair, I helped her remove her coat before she took her seat. I slipped off my coat and laid both on my booth seat. When we finished the preliminaries, the hostess presented our menus and left.

I didn't bother with my menu. I preferred feasting on Mackenzie. Evidently, she enjoyed her view, because she ignored her menu as well. I intensified my stare. When a waitress magically appeared, we snapped out of it. Embarrassed, we fumbled through our menu and ordered.

The moment she left, we retreated back into our imaginary hideaway. When Mackenzie laid her hands on the table, I swallowed them up in my hands. They were so soft, her fingers long. She shivered, her lids briefly fluttered, and her expression softened at the touch. I was just as affected, but she didn't need to be privy to all my feelings – yet. Our fingers intertwined and danced across the table.

When our food arrived, we were already sated. Mackenzie's eyes were talking to me. Our hands, still connected, didn't want to be disturbed. Somehow, I blessed our meal and Mackenzie said, "Amen." Sharing a final smile, we yielded to the aroma of oversized appetizers. Minutes later, our main course was before us. We sampled each other's dishes, teasing that the other had the better selection. Then we fought over the single serving of banana cheesecake topped with whip cream. I chuckled.

"What?"

"I don't even like bananas."

"Right, Noel. Amazing, isn't it? Considering you only let me have two bites."

Mackenzie patted her stomach in satisfaction. When she leaned back, her sweater outfit outlined a slight pouch that wasn't there before we ate. From her pouch up, I admired her assets to her curls. They defined her personality, energetic, sassy, and confident.

She opened her eyes and reached inside the small shopping bag that I had dismissed when I met her in the parking lot. She pulled out a box slightly bigger than a baseball. "For you."

"Mackenzie, I didn't get you anything. I mean, yet," which was negligence on my part. For the past ten years or so, my parents stressed that Christian Christmas was more than a commercial holiday for bargains. Most times, we briefly shopped on Christmas Eve.

"Ever heard of a surprise?" Mackenzie curved her lips into a smile. Mischief sparkled in her eyes before she winked. *"Open it before I give it to another guy."* Her eyes scanned the restaurant.

Shaking my head, I encircled her hand that held my treat. I brought the gift and her hands to my lips and blessed it with a kiss. "Thank you."

"You're welcome. I hope you like it."

The waitress appeared and fanned the bill between us. I whipped out my credit card to get rid of her.

"Open your gift, silly," Mackenzie demanded. Her eyes sparkled with excitement on the verge of a massive explosion.

"Okay." I had no shame ripping open the wrapping. A Rubik's Cube coded with deaf signs was smothered inside a cushioned box. Twisting each side, I read the messages. I was speechless. Mackenzie had shattered all components of my male pride. Humbled, I swallowed back any hint of mist in my eyes. "Mackenzie, I don't know what to say. I'm sure this wasn't easy to find."

A man appeared at our table, signing like a kindergartener who had only mastered three letters of the alphabet. With a straight face, Mackenzie and I stared at him. Helping himself to one of our unused napkins, he fumbled inside of his jacket for a pen. Mackenzie saved him the hassle by pulling one out her purse. He nodded his thanks.

The interloper scribbled, *Are both of you deaf?* When we didn't answer, he hastily unfolded the napkin and wrote the same question bigger. When we still didn't respond, he stormed away. The only word I read from his lips was idiots. I usually ignored other people's rudeness, but I wasn't going to subject Mackenzie to it. Bracing my fists on the table to stand, Mackenzie shook her head, patting my hand to stop me.

"Why didn't you answer him?"

"Because he's an idiot," she signed. "You read what he was asking just like I heard him."

CHAPTER 16

I had made up my mind that today would be the day. Sunday after worship, it would be déjà vu. I trailed a trio of ministers stuffed into black suits, who reminded me of the phrase, *short, shorter, and shortest*. We stopped at a thick dark wood door. A large brass-plate sign boldly identified it as the "Power Room."

Years ago, I had crossed over the threshold of a "Power Room," but as a confused, scared teenager, wondering what my future would be. I survived the explosion, but I was deaf, which at the time made me feel like I was dead. Back then, the tongue talking experience was another life-altering change. When God released His hold, my first word had been, *Cool.*

Today, I made myself comfortable in one of four chairs in a circle; the others joined me and grabbed my hands. A minister opened his Bible. He skimmed over the passage. He looked at me and recited, "*For he that speaketh in an unknown tongue speaketh not unto men, but unto God. For no man understandeth him, howbeit in the spirit he speaketh mysteries.'* 1 Corinthians 14:2. Brother Noel, unless God allows us to interpret your tongues, then they are unknown. We'll know that this is a spiritual conversation between you and God. It'll be mysterious to us, but plain English to the Lord."

Nodding, we bowed our heads to pray, and within the hour my hands flew up by their own volition. My mind flashed an image of Jesus as my tongue raced faster than NASCAR driver Jeff Gordon did in his DuPont Chevrolet in the Daytona 500. I had more witnesses.

As I thanked God for the affirmation, Pastor Coleman came in, waving a piece of paper. Through glazed eyes, I read the letterhead from Last Days Church of God. "Noel, this was faxed to us this morning."

I scanned the words: *I verify this soul was baptized September 14, 1992, and four witnesses heard the anointing of God spill from Noel Richardson's mouth in other tongues.*

"Brother Noel, I now have my record, and you have yours. Welcome."

The news was too good to keep to myself. Unfortunately, I couldn't reach Mackenzie. I had texted her twice. Frustrated because she hadn't responded, I was a second away from sending another message when her message flashed on my BlackBerry.

Hi, Noel. I c u text me. I was on stage with the crew ready 2 break down the set. I'm sorry. Do u have something special u want to tell me?

She already knew. I sat up from lounging on my sofa and picked up the remote to power off my TV. *Maybe, where r u?*

Leaving The Black Rep Theater. Hope 2 b home in about twenty minutes.

Call it selfishness, call it loneliness, but I wanted to see her now. *Feel up for a light meal?*

Not tonight, Noel. I'm tired. I just got in my car now so I'm signing off. Okay?

No, it wasn't okay. *I'll meet u at ur house.* Clipping my phone on my belt, I slipped into my shoes. Walking into my bathroom, I freshened up, including brushing my teeth. I went to the hall closet for my hat and coat as I re-buttoned my shirt and stuffed it into my pants. I hurried out the door to my car. I was determined to beat Mackenzie home.

It didn't happen. For once, she had beaten me. I took a chance standing at Mackenzie's front door before midnight. With trepidation, I pushed the bell, praying Mackenzie was nearby and I hadn't disturbed Mr. Norton who I had yet to meet.

Guilt pounded an upper cut to my chin when Mackenzie answered the door. Selfishness kicked me in the butt. Arrogance bit me in the leg. My body and soul ached when she saw me and her smile wasn't forthcoming.

Mackenzie's eyes drooped from tiredness. Her clothes proudly wore patches of dirt. The curls were beyond a mess. A tear clung to her lashes.

"What's wrong, baby?" I wiped the tear away and grabbed her hand.

She sighed. "News travels fast. I know Pastor Coleman received the witnesses' report from the ministers today. I called and spoke with Minister

Eddie earlier. The Holy Ghost in me knows God's power is right on the money as mentioned in the Bible. The experience reaffirms every scripture. I'm sad when some people don't want it, refuse to pray for it, and the preacher dismisses it. I want people to know for themselves that the Holy Ghost is more than tongues, it's also the anointing and power to live right."

Okay, I nodded. What wasn't Mackenzie telling me? *"That sounds memorized. What's really in your heart? I can handle your secrets."*

She shivered despite her thick sweater. Opening my wool coat, I swallowed her inside to keep her warm. "Talk to me, Mackenzie, talk."

"The woman in me doesn't want you to stop kissing me, or refrain from hugging me, disguise the desire in your eyes, or—"

"You're right. I definitely can't handle this secret." I kissed her urgently, squeezing her tighter, ignoring a tap on my shoulders. *One more kiss, God, then I'll stop. Please, one more kiss.* A shove followed another jab until I blinked. It wasn't God. It was her father—the resemblance verified it.

Everything happened so fast. One minute Mackenzie was in my arms, the next, the door slammed in my face. Her father's presence was still a blur.

The following morning's emails were full of apologies. Mackenzie was sorry she shared something she should've kept to herself about her desires that if not tamed, we could open a dangerous and powerful door. At least in two emails, I apologized to Mackenzie for showing up late, not respecting her wishes, and not using restraint—at least some. She did apologize for her father, but explained it was rather late and it was still his house. We both agreed I owed her father an apology.

We repented, prayed, and were back on track. On Tuesday, I left work early after being briefed on the forum, and other cases. I stopped by Sweetie Pies—voted St. Louis's favorite soul food restaurant.

It was hard to resist Robbie Montgomery's specialties, so I ordered two to-go dinners of fried chicken wings, corn, macaroni and cheese, and a taste of peach cobbler. Prior to opening Sweetie Pies, she had performed with and cooked for Tina and the late Ike Turner.

When I arrived at Mackenzie's school, I waited in the car and allowed the aroma of Robbie's food to intoxicate me. More than once, I thought about tearing into the fried chicken and Mackenzie would never know it.

A few minutes later, Mackenzie walked out of the doors and strutted down the steps. I climbed out of my car into the freezing temperatures. Opening the passenger door, Mackenzie bypassed her car. Squinting, she got in with suspicion. I hurried around and jumped in after closing her door. She was waiting with folded arms.

"Didn't I ban you from the premises?" she teased.

I winked, reached in the back seat, and offered her a Styrofoam container. When she sniffed Sweetie Pies' trademark peach cobbler, she grinned.

"Oh, wait a minute. I'm not supposed to be here."

Tightening her hold on the box, she conceded, "Okay, okay, okay. C'mon. I'm hungry." She laid it on her lap. *"Bless it for us."* I opened my mouth, but she shook her head. *"No. Sign to me."*

I lifted my hands, keeping my eyes connected with hers, not as an interpreter, but as a woman I cared about, loved. *"Lord, everything we have is because you've given it to us. Bless our food and our lives in Jesus' name.* When I finished, she signed, *Amen.*

We consumed our meals in silence, every crumb. After wiping her hands and dabbing her mouth, Mackenzie gathered our trash. She faced me with hesitation after tying the white plastic bag and setting it by her feet. "Noel?" she said, toying with a napkin.

"Yeah, baby. What's wrong?" I covered her hands. I really wanted to watch her lips.

"I know we've opened up a Pandora's Box with that kiss the other night, but . . ."

I smirked, knowing what she was afraid to say. "You want another kiss?"

She nodded.

"I can do that, but Mackenzie, woman, you've got to help me because I am flesh and blood and I will respond in it. I want to kiss you, too, baby, but just saying your name is temptation."

"You're right." She sighed and looked away.

I pulled her toward me and gave her the sweetest kiss my body could tolerate. Even the briefest contact was electrifying. Her lips were so soft. The kiss was sweet and too brief, but I didn't want her students catching Miss Norton necking. "Will that hold ya?"

"It'll do," she tossed back.

I never laughed so much until I was with Mackenzie. We were fighting the same temptation. If it wasn't for her quick wit sometimes, whew, only God knew. I re-directed my attention. "Tell me about your fascination for theater. I want to understand your passion. I want you to know that I'm here for you."

"I would love to have your support."

"You don't have to ask. You've got it."

"Great." Mackenzie wrapped her coat around her, not bothering to slide her arms through the sleeves, snatched her purse, and raced from my car. I rolled my eyes, swiped my coat off the backseat, and gave chase. I yelled for her to wait. "What's going on, Mackenzie?"

"Follow me," she said, whirling around before getting inside her car.

That wasn't an easy request, considering I would've failed a driving test under her instructions. Leaving the city, I trailed her to Kirkwood's Civic Center, a suburb twenty minutes away. I recognized the name Stages of St. Louis, also a nonprofit organization that received grant money. Beyond that, I knew very little about it.

Once inside and back stage, she flipped on lights, revealing an abandoned playroom where toys were left to their own devices. "This is a trash collector's nightmare." Mackenzie extended her hand and I clasped it as we maneuvered around one trap after another.

Tapping her arm, I got her attention. *"Why do*

you do this? When I met you, you were helping out at The Black Rep, then the Uppity Theatre, now Stages. Why so many places?" She guided me to a grayish stone bench and I questioned its sturdiness. I balanced my weight to protect Mackenzie in case the thing collapsed.

"Noel, each theatre house offers something different to its audience." She swept her hand from left to right, introducing me to worn furniture that my grand-parents might have owned. Dull and colorful out-fits hung from misplaced knobs in the wall. They appeared clean, but definitely outdated.

Stages of St. Louis attracts a community with limited exposure to the arts. A few years ago, they started a fundraising campaign to raise money for a new theatre.

I could relate to their efforts of matching donor contributions, writing grants for government funds, and hosting endless fundraisers.

"A theatre company's budget determines how many plays they can perform, and how elaborate the costumes and scenes are. Money determines if the company can af-ford to build a replica of a 1920s neighborhood or rent props, or—" she paused and pointed to a two-sided wall in the corner at least fifteen feet high . . ."*con-struct a collage that can be used for multiple scenes. Some of the bigger theatres can afford to build several separate backgrounds whereas here at Stages, one wall may have to be used for up to four scenes. Remember I told you I enjoy attending auctions?"*

Nodding, I smirked, too fascinated by all of this to ask questions. At the same time, I was reminded how different our worlds were. Her happiness was too contagious for me to dwell on negative thoughts. *"How could I forget?"*

She continued to sign. *"Years ago, I was an assistant on a small project. We had to find a pair of vintage wood chairs. We shopped at Goodwill and other second-hand stores—nothing. Finally, we hit some estate sales and—bingo. We got there right before the previewing ended. The deceased was a packrat. The ninety-year-old had things saved from her parents and grandparents.*

"There was a lot of old expensive stuff. Most of the people came for the jewelry. I sat dumbfounded as people in the audience raised their hands, holding white cards with a number on it, or nodded. The bid spotter acknowledged them by pointing his finger. I was really getting into it."

God, she's beautiful. You created a good thing when you made her, I thought.

Mackenzie stopped signing. "To make a long story short, we bought a set of chairs for one-hundred and twenty-five dollars." She lifted her chin in triumph.

"Can't you bid online like eBay?"

"Too boring. Now, to change the subject. Remember when I told you I liked *Dancing with the Stars*? Guess where that addiction came from?"

"I have no idea, but why should I stop you now from telling me?" My nostrils flared in amusement as I inhaled her perfume. I laughed. At times, a young girl would peep out in my woman and this was another side of her I wouldn't change.

"I'm always spellbound when theatres put on musicals. It takes hard work to learn sophisticated steps and group coordination. When I first saw *Dancing with the Stars,* I thought, wow, I would love to be in that, but I'm not a professional dancer or a star." She pouted.

"That all depends. God created the stars to shine." My hand reached for her chin to draw her closer. "Baby, there's nothing dull about you. That's why I fell in love with you. I love you." As we were about to share a kiss, the poorly constructed bench gave way. We fell into a pile of clothes.

Mackenzie looked at me before her head fell back. When she started laughing, I joined her.

"Oops, I forgot to tell you, this is my project, and I hadn't finished."

CHAPTER 17

Mackenzie's kiss, our kiss. God help me, each one was getting better and better. I couldn't last much longer. Friday morning I overslept dreaming about it. The truth was I had accidentally set my bed shaker on low. Instead of throwing me overboard, its slight vibration lulled me to sleep.

After the kiss, Mackenzie and I stayed up into the early morning hours, exchanging text messages.

Noel, do you really love me?

Yes. I waited for her declaration. After two minutes, I was still waiting. My heart sunk, but I understood she needed to reconcile her feelings.

I was about to text her goodnight when my BlackBerry vibrated in my hand.

Goodnight. O BTW, I love you, too.

Who wouldn't sleep deep after that? That was my problem the next morning. I slept too well. I rushed through my morning prayer, substituted my jog for fifty pushups, and skipped breakfast. I didn't make an appearance at PRESERVE-St. Louis until mid-morning.

I stopped at my assistant's desk for messages. Craning her neck, she studied me. "What?" I asked annoyed.

"Mr. Richardson, who dressed you this morning?"

"What? What's wrong with you? The same person who dresses me every morning—me." I jabbed my thumb into my chest.

Nodding, she stood. "You missed a few buttons."

"I knew that." Looking down, I groaned. Agitated and grouchy, I stormed away toward my office. I flung my overcoat on a chair and missed. Making no attempts at recovering it, I stepped over it as I headed to my desk. I unbuttoned and re-buttoned my shirt. My computer must've been asleep because it took three tries before I was able to boot it. I was going to get someone from the IT department to take a look later.

Finally connected, I went straight to my personal email before the agency's email accounts. Twenty messages were crammed in my inbox. Most were about the annual deaf holiday activities that I had completely forgotten about. As I clicked to open the first one, Pierce flashed an instant message.

What's up? You've been untouchable, unreachable, and avoidable for days. Still going strong with the interpreter?

I am, I typed back as another instant message popped up.

I missed the twelve days before Christmas this year.

There's two left. What do you want for Christmas? My mother interceded.

I couldn't believe it. It was a well-known fact among my family that Gina Richardson didn't start her holiday shopping before or after December 12th so this wasn't the norm. It's as if the stores had marked down specials for one day with her name on them. Christmas was a few days away.

Momma, whatever you want to give is fine, I replied as Pierce resumed his interrogation.

Pierce: *Are you sure about her?*

Pierce had a one-track mind when it came to obtaining information. My brother's mannerisms were predictable. He was probably rubbing the back of his neck while formulating his next question. Pierce was on top of his game when it came to dissecting plaintiffs' testimonies. His questions were face value. Pierce was always role-playing the devil's advocate when it came to my best interests.

Caleb's message box conveniently kept me from answering. *How does she look?* His presence meant we were only one member short of a family affair. The family circle always formed when I didn't check in for a while.

Is she saved, Noel, really saved? Pierce retrieved the conversation.

It wasn't a surprise when my dad let his presence be known, *Make sure she is, Noel, and take your time. Remember you can talk or sign to me about anything, son.*

I would love to meet your interpreter. Bring her over to the house for Christmas, my mom's message demanded as she bumped Caleb's incomplete message box off the screen.

Listen, you heard me knocking. Gertrude Penelope Richardson, my paternal grandmother, typed once I let her into the discussion.

Grandma, I'm deaf remember? I can't hear anything.

Humph! You should be more observant while you're logged on to this thing, Grandma scolded.

Yes, Madam.

Momma pressed: *Back to Mackenzie, Noel.*

Pierce: *Yes, Noel, back to Mackenzie.*

I'll ask her, but I don't want you all jumping to conclusions, I warned.

Pierce: *Noel, I'll catch up with you later. It's too crowded in this closet. I'm out of here. Love everybody. Poof.*

Grandma: *Anyway, maybe I should get McKinley a gift, too. I have plenty of birthday and Christmas gifts left over from last year that I can recycle.*

Her mind was gearing up for a monologue about what presents she would never use. If she took her Aleve this morning, her arthritic fingers could fly across the keyboard for hours. I'd try to correct her about Mackenzie's name later.

Dad: *Mother, don't move faster than Noel. I'm just glad a woman of God has captured his attention. Noel, after you get to know her, then we all would like that opportunity. And, mother, our son says her name is Mackenzie, not McKinley,*

Grandma: *It's BigMoma, Richard. BigMoma!*

I'm out of here, too. Love you. Talk to everybody soon, I pushed send and signed out of my AOL account. I loved my mother and grandma, but there were two things I learned about instant messaging with them: first, if they typed more than two sentences, that meant they were on a roll. They viewed the advance technology as a telephone call, prepared to type back and forth for hours. And the second thing is that I'd always forget until it happened next time.

My head spinning, I took a deep breath. I stood and walked to where my coat was sprawled across the floor. Reaching down, I yanked my hand back when something began to move under it. I leaped, recalling one of my employees mentioning seeing a rodent, but I was sure I had taken care of that problem.

My coat wasn't new, but I didn't have a problem getting rid of it in the process of terminating a pest. I was stomping on my coat when Keshon from the mailroom walked by.

"I heard you grunting, Mr. Richardson, and I came to investigate. Why are you stepping on your cell phone? I think it's vibrating." Without waiting for an answer, he moved two paces and swiped my coat. Digging inside my pocket, he handed me my BlackBerry.

This morning in my haste, I forgot to clip it on my waist belt. "Thank you, Keshon." As he turned to leave I saw a smile plastered on his face. I didn't give him the privilege. I laughed first. Keshon turned back and joined me.

I checked the two messages, Pierce: *I meant what I said, Noel. Fast and pray about Mackenzie.*

The man gave a new meaning to bulldog.

The other was from Mackenzie: *Noel, I'm remembering our kiss, your words, my words. And where is my morning scripture? I'm praying you have a blessed day.*

A cocky grin appeared on its own. "Take that, Pierce Richardson," I said with a chuckle before I began to tackle one request after another awaiting my approval. Once when I glanced up, I wasn't surprised to see Lana lingering near my office, but she never came in.

"You're late."

"I am." I leaned back in my seat and watched the emotions play across Lana's face. *"But I sign the paychecks."* I dismissed her.

My abbreviated day was business as usual, but before I left, I asked Lana to come to my office. *"Have a seat."* She did. *"Lana, I'm sorry if I hurt you earlier. I love you as a friend, but remember two things. No, three. I'm the boss first, I keep track of my own schedule, and we're friends last. Outside of work, we're always friends."*

"You're right, Noel."

"I know."

CHAPTER 18

God wasn't happy with me, and He let me know about it as He pushed me out of bed. "Time is running out, Noel. Valerie needs to make a change, and I'm sending you to get the job done," He clearly spoke to my spirit. I frowned, *what job?* I asked God to let me know when the time was right, throwing the ball back in His court and hopefully, letting me off the hook for the time being.

One hour later, I returned from my morning run, showered and dressed for my only Christmas shopping on Christmas Eve. Macy's was my one-stop shopping place for my family and staff—gift certificates. I had to be more selective for Mackenzie's gift. Nordstrom's came to mind. I had no idea what I was looking for when I browsed through the clothing racks. I was sure Mackenzie had perused a Harris Communications catalog that catered to the Deaf culture. It's not as if she could've picked that up in the grocery check out line. She did her homework. She deserved no less consideration.

Not a shopper and I didn't want to be one. I was about to leave when some hurried shoppers jostled me near a glass case. With all the glitter and gold decorations throughout the store, I don't know how a splinter of a sparkle got my attention, but something in that case winked at me, beckoning me closer. Leather gloves, how exciting. I examined them anyway—black, brown, red, blue, white. Some were trimmed in fur. I did a double take. I had never seen gloves trimmed in . . . diamonds?

I couldn't pull my eyes away from the exquisite items. I imagined Mackenzie's slender manicured hand appreciating the warmth of fur. As I continued my scrutiny, a chipped red fingernail blocked my view. Aggravated, I glanced up and stared into the face of a tired and agitated sales clerk. "Can I help you? Do you want to buy anything?"

Straightening my frame, I towered over her. I didn't care how many customers she'd waited on before me, I deserved a smile for the amount of money I could dish out. I pointed to the black gloves. She inserted a key to unlock the case then gently lifted the gloves from the carefully stacked pile. She reverently placed the merchandise on the counter before me.

A thin piece of paper floated out as I studied the merchandise: One-hundred percent Italian silk-lined black lambskin women's gloves with embedded Swarovski jewelry.

"How much?"

Her answer was indistinguishable, but it didn't matter. I reached into my back pants pocket for my wallet and Visa card. As she took my card, I refocused on Mackenzie's gift, brushing my fingers against the crystal bits. I signed the receipt without looking. Patiently, she wrapped the purchase in tissue paper before putting it inside a long box.

"Do you want me to gift wrap this?"

I thought that's what she just did. I nodded. She meticulously taped gold-foiled paper around the box. Still not finished, the woman considered her handiwork before reaching for a strip of red velvet she manipulated into a bow. Putting it in a bag, she handed it to me with a smile. "Thank you, sir."

Taking my purchase, I headed out of the store. Glancing at my receipt, I chuckled. No wonder I got a smile. The gloves were $300. Mackenzie was worth every dollar. I didn't care about the money with her; only my heart.

That night after the stores had closed early for Christmas Eve, the church's parking lot resembled the mall. Only coveted handicap spots were available. From a distance, I saw a space someone apparently overlooked. Inching closer, I saw why it was vacant. A Navigator bullied itself over the line.

I considered the scenario. I would be like a bear escaping from a cage, manipulating my muscles as I held my breath until I was freed. I'm sure I would rip off a couple of buttons from my suit jacket in the process. My tailor would have a fit at the thought of abusing fabric. The next insurmountable task would be to scoot between my car and the SUV without using my coat as a polish cloth. Nah, I kept driving.

Finally, I did find a space at the very end of the

lot. My strides were wide as my excitement built to see the pageantry Mackenzie helped orchestrate for the church's musical, the Night of Miracles. Once inside the vestibule, the doors to the sanctuary were propped open for an easy entrance. I crossed over the threshold, mesmerized. The already beautiful sanctuary was transformed into a majestic playhouse, and the new setting seemed to spill into the hall as if the splendor couldn't be contained.

The lighting gave the illusion that the pews had shrunk. Nick bumped into me as I walked, admiring the changes. The transformation had the Mackenzie touch.

"You don't need any interpretation. Everybody knows the story of Christ's birth," he said, suggesting another section where we were three rows from the makeshift stage. I agreed, shook off my coat and followed. I knelt to pray, then sat and rested my coat and Bible beside me. Stretching my legs, I had just thanked an usher for a program of the night's performance when Nick tapped me on my arm.

"You know I'm in love with her," Nick said, his expression serious.

"Who?"

I followed the direction of his star-gazed eyes—Valerie.

I was about to say good luck, but thought better of it. Then I reconsidered. The brother needed to know what he was getting into. "She's a piece of work."

Nick blew out a deep breath. "Don't I know it, but God knows it, too. She doesn't know that the man she's searching for is right in front of her. I'm waiting, watching, and praying for God to not only speak to her, but give Val the mind to hear what God has in store for her." He grinned and nudged me. "You and Mackenzie can't be the only happy couple in church."

I wished Nick's confession was an answer to my prayers and could possibly deliver Valerie's tormented soul. The lights dimmed to my relief. I didn't want to talk or think about Valerie until it was necessary. For the next hour, I lip-read some of the songs. When those around me put their hands together, I mimicked them. When their bodies shook with laughter, I laughed, knowing I had clearly missed the amusement.

Besides the magnificent wardrobe, the play had live animals and a borrowed Baby Jesus. I remembered the night Mackenzie gave me a tour of that theatre. I recalled the terms for each special effect, but Mackenzie achieved the illusion of iridescent stars illuminated the ceiling. Scenes changed when the wall moved like a revolving door.

A childlike angel appeared. Instead of descending, he was unrolled like a yo-yo almost to the floor, but his feet never touch the stage. I wiggled my fingers in the air, the deaf sign for applause, as others clapped. Mackenzie had her fingerprints all over that stunt.

Midway into the play, Nick elbowed me twice, blowing his breath in my ear. When I didn't respond, he nudged me again. Finally, I shoved him back, irritated. "What, man?"

"She doesn't know I exist."

I shouldn't have sat next to Nick. I was trying to concentrate on the play, plus I had no encouraging words forthcoming. Taking the hint, he turned back to the stage.

The production ended forty-five minutes later. The audience gave the cast and crew a standing ovation as each bowed when they were introduced. I don't know how she located me in the audience, but Mackenzie's eyes found mine before gracing everyone with a radiant smile. The audience waved programs in the air as wonder still danced in their eyes.

Afterward, some people rushed home to finish wrapping gifts. They weren't missed as the fellowship hall swelled with people who wanted to congratulate cast members who stood in a receiving line, soaking up the accolades bestowed on them. Mackenzie's smile was brighter than bleached sheets. Amazingly, between handshakes and hugs, she stole glances my way as I waited on the sidelines.

Eventually, she made her way to me and stopped. Her eyes told me what she wanted, a hug not meant for onlookers. As my nostrils flared and I bit my bottom lip, I conveyed with my stare that I knew what she wanted and I wouldn't disappoint before the night was over. *"You were wonderful. Mackenzie. You are truly a talented woman."*

"I know."

Tweaking her nose, I laughed. I reached for her hand. "You sassy woman, the correct answer is 'thank you.'" She playfully bumped me as we headed for light refreshments at the tables, which included holiday "treats."

As the crowd thinned, Mackenzie's high strung energy began to fizzle. We strolled to a side room where the crew stored their belongings. Mackenzie gathered her purse and I assisted her with her coat. After she buttoned the last button, I took her Bible and escorted her to her car. I spied Nick vying for Valerie's affections, but she was too distracted, watching us. I had to get the showdown with Valerie over with so she could move on. Although I had no idea why I seemed to bring out the demons in Valerie, I trusted God to help me make sense of all this one-sided hostility.

Outside, with the exception of about ten or so cars, the parking lot was deserted. At Mackenzie's car, we stared at each other until I couldn't take it anymore. I looked around for bystanders, then I stole a hug and relaxed, contented. I removed my gloves and held her cold hands, thinking about her gift. "Where are your gloves?"

She responded with an embarrassing smirk then batted her eyes. "I lost them."

I stored that information. Although my hands weren't much warmer, I stroked her fingers. "The National Black Deaf Advocates is sponsoring a holiday party the day after Christmas. Come with me." I wasn't asking.

Her eyes filled with disappointment. "I can't."

Stay calm. I dared my face to reveal anything—nothing.

"I have to pack."

"Excuse me?" I lifted my brow.

"Chicago. I'm going the day after Christmas."

CHAPTER 19

Chicago? She had to be kidding me. I would give her back the Rubik's Cube for her presence. I was seconds away from initiating an argument in the church's parking lot. This was our first Christmas together and I felt as if I should have precedence over any of her previous plans. To keep that argument at bay, I denied myself, and Mackenzie a kiss. I prayed with her, held open her car door then got in my car. We drove off the parking lot and went our separate ways home.

I was ashamed that on Christmas morning, I was still fuming while shaving—a bad combination. That must have been the same Chicago visit Valerie was fervently praying for under the guise of it benefitting Mackenzie.

Some Christmas. I wanted to introduce Mackenzie to my family. My holiday plans to spend the day with the woman I loved dwindled down to our new routine of me having the sole privilege of picking her up for church, and Mackenzie enjoying the pampering treatment. I felt like I was being forced to hand over her gift, and then send her on her way. Something was wrong with that picture. The bathroom counter received the brunt of my frustration with a pound of my fist. My chin suffered the other when I nicked it.

Could the morning get any worse? Yep, it did. Our morning emails usually pacified me until I could see her smiling face and sniff her perfume. After the scripture, we switched to instant messaging. I would try to be a man who could compromise.

What would you like to do today after service, baby?

Mackenzie: *Noel, I'm sorry. My father and I always spend this holiday together.*

No exceptions?

Mackenzie: *I love you.*

Then act like it woman, I wanted to say, but I held that demand. *I love you, too. Be ready in an hour for church.*

I signed off without waiting for a response.

I donned another one of my custom-tailored suits. In the hall, I dragged my coat off the hanger, then snatched Mackenzie's gift bag from the living room table and headed for the door. *It's not about me,* I chanted. It's about celebrating Christ first and my wants second. Make that third. She just put me on the back burner.

I had barely left my fingerprints on Mackenzie's doorknocker when she opened the door, smiling. Her trademark curls lay straight past her shoulders. *Wow.* Coincidently, she wore a brown pinstripe dress or maybe it was a coat. It covered her body, that's all I knew. Suede ankle boots showed off her legs. A large brown hat adorned her head. The sight of her almost brought me to my knees.

"Oh, my God, help me," I couldn't contain my thoughts as I towered over her, cataloging her new look.

"It's that bad?" she asked, panicking.

I couldn't answer.

"Noel, you hate it, don't you? I stayed up all night after service . . . I thought you would like it . . ." Her hand covered her lips to prevent me from understanding anything else.

"Mackenzie, you have no idea how much power you have over me. Your hair, where are all the curls?" I felt like a fool for being an idiot.

"Don't you like it?"

Reaching out, I finger-combed the straight, soft strands. "What's not to like on you? Those curls are definitely you and only you, but this woman before me is God's beauty manifested."

"Good answer." She stepped into my arms. I didn't want to let her go—period—to Chicago or to church. Kisses and loving her didn't give me a right to make demands. I was breaths away from getting on one knee. *And say what? Marriage, babies, and retirement?* Despite my feelings, we were still in the exploration stage. *Yeah, right. You confessed your love in less than thirty days of meeting her,* I thought.

Then Mackenzie worked her magic. She winked. Her lashes were longer—sassy. Her smile beamed—alluring. She shook her hair, flaunting her long mane that swished from side to side. She knew what she was doing and kept enticing me anyhow. I stepped back to keep my sanity, and I still hadn't apologized to her father.

She smirked, lifting a silky brow. *"You look very handsome. I like your hat."*

I reached to remove my Dion Saunders fashion statement, having forgotten my manners and all common sense once Mackenzie opened the door.

"No, don't." She touched my sleeve. *"It emphasizes the mysterious thoughts and looks of a man who loves me."* She innocently stroked my clean-shaven cheeks and chin. I tensed at her massage of my nick. The wound was because of her anyway. She was leaving.

Mackenzie was setting me on fire as I tried to regulate my breathing. *Lord, you can intervene at any time, because Mackenzie was making it hard to resist,* I silently pleaded. *"Mackenzie, you are seriously asking for some carnal trouble today. You're teasing me and you're leaving me. That's a bad combination. I'm not a toy so don't wind me up. Ready to go?"*

"Noel, when I come back, I'm going to make you my number one priority, behind God, of course."

"Well, Merry Christmas and hallelujah. That's what I'm talking about."

I stepped inside as she walked to a hall closet. The door was the size of a small pantry. I blinked to scan my surroundings. The room looked like something out of the Orient. There were a lot of browns—couch, toss pillows, walls. Besides the couch, there were enough chairs for a small gathering.

After twirling a cape off a hanger, Mackenzie danced on her toes to rummage through a top shelf. The hunt over, she struggled with a shopping bag brimming with gifts. Stepping behind her, I easily retrieved it for her. Before I moved back, I placed a kiss on her hair. Thanking me, she looked inside the bag and wiggled out a small box and handed it to me.

"Mackenzie," I said, gritting my teeth. How could a woman balance beautiful and fascinating with hardheadedness?

"Noel," she stopped and held up her hand. "My small gifts are tokens to let you know I'm thinking about you. I couldn't pass this up. While window shopping in the mall, I passed Crabtree and Evelyn. The cologne *Noel* was on display on the shelves, so I backtracked. The sales woman said the cologne was a way to celebrate the reason for the season, 'After all, Noel does have a biblical significance,' she had said."

I shook my head, chuckling. "My name isn't in the Bible."

Mackenzie nodded. "I know. I tried to tell her it's Noah. She said, 'Same thing,' and continued to ring up my purchase. Anyway, it reminded me of you. I bought it to remind you of me."

She had me wrapped around her finger. *God what have you given me? No wonder Adam ate the fruit Eve offered.* Instead of fruit, Mackenzie held the bag of potpourri under my nose. I inhaled and exhaled without losing eye contact. If I started on her lips, I wouldn't be able to finish. Clearing my throat, I picked up her bag and grabbed her hand. "C'mon, woman, a minute longer and we're going to need a chaperone. Speaking of chaperone, where's your father? I want to apologize for the other night."

"I've already spoken to him and apologized for you."

"Thank you, but . . . I can speak for myself and I will. Is he home?"

"No."

Inside my car, I presented Mackenzie's gift bag. "Merry Christmas."

She sucked in her breath and her eyes widened as she unwrapped her present. Meticulously, she fingered the gloves.

Mackenzie's lips moved, but I couldn't read them. Reaching out, my right hand lifted her chin. "You have to look at me."

Her eyes glistened. "I buy the best shoes, leather handbags, and stylish durable clothes, but I've never invested in a good pair of gloves because I usually lose them before the end of the season," she paused. "Noel, I'll never lose these."

"Thank you. I love you, and I'll never repeat those words to another woman."

CHAPTER 20

The choir marched into the sanctuary with their purple robes swaying. According to the overhead projector, they sang "The Hallelujah Chorus." Everyone was standing, including me. I didn't need to know the beat to clap my hands or move my feet. Midway through the praise portion of the service, I glanced back and surprisingly made eye contact with my parents. After my initial shock of seeing them there instead of attending their home church, I nodded. My dad tilted his head in acknowledgment as Momma waved frantically as if I didn't see her.

I did another head check as the choir finished and spotted Pierce a few pews behind my parents, and even Caleb was supposedly sneaking in. My brothers never looked my way, but Pierce seemed captivated with the interpreters. Ah, yes, Mackenzie had that effect.

The jubilation continued as Pastor Coleman began his sermon, *Jesus Revealed. It's time to open our gifts,* Mackenzie interpreted.

"Okay," Keisha and Daphne who wore matching dresses, signed as they tore into the presents Mackenzie gave them. I don't know what she gave them, but Mrs. Campbell warned her daughters to wait until they were home before opening them. As far as the sisters were concerned, Pastor Coleman gave them permission. They had practically shredded the wrapping off when their mother reached over and snatched both presents from them. Pouting, they made a dramatic production of folding their arms as Pastor Coleman continued.

"Not a tangible gift you got from under the tree. Open the gifts God gave you, and He doesn't need a holiday to give us gifts. After unwrapping Grace, we discover Mercy. Joy escaped and danced behind Peace. Salvation and Power stood at attention before Healing and Deliverance were uncovered. Somehow, Love seemed to be a small package, but once opened, it exploded, covering all the other gifts."

The crowd was riveted as he quoted scriptures verbatim to back up his hour long sermon. Afterward, he stretched out his hand, offering an invitation. *There is never any reason for you to leave this church hungry. There's more food on the table from where this morsel came, and you know what?"*

He waited for us to respond.

"There are more gifts, too. If you want your presents, ask. Daddy, I want the box labeled Peace, I need two packages of Power. Need Joy? Yeah, it looks like that's here, too. Come on, today is a good day to ask. Repent first, confessing your sins, not to me, but to the Lord Jesus. Tell Him you're sorry. Ask Him for help. Once you've made up your mind, come for prayer. If you want to get rid of your filthy garments, let God wash your sins away in

Jesus' name. He offers a full-service makeover. He will wash, dry, press, and dress you Himself. Come on now. No sense in wasting these gifts."

In their Sunday best, many came. God had a special message for me: talk to Valerie. After the benediction, I spied Valerie as she left her Deaf Ministry post. Inhaling a heavy dose of air, I readied myself for the inevitable. This talk could be quick and easy or drawn out and difficult. *Lord, you decide,* I prayed, locating Valerie on the other side. I wasn't far away when my mother bulldozed her way through the aisles, coming toward me.

I had actually forgotten about Mackenzie when she tapped me on the shoulder.

"You ready to go?" she signed and covered her ears.

"Funny, I hadn't noticed," I taunted.

When she reached out to inflict a harmless punch, my hand was quicker and I grabbed her fist and gently squeezed it. *"Seriously, my family is here. I want you to meet them."* My expression told her it wasn't a request. First, I needed to tell Mackenzie what I had planned to do. *"Listen, baby, I need to confess. It's about the conversation you had with Valerie."*

"Do we have to talk about that now? The one you had no business interpreting."

Clearly, this wasn't a good time for Mackenzie, and definitely not what I had planned to do on Christmas. *"She truly believes God sent me for her. You and I knew from day one that was not the case. I don't think she believed you. I've got to talk to her. Hopefully, she'll believe me."*

Opening her mouth, she folded her arms then

changed her mind as she lifted her arms. *"I should be angry with you for eavesdropping. I don't care if you can't hear. That was a private conversation. However, the air needs to be clear before my friendship and fellowship with Valerie can move on . . ."* Mackenzie paused, thinking. *"I don't know if that's a good idea, Noel. If she found out you knew what she was saying, she may go ballistic from embarrassment. She doesn't take rejection too good. Today's definitely not a good day."*

"Mackenzie, I wasn't asking your permission. I have to talk to her in order to be obedient to God."

"I understand, Noel." She twisted her mouth in torment and then lifted her fingers to comb through her curls. Mackenzie momentarily appeared shocked when she realized they no longer existed, then patted her head instead. *"Will you wait for me and we can do this together?"*

"I don't know. Personally, I'm ready to get this out of the way. I've tolerated her unjustified attitude long enough."

"She doesn't know you know. Okay. Let me talk to her first. Promise me, Noel."

I could use the buffer and Mackenzie would only be gone a few days. I shrugged. *"Okay."*"

"The service was inspiring." My mother appeared, ending my conversation with Mackenzie.

"Noel's inspiration not from message," Caleb gibed in broken American Sign Language. I got tired of reminding him that English Sign Language was much easier, but what do I know? I'm only his deaf older brother.

My dad and Pierce were exchanging Christmas greetings as they made their way to us. Linking my fingers with Mackenzie's, I pulled her closer.

"Mom, Dad, Pierce, and Caleb, this is Mackenzie."
I couldn't help from worshiping the woman, and I
wanted my family to see it.

"Merry Christmas," she greeted, shaking their
hands one by one. That wasn't good enough for
my mother as she gathered Mackenzie in a hug.

"Dad, I'm glad to see you all, but why are you
here instead of at your church on Christmas?"

Momma shrugged. "Since Mackenzie is coming
over after church, I thought it would be nice for us
to fellowship with you two beforehand." She
peered at Caleb. "I'm glad your brother decided to
join us." Momma proceeded to bombard Mackenzie with question after question about our relationship, and her age. I tried to intervene before
she asked what high school Mackenzie attended—
a ridiculous "St. Louis thing" to define the status
of a person. I tried to tell Momma that Mackenzie
wasn't coming, but Momma shooed me.

Then Mackenzie broke the disappointing news.
My mother was crestfallen. Pierce lifted a brow in
scrutiny, and my dad nodded his understanding
after Mackenzie explained she had to pack.

While all the activity was centered on Mackenzie, Caleb gave me the oddest expressions, frowning and gritting his teeth. I shoved Caleb aside.
What's your problem? I signed with my back to
Mackenzie then realized he probably didn't understand me, and I wanted Caleb to hear my question.

My nostrils flared as I grimaced in irritation.
"Why the faces, man?" I sat against a pew with my
arms folded, waiting for his response.

"Mom, Dad, and Pierce were being polite. You'd
better be glad you can't hear. She has a soft voice,

but it's whiny and irritating. If a woman's voice doesn't attract me, then nothing else will, because regardless of her physical assets, she would drive me crazy during sex."

I prayed to God that nobody heard what my brother was saying, especially in church. "Careful, Caleb, that's my woman you're talking about."

"*Whatever*," he signed back with perfection as I broke up the family conference to take Mackenzie home.

CHAPTER 21

Traditions, Mackenzie had said. I twisted my lips mockingly. *Let me tell you about my holiday traditions, Mackenzie,* I fumed to myself.

When I was younger, my family believed in Santa Claus. Not the jolly old guy, but the sky is the limit credit card spending. Momma and Dad had to work overtime for months afterwards just to get the balance down for the following Christmas spree. Of course, my brothers and I never knew that as we indulged in our heart's desire of every requested item under a seven-foot tree.

After we embraced the Lord, my dad instituted new guidelines. If we spent one-hundred dollars on anybody, God had to get one-hundred and one dollars. It took a while for us to adjust to the new rules, but eventually, we did. *Traditions.*

Momma made contributions to the Sickle Cell Disease Foundation of America for Pierce, United Negro College Fund for Caleb and the National Black Deaf Advocates for me. Every year, a differ-

ent homeless shelter received a check with my
dad's signature. *Traditions.*

After depositing sizeable portions of turkey,
dressing, homemade rolls, potato salad, mustard
greens, and sweet potato pie into our mouths, our
stomachs rebuked further abuse. To lose a calorie
or two, the men cleaned up after Momma's Southern cooking mess before heading to the family
room. Claiming a spot, we unbuckled our belts
and kicked off our shoes. We were ready as Dad
pointed the remote toward the TV.

Most programs were broadcast in closed-caption,
and sometimes, it was *tradition* that the station hadn't
reset the closed-caption after a local commercial
spot. I knew the routine. It happened at least a couple of times during the month. Using my Blackberry, I retrieved a previous e-mail to a station,
changed the date, and forwarded it on. If I were
lucky, the service would be turned on before the
program, or in this case, the football game ended.

Finally, the closed-caption was activated about
an hour into the first game. Only then, the letters
were too small. The bigger the screen, the more
readable the sentences, and Dad had a big screen
plasma TV that wasn't working, but was still under
warranty. Repairs weren't available until after the
holiday, so I lip-read as much as I could.

Concentrating on the plays, we leaned forward.
My heart pumped in anticipation with three minutes left in the second game. The quarterback
scrambled, looking for an open receiver before
taking off to score the touchdown from the fif-
teenth yard line. He passed the twelfth, the tenth,
the fifth . . . then Momma intercepted the play,

blocking our view with the universal time-out sign. We threw up our arms, yelling. *Tradition.* She did it every year for attention.

"You guys ready for dessert?"

"No!" we said. When she moved, a commercial was airing.

Later that night, Pierce nudged me as I dozed on the sofa. "Hey, got a minute?" I nodded. "I wanted to talk to you about something." He glanced at my dad and Caleb. *"Alone. How about a cup of coffee and a slice of pecan pie, and I'll meet you down the hall?"*

Standing, I headed down the hall to one of our old bedrooms that Momma had converted into an anything room—sewing, library, home office, and God knows what else.

After taking two steps into the free-for-all room, I yelled. Steadying my left foot, I lifted the other. I yelled again. Like a dart, a safety pin was clinging on my silk sock. I yanked it out and cautiously laid my left foot down. I examined the other and pulled out a straight pin. Exhaling, I rested that foot only to be attacked by another pin. Biting my mouth to keep anything ungodly from escaping, I dropped to the floor, only to discover a bent pin was strategically pointed at my butt. That's it, the room was booby-trapped, and this would definitely go down as my worst Christmas on record.

Momma barged into the room, drying her hands on a kitchen towel. She bent until we were eye level. "Noel, what's wrong with you?"

I stole a deep breath as I massaged the waves in my head. "You have a war zone in here. I should've known better than to come in here."

"I'll have you know, I vacuumed this room thoroughly last night after I made the place mats. She spun around in her house-shoes and left as Pierce strolled in with our snack, laughing.

"She got me last week. It is a battle field." As he set our pie and coffee on the table and backed up, that's when a pin got him. I barked out a laugh as I rubbed my butt, walking on the sides of my feet to the sofa.

We engaged in a few more episodes of teasing before slapping each other's back. Pierce ate his dessert and waited for me. His face was unreadable, so I had no idea what was on his mind. After gulping down my last bit of coffee, I waited.

"She's pretty."

I didn't have to guess. "Yes, Mackenzie is very pretty. I can't believe no one has snatched her before me."

"She's the one. I can tell by the way you watched her at church, and you've been a pain in the butt—and I don't mean that pin either—since you've been here."

I looked away to keep Pierce from reading the emotions that played across my face. I couldn't help but smile as I faced my brother again. "Mackenzie's everything a man could want. She's fine, wears her own hair that isn't detachable, and has legs that peek out every now and then. She's sweet, confident, professional, but when we're together, we're laughing, teasing, praying, and battling the devil to keep our carnal lusts out of the way."

Pierce stopped me. "I wonder what's keeping

the right woman from crossing my path. Congrats on a good choice. Does she love you?"

"She says she does, and I believe her. Hey, mind if I ask you something?"

He shrugged and nodded.

"Caleb says Mackenzie has a high-pitched, annoying, and whiny voice. Does she?"

"Yep."

A few days after Mackenzie left, I texted Lana and invited her to lunch. Relaxing inside Tony Roma's at the St. Louis Mills, we sampled each other's food as we exchanged amusing tales from our past. I paused when I glanced over Lana's shoulders.

Pierce was strolling toward us accompanied by a very attractive woman. I smirked. Boy that was fast finding the right woman. *"There's my brother. I didn't know he would be out here. You remember Pierce."* I stood and waved to get his attention.

"Noel, invite them over." Lana also stood.

Nodding, I squeezed from the booth. Taking long strides, I blended with others in the food court until Pierce noticed me and grabbed his acquaintance's hand. Face-to-face, Pierce and I exchanged hugs and slaps on the back.

The woman's face was in awe. "You two look just alike."

"Yeah, we get that a lot. I'm Noel," I said before turning and leading them to my table. Lana gave Pierce a warm hug.

Turning to his date, Pierce made the introductions, "Donna, this is our good friend, Lana. Lana, Donna."

"If you haven't eaten, come join Lana and me," I offered and made room for them.

"Are you buying?" Pierce teased me.

"Absolutely."

Lana and I resumed eating while Donna and Pierce scanned the menu. His date said something that caused Lana and me to exchanged bewildered looks. Pierce turned to us and signed. *"Donna said your ribs look good, but she just got her nails done, and she'll probably remove her polish licking the barbecue sauce off her fingers. She was joking."*

Donna's confused expression blinked to disdain. Pierce saw it, too. I didn't have to read his lips to understand what Pierce's eyes revealed. Donna would be history. She wasn't the one.

Pierce wasn't picky when it came to a woman's looks. Yes, she had to be pleasing to his eyes—not necessarily a bombshell or knockout—and a Christian woman with a sweet spirit.

Plus, the woman had to be comfortable with my deafness. If the "right woman" wasn't willing to even learn finger-spelling, she wasn't the one. His stubbornness was humbling.

CHAPTER 22

I must work the works of Him that sent me, while it is day. The night cometh, when no man can work. It had to be God's voice.

"Okay, Lord, I'll talk to Valerie the next time I see her," I said, groaning as I parked in front of Barnes & Noble. I had time to skim through some sport magazines until I met Caleb and Pierce to roll a few games of bowling,

Bypassing the bestsellers table that greeted me at the door, I plucked copies of *Sports Illustrated, ESPN,* and *Sporting News* off the shelves. Strolling to the café, I ordered a tall espresso. With a steaming cup in one hand and magazines under my arm, I dropped them on a nearby round parlor table, removed my coat and took a seat. I offered a thirty-second prayer over my drink before taking a cautious sip. Sighing, I closed my eyes and enjoyed the warm brew on a cold winter day.

Two magazines later, I checked my watch as I finished an article on Tiger Woods. Standing, I gulped down my remaining espresso, grabbed the magazines, and headed to the register. On my way out, I literally bumped into Valerie, who was gracing Barnes & Noble's doorway. I cringed. *Now, Lord?* I didn't really have time to talk to her now.

God spoke, "Fool, this is your time and place." Reluctantly, I opened the door wider.

She tried to pass, but I blocked her. "Excuse me."

When I didn't move, Valerie looked up. "Noel?"

"Hi, Valerie, I need to talk with you." I was ready to open my mouth and let God's words spill out. "We need to talk," I repeated, hoping I wasn't too loud to draw attention, or too low where she wouldn't hear me.

She had cleared the door when she spun around. "About what, Noel?" She torpedoed daggers, her nostrils flared, and her hands balled into fists. The idea of using Mackenzie as backup wasn't so bad a idea after all. *How ugly is this going to get, God?*

"You." I chided myself for my bad choice of one word that was so accusatory, it was sure to put anyone on defense.

When I moved out of her way, she kept walking, so I followed her to a display table of sale books. I couldn't make out what her lips were saying, and she didn't bother to sign.

God, you're not going to make this easy for me are you? I asked. He commanded me to talk to her, but He didn't give me what to say. Basically, I was on my own. Scanning faces, I searched for some divine intervention for the perfect words. Of course, my vocabulary had abandoned me.

"To be truthful, Valerie, I want to get to know you, and for you to get to know me." That was the best that I could come up with on short notice.

Valerie faced me with a smile. "So you're finally coming to your senses? It's a little late for that, don't you think? You did choose someone else that God didn't send you." I couldn't tell if her voice was raising, but I did catch a few stares directed our way. Yep, that's what it meant.

"Listen, Valerie, I'm trying to be pleasant and settle a score we must've created in another life." I checked my watch. She had fifteen minutes and then I was out of here. "Come on, we can have a seat in the café. A cup of latte is on me."

After a brief hesitation, she squinted. Finally, she shrugged and led the way. I trailed her. At the counter, she considered the menu box posted above the workers' heads. Turning around, she grinned at me mischievously. "I never pass up a free meal."

A cup wasn't a meal. Valerie was a leech. She tried to get one over on Nick. I'm surprised he didn't let her. I angled my head to read her lips so at least I knew what I was paying for.

"A caramel latte, I want a slice of the cherry swirl cheesecake, and double chocolate brownie," she paused again, thinking as she tapped one clear-polish finger to red glossy lips. "I'll take a bottle of cream soda for later."

Valerie appeared to be finished when she took a breath, but she regained strength and kept ordering. The cashier continued punching items on the register. "Anything for you, sir?" the woman asked, amused.

I shook my head. I wanted to say, *Are you kidding? I might suffer an upset stomach watching Valerie digest all this food,* but I kept that thought to myself.

After paying for her purchases, I accepted her tray laden with enough junk food to energize a kindergarten class. With only three customers in the café, Valerie circled tables before settling on one. Setting the tray down, Valerie patiently waited as I helped her out her heavy winter coat and scooted her chair back. Settling in the seat across from her, I forced a smile. "Are you sure this is enough? I wouldn't want you to starve."

Her eyes brightened. "You're right. I might need a few items for later. Shall we pray?" Valerie suggested.

I nodded. "Go ahead."

I held my breath in annoyance. If she was stalling this conversation, she was doing a good job. Unfortunately, I had to meet my brothers and I needed to get this over with so I could leave.

"Why don't you bless my food? I want to hear you pray," she requested.

Shrugging, I bowed my head, said grace, and I opened my eyes, "Amen."

"I wanted to hear you pray."

"You heard me. Amen."

She meticulously lifted her napkin and let it drift to her lap. I was amused and getting peeved. Somehow I knew I wouldn't be bowling with my brothers if Valerie treated a paper napkin as if it was white linen from a five-star restaurant.

In no rush and with much fanfare, she peeled the paper from her straw and sipped her cream soda before tasting her latte. The combination of drinks was weird, but the method seemed to match Valerie's unusual personality.

"Mackenzie was right about you," she said, giving me the first genuine smile since I had started attending the church.

"She was?" Curious, I sat back. Massaging my chin, I watched her lips.

Valerie nodded. "I had no right to judge you before I got a chance to know you. God never makes a mistake."

Finally, she got the message, so why had she walked around church with a chip on her shoulders? Tapping my fingers on the table, I waited for her to continue.

"I prayed unselfishly and fasted, too, for a friend. The deal was that my prayer partner, supposedly Mackenzie, would ask the Lord to send me a husband, a good and a kindhearted man who would learn my ways and be patient with my imperfections."

Whew, I wasn't expecting her poetic response. "I see, but—"

Valerie waved her hand to stop me. "Noel, you are that man. You're good looking, I heard you have a good job, you're faithful in attending, but you're as imperfect as I am. God has a bad sense of humor, doesn't He?"

I ignored her remark. I was as perfect as God wanted me to be. I stroked my mustache as I chose my words carefully. Leaning back, I studied her features. She was serious with her declaration. "Valerie, why do you feel I'm that man? One minute I feel you hate me, within minutes you almost love me."

"I do love you, Noel."

I refrained from chuckling. Her latte had to be spiked. When I didn't respond, she stopped eating and folded her hands.

"God spoke to me. I know it was Him. When I got off my knees, and I was not praying for myself, mind you—" she paused and patted her chest—" God spoke to me and said, 'His name is 'N.' God told me I had to look through the man and find his heart, so I kept looking at you. I couldn't see past your deafness to see your heart."

Talk about calling the wrong number, I knew God didn't send me. I could tell her it was Nick who had a crush on her, not me. Nick was probably one prayer away from asking Valerie for her hand in marriage and having three point-seven kids or whatever the saying was. There was no way I was getting in the middle of that. I doubted Valerie would believe me anyway. I drummed my fingers against my thighs, thinking how to respond.

I had to make this woman understand, so I signed. *"God is faithful. Please don't let me be a distraction to the magnificent blessing that God has for you."* I pointed at her. *"I'm not the one, Valerie. My spirit doesn't bear witness."*

She resumed eating as if I hadn't said a word, which technically, I hadn't. She reached for a napkin, dabbed her lips before sipping her latte, then her soda. When she lifted her brow, I braced myself.

"So I guess Mackenzie is your heart's desire?" Squinting, she tightened her lips and imaginary steam flared her nostrils. When she folded her arms, I knew she was gearing up for a fight.

I didn't back down as I had wasted enough of my time. The only reason I was missing bowling with my brothers was because this was God's doing. There was no lesson in this for me except a blessing, which I would be a fool to turn down. Without blinking, I leaned forward. "You're right. Mackenzie is the desire of my heart, but you've doubled your prayer request to send her packing to Chicago. I've already got a preview of her leaving me this week, and I don't like it."

Valerie calmly pushed away the remnants of her meal, which wasn't much. She unfolded her arms and re-crossed them. "Brother Noel, how do you know I was praying for Mackenzie to move to Chicago?"

"You said so."

"Not to you, I didn't. Either you two have been discussing me behind my back or you've been lip reading our conversation." She stood, almost knocking over the chair. "You've got some real issues, Noel. I suggest you resolve them before we can further develop a relationship." Grabbing her handbag off the table, she stormed away. I'm sure if I could hear, her footsteps would have been deafening.

Exhaling, I bowed my head. I was back to square one. "Lord, I hope that turned out the way You expected, because I'm not feeling it."

CHAPTER 23

Flight 134 from Chicago O'Hare was late. I waited impatiently at Lambert St. Louis International Airport under the pretense of being patient. I thought about bringing her a flower, but I could get her a dozen if she wanted them. I considered a box of candy, but that stuff was bad on the teeth. I guess I could've bought her a trinket or something, but if she wanted that, I would take her shopping. My arms were free for one reason only—Mackenzie to fill them. So I paced with my hands stuffed into my pant pockets, waiting for Mackenzie to make her grand appearance.

Then I saw her—the walk, the confidence, the glow, even her mass of curls—all Mackenzie's signature. Like a telescope, I followed her every movement. My lips curled into a grin as Mackenzie searched for and then found me. *God, she is definitely one of Your marvelous works, and I praise You for my eyes to behold such splendor,* I thought, pushing off the wall to meet her. The initial hug released the build up of stress that I had suffered all week. The second contained kisses suitable for a G audience. Finally, during the third one, I told her I missed her. After the preliminaries were completed, I asked, *"How was Chicago?"*

"It was wonderful. I missed you a little." Mackenzie wrinkled her beautiful molded nose. The longing in her eyes revealed she was holding back.

"Only a little?"

"Let's just say, Mr. Richardson. I looked forward to coming home."

"Good answer, woman."

"I thought so, too," she teased. *"My friend, Rhoda, and I shopped, ate, then shopped some more. Yesterday, we attended an exhilarating gospel play."*

I chuckled at her animation. Squeezing her hand, I linked hers with mine as we rode the escalator downstairs to the baggage claim area. At the carousel, she pointed to her luggage and I retrieved it. After the sixth piece, I turned and waved for a sky cap. *"Woman, you've only been gone for six days. You checked one bag and had one carry-on. How did you manage all this?"*

She shrugged as if it wasn't anything out of the ordinary. "This is a holiday ritual. I usually stuff my new purchases into Rhoda's luggage, and once I'm home, I empty them, and ship the suitcases back to her."

I shook my head in disbelief. Only a woman would devise such a scheme. Once seated inside my car, we shared a fourth hug and private kiss. It was PG-13, but barely. When we parted, I squinted at her bare hands for the first time.

"They are in my purse." Mackenzie teased.

*   *   *

"Ready to begin a new year?" I asked Mackenzie as we shared a light lunch after leaving the airport.

"Absolutely."

Although I preferred to sign in a restaurant because I couldn't control my volume, I had to speak. I needed my hand as a point of contact with Mackenzie so we played with each other's fingers. "I'm looking forward to spending it with you, baby."

Mackenzie didn't speak or sign, but the reflection in her eyes told me everything I needed to know—that she was deeply in love with me. Good, I smirked, because Mackenzie had taken her last trip to Chicago without me. Reluctantly, I dropped her off at her home, carrying her luggage in two trips, for her to rest before Watch meeting.

Hours later, I gave my reflection in the bathroom mirror a critical eye before jumping into the shower. My life up until tonight flashed through my mind. I couldn't help but smile. "I told her I loved her. She agreed to explore my world. My family knows I'm crazy about her . . ." I frowned. I had yet to meet the elusive Mr. Norton. Before the stroke of midnight, I would.

After dressing, I was a man on a mission as I headed out of the door. Twenty minutes later, I parked in front of Mackenzie's house and eased from under the wheel of my car. Colorful Christmas lights twinkled against a clear sky night, lighting the street for a last go-round before they were packed away until the next year. I pushed the doorbell and counted to ten. I was about to push it

again and then count to twenty, but Mackenzie
opened the door.

Greeting me, she hugged me as if we hadn't
been together in years instead of hours. Once wasn't
enough, so I squeezed her a second time as she
struggled to separate from me as she invited me
in. Closing the door, I shook off my coat. When
she reached for it, she gave my attire an appreciative nod. *"Nice outfit."*

"Yours, too." We both wore dark gray turtlenecks.
She matched my gray slacks with a darker gray
skirt and boots.

Reaching for and grasping my hand, she tugged
me to a small kitchen that would have disappointed a treasure hunter. What the room lacked
in size, it compensated in bright colors: curtains,
place mats, stool cushions, and other accessories.
For Mackenzie and her dad, it was accommodat-
ing.

Two glasses waited for our attention. A punch
bowl and a platter of stacked tiny sandwiches were
nearby. "Hmmm, so we're having our own private
party before service tonight, huh?"

"Yes." Mackenzie picked up a glass and handed
it to me before taking the other. We exchanged
smiles as if we were the lucky bride and groom
about to drink from each other's cup. Maybe, it
seemed we were heading down that road. Pinching a triangle-shaped sandwich, she coaxed me to
open my mouth. She shoved it in and stole a quick
kiss. I nibbled, enjoying I dare say, the seduction of
a woman whom I loved.

"I did miss you, Noel," she confessed while I
chewed.

"Good," I said after swallowing. I didn't offer my confession. Let her stew after the torment she caused me this past week. We grabbed a few more sandwiches and washed them away with punch before going back to the living room. A stack of papers, a package of gold-foiled stickers, and a red marker occupied a glass coffee table.

I lifted a brow. "School work during the holidays, Miss Norton?"

I'm playing catch-up before school starts again. "She offered me a seat in an overstuffed chair that could fit two. Sinking down, I stretched my legs and checked my wrist watch, pleased that we had an hour before the start of service.

Patting the spot next to me, I beckoned for Mackenzie to join me. Warmth from flames in a gas fireplace serenaded us. Content and relaxed, I closed my eyes and let my mind wander back fifteen years; then without any prompting, I started talking.

"The last song I remember was Peabo Bryson and Regina Belle's *Whole New World.* How appropriate. One day I was a normal curious teenager, and the next morning I woke a deaf mute. I couldn't hear and I was speechless. I suffered burns—the worst on my chest, and other injuries. Rebellious couldn't even begin to describe my attitude."

Mackenzie nudged me, and I opened my eyes to see water in hers. I patted her hand. "It's okay, baby." Shutting my eyes again, I dropped my head back as my elbow rested on the chair arm. "My parents and brothers were there for me as we enrolled in sign language classes. I had to endure therapy, psychological and medical testing.

"My family and doctors believed that with the advances in implants and hearing aids, something could be done, but not in all cases." My thumb jabbed my chest. "I was one of those 'not in all cases.' "

She squeezed my hand as I unearthed the past, releasing pent up emotions. "I have two strikes against me, Mackenzie. I'm a black man and I'm deaf. Although I was secure being me, sometimes I didn't know if one or the other or both played against me."

Mackenzie rubbed my arm, adding pressure that made me look at her again. "I'm confused, Noel. Whom were you talking about a few minutes ago? I don't know him. I see a confident, educated, and a very handsome man who turned his life over to Christ. I fell in love with that brother."

I chuckled. I thanked God for giving me my own Biblical character. Ruth: loyal, loving, and strong. No wonder Boaz had snatched her up. *"What do you know about living in my world—the deaf community, really?"*

"I live it in now, Noel."

"No, baby, you can turn it on and off when you want. Yes, I can talk. I don't know how I sound, but my world . . ." I pointed to my chest again. *". . . is quiet all the time. I want you to experience my world, and see if it's a proper fit. Will you do that for me?"*

Mackenzie edged away. When I was about to protest, she stood and backed away with the oddest expression that almost bordered on defiant. Her reaction was unexpected, which made me uncertain and her lips didn't move, neither did her hands. I ignored it as my eyes coaxed her as my thoughts gave her the words to say, *come on, baby, say it, say, yes, I'm positive that I can fit in your world. C'mon, talk to me.* My face gave nothing away of my internal battle, but I waited for her to say the words or sign. I'd take either one. I never spoke my thoughts because she had to speak whatever was in her heart.

Something behind me got her attention, and she didn't appear to be too happy about it as she positioned her hands on her hips. Glancing over my shoulder, a bear-size man, who wasn't smiling, briefly startled me. Evidently, there was another hiding place beyond the kitchen.

He squinted as curiosity filled his eyes, then anger. Sternness puckered his lips, and balled fists at his side. He defined a man who would not to be crossed or tolerate much, including people—me, perhaps. Maybe I was reading him wrong. I didn't need Mackenzie to make an introduction.

Also standing, I stepped forward, extending my hand. "Mr. Norton."

"Noel Richardson, huh? Mackenzie said I'd be pleased and impressed. So far, I'm waiting for both."

When the bearded man didn't stir to reciprocate my greeting, Mackenzie moved to my left side, took my hand, and gave it a squeeze, a gesture Mr. Norton didn't miss or seem to like. Pulling back my hand, I stuffed it in my pocket while he sized me up. The man didn't know me besides a name, yet his expression showed nothing but contempt.

"Stop it, Daddy. I'm not nine. I'm twenty-nine," Mackenzie ordered.

"I'm sorry, sir, I meant no disrespect." The kiss

outside his door must've really angered him, but apologizing seemed the proper thing to do. I wanted to get beyond that.

"Well, Mr. Richardson, sit down. Let's get this show on the road."

"Show on the road?" I frowned and looked at Mackenzie for an explanation, but she shrugged. Mr. Norton's body language told me I'd missed some of his words. When I turned back to face him, I lip-read ". . . you're going to hit the road."

Stepping carefully in front of him, I cupped my right hand and pointed it down into the palm of my flat left hand, signing repeat. "I'm deaf."

"Ah, naw," Fred Norton responded, rolling his head as he dived for me.

Mackenzie jumped and barricaded me. I gently pushed her out of harm's way. I would try my best not to hurt the man, but I steeled my body for him to get his best shot before I would restrain him.

When I dodged his first swing, I had to admit this wasn't how I imagined my year would end.

CHAPTER 24

I had seen Mackenzie mad before, but she was so upset her body was shaking. Her focus switched from her father to me and back again. She took a deep breath as she shoved me to the closet where she dragged our coats off the hangers. Before we walked out of the door, she and her father engaged in a heated argument.

It was ludicrous. Was her father for real? I'm not a man easily frightened, but I was unprepared for his wrath. How I got out of Mackenzie's house unscathed was a miracle. Any other man besides Mackenzie's father, would have been going down. *God, I did not return to church to fight this kind of battle*, I thought.

Gripping the steering wheel, I couldn't face Mackenzie as I drove to church. Her dad was crazy, I was angry, and Mackenzie was embarrassed. "What just happened?"

When the light turned red, she tapped me. "It's not about you, Noel. Daddy acts like that with all the guys who want to take me out. I'm way too old for this and to be humiliated repeatedly."

"Well, it's about me now." The light changed. I proceeded with caution, not just with my driving. I didn't care about the men before me, or if they lived to tell about it. Her father really didn't want to tangle with me, because instead of Mackenzie holding me back, God would, and I didn't want to have to apologize to her or repent to Him. Another light flashed red. I angled my head when she tapped me again.

"I'm really sorry. I've never seen him so hostile. I thought he was going to have a stroke. He just forced my hand. I'm going to look for a condo immediately."

Still fuming, I didn't encourage her one way or the other. The last fight I had was in high school when evidently, I had shouted too loud from the stands during a basketball game. The game had barely ended when a giraffe-tall player rushed into the stands and accused me of making him miss a crucial basket. At seventeen, I had height, too. The stadium seating gave me more. He threw the first punch and missed. I threw the second and didn't miss. After his swollen jaw and a black eye, we were cool.

"Mackenzie, if there is a next time, don't get in the way." I pumped my brakes as a third red light caught me. *God, are you trying to tell me something besides slow down?* I thought, glancing at Mackenzie again. I prayed that I wouldn't physically fight her father, but I was a man just like Mr. Norton. It was in his best interest and mine that he respected that.

I frowned at Mackenzie's last readable words to her father. "Daddy, he's a committed man of God who I've chosen to love. Noel is a good man. It's not like we're getting married."

The woman had no idea of my intentions, and neither did her father. They would know when I knew for sure.

I cleared my mind, or I tried, to prepare for my first Watch meeting. I knew Catholics had a midnight mass on Christmas Eve, but this was a first for me. The hour was late, but the crowd's energy wasn't lacking as they made a mad rush into the sanctuary. Many were dressed for some serious celebrations: expressive hats, expensive suits, and fresh haircuts. There was definitely a party going on, and I didn't want to miss it. I pushed the incident with Mr. Norton to the back of my mind.

Although Mackenzie's obligations wouldn't allow us to sit together during service, we always prayed together on our knees before she reported to her designated spot. I would never get used to the house of worship as being our place of separation.

Valerie entered the sanctuary and eyed me with an unreadable expression. Some things never change, I thought. *God, I sure hope this drama tonight is for Your glory because from where I'm sitting, there must be a miscommunication.* Opening my Bible, I flipped through the pages, looking for a scripture, anything that would give me a clue of what was happening with Valerie. Romans 5: *And not only so, but we glory in tribulations also, know-*

ing that tribulation worketh patience. God, come on, patience is definitely not my strong point. Closing my Bible, I looked up to see Mackenzie and Valerie staring at each other. I groaned. Now what? I relaxed when they embraced in a hardy hug.

The choir was massive, swelling with people I'd never seen. Their purple robes had one wide streak of red. I don't know how many songs they sung, but the vibrations were powerful. A peace descended on me, causing my lids to drift close as my spirit worshipped God in a secret place, a place where neither Mackenzie nor the pastor could take me. Then I heard the voice of God. *Noel, the work that I have performed in you, I will finish.*

Lord, help me understand what that work is exactly, I pleaded. But when God didn't respond, I opened my eyes as Pastor Coleman began his sermon. "*Turn to 1 Corinthians 15:51, Behold, I show you a mystery. We shall not all sleep, but we shall be changed. Listen church, God's referring to those who died believing on His promise. For those of us awake, let us not go into the new year sleep walking, spiritually asleep. That won't cut it, be on full alert. We are closer now than we were this morning.*

"*Don't take a nap on Jesus. Be ready in season and out, night, day, by the minute or hour. Verse 52: In a moment, in the twinkling of an eye, at the last trump. For the trumpet shall sound, and the dead shall be raised incorruptible, and we shall be changed. If I die, let me die in Christ. If I live, let me live for Christ. Remember in a twinkling, a blink, some will be raised to live again. Others,*" he paused, rubbing his chin, looking out in the audience, "*well, let me just say this on the authority of God. Others will rise in a corruptible body that will continuously die corruptible again and again and again,"* Mackenzie signed.

Finally, Pastor Coleman closed his Bible and bowed his head to pray. I also briefly closed my eyes and vowed to spend more time with God. Mackenzie's eyes met mine as soon as I opened them, asking for forgiveness. I nodded, conveying that I was trying to forgive and forget, but for her I would try harder.

I checked the wall clock in the back, which was the size of a window. It was synchronized with my watch, exactly twenty minutes before midnight. The crowd was lively and waiting.

When the choir stood, there was a surprise waiting for me. The vibrations of their voices rattled my chest cavity. On one accord, they lifted their hands and signed a song called "Celebrate." I wondered at the words. I marveled at the possible melody. The scene was awesome. I glanced at Mackenzie. Her smile was so sweet.

Impressive was the only way to describe the service from beginning to the end. Afterwards, Nick slapped men's backs in greeting, kissed babies, and hugged church mothers before approaching me. "Happy New Year, brother," he said, slapping his right hand into mine in a gripping handshake. I challenged his with a crush of my own. He smirked. "It's going to be a great year. I feel it."

After the clutch I gave Nick, I wondered if he still had feeling in his hand. "Yes, it is."

Nodding, he turned to walk away, and then paused. Glancing back, Nick continued to grin at me then left. I raised my brow. Peering over heads, I located Mackenzie swallowed up in the crowd.

When she resurfaced, Valerie pulled her aside. Within minutes Nick pulled Valerie aside.

My little girlfriends tugged on my pants. Kneeling, I welcomed Keisha and Daphne's kisses and hugs. Despite their exhilaration, their eyes drooped with sleepiness. Mrs. Campbell introduced me to her husband who seemed to be just as drained as his daughters. "Honey, I told Brother Noel that the girls think he favors your brother and that's why he can't get rid of him."

"You do. I'm Albert and it's nice to meet you." I stood and we shook hands before the girls gave me one more wave goodnight.

I made eye contact with Mackenzie who shot me daggers. I grinned at her mocked jealousy, but then she whirled around and stormed away. Surely, she wasn't threatened by the Campbell sisters. Perplexed, I weaved around saints to gather our coats and my Bible. When I caught up with her, she gathered her things from me and pushed the church door opened, dismissing my attempt at chivalry. She walked ahead of me. Clueless, I slowed my gait. She rode with me so she wasn't going anywhere.

"Mackenzie, it's a new year, what's wrong?" I asked when I was near my car. God, deliver me from moody people.

She did an about face. Walking back, she came within inches of my face. Her lips moved slow enough for a new student of interpretation to understand. "How could you do what I asked you not to do?"

It was almost one o'clock in the morning, my energy was fading fast and my irritation was building. My mental capacity could only hold so much. "Talk to me, baby."

"I'll talk to you all right. Noel, I asked you not to mention anything to Valerie."

Grimacing, I rolled my eyes. "God spoke to me, Mackenzie, not you. I had to do His bidding." I pointed to my chest. "With you or without you, it was God's timing, not ours."

"Then you shouldn't have promised me," she argued, finding her hip under her coat and planting a fist on it. "If I recall, I didn't force you to say it. Valerie seemed down tonight after service. God may have told you to talk to her, but at least I could've told you how to approach her. I've known her longer than you, Noel."

I checked my watch, which infuriated her more. I grabbed her hands that were wearing the gloves I had bought. After I had her attention, I released them and began to sign, *'Baby, get rid of the attitude. It's not all about you, you, you! I'm deaf, Mackenzie, but I'm not stupid, and the voice I hear is God's. For weeks, I've been yielding to your wants, needs, your feelings, and shutting out my world for you. That's one-sided. I don't need your permission. I'm not a puppet. I let you call the shots because I love you, but you don't call all the shots. If you really care about me and are committed to this relationship, then let's make some changes. To start, what's stopping you from coming into my world, Mackenzie? Or is it too quiet?"*

Indignant, she snarled. "Of course not, I'm an interpreter, remember?"

"Yeah, how can I forget? I fell in love with your hands first, then those sexy eyes and everything else that is you,

and finally your heart. I'm not going to beg you, Mackenzie. You say you love me, and I believe you. I don't need you to prove it. I'm asking, as a man who wants to fall deeper in love with you, that for the next month, you'll explore my world. Finished with what I had to say, I opened the car door and drove her home to her crazy father.

CHAPTER 25

A week later, it was business as usual. Mackenzie was back in the classroom. My staff and I were tweaking proposals for this year's government grants, reviewing our lists of contributors, contemplating fundraising events, and mulling over requests for our agency's intervention.

Since that day in the church parking lot, Mackenzie and I had reconciled that we would allow God to direct our paths through prayer and more scripture reading. This commitment came after we kissed and made up. One Friday night after we placed our orders at the Pasta House, we munched on breadsticks. When Mackenzie gave me an angelic expression, I knew she was concocting something.

"Noel, I was thinking,"

I shook my head. *Here we go again,* I thought, Mackenzie was trying to negotiate.

She swatted me on my hand. *"Hear me out."* She grinned. *"Sorry, figure of speech. Come to my classroom. Talk to them about contributing factors to hearing loss,*

tell them what it is like to be deaf. You and I could dem-
onstrate sign language communication. I'm sure Moses
would like to see you." Her eyes twinkled with mischief.

I chewed on the lump of breadstick and swallowed. I felt we were going down a path of resistance. We were having problems meeting at a
common ground, which I'm sure thrilled Mr. Norton. Since that last incident, he seemed never to
be at home when I arrived. I refused to bow to his
intimidation. Mackenzie didn't offer any explana-
tions for his absence, and I didn't inquire. *"Is it too*
much to ask for spending time in my quiet world?"

"Maybe," she surprisingly signed back, either in
a challenge or a tease.

I wasn't going to let her bait me. Fuming, I bit
off a bigger piece of bread then another without
swallowing the first piece. I kept biting off bread
and chewing it until I nipped my finger, signaling
the bread was gone.

When our waitress slid our salads in front of us,
I thanked her and bowed my head and silently
blessed our food. *Tell a woman you love her, and she*
starts working your patience, I thought, recalling
James 1:4: *But let patience have her perfect work, that ye*
may be perfect and entire, wanting nothing. There was
that scripture again. I really did love her. I prayed
we could get through this spiritual roadblock.

After stabbing bits of my salad with my fork without responding, our meals arrived as I squinted at
Mackenzie. She slid her spaghetti in front of her
and ate with gusto. I wondered if this Holy Ghost-
filled woman would always drive me crazy. "Listen
beautiful, thanks for the invitation, but I won't be

coming to your school anytime before you accompany me to one of my deaf events. I mean that, Mackenzie."

The night went downhill from there. For two days, I questioned if I had been too demanding, too hard on her, too anything. I couldn't shake the look of hurt that had flashed across her face. Minutes after my referendum, she chanced a wounded glance at me. She didn't cry, but her eyes were glazed. Man, why did God create women to be sugar and spice and everything to drive a man crazy? Reaching for her hand, I brushed a kiss in her palm, but I still stood by my edict. I wasn't bending to her will.

At work, I was miserable. My employees noticed my irritability and kept their distance. The light flashed, alerting me that someone was at my office doorway. I ceased drawing meaningless shapes on a pad of paper and looked up. Lana stood there, waiting for an invitation. I beckoned her in, but she didn't take a seat.

"Noel Richardson, I don't know why I'm saying this, or if she's worth it, but you need to make a decision and then stick with it. If she truly wants a relationship with you, she better run to home plate or some other woman is going to call her out. That goes the same for you. Remember that," she signed and left.

Women, I thought. *I love them.* I was unproductive so I did make a decision as I cleared my desk. Like a robot, I shut down my computer and switched off the lights. With my coat and keys, I walked out of my office, nodding at my assistant. *"I'm out of here for the rest of the day."*

"I hope you enjoy it," she signed back.

I detoured to Lana's office. She looked away from an interpreter on the plasma screen who was signing a video conference call.

"Thanks." I winked.

She winked back.

I hadn't prepared my "I'm sorry that I'm an idiot" speech by the time I arrived at Mackenzie's school. Following the procedure, I headed to the office to sign in. The same woman was there. When she saw me, she puckered her lips and quickly applied lip gloss. *Women,* I thought again, smirking. "I know the way unless you have to escort me every time."

Her shoulders slumped as she gave me a badge, picked up a phone, and waved me on. When I reached Mackenzie's classroom door, I was poised to knock, but froze. Dumbfounded, I couldn't believe my eyes.

Mackenzie's class was communicating in simple sign language phrases. It wasn't ASL, but ESL, the English signing, which forces students to sign each word that is spoken instead of using shortcuts or slang. If my leg was long enough, I would've kicked myself. That woman loved me and supported me despite my arrogance. Opening the door, I met her eyes and signed sorry. Her students' arms flagged the air as they shouted, "He says he's sorry, Miss Norton."

She faced her class again, signing, *"I know."* Mackenzie wiggled her fingers in the air and they followed. *"Okay class, you have a five-minute recess, hurry."* Two boys nearly tripped, trying to beat the girls out of the room. I didn't know where they were going and didn't care.

Cautiously, I stepped closer to Mackenzie until I could reach out and touched her cheek. "I don't know what to say."

Her finger touched her lips to silence me.

Maybe it was her magnetism or my guilt for acting like a jerk, but I knew I couldn't love her any deeper. I knelt. "Marry me."

It was her turn to stroke my cheek. I sniffed the faint scent of her sweet hand lotion before she signed. *"Noel Richardson, if you think I'm going to accept a proposal in my classroom, in the middle of recess, think again."*

I exhaled. My baby was back, attitude and all. Mackenzie reigned, and I would let her because I liked her just like that.

"If and when you ask me to marry you, again, I want the whole nine yards, music, whether you can hear it or not. Dinner—Denny's isn't an option—and you do have to ask my father for permission so you better work that part out. Some women get one proposal. You've got two chances with me."

I chuckled, afraid that my laughter of joy would shake the school. She had become my heart, and it couldn't pump without her. Mr. Norton wouldn't stop me. *"Yes, Madam."*

"Good. Now, get off your knees because your friend, Moses, is coming, and I'm sure you don't want him to see you in such a submissive position."

"Why are they signing?"

"For an educated, successful entrepreneur, Noel, you're clueless. During the month of January, every day, I've incorporated into the curriculum two hours of communication by signing only. It's not about me all the

time, sometimes it's about you. I'm doing it because I love you."

She always knew how to get to me, saying all the right words. Smirking, I bowed to the queen. As her students filed in, I knew my time was up. *"Dinner?"*

"Will it be a silent supper, Noel?"

"Definitely."

Mackenzie signed, *"Yes,"* then addressed her classroom to stop talking and sign.

Walking out of the building, I pumped both my arms in the air in victory. I still wanted to kick myself.

CHAPTER 26

January's bitter cold temperatures didn't stop our marathon dates. She even decided to skip taking classes for the winter schedule. Mackenzie kept pace with my deaf-related activities without one complaint. Whenever I picked up Mackenzie for a date, I always inquired about her father's whereabouts. I wanted him to know I wasn't backing down to get to know him. The last weekend in January, Mr. Norton surprised me when he answered the door.

His staunch expression was set like baked cookie dough, but my determination was covered by a spiritual breastplate geared for battle. What threw me off was his signing a greeting and bidding me entrance

"Good evening, Mr. Norton," I signed back as if it was normal between us, disguising my shock.

I knew it was too soon to say hallelujah. Once inside the living room, he turned his back to me. I excused his lack of proper deaf etiquette. When he sat on the sofa, I followed because honestly, I didn't expect two invitations in one day.

We eyed each other, daring to see who would cower first. Mackenzie briefly made an appearance. *"Hi, Noel, I'll be ready in a minute."* She blew me a kiss and disappeared. As her father and I resumed our macho standoff, I suspected a Mackenzie setup.

"Don't get too used to this. I'm not taking any deaf classes. I'm only doing this to appease my daughter. She seems to think you're worth something. Personally, I know you're a waste of her time. Like the others, I don't expect you to stick around that long," he strung along the words in one breath.

Making myself comfortable, I crossed my ankle over my knee. *Lord, this is going to be a hard nut to crack, but you're a way maker and heart changer. Please allow Mr. Norton to see nothing but You in my life. Amen,* I prayed to myself before Mackenzie returned. We left a few minutes later.

Our first stop was at my parents. They insisted—no, nagged—no, demanded I bring Mac-kenzie to their house. They had instantly liked her from their brief encounter on Christmas Day. Even Pierce, who I sometimes nicknamed Fierce because he could be brutal when it came to women, couldn't find fault with Mackenzie.

Caleb took our coats as Momma directed us to the living room. A roaring fire was set to entertain us. I chose a spot in the corner of a sectional and patted a spot next to me for Mackenzie. She obliged.

Less than sixty seconds after Mackenzie smoothed the wrinkles out of her skirt, my mother began to fire off questions. "So, Mackenzie, is there anybody deaf in your family? What made you want to learn sign language?" she asked with curiosity.

I hadn't appreciated it before, but Mackenzie demonstrated how important my deafness was to her. She turned and looked at me, while answering my mother. "Mrs. Richardson, no one in my family is deaf." Her eyes twinkled. "I always thought the language was beautiful, expressive, and I was curious. I wanted to be included in their world, not excluded." Mackenzie faced my mother and finished with, "If that makes any sense."

Momma shook her head. "No, but we all have our reasons."

Dad strolled into the room with two glasses of his homemade root beer floats, forcing an intermission. He handed a glass to Mackenzie and the other to me.

Taking a seat on the sofa near Momma, Dad stretched out his arms, encouraging her closer. *"So, Mackenzie, do you only interpret at church, or are you certified?"*

My mother smacked his leg as if scolding him. "Honey, you don't have to sign. There is nothing wrong with Mackenzie. She can hear us."

Dad frowned as Pierce signed,*" Momma, there's nothing wrong with Noel either. He's sitting right here in front of us."*

"I agree with Momma. If we can all hear, why sign? Noel can lip read," Caleb added.

A disagreement brewed before an argument exploded. Discreetly checking my watch, I took

Mackenzie's hand and squeezed it. I stood and helped her up. "Well, it's getting late everybody. Mackenzie and I are going to head out so we won't be late for the play."

While my parents fussed over Mackenzie and gave her hugs, Pierce pulled me aside. *Wow, was she your choice or God's?* Pierce signed with his back to Mackenzie.

"Both." Our fists met in agreement. I grabbed our coats and helped Mackenzie slip into hers. We left for the Fox Theatre where "Big River," featuring some deaf cast members, was touring.

As I expected, the stage production did woo Mackenzie. Inconspicuously, I watched as her eyes followed the actors' hand movements. While some clapped at the conclusion of a scene, those who were deaf in the audience raised their hands and wiggled their fingers. Mackenzie wiggled her fingers with me.

Hours later, in a nearby restaurant, Mackenzie recalled her favorite scenes as we sat around the table with two other deaf couples. When the waitress placed meals in front of one couple, they dug in without waiting for us. The second couple prayed to themselves. Mackenzie reached across the table after the waitress delivered our orders. My rough hands swallowed up her soft, moist ones.

"Pray for our meal, Noel. If we speak no other words tonight, I love to hear you pray," Mackenzie requested. As she bowed her head, I followed.

"Father God, in the name of Jesus, I thank You for this incredible woman who has become a joy, a friend, and the love of my life. I ask that You bless her food and mine, and provide for others less fortunate, and I thank You for our fellowship in Jesus' name. Amen." Opening our eyes, we met the others' stares. Mackenzie and I shared a secret smile, lifted our forks, and attacked our food.

Mackenzie was definitely the best person to walk into my life. February had arrived and our love had grown stronger. Mr. Norton became less hostile as I arrived to take Mackenzie to Bible classes, prayer meetings, or dates. I believed it was a result of my prayers and my resolution to remain in Mackenzie's life.

When a snowstorm forced school closings and Mackenzie was holed up in her home, we exchanged so many text messages, I lost count. As snow threatened to shut down businesses, including church services, we logged on to our computers to watch videos and deaf movies on You Tube.

As Valentine's Day approached, I toyed with the idea of proposing again. Mackenzie demanded the whole nine yards of romance. When I looked at Mackenzie, I saw seduction and temptress. I loved her, yes I wanted to marry her, and I even asked once, but I should've consulted God to make sure the timing was right. Mackenzie was the right fit, and I was at the spiritual level to meet Mackenzie's needs.

I searched the scriptures for answers. When none came, I fasted for two days. I shied away from Mackenzie so she wouldn't distract me. A man could suppress his carnal desires for so long, so I continued to fast for spiritual dominance, then God spoke. I had expected an Old Testament Proverb or New Testament Hebrew scripture like "marriage is honorable in all, the bed undefiled,

but whoremongers and adulterers God will judge."
Lord, help me to hold out until the honeymoon!

God had other plans as he forced me to study beyond verse one in 1 Peter 3. Would I be a man who Mackenzie felt comfortable yielding to my decisions without question? I knew my role as the head didn't call for me to boss Mackenzie around. I chuckled. Mackenzie wouldn't stand for it anyway.

God wanted me to understand the meaning of "dwelling with your wife according to knowledge," "giving honor unto the wife," "[Mackenzie] being the weaker vessel—not the weakest," "heirs together," and "prayers be not hindered."

CHAPTER 27

My creativity in a marriage proposal was in trouble. I needed help. I had ruled out the red rose petals from her house to my waiting car thing. It would be just my luck she'd slip and fall. Writing a message on her classroom chalkboard probably wouldn't work either. If Moses saw it first, he would erase it or add something like 'don't marry him.'

I was oblivious about choosing the engagement ring, so after watching countless commercials for Jared the Galleria of Jewelry, I went to Jared's. If it wasn't sparkling, it was dazzling. I peered through every glass counter, bypassing gold, silver, and the solitaires. The clerk looked relieved and impressed when I settled on a 14K white gold one-carat three-stone diamond ring. She was blissful when she scanned the price tag.

Purchased, wrapped, and secured in my blazer's inside pocket, I sent a text to Pierce and confided in him that I was I ready to pop the question, and after the ring what was the next step.

Luther, Pierce typed.

Luther who? Vandross?

The late Vandross, his love songs are legendary and I haven't known one woman who didn't like him. I had planned to play it in the background when or if I even proposed. It will set the mood where she'll tear up and will say 'yes' before the song ends. Pierce typed back. *Buy something that has the song 'Here and Now.'*

Sounds like you have a plan, Pierce.

Yeah, a plan that's waiting to be put in action. Poof.

Once I was at home, it wasn't hard to find the song online. I purchased it with an overnight delivery. I surfed the net to create a Hallmark e-card. I chose an opened red rosebud in the background. Separate images of a black man and woman faded in and out. They didn't look like us, but Mackenzie would get the message. I clicked yes to music, hoping the selection would match the card's theme. In the message box I typed, *You have been my Valentine waiting to be opened. Mackenzie, please spend this special day with me at a special place for special memories. Say yes, Noel.* I pushed send.

Less than a minute later, my BlackBerry vibrated. Mackenzie had me guessing what *she* meant with her one word answer: *Yes.*

I made reservations at Bissell Mansion Restaurant & Murder Mystery Theatre, a historical St. Louis landmark known for its hilarious murder mystery performances, as a tribute to Mackenzie's ambition in the arts.

Throughout Valentine's Day at PRESERVE-St. Louis, floral deliveries, chocolate molded lips, and early departures told stories I didn't need to hear to understand. Lifting my TV remote, I pointed it toward my wall plasma monitor. Deciding against that method, I opted for my computer web camera where the interpreter could see me sign, relay the message via headset and sign back, which I could watch on my computer. I requested he dial Mackenzie's home number. When my party came on the line, I was instructed to go ahead.

"Mr. Norton, this is Noel Richardson. I need to speak with you as soon as possible, sir, concerning your daughter," I signed to the interpreter.

"What's wrong with Mackenzie?" The interpreter's facial expression let me know that panic was heard in Mr. Norton's voice.

"Mackenzie is fine, but I do need to ask you a question in person man to man."

"If I say, no, will that keep you from asking Mackenzie?"

"Mr. Norton, please, I just need a few minutes of your time. I can leave work early and stop by."

"Never mind that," the interpreter's expression showed irritation heard on the line. *"Tell me where you work and I'll stop by as soon as I can while I'm out."*

I gave him my company's address and waited.

When the motion sensor under my door mat alerted me that I had a visitor, I glanced up to see Mr. Norton strolling through the doorway. He didn't wait for an acknowledgement. His soon-as-soon arrival turned out to be later-than-late afternoon as if my work day revolved around him. That day, it did.

He scrutinized my furniture and every device. Finally, he dragged a leather cushion chair to my desk and sat. He waited; I waited. Taking an exaggerated visual breath, he twisted his lips. "Okay, let's get this talk on, Richardson. Talk to me."

"I love Mackenzie. She trusts me to be there for her and to make her happy."

Mr. Norton held up his hand to stop my rehearsed speech. "Can you be there for her really? What if she falls and you can't hear her? What if you two have a child, can you hear your baby crying? She may trust you, but I don't, Richardson. She's a grown woman and stubborn like her mother. I could never talk her mother out of anything either once her mind was set." He threw his arms up in frustration.

I stole his temporary reprieve to defend myself. "If she falls, I pray God will pick her up. My hearing may be zero, but my love is more than one-hundred percent. As for children, Mackenzie will use her ears. When she isn't home, I'll depend on God and a baby cry analyzer, which tells me if my child is sleepy, hungry, or wet." I raised my finger. I wasn't finished. "Then there's this thing called portable video monitor with infrared night vision. People who hear use something similar to it. Also, hearing parents teach their babies sign language as an early form of communication even if they aren't deaf."

"Humph. Mackenzie believes in you, but frankly I don't. You're black, you're a male, and you're deaf. That's three strikes against you."

"Without Mackenzie, that's four strikes. Mr. Norton, you fail to acknowledge I hold undergraduate and graduate degrees. I don't use my deafness as a crutch. It's my motivation from the time I wake each morning. I'm the CEO of this organization that has assisted local, federal, and state governments, company vice presidents, and small business owners form a better relationship with the community. I own property and stocks. I'm physically and spiritually healthy. Mr. Norton, I've sought the Lord on this, and I love your daughter. I want your blessings, and man-to-man, you'll have to give me a better reason than my deafness to say no. Admit it. I have an impressive resume. I'm more than qualified to take care of my woman."

"I don't have to admit anything. You'll only have one shot at protecting my daughter. You fail, I'm coming for you." He stood and stalked out of my office.

I'll take that as a yes, I grinned, thinking.

CHAPTER 28

That evening, I stood confidently on the Nortons' front porch and knocked. The dusting of snow glistened on the sidewalk. Mackenzie opened the door, smiling. Her head was covered with a fur ball. Upon closer inspection, it was a globe-shaped hat that reminded me of a squirrel's coat.

A long black coat with a fur collar hid what she was wearing. I couldn't help it, but yes, I did a glove check. I was thankful that she hadn't lost one or the set. I stepped up into the foyer, forcing her back.

"Happy Valentine's Day, Noel Richardson, will you be my Valentine?" Mackenzie methodically slid a card from her coat pocket. The longing in her eyes made me want to drop to my knee, ask her to marry me, and open City Hall to wake up the Justice of the Peace.

Begrudgingly, I broke eye contact to take her card. The black man on the Mahogany Card didn't look like me, but his bare chest with firm abs and biceps did resemble my body. The only difference was I had the burn scars and this guy didn't, and the woman in his arms wasn't as beautiful as Mackenzie, but I held my breath as I read the words: *I never knew what I was missing until you. Your smile . . . your walk . . . and your hugs. You're my Valentine all the time.* Then in the corner of the card, she had scribbled *"Yes."* I bit back a smile. So my woman was into playing games with me again, thinking I was going to propose and trying to steal my thunder by saying yes beforehand.

I grabbed her in a hug and squeezed until she fought against my embrace. "Woman . . ." I paused when Mr. Norton appeared before me. I released Mackenzie, but kept her close. Extending my hand, I acknowledged him. "Good evening, Mr. Norton."

Surprisingly, he gripped my hand in a shake. "Call me Fred."

Fred? Who would have thought? Let patience have her perfect work. Leaving, my steps were lighter as I escorted Mackenzie to my Cadillac. Behind the wheel, I pushed the play knob where I had the radio programmed to Mackenzie's favorite station.

As my chest vibrated, I frowned, but kept driving. Mackenzie said she liked instrumental gospel. We hadn't gone a block when Mackenzie tapped my arm. *"Why are you playing heavy metal on FM 97.6?"*

No wonder it didn't feel the same. That explained it. "I thought it was the jazz station FM 96.7."

Mackenzie shook her head. A smile peeped before a contagious laugh. She found the station, leaned back, and crossed her arms in triumph. A few minutes later, she tapped me again. "Where are you taking me?" she asked before I exited onto the highway.

"It's a surprise," I answered, glancing at her. I appreciated every beautiful thing God used to create her. She was stunning, more beautiful than a woman had a right to be, and soon she would be mine.

Mackenzie's eyes twinkled in merriment. She didn't ask any more questions until I exited from Interstate 70 to Grand Boulevard. Weaving through deteriorating neighborhoods in North St. Louis, I turned onto Randall Place. Our destination was no longer a surprise. I parked, shut off the engine and faced Mackenzie whose eyes were misty.

"Noel, I haven't been here in a long time."

"You wanted the whole nine yards. I hope tonight I'm giving you ten."

A single tear created a trail down her face. I wiped away the wetness with my thumb. "For the past seventy-four days, your smile—" I paused, tracing her lips until she smiled. I responded with a cocky grin—"your presence—" I stopped again, intertwining her fingers with mine and bringing them to my lips—"and these incredible hands God gave you enchant me." Another tear spilled. "Mackenzie, you haven't mentioned anything about theater projects, and I know you put that on hold because of me, so tonight is yours." I braced my muscles when my sweetest, weaker vessel of a woman bowled me over in a gripping hug. I received my blessing with enthusiasm and laughter. "Ready?"

"*Yes.*"

Outside the car, we walked hand in hand a few

yards to the steps of the former mansion converted to a theatre. The commanding brick structure reigned on a hill, overlooking the interstate. City records showed that Captain Lewis Bissell built it in the 1820s and it was possibly the oldest home in St. Louis.

Bissell Mansion was considered St. Louis' original audience-participating comedy/mystery dinner theatre. Leaning into me, Mackenzie smothered her face in my coat in an attempt to shield herself from the harsh elements.

"Cold?" I asked, looking down as the wind danced in her fur-ball. When she nodded, I held her tighter.

Once inside the old mansion, an unassuming older gentleman welcomed us. "Good evening sir, madam. These are your characters, Eloise and Sebastian." He leaned closer. "Keep your identity a secret." Nodding our understanding, he continued, "Someone in the audience will be randomly called to act out their parts. Who knows, one of you could be the murderer, or a suspect, or a witness to the deed. Hope it's not you," the man warned, wiggling his bushy eyebrows. What Mackenzie didn't know was that she would be in the spotlight tonight. The staff was more than willing to be included in the scheme.

Anticipation lit Mackenzie's face as we entered into a large living room that had been transformed into a restaurant. I helped Mackenzie remove her coat. She was about to take off her fur ball when I stopped her.

"Don't. I like it. It matches your sassy attitude."

She looked at me with a glint in her eyes. Wrinkling her nose, she prepared to respond. I smacked a quick kiss to stop her. "Sassssyyyyy," I teased.

White-linen tablecloths were draped over numerous tables. Thick wood-paneled double doors matched the mantle-top fireplaces. Choosing a table, I pulled back Mackenzie's chair and waited for her to be seated before I sat across from her. Her eyes sparkled as she glanced around. Folding her hands, she leaned forward, prompting me to meet her halfway. "Noel, this is so exciting. This was a wonderful idea. Just think; we'll help the detectives solve a mystery."

"Yeah." Her shoulders slumped as she covered my hands. They were so soft. "Noel, I wanted to prove that you mean the world to me."

I swallowed as my heart pounded faster. Who was proposing to whom tonight? "Mackenzie," I stopped. I didn't know what to say because that's exactly what I wanted Mackenzie to do, prove to me she could live in my world. I dropped my head in shame.

She tapped my arm to get my attention. *"For the record, Noel Richardson, it's a good thing I love you."* She grinned. "Since you're such a winner, I think I'll keep you."

Our flirting ceased as the room filled to capacity for the performance. Attendants began serving the appetizers of crab Rangoon, toasted ravioli, and a cheese ball with zucchini bread. I reached across the table for her hands. "My Valentine, would you do the honor of blessing our food?"

Batting her lashes, she bowed her head. I followed. When she squeezed my fingers, I looked up and together we mouthed, "Amen." We feasted on the finger foods until our main course of baked white fish with an unusual seasoned sauce, Greek salad, sautéed vegetables, and twice-baked potato arrived. Twenty minutes later, the lights dimmed for the production of "Mayhem in Mayberry."

The theater actors were hilarious. Although some guests received character cards when they arrived, their lines were altered. Yet, they were encouraged to play their roles convincingly. Those who didn't receive character cards were still informed of tonight's surprise and to be on the lookout for the mystery couple. Sinister eyes bounced from table to table. Nobody was above suspicion as victims of Cupid's bow.

Just when the audience thought they had the plot solved, there was a new development. A woman screamed for the police. When heads turned, I turned around to see a man across the room stand. "I'm the sheriff." He definitely fit the profile with an emotionless face, but he stumbled over his lines almost incriminating himself. The crowd laughed. I laughed, too. Not because I got the joke. I simply read the man's facial expressions. While most guests applauded, Mackenzie and I raised our arms in the air and wiggled our fingers.

A man dressed in a head-to-toe jailer costume with a ridiculously long, questionably fake mustache and goatee, raised his hands to hush the crowd. "Not so fast. It appears we have another possible suspect. With his hand shielding his eyes, he looked out in the audience. "Eloise McDuffy, where were you the night Miss Bea was kidnapped?"

Mackenzie looked at me for answers. I simply

shrugged as a spotlight formed around Mackenzie as she was summoned to turn herself in to the jailer. All eyes were on her, including mine as I leaned back, praying this was the special moment Mackenzie had waited for all her life.

The room grew darker until the guests' faces faded. Mackenzie's eyes searched for mine, but I was no longer seated. I slid from my seat and squatted as I moved from table to table until I stood by the door. Don't ask me why, I just thought when she looked for me it would add to the mystery. When the lights flickered briefly, a petite elderly woman with silver hair ambled her way into spotlight. She thrust a gift box into Mackenzie's hands. "Are these not the jewels you stole from my bedroom, Eloise?" She pointed for Mackenzie to open it, and she did.

Even when I'm an old man with trifocal lenses, I'll always recognize my name on your lips. Whatever is asked of you tonight just say yes, my note read. Her hands began to shake when she realized this wasn't about "Mayhem in Mayberry," but her. "Oh, Noel."

The jailer pulled out toy handcuffs. That was my cue that "Here and Now" was playing. When I had dropped off the Luther CD earlier, the manager and I agreed that the handcuffs would be my signal. Pierce came through for me. Reading the words to the song inside the CD jacket expressed what was engraved in my heart. I couldn't look into her eyes without seeing what she meant to me— happiness, sweetness, faithfulness, and making my dreams come true.

Mackenzie's spotlight shut off. As the flames from candles danced throughout the room, I squatted to weave between the tables, making my way to the front until I bumped into a chair, and dropped the ring box. In the dark, crawling on my knees, I fumbled for the velvet-covered square. I guess when I missed my cue, the lights flashed. Three guests, including one woman, were scouring the floor, helping me find the jewel box. I bumped heads with one man. When the room went dim again, I clashed with more bodies as they joined the search under tables and chairs.

When lights flickered a third time, a very pregnant woman lifted her hand in the air with the ring box. Thinking the mystery was solved, the audience clapped as Mackenzie looked in the direction of the commotion. The mommy-to-be slammed the treasure into my fist before the room went black again.

With the prized possession clutched in my hand, I stood. Composed, I straightened my suit and prayed that no one or any other object got in the way of my proposal mayhem. Exhaling, I stood behind Mackenzie when the lights brightened the room. Gently, I wrapped my hands around her arms. She jumped as I coaxed her to turn around and face me.

On one knee, I carefully laid the box next to me and patted it for good measure. Lifting my hands, I began to sign, *"Mackenzie Norton, there's only one you. No other woman could ever occupy the space in my heart, but you. Here and now on this Valentine's Day, I'm asking you, as a man who is only complete with you, to marry me. Say yes, baby. We've been together three months, but I need more. I need a lifetime."*

"Noel Richardson, thank you for walking out of my dreams and into my heart. Yes."

My eyes never left hers as I lifted the box, fingered it open, and gripped the ring from its spot. With urgency, I slid it on her finger before standing. In the background, hands waved in the air instead of clapping. I'd have to thank the owner later for instructing patrons to lift their hands and wiggle their fingers as a silent applause.

I wanted to kiss Mackenzie as if it was our wedding day, but she had me constricted in a bear grip. As she cried, her furball tickled my nose.

CHAPTER 29

The news of the Norton and Richardson engagement traveled fast. Pastor Coleman tracked me down on Sunday morning before service. "Make your prenuptial counseling appointment soon, Brother Noel. I only marry couples who plan to stay together, and are willing to compromise, forgive, and love until the end," he advised then congratulated me. "I wish you both so much happiness."

"I will and thank you." Instead of shaking my hand, he slapped me on my back, bumped his fist with mine, and then walked away.

As Pastor Coleman preached on "The New City" from Revelation, praise rose continuously throughout the sermon. He finished by asking, *"Do you have permanent residence? If not, hurry. There are limited vacancies left before the flight takes off."* People rejoiced and repented. Many were baptized after they changed into white garments. The benediction came some time later.

Nick approached me, pumping my hand. In friendly retaliation, I gripped his hand until he winced. Since I had spent so much time with Mackenzie the past months, I hadn't noticed Nick's transformation. He had dropped weight, buffed up, and sported a shaved head. Even Nick's teeth looked whiter.

"Congratulations, man. You know I'm in love with Valerie. I've been working my charm, but man, it's going pretty slow."

I frowned at Nick's worried look. Stroking my chin, I debated. Did I consider Nick close enough of a friend to share my concerns? I shrugged. "Honestly, I don't see Valerie as your type."

"You notice that, too, huh?" Nick nodded. "I hear ya, man. Right now, she's not the woman I want yet, but I love her. Love is patient, love is kind, love is longsuffering, and more. So I'll wait for God to change her. At least she let me take her out a few times."

Let patience have her perfect work, I thought, but I didn't want to discourage Nick, nor be a stumbling block to his patience for Valerie.

"I think I'm close though, man. Casually, we talked about prayer, hopes, dreams, you know. She's adamant that God has a man for her whose name begins with the letter 'N.' He elbowed me in my side, grinning. That's me man, that's me. It may seem slow, but Valerie and I will get there. Who knows, we may beat you and Mackenzie to the altar so start praying for us, especially Val."

"You got it. I've already started."

Planning a wedding was invading our privacy, especially with all the "must dos" of picking dresses, tuxedos, invitations, and other stuff women told me I had to do. Plus, with spring approaching, Mackenzie and I alternated between our deaf and hearing activities. She attended Deaf Awareness Night at Busch Stadium with me to watch the St. Louis Cardinals.

A few times, I tagged along to some estate auctions with her. One time, we laughed through it, and didn't get a chance to bid on one item. She accompanied me to fundraiser events for PRE-SERVE-St. Louis in exchange for me going roller skating. After two falls, a shove to the side, and a crash into a wall, we both agreed that the sport wasn't for us.

While I was at practice with the male deaf softball team, she was elsewhere helping to design and construct stage backgrounds. Throw wedding plans into our mix, and we no longer had our usual laid back downtime. After reading an email from my mother, I sent a text message to Mackenzie: *Hi, baby. Momma wants us to stop by for dinner Friday so you two can talk about the reception, invitations, yada yada yada.*

Hi yourself. I would love to, but we're putting the finishing touches on The King and I set, which starts next week. I'll be late. I'll meet you there.

I'd rather pick you up.

I'd rather already be your wife so . . . we have to give a little, Mackenzie typed back.

Okay, smart lips. I'll see you about nine. Love you. Be careful, and be blessed.

Need I remind u that u happen 2 love my smart, beautiful lips? Love u, too. Bye.

Friday night at my parents' home, I alternated

between watching a basketball game and peeking out for Mackenzie. The woman caused me anxiety when I didn't pick her up. Snatching my Black-berry off my belt, I sent her an IM, *Where r u, baby? It's getting late.*

I'm around the corner. 2 minutes, tops, she sent back. I grimaced at her famous line. My mother tapped me on the shoulder.

"Where is she?"

"Oh, she says two minutes away, so basically ten minutes," I informed my mother, retracing my steps to the couch. I slumped down.

Thirty-five minutes later, my father opened the door for Mackenzie. They exchanged hugs. Pierce stood at the same time I did. Caleb dozed in a cor-ner chair. As I hurried to Mackenzie, my mother cut me off and embraced her before I could scold her for making us wait and me worry.

Momma ushered us to the table for a light din-ner of baked chicken, brown rice, and salad. After eating, we cleared the table for Momma to dump a stack of catalogues with pages ripped out. Caleb made his escape, but Pierce and my dad stayed so I wouldn't be outnumbered.

The planning meeting got off to a great start, but steadily went downhill. Momma was the loving mother most children would envy. Her only un-manageable habit was saying things without think-ing. Mackenzie did think and still spoke her mind, regardless of the consequences.

"I think it's so romantic that you want to be mar-ried on your one-year anniversary when you two first met. The weekend after Thanksgiving is per-fect!"

"Thank you, Mrs. Norton," Mackenzie replied and looked directly at me, and mouthed, *I'll never forget that day either.*

I scooted closer to Mackenzie and rested my arm on the back of her chair. Reaching into her hair, Mackenzie relaxed as I massaged her scalp, snaring my fingers in her curls.

"For a long time, I worried about Noel living alone. I'm so glad now that he has someone who can look out for him. What he's lacking, you can make up for."

Mackenzie balled her hand into a fist. Systematically, she disengaged my hand from her hair, one finger at a time. She sucked in a deep breath. Probably to transform it to steam like a dragon.

"Mrs. Norton, you must have our relationship somewhat confused. I said yes to Noel because I expect him to take care of me, provide for me, be the head of our home, to establish the tone of holiness in our house, and to do whatever God instructs him. Noel is a man who doesn't need a babysitter," she stated then signed for me so there would be no misinterpretation of her words. "I'll love and take care of him as a wife, not a caregiver."

Dad looked at me, and I glanced at Pierce. Even Caleb re-entered the room with trepidation. Both with strong personalities, I knew it was a matter of time before they would clash. Momma sat speechless. I don't know what tone Mackenzie used, but Momma's shocked expression indicated Mackenzie had issued fighting words. And I thought Fred was dysfunctional. I forgot about Momma when she wanted the first and last word.

"Listen, young lady, you must've forgotten to whom you're talking and that you are a guest in my house. Yes, my son is a man, a very capable man. I'm confident he will make an excellent husband and father, but," Momma leaned forward and continued, "I do expect you to accept the extra burden. There are some things Noel can't do, because he's deaf."

"Enough!" Dad intercepted and both women froze.

"Mackenzie, you'll soon become our first daughter. We'll love you. With that said, you're expected to give Gina her honor, respect, and your love." Dad waited for the words to sink into Mackenzie's heart. I wrapped my arms around her shoulders and squeezed. The last thing I wanted my woman to think was we had ganged up on her. I kept quiet.

Facing each other, my parents shared a silent communication before he added, "Honey, Mackenzie loves our son, not as an invalid, but as a man. We will not interfere."

CHAPTER 30

The confrontation was short-lived. Thank God, because I wasn't going to allow them to put me through any Momma-fiancée drama. Prayer changes things. After a few days, they reached out to each other. I was jealous because the closest I had gotten to Mackenzie's dad was to call him Fred.

At church, I sat farther from the front in the deaf section. Although Mackenzie was a feast for my eyes, she became a distraction for my soul. More than once, I had to ask her for the scriptures after service because I couldn't concentrate. The other blessing was Valerie. We weren't buddies, but thank God she stopped treating me as the adversary.

From my point of view, things didn't seem to change for Nick. Valerie still didn't seem interested in him beyond friendship. He had to either trim down and buff up some more or pray harder. At their snail's pace, they might be engaged by the time Mackenzie and I became grandparents.

One morning after I finished my jog and weight lifting regimen, I clicked on my television and requested a video relay to call Mackenzie. Although I used the service for business and a few personal calls, Mackenzie and I often didn't use it because we didn't feel comfortable having someone in the middle of our conversation.

"Wake up, my sleeping beauty fiancée," I signed to a female interpreter.

The interpreter advised me of Mackenzie's yawning and stretching sound before Mackenzie responded, *"Leave me alone, Noel. Sleeping is a beautiful thing."*

I chuckled at the interpreter's interpretation of our conversation. *"Come on, baby. It's been a long time since we've spent an entire day together. You've got one hour and fifteen minutes to be ready,"* I signed and waited.

"I don't want to stroll. I want to eat. Bring a picnic basket and I'll be ready in one hour and forty-five minutes. Goodbye." The interpreter smiled and signed, *"Call disconnected."*

Shaking my head, I thanked the woman and clicked off my television. "Always the negotiator." While Mackenzie got up, dressed, and whatever she did in the morning, I scanned through my Bible then turned on *ESPN* for the sports highlights until it was time for me to leave and get her.

As I backed out of the garage, I jammed on my brakes when I spied two bicycles dangling from a loosened metal hook. Pierce never reclaimed his bike since my move into my house. Shifting my Cadillac into park, I walked around to the back of my car. Deciding to take them with me, I lifted them like a small dumbbell.

I secured them on my bike rack before heading to Dierbergs, St. Louis's family-owned chain of neighborhood grocery stores. Without a basket, I scanned through the plants section. A perky woman kindly told me they weren't for sale unless I also purchased flowers. I didn't need convincing. After I paid the woman, I got busy, throwing stuff into the makeshift picnic basket.

Checking my watch, I groaned in defeat. Once again, Mackenzie had bent me to her will. I would arrive at Mackenzie's house exactly at the time she wanted. I didn't know how she did it, but Mackenzie secretly wound me up like her personal clock.

At her house, she still wasn't ready, so I endured a strained conversation with Fred. Today, he wasn't in a mood to sign. No surprise there. Mackenzie didn't make her appearance until another fifteen minutes. My jaw slackened, and my hands went numb. Thanks to the warm weather and shorter skirts, I'd seen even more of Mackenzie's great legs. Thank God she didn't wear those skirts to church. Her legs and signing would surely be a distraction to any man.

The skirt was long, but I still stared. She seemed to float, stopping in front of me, enjoying her dominating stance as I sat perched on the sofa. Mackenzie broke the spell when she brushed a kiss on my forehead. Blood rushed to strengthen my legs as I stood, towering over her, switching the dominant role.

She wrinkled her nose. "Hi, Noel."

The first words out of my mouth were, "Let's move the wedding day up to tomorrow?" I wasn't joking either, and I didn't care what Fred said as he watched our interaction.

She laughed and swatted my arm. "And end your torture? Never."

No way was I going to confirm that she was right. She may count the months, but I was counting down the days, and that was torture. Her heeled sandals and long skirt weren't bike-riding friendly. A matching scarf somewhat tamed her curls. I liked the way she looked. I didn't dare ask that she consider changing for a bike ride. I would be satisfied with a picnic. Wrapping my arm around her waist, I steered her to the front door. Fred also stood. He did a poor job of hiding his amusement of our exchange.

I dropped my arm from Mackenzie's waist when Fred extended his hand. His gripping handshake was a reminder that Mackenzie was still his baby, and that he was still in control. Holding my own, I met his stare and nodded. Fred Norton wasn't going to let me soon forget.

Inside the car, I handed Mackenzie the flowers the woman at Dierbergs talked me into buying. Mackenzie's smile was worth it. Less than fifteen minutes later, we arrived at Heman Park in University, minutes from the city limits. Parking, I helped Mackenzie out then grabbed the basket from the backseat. I pushed the remote until I saw my headlights flash.

When I turned to Mackenzie, she was watching me with amusement. "What?"

"Locking your car once is enough, you know."

"True, but how was I to know? If it takes ten times for my lights to flash, then ten times it is."

Mackenzie agreed, "Good point."

Hand in hand, we began a search for the right picnic table under the right tree. Mackenzie tugged on my hand and pointed. I was about to walk off the narrow trail onto the grass when Mackenzie stopped me to rummage through her shoulder bag. The prize was her well-worn flats.

I shook my head and laughed. Mackenzie dropped the raggedy things to the ground and reached for my arm. Balancing herself, she changed shoes. I reach for her sandals.

She shook her head. *"I can carry them, Noel."*

"You could, but I can carry our basket, your shoes, and still hold your hand."

The perfect spot was near a playground. University City was nicknamed the city of trees and Heman Park didn't disappoint as a tower of Babel tree sheltered a lone picnic table. I placed the traditional brown *Wizard of Oz* basket on the table as Mackenzie was about to sit. *"Wait."*

"Why?"

I unlatched the basket buckle and whipped out an oversized cloth napkin. It was wide enough to cover a baby's bottom for a diaper change.

"What are you doing, Noel?"

"Isn't it obvious? Protecting your skirt."

She accepted my answer with those worshipping eyes. *"Thank you."*

After unloading the basket, I checked the bench to be sure a bird didn't beat me to it and left his evidence. I sat across from Mackenzie and reached for her hands to pray, but she stopped me. "Let me."

I obliged without blinking as her hands danced.

"Lord Jesus, I'm in awe of Your power and divine will. In the midst of this world, You gave me happiness with Noel, and I thank You. I also thank You for allowing me to share a meal with him. Please bless it . . . Amen." Smiling, she rested her hands on her lap.

Meeting each other halfway, our lips touched. When I wanted more, Mackenzie teased me with a shake of her head as she laughed at my disappointed expression.

Ham, turkey, Swiss cheese, and tomato were stacked between two slices of wheat bread. After they disappeared, we dipped celery, carrots, and cucumbers in Ranch dressing then drained our bottles of fruit drinks.

At times, the tree turned its leaves for the sun to peep through as the wind stirred. We closed the empty basket, and I discarded our trash as I stood. I stretched and flexed my muscles before I joined Mackenzie on her bench. With our backs resting against the table, I put my arm around her shoulder. She snuggled closer. For uncounted minutes, we stayed that way until Mackenzie broke free.

"Noel, when was the last time you were on a jungle gym or slide?"

Shrugging, I lifted my brow. I know she wasn't suggesting what I thought. I scanned her attire. *"Don't even think about it, Mackenzie. You're not dressed for horsing around."*

"I know I'm supposed to be this refined teacher, but

when I'm with you, the teenage carefree girl comes out, and I let her." Mackenzie pouted. "*Okay. I just thought I was marrying a young man. Maybe your mother's right. You are marrying me to push your wheelchair and give you your medicine.*" She took off running. I glanced around to make sure a dog wasn't chasing her. By the time I turned back, Mackenzie had made it to the playground and was climbing to the top of a slide.

She waved, tucked her skirt under her legs and began her descent. When her shoes kicked dust in the sand, I was there waiting. Lifting her in the air, I blessed her lips with the kiss I wanted earlier before planting her back on the ground. "Okay, Miss Norton, since you want to play, how about the swings? Hopefully, you won't hurt yourself on those."

Mackenzie grinned as she wrapped her arms around my waist. With synchronized steps, we strolled to the swings.

"You know I love you, don't you?"

Nodding, she kicked off her shoes as soon as I gave her swing a slight nudge.

I scanned the park. Kids were playing baseball, a young man was throwing a Frisbee to his dog, and then there was us. I sighed, somewhat content. "I wish I could hear the music to dance. I want to be your partner on *Dancing with the Stars,* and not miss a step. I want to sweep you off your feet and do a tango, salsa, or any dance no one could duplicate. I want to be your choreographer."

Once before, Mackenzie had consoled me when I spoke of my insecurities. She had said the soul of a man is through his mouth. Since then, I never tried to hold back my thoughts from her. Sometimes my heart's emotions spilled just for Mackenzie's ears, especially when signing wouldn't do. This was one of those times.

As her swing descended from the air, Mackenzie dug her heels into the sand. Twisting her body, Mackenzie's soft hands touched my face. Her fingers massaged the coarse hairs on my chin that my electric shaver missed.

"Noel, if you want to dance again, we'll dance. I promise. I promise you. I love you, and I can't change that ever, even if I wanted to. There'll never be a Donna Summer's last dance for us."

Then she turned around and wiggled, signaling like an impatient child that she was ready for me to push her again. Instead, I bent and nestled my chin into her shoulder and gently swayed the swing. "And I . . ." when she jumped, I paused, thinking I was speaking too loud.

Twisting her body, Mackenzie stood on one leg and used the seat to steady her other one. I grabbed her waist to support her. She released the swing chains to free her hands to cup my face. She inched closer until I almost couldn't see her lips. "Noel, there is nothing to be sorry about."

"Baby, I didn't mean to hurt your ear."

"Noel, you didn't hurt me." She smoothed her fingers over my ears. "It's your tenderness that makes me shudder. You're never too loud, never when you're around me."

Lord, I love this woman. My heart spoke to my God. "I want to bless you, Mackenzie." I prayed a short prayer for God to keep her safe, give her wisdom, and in good health.

Mackenzie's hands began to fan the air. *"Noel, I pray that God will bless you, your heart, mind, livelihood, and most of all, your hearing. God will restore as a testimony of His miraculous works in Jesus name. Amen."*

CHAPTER 31

Women. I can't live without them, and I wouldn't want to. Mackenzie was determined to shop, and shop, and shop until she had chosen the perfect Mother's Day gift from the both of us for my mother.

"Personally, a gift card to Macy's would've worked for me," I said more to myself, but Mackenzie's bionic ears heard me.

"Lesson number one, Noel Richardson. It's that extra thoughtfulness that a woman always remembers."

"Really?" I mumbled as we left the fourth specialty store within the past hour empty handed.

"Really."

Glancing around, I spotted an unoccupied bench camouflaged by several plants in silver canisters. I steered Mackenzie to it for a respite.

So what's number two? I signed, dumbfounded.

I'll keep you guessing.

* * *

"Happy Mother's Day," Pastor greeted from the pulpit. "The Word says it's a blessing to be a mother. Yet, I'm encouraging everybody today to get adopted." He picked up his Bible and began to pace. I couldn't follow his mouth so I looked to Mackenzie. *"A good mother will give you her best. So why would you want to be adopted? Because the mother you're sitting next to today is in the flesh, corruptible flesh.*

"Mothers, plan for your children's future. Make preparations now for them to be secure in the Spirit. Make sure the adoption papers are signed so they can become children of royalty." When he paused, I looked back at him. "Children, did you know you are heirs? Not yet," he said, holding up his hand and shaking his head. "Where's your connection to this King? You know how you're related to your parents, but how are you related to God? The Lord will not claim you until after your adoption takes place, the papers are signed, and the document is sealed. Your connection is sure in the Holy Ghost. Make sure you've got it because an imposter won't receive the inheritance. Romans 8:16 says, *The Spirit itself beareth witness with our spirit, that we are children of God.* Get adopted today so you can collect your inheritance."

The sermon ended with Pastor Coleman inviting anyone who wanted to be baptized that afternoon to come without an appointment necessary. So many people yielded to the spontaneity and repented that ministers were submerging three people at a time in the baptismal pool once they changed into white clothing in the preparation room. The Lord's power continued to explode throughout the church. Hats twirled in the air and bodies spun, rejoicing. Some men leaped from their seats and danced the holy dance. Mackenzie's hands were no longer signing, but lifted in praise. God must have lifted my body like a puppet, because my mouth couldn't control my tongue. It vibrated in my mouth before stopping of its accord. Remnants of the outpouring of the Holy Ghost lingered. It took a while, but eventually most of us regained our earthly control.

Pastor Coleman returned to the pulpit. *"Before we leave today, I want to remind the saints of our annual foot washing, communion, and Holy Ghost Explosion revival. The weeklong services will end with a special healing night. Saints, you don't want to miss any of this! We'll wash one another's feet as Jesus did in John 13:14."*

He scanned the sanctuary. *"How many of you can use a miracle, need a blessing or a healing? Our revival will culminate with a special healing service."* After the benediction, I waited for Mackenzie to gather her things. Daphne and Keisha, dressed in matching outfits, hurried to my side.

"Happy Mother's Day, Brother Noel," Keisha signed, grinning with a gap between her front teeth.

Daphne nudged Keisha aside. *"He's not a mommy. Happy Father's Day."* Before I could correct them, Sister Campbell and Mackenzie walked to us.

"Happy Mother's Day, Sister Campbell."

"Thank you, Brother Noel."

Mackenzie stepped forward and linked her hand through mine, prodding me to the lobby. On the parking lot, she signed nonstop at the car. *"I'm so excited, Noel. I always make sure I'm finished with my theatre projects in time for the special services. Will you be able to make it every night?"*

"*I wouldn't miss it.*" I smirked.

"*Noel, you could be healed. Let's fast and pray that God will perform a miracle. I believe God can heal you.*" Mackenzie signed before I opened her passenger door. Her expression was so tender and confident that I would believe anything.

"*I believe God can do anything He wants.*" I shut her door and slid behind the wheel, I checked the rearview mirror before driving off. I made a detour to Dierbergs's floral shop. While Mackenzie waited in the car, I went inside to pick up two bouquets. *Take that, Miss Norton. I do know how to make a woman feel special,* I thought, mentally patting myself on the back.

The next stop was Mackenzie's house. She had insisted on preparing a meal for her "almost mother-in-law." Considering she never offered to cook for me, I had to see and taste this food for myself. Together, we carried warm dishes and placed them in my trunk.

Once Mackenzie and I were officially engaged, my family wanted Fred to be included in every holiday gathering, so he was riding with us. At my car, he folded his arms. "This is the first time, young man, that we're a passenger in a car with a deaf man driving it." He didn't hide his hesitation. "Just remember, Mackenzie isn't the only precious cargo."

"Yes, sir, I'll guarantee you, I'm safer than riding with or following your daughter's car," I tried to assure him as I placed the last dish in my trunk.

"You've got a point," Fred replied.

Fred opened the back door, jumped in and latched the seat belt. I ignored Mackenzie's indignant expression as I opened her door.

A half hour later, we parked in front of my parents' home. I ushered Mackenzie into the house, refusing to allow her to carry anything except the box she had gift-wrapped at the mall. I still didn't know what "we" got my mother.

My brothers and Dad greeted us in the foyer. After they shook Fred's hand and hugged Mackenzie, the men trailed me to my car for the food. Once I took the last dish from the trunk, I got the flowers from the backseat. Balancing a pan in my arm, I checked the sidewalk. It would be just my luck that I would get run over by a skateboard, fall, and feed the ants.

Inside, everyone was crowded in the kitchen, rolling back aluminum foil from the pans. "Mackenzie." When she looked my way, I signed, *Did you give Momma our gift?*

We excused ourselves and escorted Momma into the living room. Mackenzie and I sat on the sofa with Momma in between us.

"Mrs. Richardson, I hope one day to be called mother. This is from Noel and me. I hope you enjoy your gift. Happy Mother's Day."

It looked like a hat box to me, and my mother accepted it with reverence. She removed the lid, and I leaned closer to get a peek at our gift. So far, all I saw was plenty of colorful tissue paper.

Digging deep in the box, Momma pulled out three envelopes. Frowning, I glanced at Mackenzie who winked. Each contained a gift certificate for day spa, manicure, and pedicure. *Well, that was cre-*

ative. I could've bought those without wasting that big box, I thought.

With misty eyes, she was about to hug us when Mackenzie stopped her. "There's one more."

"Oh?" Momma fingered the bottom until she found another envelope.

So far, I wasn't impressed until her eyes widened, her lips curled into a smile, and she blushed. When I tried to peep, she hurried and stuffed it back into the envelope.

"What is it, Momma?"

She shooed my hand away. "A gift certificate."

I lifted my brow in curiosity. She lifted hers higher in superiority. I let the question drop as I presented her with flowers. She sniffed them and smiled.

Then I looked at Mackenzie and scooted closer. When I grabbed the remaining bouquet, my mother took her cue to leave us. When we were alone, I said, "It's my desire to make you the mother of my children."

Mackenzie's eyes misted as she hugged me.

"All five of them," I added as she swatted me up side my head.

CHAPTER 32

God's Grace Apostolic Church made a big deal about the communion service as if it was a holiday celebration. Everyone dressed for the occasion. The women were in gleaming white dresses while the men were confined in suits, and the congregation had complied with Pastor Coleman's fasting request. The service was lively, considering we hadn't consumed water and food for twenty-four hours.

I couldn't recall many churches that practiced foot washing. My parents' church performed the special service, but I had never seen it. Pastor Coleman came to the podium, *"Our feet kiss the ground every morning. Some blister from overuse and abuse. Unless your feet have pedicure maintenance, usually they're dirty, crusty, smelly, and even ugly. They're the lowest part of your body."* Stopping, he bowed his head. After a few minutes he looked out into the crowd. *"Is anybody listening to me?"*

Many nodded. Mackenzie's brows were tight as she focused until the pastor spoke again.

"Tonight, let us do as Christ commanded in John 13. Remember, without humility, there is no conversion or salvation. If you can bend your knees, let's pray before the Lord."

I had never equated humility with salvation. Weren't all Christians humble? If not, did that mean they weren't Christians? I pushed the soul searching to the back of my mind to be considered later. Mackenzie stood and walked to my pew. Reaching for her hand, we linked fingers as we slid to our knees and prayed together.

Shortly, Mackenzie tapped my hand. "It's time for the foot washing."

The mood was reverent as members filed out of the sanctuary. No one pushed, shoved, or rushed. Once we were in the vestibule, Mackenzie and I separated. Women turned toward the fellowship hall. I followed the men in the opposite direction.

Clutching my Bible, I prepared my mind for this portion of the service. I jerked my head around when I was slapped, not tapped, on my back. Nick's hands flew up in surrender, mimicking sorry. That's when the men's line slowed at the entrance of a small chapel with chairs set up in rows. Since Pastor Coleman instructed us not to wash friends' feet, I chose a seat a good distance from Nick.

A young teenager limped toward the chair in front of me. I nodded. He returned a quick smile. Formality done, I unlaced my expensive leather shoes and slipped them off before peeling off my silk designer socks. He did the same with tennis shoes that were worn, but clean. His attire wasn't a suit, but faded tan khakis and a white shirt.

In the confined space, he knelt and scooted a rubber baby size bath tub toward me. With surprising tenderness, he lifted my feet one by one and placed them down in warm water. My feet weren't crusty, ashy, or dirty, but it was as humiliating as it was humbling. He didn't scrub them, but scooped up water and poured it over my feet as he appeared to pray. He finished in minutes, and never looked up.

On my knees, I performed the same ritual. Afterward, I was awestruck. I couldn't believe I had washed another man's feet and he had washed mine. Only for Christ would I participate in such a task.

When I stood eye-to-eye with the young man, we patted each other on the back. "I'm Noel Richardson."

"Brian Tandy, but I'm not a member here. I saw the sign outside the church welcoming everyone to the weeklong service. I wondered about it. I wasn't looking for a church, but here I am."

Soon, we parted as I walked and he limped back to the sanctuary. I felt exhilarated. Mackenzie met me in the aisle. Her eyes were bright. Her smile was radiant and it pulled me into a trance. I nearly tripped over my newly cleaned feet, which would've been more embarrassing.

"Well?" she signed.

"I'm glad I'm here and experienced it for myself."

Days later, I greeted Mackenzie at her front door with a kiss and a bulging bag of meat lasagna, spaghetti, and ziti—the ultimate platter sampler.

Of course, no meal would be complete without hot buttery breadsticks from Fazoli's, a chain of Italian restaurants in various states. "Hey, baby."

"I love a man who brings me food and flowers," she said, snatching my offering and rewarding me with a hug as an afterthought. She carried our meal, which included enough food for her father, into the kitchen, leaving me to shut the door and find my own seat. Mackenzie returned in minutes with plates laden with spaghetti and breadsticks.

Reaching across the table, I nestled Mackenzie's soft moist hands securely into mine. I prayed and blessed our food then added, "Lord, do something special for your people tonight. Amen."

When I looked up, Mackenzie replied, "He will," before seizing her first bite. It didn't take long before we had scraped our plates.

I checked my watch. Although it was five-thirty, it felt more like nine o'clock. Mackenzie and I were tired. For the past three nights, our bodies had labored double-duty, attending service in the evenings and being sleep deprived the next day at work. With a stack of papers awaiting me on the table, I felt like a substitute teacher without the pay. I agreed to help Mackenzie check her students' homework so that we could go every night.

The revival, aka Holy Ghost Explosion, was the buzz around St. Louis. Mackenzie informed me that some people had attended last year and witnessed a powerful spiritual stirring. People were healed one night and doctors verified it the next day. Addicts were delivered of drugs and alcohol. It was like Bible mania.

Latecomers were directed to the cramped quarters of the balcony. The sanctuary wasn't mega-church spacious, so it didn't take long for every seat to be claimed. Evangelist Sara Langham, nick-named Sister Dynamite, preached until the Holy Ghost released her. People spoke in tongues, some with an interpretation while others uttered in un-known tongues, not deciphered by the devil or man, to God. The young and some of the older people danced in the Spirit with uncommon en-ergy.

I couldn't wait for tonight's service. As I reached for a red marker, Mackenzie stopped me. "I really do appreciate you, Noel. You didn't have to offer helping me grade these papers so I could attend, but . . ." she paused. "Please be careful tonight. These are final tests to determine if the students will pass to the next grade."

"Yes, teacher," I said, smirking.

"You're the sweetest, sexiest, and most wonder-ful man I've ever met."

If I was eight years old, I would've blushed. In-stead, I released the cocky man inside of me. *"I like the sweet and saved, but I'm especially feeling the sexy."* I squinted. *"You're buttering me up for something."*

"I am because you made a mistake on a student's paper for two nights in a row."

I lowered my head and started to check off the answers. Without making eye contact, I owned up. "It wasn't a mistake. Moses should've put periods behind his whole numbers."

Mackenzie reached across the table and stilled my marker until I looked up guiltily. "How did you know I was talking about Moses?"

Gritting my teeth, I shrugged. *"Lucky guess?"*

Her eyes told me she wasn't buying it.

An hour later, after Mackenzie had made numerous mistakes herself, she called it quits. *"That's enough, Noel. I'm too excited to concentrate. Let me freshen up and I'll be ready for my free ride to church."*

I balled up a used napkin and threw it at her back, but she had already made her escape. Mackenzie's excitement continued to build on the ride to church. Each stop light was an opportunity for her to spill another thought. After six lights, I turned to her, waiting for her next comment. She didn't disappoint.

"Noel, tonight could be our night—your night. The evangelist said God is going to work miracles that many will talk about for generations to come. I remember the anointing she was under when the words were spoken, and I believe it."

Smiling, I turned and focused on the road as the light changed. When the next light caught me, I placed my elbow on the steering wheel and glanced at her. "Well?"

"Well, what?" She wrinkled her nose and her eyes widened with excitement. "Noel, I believe you're going to get healed tonight."

My heart skipped a beat. "Sweetheart, I feel fine. Did God tell you I'm sick?" The light changed. Driving under the speed limit, hoping for a red light so that she could explain, it was just my luck that the lights were now synchronized. The suspense was getting the best of me, so I pulled into a McDonald's restaurant lot.

Mackenzie tilted her head. "Noel, I know you're not hungry. We just stuffed ourselves with all that pasta."

Turning off the ignition, I twisted in my seat to face her. I didn't want to misinterpret her lips or hands. "Okay, baby, talk to me. What sickness?"

"I'm talking about your hearing, Noel."

I stared at her until realization hit. *"Baby, I have to be sick be healed. I'm not sick, I'm deaf."*

"What are you saying, Noel, you don't believe God can heal you—I mean restore your hearing?" She swallowed and her chest fell in a frustrated exhale. Mackenzie looked away before turning back. "Maybe that's why you haven't gotten healed all these years." *"Sorry. I didn't mean to say that."*

But you thought it, I wanted to reply, but I held my peace while my heart stopped. Is this what she was secretly hoping and praying?

An argument was simmering, and like a wildfire, I had no problem in striking a match. This wasn't one of our regular tit-for-tat disagreements. "Mackenzie, I love you, but you're crossing the line," I spoke and signed. My nostrils flared as I squinted. "Miss Norton, you know the scripture, *Faith comes by hearing and hearing by the word of God.* He hasn't spoken healing to me yet!"

I had stirred the pot. Now it was boiling as Mackenzie twisted her mouth, locked her brows, and her nostrils swelled back at me. *"Noel, don't use your deafness as an excuse. Are you saying you're going into a healing service, but don't expect, no—don't have enough faith in God that He will heal you?"*

I swept my hand down my face, but I couldn't rub off my frustration. Yes, I was deaf, but Mackenzie's hearing was definitely malfunctioning. *"What I'm saying is my faith in God is not dependent on my hope to hear again,"* I paused then began speaking,

"My faith is much bigger than that. I don't need God to perform a miracle for me to believe that He can whether He chooses to or not," I said, agitated. "Hearing God's voice is not physical, but spiritual."

"You don't have to yell, Noel."

Inhaling, I measured my breathing and apologized. *"Listen, baby, people who don't know God are healed every day. Christians who know God die every day, hoping for a healing. God is God, and He does what He chooses."*

"It sounds good on paper." Mackenzie folded her arms with too much force. "Just drive." She turned away and stared out of the window. I pounded the steering wheel with my fist, causing Mackenzie to jump.

"I can't believe this. Two people who love each other, on their way to church, and arguing like this." I spoke my mind whether she heard me or chose not to. That was up to her.

Frustrated, I turned the ignition. Mackenzie grabbed my hand, pointing to the gear. I never turned my car off. This was not a good example of why I needed to hear. Shifting into drive, I pulled out of the lot, praying for green lights all the way.

CHAPTER 33

"Noel, don't let your lack of faith keep you from getting your healing tonight. Without it, it's impossible to please Him," Mackenzie stated before opening my car door the moment I pulled up to the church entrance and shifted the gear into park. She nodded her thanks as a brother opened the church door. With too much attitude in her walk, she crossed over the threshold without looking back.

I was really getting tired of Mackenzie's on and off moods. When I couldn't find a vacancy in the parking lot, I exited to cruise the neighborhood for curb parking. It also gave me time to clear my head. I didn't want to enter God's house like this, and I would be a fool to turn down anything God gave me, including faith. Did I see pity in Mackenzie's eyes? I hoped not, because *hate* was a strong word and I hated to be pitied.

Parking some distance away, my mood improved with each step toward church. Mackenzie may have had good intentions, but she hadn't walked

in my shoes. Once inside the vestibule, I had to negotiate around people to enter the sanctuary. The
church was already packed and we had twenty
minutes before service began. The energy was
high, and the beat of the music vibrated through
my body, calming the conflicts that battled in my
mind. I searched the interpreters' chairs. Valerie
was already there, but Mackenzie was absent.
Where was she? I wondered.

Not far away from the Deaf Ministry's section,
Mackenzie stood clapping in a pew. She craned
her neck as she kept a watchful eye out for me. All
the times I wanted my woman sitting next to me
during service, this wasn't a good time. Would our
disagreement continue in church? I started to
turn back and find another seat when a brother
tapped me. Most of his words were indistinguishable, but I understood, "The lady says there's
room." Schooling my expressions, I thanked him
as I crawled over people's feet to get to Mackenzie.

We stared at each other and Mackenzie apologized. When I didn't, she stepped on my shoes.
I'm sure it was an accident, so I ignored her blunder. I laid my Bible on the seat and knelt to pray.

When I stood, Mackenzie was waiting for me so
I signed. *"Okay, I'm sorry. Thanks for sitting with me
tonight."* We avoided a full fledged war, but I still
wondered about the things she had said.

*"Noel, it's a special night. I wouldn't want to be in
any other seat with anyone else."*

Hmm mmm, I thought to myself.

The spiritually charged service was underway
when Nick strolled in with two attractive ladies. He
winked as he passed me. *What was he up to?* I won-

dered. Valerie inconspicuously shot daggers at Nick when he sat in eye's view of the deaf section.

When Evangelist Langham stepped to the pulpit, Valerie began signing. *"Praise the Lord everybody in this Holy Place. Let him that has breath, praise the Lord. While you're still standing, turn your Bible to 3 John 3. Beloved, I wish above all things that thou mayest prosper and be in health, even as thy soul prospereth.*

"Tonight we're going to ask and believe God to not only prosper our bodies for whatever they need, but our souls that we can be more like Him." Valerie continued to sign, but her fingers didn't dance like Mackenzie's. *"Please turn to the Book of Acts. Although I'd love to read every example of people being healed, time will not permit me; but Acts 14 gives us a good example about a crippled man and his faith to be healed."*

Nudging me, Mackenzie gave me her best angelic look, which warmed my heart. Then one dark, fine eyebrow lifted. "I told you so."

Exhaling an agitated breath, I refocused on Valerie without responding.

"Okay, let's allow the Holy Ghost to explode in this place. You've heard the Word, now let's believe it as you hurry to the altar. C'mon, c'mon, move quickly. God's already got His number who He will heal. Let it be you."

Valerie ceased signing as people moved uncontrollably to the front. Pride aside, men ran, but some women beat them. A few wheelchairs began to roll. Instantly, I thought about my foot washing partner, Brian, and wondered if he was in the sanctuary. I felt like a hypocrite, wondering whether Brian was content with his limp or would he go to the altar for a miracle.

Mackenzie elbowed me again. As I stepped back

so she could scoot past me, she grabbed my wrist in a hurry, tugging me to the front and mouthed, "Noel, let's see what God is going to do."

This time, I encircled both her wrists. "Let the people who need to be healed go."

We stood in the pew with a stalemate as others jostled us. *"Mackenzie, I'm a man, not a child who needs to be led around."*

"I'm sorry." She rubbed her fist circular in her chest.

"Good." Then feeling like the bad person, I took her hand and tugged her to the front. We joined others who hurried as if it was a one-day sale at Nordstrom. While we inched closer, Evangelist Langham lifted her hand and touched a school-aged boy who wore eyeglasses as thick as a piece of bread. A tight strip of black elastic band held them in place.

"Remove your glasses, child." He obeyed. She touched his eyelids with two fingers in a manner I could only describe as a Three Stooges stunt. The boy jumped in his place. Minutes later, he was rejoicing. When he raised his hand, the evangelist grabbed it and raced up the pulpit steps.

She asked someone one row from the front to hold up his Bible. The brother did. "Now read," she commanded the boy.

"Come unto me, all ye that labour and are heavy lad . . . lay . . ."

Patting him on his shoulder, she stopped him. "That's all right, baby. The word is laden. That means weighed down. "Did he read it word for word?" She asked the Bible holder. When he nodded, an explosion erupted. The saints worshipped God, including Mackenzie and me.

When Mackenzie stumbled, my arm encircled her waist. When I looked down to see what had blocked our path, I was shocked. Brian! He was dragging his leg as he walked. Holding onto Mackenzie, I steadied him.

He gripped my belt and used me as his support. "Thanks, Brother Noel. I was getting tired and my leg hurts if I stand too long."

"Not a problem," I reassured him as my arms held on to him on my right side and Mackenzie on the left. That's when the line seemed to advance.

When it was Brian's turn, I released him as he limped his way to Evangelist Langham. Mackenzie began to pray. The evangelist laid hands on Brian and had him stretch out his arms. She squatted and appeared to punch him in his knees. "Ouch," I said for him.

When I blinked, I missed what happened for Brian to land on his feet. He leaped a few more times before he raced off around the church, scrambling as he moved from left to right. Before my eyes I had just witnessed God's healing power.

Soon it was our turn in front and Mackenzie lifted her hands as she received prayer. A few minutes later, I stood before Evangelist Langham. She looked me squarely in my eyes. "What are you seeking from God?"

"His will in my life, and my hearing restored if that is His will," I answered.

Nodding several times, she laid her hand on my forehead. As her lips moved rapidly, I prayed until she removed her hand, which seemed a bit long with others waiting. "God is pleased. Let your blessings be according to His Will."

The healing service lasted for three hours until the aisle was clear of seekers, and I witnessed more people be healed.

Finally, Pastor Coleman gave the benediction. Taking Mackenzie's hand, I led her to the foyer to wait while I went for the car. When I saw Brian, I made a detour. We hugged, grinned, and I looked him over. He showed off the handiwork by shaking his leg. "God did all right, didn't He? Look what a little faith can do."

CHAPTER 34

Friday morning, I logged onto my computer after completing my morning ritual. I expected emails from Mackenzie, but there weren't any. Surprisingly, Nick had emailed me. Although we exchanged email addresses a while ago, we had never emailed each other.

"Noel, she's jealous, man. Can you believe she actually came up to me last night after service? She played hard to get for about fifteen minutes before she allowed me—according to her—to take her out next week. I can't believe I'm in love with that snobby woman, but I am. It was worth bribing my cousins to come with me, but after last night, they said they'll definitely be back. Nick."

I chuckled. I didn't have to guess that the "she" he was referring to was Valerie. I had to give him credit, Nick was tenacious. Before logging off, I sent Mackenzie a "thinking of you" e-card, proposing a dinner date for later to celebrate her last day of class for the school year.

At work, my executive meeting ran longer than

expected. Then I missed the opportunity to send Mackenzie an instant message while her class was at recess. It was almost eleven before I was able to fire her off an email, suggesting any Italian restaurant of my choice, I joked, knowing she preferred Chinese and Jamaican dishes.

By early afternoon, I had cleared my desk to leave. I stopped to see my assistant on my way out. *"If the building catches on fire, call the fire department, our insurance company, and then me. In other words, I'll be unavailable.*

She gave me an "aye, aye, Captain" salute.

Thanks to road construction, class had already dismissed for the summer by the time I arrived at Mackenzie's school. Girls raced across the campus, flinging their mandatory sweaters from a chilly morning into the air and dumping stuffed backpacks to the ground. Not to be outdone, the boys ripped off their ties as they barreled toward the playground. Since the day was breezy and sunny, I decided to wait outside for Mackenzie as I leaned against the hood of my car.

Soon the vision of my thoughts descended the school steps with her hair whirling in the wind. I jogged to meet her as she struggled with a large box with a year's worth of material.

"Hi," Mackenzie greeted, releasing her load.

"Hi, baby. Did you get my email about dinner? You know I was kidding about Italian, but we can go wherever you want."

"How about my house and we can order in?" She didn't look happy.

"Only, if you show me a smile."

Mackenzie obliged, but I learned from my mother when a woman wants to talk, let her or you will regret it later. "Okay. Why don't you call something in on the way home and I'll trail you."

The delivery driver from Chinese Wok beat us to Mackenzie's house. Once we were out of our cars, I retrieved her box and carried it inside. Fred and I exchanged hellos as he left. I returned and, the man was scratching his head as he shuffled through the orders. I tapped him on the shoulder, startling him as he fumbled with a bag.

"Sorry." I should've known better. The gesture annoys me when someone sneaks up on me. "Mind if I take a look?"

Shrugging, he moved aside. White bags with handwritten tickets stapled on the outside were lined up in a box. I could see his aggravation as I squinted to make out the scribbled notes. I grabbed two sacks that appeared to be ours and reached into my pocket. I gave him a twenty dollar bill. "Thanks, keep the change, man."

When I walked into Mackenzie's house, she already had utensils on the table. We blessed our food and ate until the last morsel had disappeared. Together we cleared the table, I rinsed the dishes and she loaded them into the dishwasher. Once in the living room, I sat on the sofa, and patted the spot next to me. When she declined, I frowned.

"Noel," she paused, struggling for a deep breath. Moisture glazed her eyes as she began to pace. A grave burden seemed to have suddenly weighed her down.

My heart dropped in concern. Something wasn't right. I stood to hug her, but she refused me.

"Noel, you know I want whatever God has for you, which includes your healing. I really feel—no—I know if you would've asked God and really believed, He would've healed you."

Instead of towering over her, I threw my arms up and sank to the sofa. "Oh, we're back on this again?" Did this woman have any idea what "let it go" meant? I doubted it.

"Noel, I had to practically drag you to the altar. What was wrong? Do you want to remain deaf? Last night was your window of opportunity. God was healing people right before our eyes," she pleaded then frowned. "If I hadn't been sitting next to you, nudging you along, you wouldn't have even gone, would you?" Folding her arms, she drew the line and waited for my response.

"I've never lied to you, Mackenzie, so the answer is no." She didn't say anything, but her shocked expression told a lengthy story that she couldn't wait to share. Leaning forward, I rested my elbows on my knees. "I sought the Lord to make you happy. God had already ministered to me years ago. Is that the only reason you sat next to me?"

"I can't believe you said that. It was a healing service. Why wouldn't you go?"

My nostrils flared. This time I did stand. "Why did you go?"

"For you," she pointed, accusingly.

"That's where you made a mistake. Mackenzie. You should've gone for yourself."

Tapping her forehead, she inhaled. "Listen,

that's not the only reason I sat with you. I wanted to share the experience of the service with you . . ." Frustrated, she stopped. "I wanted us to believe together. I prayed that God would give you enough faith."

She grinned to appease me. It didn't. With a concentrated effort, I shook off my accelerating anger. Any other woman, I wouldn't have even dignified with an answer, but I loved Mackenzie. I didn't realize she had such little faith in my relationship with God. "Had it ever occurred to you, my sweet little woman, that I'm the head of my household—me? I don't need you to run the show for me. I've allowed you to run our relationship because I enjoy letting you think you're controlling it. Second, faith to be healed comes by hearing, and I didn't hear any words from God."

She reached for my arms and I welcomed her touch—that was the lover in me, but the man in me wanted to keep my distance, sulk, and leave, slamming the door on my way out.

"Sweetie, the Bible says we have not, because we ask not. Ask and it shall be given, whatever you ask in prayer, ask in His name, ask in faith . . ."

"Enough, Mackenzie! Enough about you questioning my faith," I said, gritting my teeth. "I know a few scriptures myself, Miss Norton. How about . . . *faith is the substance of things hoped for, the evidence of things not seen, and without it it's impossible to please God.* I'm here to please God, Mackenzie, not you. Only God knows the number of times I hoped for me to regain my hearing. In Hebrews, I know, *By faith the elders obtained a good report. Through faith, we understand that the worlds were framed by the word of God, so that things which are seen were not made of things which do appear."*

Mackenzie opened her mouth to interrupt, but my hand stopped her. "No," I said, "You questioned my faith. *By faith Abel offered God a more excellent sacrifice.* Don't judge my sacrifice, Mackenzie. *By faith Enoch was transformed that he should not see death. By faith Noah, being warned of God of things not seen yet, moved with fear and prepared an ark to the saving of his house. By faith Abraham, when he was called, obeyed.* Wait a minute." I held up my finger as her mouth again opened to interrupt me. She was going to listen about how I studied, learned, and prayed for that intensity of faith as I continued to rattle off quotes, *"By faith Abraham, when he was tried, offered up Isaac,* but Abraham believed God's promise. *By faith, Isaac blessed Jacob and Esau concerning things to come. By faith Joseph, when he died, made mention of the departing of the children of Israel.* See, baby, faith . . . it's a generational thing and it can be passed down." I lifted my hand to God for all the scriptures that I had recalled when I needed them.

"Moses used that same faith to pass through the Red Sea. By faith, Joshua followed God's instructions to crumble the walls of Jericho with a shout and trumpet blast. The faith of a prostitute, Rahab, saved her from death. Don't get me started with Samson, Samuel, and prophets. Don't get me started, Mackenzie, because I'm on a roll and I'm about ready to shout and tear down some walls that I didn't construct, right here and right now. By faith, I, Noel Richardson answered when God called me, repented, and was baptized."

I was so mad I could've choked the devil himself. Fuming, I spun around, searching for the door, which was right in front of me. Without looking back, I opened it and stormed outside, forgoing the childish thrill of slamming it.

BOOK TWO

There're two sides to every story. Here's Mackenzie's . . .

CHAPTER 35

I had waited my entire life for Noel Richardson. He was perfect in every way that mattered to a woman: job, appearance, and spirituality. His skin color reminded me of maple butter syrup. Lord knows, Noel was pleasing to my eyes. I couldn't help but fall in love, but that wasn't the only reason.

Noel's scent was hypnotic. He didn't think I had noticed when he tested new colognes, but I did. His shirts did a poor job of concealing his bulging muscles. The cuffs of his pants never, ever touched the dust of the ground. It was as if he had them trained to obey. Noel's strength was attractive, his desire to seek God was endearing, but it was his honesty that nurtured our relationship. I doubted Noel knew when he whispered. Although Noel was deaf, his heart never failed to hear me. I fell in love with his heart. So what happened?

That was a million dollar question that I didn't have a ten dollar bill to answer. I shook my head to scatter my memories. It didn't help. Staring out of my kitchen window, I couldn't seem to focus on anything. I turned around, remembering to sip my coffee. The flavor was bland, not doused with my regular heavy hand of sugar, and it was tasteless like my life. I was about to make me a new cup when the phone rang. "Hello?"

"Hi," Rhoda Brownlee greeted. "I'm just checking up on you. Still no word?" she asked cautiously.

"Nope, still no word since the last time you called." I checked my watch. "Which was how many hours ago?"

Rhoda and I had become and remained best friends since our freshmen year in college. She was the most exotic rich-black-skinned woman I'd ever met. Rhoda wore her darkness as an Egyptian queen with a magnetism that people couldn't help but gravitate toward. That was a welcome contrast in our imperfect world where dark skin could oftentimes be subjected to prejudices and misconceptions.

She was the exception. Many were in awe of my best friend's flawless covering. A day never passed without someone inquiring about her country of origin. "Jersey," she always responded with a thick East Coast dialect, dumbfounding everyone.

Months ago Rhoda had rejoiced about my bliss with Noel, so the day of my argument with Noel, I concealed my inner turmoil. When she called, our chat—or rather her chatting—was well underway until five minutes into the conversation when Rhoda used the "N" word. I felt that I might throw up. She hadn't stop singing the praises of a man whom she had never met. Gagging, I raced to the bathroom. I really did regurgitate. I think it was from the day-old Chinese food, not Noel—the "N" word.

When I called her back, I was bawling within seconds. For two uninterrupted hours, Rhoda listened, sympathizing with my raw emotions as if I was a sixteen-year-old, losing my first love. At almost thirty years old, I could truly say Noel was my first love. Unfortunately, my therapy session came to an abrupt halt when her fiancé beeped in, reminding me of his priority in Rhoda's life. So she bid me a good night.

That was almost a week ago. Fast forward to now, and like clockwork, she called several times during the day armed with scriptures, ready to dispense at any moment.

"Rhoda, I don't feel up to talking—"

"I understand. Whenever Heath and I have disagreements, you know I don't like to talk about him for at least twenty-four hours, too. Girl, let me tell you, that man made me so mad . . ."

I loved Rhoda, but sometimes she only understood other people's problems by recalling her own, overriding someone else's despair. "Rhoda," I lifted my voice to pull her back to my situation.

"What?" She had the nerve to sound annoyed. "Oh, sorry, you know whenever you're ready to talk, I'm here for you."

Gripping the phone, I bowed my head and closed my eyes. "I really did expect Noel to burst through the door with his arms stretched and lift me up like one of those figure-skaters before kneeling with puppy-dog eyes to apologize."

"Mack, the Winter Olympics are over."

"Yeah, I know, but you're aware in another life, I

would've been a champion skater, right? I should've never stopped taking those skating lessons. Anyway," I said, swallowing a sigh, "my tears had a mind of their own. My pride had crumbled, but I was determined to be the first person to say I'm sorry. After almost a week, I accepted that he wasn't coming back."

"Oh, I remember when Heath and I had our first argument. He was the first one to say he was sorry. That's why I love—"

Gritting my teeth, I counted to three. "Rhoda, it's not always about you."

"But love is kind, love is patient, and it keeps no record of wrongs. Maybe that's why I can't help but talk about *him,* not me," Rhoda defended.

"Love also hurts. I'm a first-hand participant, remember?"

"Mack, stop it. Stop torturing yourself. Look, I've got to go. Heath's at the door and we're going sailing with friends on Lake Michigan."

Although I wasn't ready to say goodbye, I didn't stall. I thought my tear ducts were depleted, but drops trickled down my cheeks. Pulling myself together, I haphazardly strolled to the bathroom, and splashed cold water on my face before blowing my nose.

After days of gut-wrenching cries, my reflection in the mirror was unrecognizable. I lifted a pocket Bible from the vanity and sat on the commode, trying to re-focus. "Lord, talk to me."

Wrestling with the tissue-thin pages fused together, I stopped at Romans 8: *And we know that all things work together for a good to them that love God, to them who are the called according to His purpose.* Closing my Bible, I prayed. That's when Peace commandeered my spirit, requesting permission before settling into my soul. Shoving Doubt aside, Confidence took its post. "Okay, God, so now what?'

CHAPTER 36

Sunday morning, I dressed meticulously in my favorite color—white. I wanted to catch and keep Noel's attention. I dabbed my makeup until perfection. Oil sheen covered curls obeyed their holding position until a gust of wind tango and my curls spiraled. When a piece of dust attacked my eyes, I rubbed gently, but smeared my mascara anyway.

Once inside the church, I repaired whatever damage I could in the women's restroom, then with my head held high, I stepped in the sanctuary. Shielded by my lashes, I performed a quick surveillance. Arriving earlier than usual, I readied my smile, and waited for Noel's confident gait to make an appearance.

Noel never showed. Even the Campbell sisters were antsy, looking back several times for him. It was hard to digest a sermon when my heart was heavy. Instead of seeing the Master Physician, I left without filling the spiritual prescription.

Wednesday arrived and faded. Again, Noel

didn't bother making the Bible class. His absence sparked curious murmuring among the saints, but only Valerie voiced her questions. Pulling me aside after class, she stalled my escape.

"That's two for two, Norton. Where's your man?" her tone a notch stronger than an innocent inquiry as she slithered next to me.

"I don't know," I whispered, praying our conversation wouldn't attract attention. I turned to escape Valerie's inquest, but her hand encircling my wrist restrained me.

"Wait a minute," Valerie said louder than I would've preferred.

Leaning closer to her face, I inhaled the barbecue sauce that lingered from an earlier meal. "If I wanted an audience, Valerie, I would've made an announcement."

"Fine." She whipped her neck around, scanning the perimeter. "As a friend, I have a right to ask about your well-being."

Folding my arms, I stood back. I lifted one brow and enunciated each word. "I wouldn't take that right for granted. Now, I'm tired and I just want to go home."

"Okay, okay." Valerie held up her hands as if deciding whether she should sign or talk. Shrugging, she spoke in a hushed tone, "Listen, you've got a ring on your finger, and you don't know where your ying-to-yang, your pot-to-your-pan, your polka-dot-to-stripes is?" She glanced at my diamond engagement ring, lifting my hand like a manicurist, as if she hadn't seen it before.

"Valerie, don't start, and . . . polka dots and stripes don't even match." Snatching my hand back, my mind and body took a defensive stance. Before Valerie could further insult me, Nick approached. "Praise the Lord, Valerie," he said with a tender smile and a sparkle in his eyes. A noticeable gentleness replaced Nick's known joking character.

"Hey, Mackenzie, where's Noel? I called him several times and left a few messages with a relay operator. Your man doesn't know how to return calls?"

"Nick, next time try IM or text message. Noel only uses relay calling as a last resort. Excuse me, saints." Gathering my Bible and purse, I hurried from the sanctuary. Slow enough to appear that I wasn't running, but fast enough to get away. I didn't stop until I exited through the church's door, joining others on the parking lot.

The night sky offered a dim path to my red Mazda. It didn't match the security Noel gave me as my escort, and it had nothing to do with physical protection. I wished I had counted the number of times Noel and I strolled to my car. Valerie was wrong. Noel was my peanuts-to-jelly beans—one of my favorite munchies.

Whenever we drove separately to church, Noel always seemed to beat me, although I was usually just around the corner. Okay, several blocks away. Maybe ten minutes at the most before I pulled into the parking lot. Noel was always posted at our self-designated spot, leaning against his car. Even in the cold! He would patrol the space next to his Cadillac, daring anyone to think about claiming it.

"I miss you, Noel," I whispered as if he was present and his eyes could read my lips and his heart could feel my emotions. Yes, I guess he was the ying-to-my yang because the man could feel my emotions.

At the following week's Bible class, Valerie's 'I told you so' look mocked me as if a pit bull was locked to my ankle.

Amen, I signed the benediction. Again Valerie cornered me, and had the good sense to keep our conversation discreet. She tapped her chin. "You know, Mack, I've been thinking."

"Should I be concerned?" I was irritated from being irritated.

Valerie shook her head, offended at the suggestion. "Of course not, but—" her finger left her chin and paused in the air between us. "I'm convinced that God sent Noel to me. Hear me out," she added as I readied for an argument. "C'mon, Mackenzie, maybe he was an angel of light. Aka Satan Noel couldn't trick me, so he tried to seduce you until God intervened. The Word says God will never leave us nor forsake us. Jesus was right in the middle of that! I mean, Noel vanished. The scripture does say resist the devil and he'll flee from you, girl."

My jaw just dropped. Emotionally I was hurting and Valerie was sealing my coffin with Krazy Glue before nailing it. She didn't know how to let things go. She was piecing scriptures together tighter than a knitter perling yarn for a sweater.

Now I was more than ready to lash out. "Valerie Victoria Preston, it's good to quote scriptures, it's better to live them." Lifting a brow, I considered my next comment that would qualify me as a Christian hypocrite. God was telling me to hold my tongue, but I opted to use my free will. "Did you ever think that Noel wasn't meant for you either? Ben's name is tattooed on your chest. Maybe you better look for a man that has B-E-N in his first, middle, or last name."

Gasping, Valerie quickly crossed her arms against her breast. Leaning forward, she whispered, darting her eyes around us. "You know about that?"

"Yeah, me, and anyone else with eyes can see Ben's name winking at us from your revealing tops. How do you think your husband is going to feel making love to his wife and seeing another man's name on her body?

"You won't find a B in Noel Allen Richardson. Goodnight, Valerie." Before I turned to leave, tears glazed her eyes. I understood the pain I inflicted, but I was too tired; tired of the drama, tired of Noel's absence, and tired of Valerie's insensitive statements. I was almost out of the sanctuary door when I felt God's conviction.

I glanced over my shoulder as the deacons shut off overhead lights. Valerie was rooted in the same spot as if waiting for my return, or in shock. Condemnation pricked at my heart. Whirling around to apologize, I had taken three steps when Valerie waved a hand in the air before it settled on her hip.

"It doesn't matter anyway, Mack. I happen to know a brother whose middle name is Benjamin, and I'm sure he'll be thrilled to see his name on the top of my breast. He has had his eyes on me lately. Nick's dropped some weight, buffed up, shaved his head, and even had his teeth bleached.

At least he can hear God's voice. Admit it, Norton, you've been played."

I should've kept my mouth shut earlier, so I did now.

"Mackenzie, come sit down," Daddy requested. He pulled a kitchen chair from the table, waiting. I did as I was told without meeting his eyes. His tone hinted this wasn't going to be a light-hearted morning conversation before he left for work.

Chewing his food, Daddy poured orange juice into his glass. "Want some?" He offered. I shook my head. He took a gulp, smacked his lips, and squinted. "I haven't seen that fiasco named Noel in weeks."

I nodded and rubbed my hands.

"Listen, princess, I had tolerated Noel because I love you, but I've always felt you deserved someone better. He is not the man to whom I'd imagined walking my only daughter down the aisle and giving away. Now you know I'm not as churchy as you, but maybe this is God's way of saying, no."

Tears blurred my vision, but I remained silent. Daddy didn't need to know I had texted, emailed, and even sent Noel instant messages. I drew the line at showing up at his house or job. I was too old for that kind of drama. Instead of planning a wedding, I was burying my feelings.

Scraping up the last portion of eggs, he stuffed them in his mouth and pushed his plate away. "You'll be okay. You'll be glad you waited for the man the Good Lord and I wanted for you."

I couldn't accept his last statement. "I received a letter from Goodman Theatre for a summer project. It's my open door, Daddy."

He rubbed his chin. "You going?"

"I'm thinking about it."

"Good," he replied, standing. Scooping up his plate, he deposited it in the sink. Without another word, he swiped his lunch bag off the kitchen counter, planted a kiss on my head and left.

I stopped keeping track of the number of times I wound up in Heman Park, crying and sitting on the same bench Noel and I had shared that picnic lunch. In a blurry distance, a couple strolled hand in hand. I was developing a brain freeze, not from memories of Noel, but from one of my summertime favorites, a 7-Eleven Slurpee. I had to stop torturing myself, which would trigger more tears and trips to 7-Eleven. I could only endure so many daily brain freezes.

I was becoming pathetic. I did have other options like Chicago. On my previous Christmas break, Rhoda and I attended *The Black Nativity: A Gospel Song Play*. The pageantry and the characters' revelation of their faith were a captivating portrayal of a Langston Hughes work. Days later, we dragged Rhoda's fiancé to see the *Christmas Carol*.

For so long, I worried God about an opportunity to say that I once worked on a renowned production. Every night, I had prayed, "Lord, bless me with this desire of my heart." When Noel came into my life, God placed the desire of my heart before my eyes, or so I thought. My mind automatically asked, "Goodman who, what, where?"

"Who you talkin' to lady?"

I blinked and met the curious clear brown eyes of the cutest little boy. His two-piece short set was clean except for a faded pink stain below his chin, the evidence of a Popsicle or juice. His brown skin and black hair would make any mother boast for producing good genes. The wandering youngster couldn't have been any more than four or five years old.

Embarrassed, I grimaced and dropped my head, mumbling, "Nobody."

"That's what I tell my mommy when I'm playing with my friend. He's invisible."

I shook my head. "I don't hav—"

Looking around the park, the child teetered closer. "You think your friend wants a cookie?" He didn't wait for my answer as his small hands plowed into his bulging side pockets. Granules spilled as he presented his fist of crumbs. He whispered, "I'll share. My friend likes Oreo cookies so I always get extras for him."

Before I could decline his offer, a high-pitch echoed through the park, "Jonathan, Jonathan! Boy, you better get back over here, right now."

Jonathan made a quick decision as fear covered his face. He dumped his donation in my lap, and sped off. His feet propelled him faster and farther than a tricycle without training wheels. He was an Olympic medalist in progress.

Humored, I shook my head, scraping the crumbs to the ground. Alone again, my mood became somber. I never realized how my mind and heart battled for dominance. I didn't want to think about Noel, but my heart did, so memories resurfaced. When Noel proposed, my other prayer requests ceased. Nothing else seemed more important. Noel was a perfectionist at balancing show and tell. His eyes, smiles, and arms showed me how much I meant to him. His lips told me how much he loved me.

"Okay," I mumbled, patting my thighs. One more thought about him would drive me to drink another Slurpee. Let it be known, I wasn't budging. I could be the mistress of hold out. "God, I appreciate every detour that you made in my life. Enough of Memory Lane, I'm ready to get back on the main road." Deactivating my car locks, I got in. By the time I clicked my seatbelt, my mind was made up. I was packing. Who knows? The opportunity could turn into something permanent.

CHAPTER 37

Three days later

Chicago, home of the Cubs, the White Sox, the Rams—oops, that's a St. Louis sports team. Home of Garrett's Popcorn, catfish at Priscilla's Soul Food, Michigan Avenue, white stretch limousines, and the onslaught of homeless beggars. It was also a place where Noel Richardson didn't live. I stretched a replica of a smile across my face.

The Windy City also served as a breeding place for artists from all over the world. The Theatre District was home to the Cadillac Theatre—where *The Color Purple*, attracted bus loads; The Chicago Theatre, The Ford Theatre, and others. Even the Arby's boasted a red awning that was trimmed as if it was another theatre company.

Okay, enough of the history lesson. My predictable and boring four-hour road trip to Chicago turned into a five-and-a-half hour drama packed adventure. "Gertrude," my once dependable car, picked the wrong time to experience hot flashes from a radiator leak to a flat tire. I refused to accept the mishaps as a sign from God to turn around. God opened the door to Goodman Theatre, and with my head tilted high, I planned to step through it.

When I finally parked in Rhoda's driveway, she was standing in the doorway of her townhouse, choking a cordless phone. Seeing me, she dropped it and rushed to my car then backed away as smoke huffed beneath the hood. She hesitated, bracing for an explosion.

I turned off the ignition and got out. Determining the coast was clear, Rhoda barreled into me. "Mackenzie, girl, you had me worried. I see why now. Your cheap butt needs to dip into your bank account and buy a new car. You could easily afford an Escalade. You've been saving money since college. Anyway, when I couldn't reach you, I called Mr. Norton, who also panicked. Before we knew it, we were praying."

"Oh, Rhoda, I'm sorry. My cell phone had a weak signal and I brought the wrong charger. I'll have to buy another one while I'm here. Wait a minute. Daddy was praying? Well, praise God. I better let him know I made it."

"Yes, praise the Lord. Maybe one of Heath's mechanic-friends can take a look at it tomorrow." Rhoda peered through the car window. "Did you come for a visit, or to stay? I haven't seen this much stuff since we moved off campus, and don't think I didn't notice the bags under your eyes, the weight loss, that dingy half-smile, your unkempt hair, wrinkled clothes, and—"

"Geez, Rhoda, sure you don't want to check to see if I've got on clean socks? I've been driving for five hours. How do you expect me to look? I'm not about to walk the red carpet for a premiere."

With one hand on her hip, she squinted. "If that piece of rock wasn't blinding me, I wouldn't have noticed the other stuff." She lifted my hand as if she was Valerie's assistant manicurist. "Mack, this is some serious love going on here. This rock is telling me it ain't over."

I snatched my hand back, briefly looking away. "At one time, I thought so, too. C'mon, Rhoda, no questions."

Looping our arms, we matched our steps as we strolled on the curved pathway to her porch. "Hmmm mmm, right, so how long are you staying before school starts?"

"Honestly, I haven't made up my mind," I said with a sigh.

"Well, you know my hospitality is legendary, but I will put you out," Rhoda joked followed by the melodious sound of her laughter. The pitch, the tone, and the duration never changed.

As soon as we walked through the door into her living room, I used Rhoda's cordless phone to call Daddy and assure him I had made it okay.

"It's time for you to get a more dependable car. Get something like Noel's Cadillac. I'm thinking about buying one myself."

I ignored the reference to Noel's car. "I'll think about trading Old Gertrude in for something else, but not a platinum Cadillac CTS."

Rhoda leaned against the back of her sofa and chuckled at my Mazda's pet name. Although it was my third car since college, I called them all Ger-

trude. I figured if George Foreman could name all
five of his sons George, then I hadn't broken any
records yet. When I disconnected, I looked at
Rhoda unfazed. "Hey, let me grab my stuff and—"

Frowning annoyance, Rhoda shooed her hand.
"Girl, please; Heath can get that."

Heath. Of all the names to call her man, Rhoda
picked one synonymous with a candy bar—a deep,
dark chocolate treat. As if hearing his name,
William "Heath" Wilkerson's rich booming voice
responded. The fantasy voice of a sexy black male
radio announcer preceded heavy-hitting footsteps,
but a white guy stood in Rhoda's doorframe. Shirt
sleeves rolled up and a dish towel in his hand.

"I can get what, baby? Hey, Mack, when did you
get here?" Taking one step, he grabbed me around
my waist and lifted me in the air as if I was a tod-
dler enjoying a thrill ride or an ice skater.

"Put her down, Heath," Rhoda fussed as I
screamed in jest. "She has stuff in that raggedy car
of hers.

Upon my descent, William smacked a bruising
kiss on my cheek.

"Little Mack, it's good to see you, girl. You had
my woman worried. Welcome back to the Windy
City. I was heading out anyway so I'll grab your
things." He paused, patting a stomach that was one
meal away from tipping over his leather belt. Besides that minor imperfection, he was very pleasing
to any woman's eyes. "My baby cooked me some serious oven-fried chicken, mustard greens, and—"

"Just get my bags, Heath," I teased. "I can taste
test my own food."

Once in her updated kitchen, compliments of

William, Rhoda made a beeline to a steaming pot on the stove. I walked to the sink to wash my hands. Afterward, I climbed on a barstool, balancing myself on the thick cushion. The makeover in the room was phenomenal. William's skills as a homebuilder and eye for remodeling were unmatched. Even though he designed and was constructing their new house, he insisted on remodeling Ronda's townhouse so that she would get the maximum re-sale value.

"What's the latest on 'Gone-without-a-trace' Noel?" Rhoda demanded, taking a crystal pitcher from her refrigerator. After pouring lemonade into two tall glasses from the cabinet, she turned around, walked to the table, and slid a drink in front of me like a bar waitress.

William's return kept me from answering her. I grinned at him. "I love you, man," I flirted.

"Sorry, Little Mack. I'm a one woman man." He deposited my bags outside the kitchen door. He kissed his fiancée, waved goodbye, and with his signature bow-legged walk, strolled out of the kitchen.

"I still can't get over you marrying a white guy."

Huffing, Rhoda rolled her eyes, feigning insult. "Heath isn't white. Don't let the skin fool you. He's definitely got some black blood, unlike his younger brother, Sam, who's convinced he is white. That man has cut ties with his black family, moved to Ohio, and started a small hotel chain or business or something like that. You'd think that he was living in Mississippi before the Emancipation Proclamation where it was commonplace for mulattoes to claim they were white to escape slavery." Rhoda shook her head. "Heath has a little black blood, maybe about twenty-five percent. Doesn't matter to me, I would love him anyway and he loves me."

"I never questioned that," I said.

"Sorry for the genealogy lesson." Rhoda apologized, shrugging. "Blacks and whites make too many assumptions. Sometimes, I find myself defending our relationship. I only let *you* tease me, but don't push it."

"I always forget about the stark contrast. You're this Egyptian Nubian queen who escaped from one of Pharaoh's tombs. Despite the stares and the inquiries, is it really worth it?" For the first time, my question made me wonder if Noel and I received stares. Unlike William, Noel didn't draw attention until he signed, but then I was too infatuated to really notice.

Rhoda sipped her drink and frowned, thinking. "I want people to be envious of our love. I want our love to be the showstopper, not a taboo vanilla and double-dutch chocolate couple who should know better than," she paused and made quotation mark with her fingers, "crossing the color line." He's the man I adore. Yeah, he's good looking, sexy as God made him, smells good, bow legs—"

"Rhoda! I didn't ask for a biography of William Wilkerson."

She fanned her face. "When it boils down to it, we both love the Lord. We've attended the same church for almost two years. When God filled him with the Holy Ghost and he experienced the fire that exploded in unknown tongues, I rejoiced something fierce. I had no idea that I was rejoicing for the man who would become my husband."

Nodding, I exhaled. Rhoda was too cheerful when I was looking for misery to keep me company. I got up and walked to the stove. Focusing on the feast set before me, I shamelessly helped myself to hefty servings of Rhoda's chicken, mustard greens, and yams. Returning to the table, I bowed my head. I prayed for God's blessings on my food since my love life seemed to have missed it.

CHAPTER 38

A few weeks later, God was telling me something during my morning prayer. The Holy Ghost possessed my tongue and manhandled it like a cowboy in a rodeo. I welcomed God's control as a reminder that I wasn't alone. I covered myself in toughness as if I was unconcerned about what happened, but I was naked before God. "Lord, only You can heal my broken heart. Please help me get over this first love and find my true love. Amen."

Thank God, He gave me another focus. In the mornings, I worked alongside the set designer in the studio. Occasionally, we visited the theatre shop in the afternoons. Then there were the production meetings that sometimes lasted late into the evenings. A job at Goodman, if offered, would definitely be worth relocating.

One evening, while in Rhoda's kitchen, sipping on coffee after dinner, she started a cross-examination, which meant a serious discussion was forthcoming. "Talk to me, Mackenzie. Things just aren't adding

up. A man doesn't walk away from a committed relationship, especially not from his fiancée after a
disagreement."

Ever since Rhoda solved a Rubik's Cube puzzle,
she thought she was a sleuth at anything. She hadn't
taken my previous hints that the subject was off
limits and detrimental to my mental recovery, so I
changed the subject to what I wanted to discuss.
"The upcoming production of *The Boys are Coming
Home* is a little more than a month away, but the
rush to complete the stage is demanding, and—"

"Friends don't play games with each other,
Mackenzie. Sister-girls don't speak in Morse code,
and saints don't shy away from the truth. Instead
of planning a fairytale wedding, you're in my
kitchen." Rhoda stood and began to pace the
floor, rubbing her chin. "We had to have missed
something."

Missed something? Evidently I missed a whole lot, I
thought to myself, but didn't voice it. "Should I remind you I'm in Chicago to work at the prestigious
Goodman Theatre for an opportunity of a lifetime?"

"Mack, I thought the chance at love was the opportunity of a lifetime. I remember one minister
saying, in a lifetime, a person must seize the opportunity."

"Rhoda, I've dissected and reconstructed the
scenario I don't know how many times." Closing
my eyes, I rubbed my temples. "I still can't get over
my shock that he yelled at me then the coward
left." I sniffed. "Do you have something in the
oven?"

Rhoda jumped and raced to the stove. "Girl, the man is deaf." She pulled a charred apple pie from the oven. There went our dessert.

"Small technicality," I said with as much attitude as I could put together on short notice. It was a toss up if my friend or the conversation was beginning to annoy me. Her interrogation was making me think twice about making Chicago my home. Rhoda was determined to be multiple thorns in my sides and back. Suddenly, Momma's wise words floated through my head—all things in life are important, but go after the most important. *That is exactly what I plan to do, Momma,* I thought. Although the seed of Noel's love would continue to grow, that didn't mean I couldn't constantly prune it.

"What's the worst thing the brother could've done?" Rhoda was determined to pry until I totally confessed.

"Without faith, it is impossible to please God. Noel knew every scripture about faith, yet he lacked the evidence to believe God for his own miracle."

"Excuse me?"

"Noel missed his opportunity for a healing, Rhoda. If it was me, I would've been the first one in line. I just don't understand."

"I see."

I waited impatiently for Rhoda to become as outraged as I had. "Is that all you have to say?" I hissed, lifting a curious brow.

"Well, faith does come by hearing."

"Rhoda, tell me something I don't already know."

"I'm not talking about hearing physically. I'm talking about spiritually. God gives us allowance for our imperfections. You didn't. Noel has insecurities, and you should've respected his right to work it out."

"Listen, Rhoda, don't tell me couples don't have disagreements. I know you and William haven't always agreed on everything."

"Very few, but we've never stopped talking to or loving each other."

"You're not hearing me. All this time I thought Noel was walking by faith, seeking God in every area of his life. Where was his faith that night?"

"Is that what you truly believe, Mackenzie? Because the Bible says God gives everyone a measure of faith, a measure." She demonstrated by calculating the small space between two fingers again and increasing the space. "Does every person who is involved in an accident recover? People who are sick and dying are begging for a healing to live, and some have not only faith, but also have confidence in God that He will do it. I think you were wrong to question his faith."

Fingering my napkin, I was embarrassed to admit it. "I thought about it after the fact, but I mean, even if God didn't heal him, I think Noel should've still walked to the altar and proved God. Anyway, as I've told you, I tried to apologize. I wanted to understand what was going on in Noel's mind, but he didn't return my texts or emails. If the man holds that type of grudge, then maybe Noel wasn't meant for me." I sniffed.

"A man doesn't profess his love, empty his pockets for a diamond ring, and then—" She reached across the table. For small delicate hands, her grip was tight and unforgiving. "Then explain this," she said, pointing to my ex-engagement ring. "The thing you keep twisting when you think I'm not looking. Why do you keep wearing it?"

"To keep hope alive?" I offered as a plausible guess before gritting my teeth.

CHAPTER 39

I removed my ring, and purchased a gold chain to wear instead. I didn't want to think or focus on anything but Goodman Theatre, which housed the Albert Ivar Theatre. The larger one had more than eight hundred seats; down the hall, doors opened to the small, more intimate Owen Bruner Theatre.

I couldn't wait to see how the individual efforts of the cast, stage crew, and director would eventually come together to transform Shakespeare's *Much Ado About Nothing* into the musical *The Boys are Coming Home*.

I arrived downtown after an hour commuter train ride. I answered my cell phone when it chimed without checking my caller ID. "Hello?"

"Guess who was at church yesterday? Noel," Valerie snitched before I could guess. When she got a hold of a piece of gossip, I was her first depository, which most of the time, I ignored. Sometimes, I did absorb the nonsense.

God, You know I can't handle it if Valerie's next

words are, and he was with . . . , I conversed with the Lord.

"Want to know what he asked me about?" Valerie supplied the answer. "You," she said displeased. "Yep, you heard me right."

"Me?" My hand patted my chest to soothe the unexpected palpitations. A few commuters gave me concerned stares, probably hoping I wouldn't suffer a heart attack and disrupt their rehearsed walking route to work. I couldn't decide if my estranged fiancé's query annoyed me or flattered me. "Valerie, please don't tell him anything."

"Don't worry, I won't. Girl, I've got your back. Hey, I've got to go. I just got to my desk." Valerie disconnected without a goodbye.

Curiosity nagged me, but pride slapped some sense in me not to linger on that call. I walked through Goodman's glass doors as if I hadn't spoken to Valerie. Later, I fought back tears as I watched the portrayal of the interracial love affair between Brad and Maggie in *The Boys are Coming Home.*

Valerie didn't call again that week, and Sunday morning, I looked forward to whatever sermon Rhoda's pastor delivered. Mark 4 was a simple message, but he gave it a whole new meaning.

"Saints, did you ever notice that when you plant grass seeds, weeds will sprout and try to choke out the grass? How could that be when we don't plant weed seeds? As a matter of fact, I don't know any nurseries that sell bags of the landscaping nuisance, but with every good blade of grass, watch out for the weeds. Seeds need to be monitored and nourished," Elder Melvin Clark preached, waving his Bible in the air from the pulpit.

He continued, "God talks about the ground or the receiver of the seed, but I'm challenging the planter today—yes, you. Are you throwing God's Word out there, or are you taking your time and searching for the perfect spot to build your garden?"

While I performed a self examination on my techniques of witnessing, my gaze strayed to the church's Deaf Ministry, made up of three people and one interpreter. My heart yearned to participate.

Rhoda nudged me. "You're missing him, aren't you?"

I blinked, irritated by her intuition more than the interruption. Shrugging, I looked at the preacher. "I miss interpreting," I corrected.

Rhoda lifted a brow, twisting her lips. "Humph, lying in church."

William, who was sitting on the other side of Rhoda, squeezed her fingers, shhhing us before winking at Rhoda, then me.

After the benediction, William treated us to dinner. An hour or so later, we returned to Rhoda's townhouse where we relaxed in the living room. The pair huddled on the sofa. I chose the ottoman as my back support and the floor as my cushion as we enjoyed the jazz music serenading from Rhoda's High-Def TV.

"What attracted you to Noel?" William asked out of nowhere.

I lifted a brow in suspicion. Now, Rhoda was

putting William up to do her dirty work. What more was there to tell? So I rehashed what Rhoda already knew. As a smart aleck, I closed my eyes and lifted my hands and signed, *"Noel approached me after I helped serve Thanksgiving dinner at church and manipulated his voice to a hushed tone, almost like a whisper in my ear. I could've slid off my chair like spilled milk. After that, God is my witness. I was hooked. The magnetism was strong from the beginning. I enjoyed signing to and with him, yet I would rather talk to him just to listen to his voice."*

"Yeah, I could tell from our conversations you were hooked," Rhoda interrupted.

My lids shot open. "You understood me? When did you . . . how did . . . why?" I stuttered flabbergasted.

Shrugging, Rhoda played the game. "I figured if my best friend's man was deaf, then it was my responsibility to learn how to communicate on his territory. I only recognized a few phrases, but enough. I took an introduction class and I have a few how-to-sign books."

Tears floated in my eyes. I sniffed to contain them. I was overwhelmed with so many emotions. "Rhoda, I don't know what to say except thank you. I'm just sorry it was in vain."

CHAPTER 40

My mouth confessed that Noel Richardson was history, but my heart—the stubborn thing—tightened its muscles and refused to provide life support. It became mental warfare as the two battled for dominance, and Matthew 12:34-37 gave my heart the ammunition. . . . *out of the abundance of the heart the mouth speakeath . . . every idle word that men shall speak, they shall give account thereof in the Day of Judgment . . . and by thy words thou shalt be condemned.* That was enough for me to shut my mouth until the rapture.

In the kitchen, Rhoda saluted with a smile.

"Good morning to you, sista," I responded, grinning. As a fellow teacher, Rhoda frowned upon the use of slang. I did, too, but it was fun to tease her. She occupied her summers teaching English as a second language to recent immigrants.

She removed blueberry pancakes from the skillet, buttered them, and created a lopsided masterpiece. As she carried two plates to the table, I did my part by filling two glasses on the counter with grape juice. Tasks completed, we took our positions.

With our heads bowed, Rhoda blessed our food. "Amen," we said in unison.

Squinting, Rhoda scrutinized me before she spoke. "You look cute today, Mack. As a matter of fact, you've been a different woman lately . . . your choice of clothes are colorful, and airy. You even have coordinating shoes, you're wearing your hair long and straight, and you seem more content. Hmmm, something is up with you."

Smiling, I accepted her compliment and kept eating. Rhoda sighed as if she was waiting for me to divulge a revelation. I had nothing new to report. I was becoming my old self again.

"So, how's work?"

Swallowing the last of my spongy pancakes, I dabbed my lips. "Awesome. The theatre has sophisticated trap doors, and fly spaces to create vibrant, reach-out-and-touch scenes. One stage manager borrowed her great-grandmother's bed for a 1945 scene."

"You're kidding." Rhoda rested her elbow on the table and listened with fascination.

I shook my head. "Then, there's the cast who are born singers. They dance as if their first steps were in tap shoes."

Shaking her head, Rhoda chuckled. "You get so excited about the theatre."

"Not any more than teachers when their students excel."

"I would've fought for my man."

"What?" I frowned.

"There is no way I would've let Heath pull that stunt on me. Girl, I would've gone to his work site and shut down the entire construction job until he and every worker heard me out," Rhoda paused, laying her hands on top of mine. "Mack, don't be mad. I'm just telling you what I would've done."

"You've known me long enough to know that I don't chase after a man. I'm not a desperate housewife, fiancée, or hoochie mamma. I've packed up, shipped out, and moved on."

When God closes one door, another one opens. Alexander Graham Bell perhaps knew what he was talking about, and despite who said it, I welcomed a crack in the door.

Maybe my co-worker, Todd Daniels, was that crack. He was a nice guy, good-looking, and church-going. A transplant from Houston, he was a designer's assistant at Goodman. A day didn't go by where he didn't compliment my attire, encourage a smile, or engage me in a production decision.

More than once he invited me to lunch, which I always declined, but Todd was wearing down my resistance as he cornered me the moment I stepped off the elevator.

"Hey, Mackie," Todd teased. At first, I considered his pet name a pet peeve. Now I enjoyed hearing the endearment. His habit of invading my space forced me to come in contact with his nameless cologne. At least he smelled good. "Are you hungry?"

My stomach growled; answering before my lips lied. Grinning, I blushed with embarrassment, which made his eyes danced with mischief.

Grabbing my hand, he tugged me toward the lobby. "I'll take that as a yes. A bunch of us are going around the corner for a quick bite." He smiled, exhibiting a slightly chipped front tooth.

I squinted and admired his clean-shaven face. *Maybe,* my mind softly suggested, *just maybe it was safe to dive into the dating pool. If nothing else, I could dip my toes in the water.* It was time to let my guard down. Todd and I were becoming more than casual co-workers, we were on the road to being good friends.

"You look pretty today and . . ." he stopped, holding up a calloused finger, "you smell good and . . ." he paused again and wiggled another finger, "I like your hair straight." He leaned closer. "Are you flattered?"

As a matter of fact, I was, but I would never admit to it. I imagined that instead of tagging along for lunch, we were practicing a prelude to an "I'll pick you up at seven o'clock" date. That's when my heart called for intermission, slapping vessels together to rush blood to my brain. It wanted to remind me that Noel's ring was dangling from a chain close to my heart. Actually, it was stuffed in my brassiere. A woman can never be too careful.

Slapping his arm, I laughed instead of giving him an answer as my stomach roared again. "If we don't eat soon, I'll go to the vending machine and buy a bagel."

"Never on the first date."

Date? I silently repeated. It was just a figure of speech, nothing more than friendly banter. He continued to escort me to Goodman's main entrance where we met other crew members. Once outside on North Dearborn, a tall, nicer looking, and better dressed man approached Todd.

Recognizing the stranger, they engaged in the fist toast and quick hug, completing the indoctrination with the thumps on their backs. When they stood back, Todd acknowledged my presence. "Mackenzie, wait. I want you to meet a friend of mine—"

He cut Todd off, extending his hand. "Friends call me B. Feel free."

"Okay. Hello, Dee." I accepted the handshake that seemed more as a caress.

His chuckle reminded me of a grunt. "It's B as in better." His wandering eyes suggested he wanted to say more.

I left them to their reunion and caught up with the others. We rounded the corner to our destination then came to a disappointing halt. The café was crowded. Barely inside, we squinted, strained our necks, becoming vultures as we scrambled to claim two tables as soon as patrons stood and evacuated the coveted spots.

Some of us were makeshift post guards at tables while Todd and others eased into line to place multiple orders. When Todd finally brought our orders to the table, he commanded the attention of more than one woman's eyes without trying, and I joined them in admiration.

I returned Todd's smile as he laid down the tray laden with food. Todd's persona outside the the-

atre walls was very appealing. *Humph, Noel, who?* I
teased to myself. Fondling with the chain on my
neck, my hand brushed against the outline of the
ring under my blouse. *Yeah, you know Noel who,* my
heart tossed back.

Katie Bell, a sweet, quiet, and talented set designer, scooted me inside the booth, forcing Todd
and his friend to sit together. I bowed my head to
say grace, but crunches and smacks interrupted me.
Still, I refused to open my eyes until I said, "Amen."
Across the table, two pairs of eyes competed for my
attention.

"Mackenzie, you have a dazzling smile," Todd's
friend stated, grunting.

I almost spilled my chicken and wild rice soup at
the unexpected compliment. "Thank you, Paul,
right?"

"It's B. I know how initial introductions can be,
so let me give you a few tidbits about me, so I'll
stand out from the competition. I'm an analyst at
Citadel in the Financial District a few blocks from
here." He paused, releasing a slight grunt. "I've
paid a pretty penny for a condo on Lake Shore
Drive. My other assets—"

Todd cut him off with a slight shove of his
elbow. "So, Mackie, are you planning to stay in
Chicago for the winter production of the *Christmas
Carol?*" he asked after stabbing his salad burdened
with every conceivable artery clogging enhance-
ment and high sodium topping that was off limits
to health conscious eaters.

Opening his mouth, Todd widened it to swallow
every portion of blue cheese, olives, chunks of

bacon, salami, ham, and heaps of poppy seed dressing that could fill a soup bowl. I'd never seen a person barely chew and swallow with ease.

After taking a few bites of my ham sandwich, I dabbed my mouth. "I haven't made up my mind."

Todd lifted his glass of ice tea. If he took a sip, I missed it. "Well, let me help make up your mind. You know the *Christmas Carol* is a props-heavy production, using more than one hundred pieces to make the scene come alive.

I'm sure he could see my mouth salivating.

His nostrils flared. "Oooh, I love it when I have your undivided attention. Mackie, I know you can visualize the scenes, locations, and time periods. The director is meticulous about detail—pillows, slippers, a tissue box on a nightstand, coins from a man's pocket, old furniture, squeaky floor planks, and on and on. Of course, the production could take months, but . . ." he paused and shrugged. "Perfection takes time . . ." An untamed belch interrupted his spiel and our appetites.

As if on cue, Katie Bell and I slid our meals closer to us, fearing contamination. Two smaller tremors followed before he begged our pardon.

"Sorry, I don't have a gall bladder."

I nodded, scribbling a mental note. *Never go with Todd to breakfast, lunch, or dinner again, and get him some Tums.*

His friend tried to recover the repartee after Todd's temporary medical emergency. "I hope you do. I personally would like to see more of you, Mackie."

"Well, that's not going to happen. She'll be busy

working with me, and don't call her that. To you, it's Mackenzie," Todd finished with his signature grunt.

Oh, boy. I tried not to roll my eyes. Todd needed to switch to a high protein diet. I hoped B didn't have gas, too, as he laid his fork quietly on a napkin. His mannerism was a stark contrast from Todd's. When he smiled and tilted his head, his five-o'clock shadow flirted with me. His voice was almost as baritone as Noel's.

"Actually, my name is Ben."

My eyes bucked. *Oh no,* I groaned inwardly, the name synonymous with Valerie's fantasies. If she was here with me, she would accuse me of being a career man stealer. Back to opening the doors, Lord, please shut these quick.

It was almost eleven at night by the time I returned to Rhoda's home. I let myself in, and climbed the steps. I smirked when I checked in on Rhoda, who was snoring. Wait until William discovered that not only was he getting a sleeping beauty, but a snoring one at that. Closing her door, I went across the hall and retired to my bedroom.

The next morning, I hummed as I walked through the door to Rhoda's kitchen. Despite me getting into bed late, I woke refreshed and had a good morning prayer. "Good morning, my sista."

Rhoda whirled around and braced her back against the counter, startling me. "I was praying last night, Mack."

Squinting, I patted my chest. "Whew, girl, you scared me." I relaxed and strolled to the stove. I filled my plate with turkey sausage, biscuits, and hash browns, but if I developed gas, hash browns would be history. "Yeah, me, too, and I think God is telling me to stay in Chicago. Instead of putting your townhouse on the market, you can sell it to me. I may even continue graduate school at Roosevelt University and splurge to buy a new car." I stopped rambling, blessed my food, and walked to the table.

"No."

I chewed and swallowed, trying to digest what Rhoda just said. "No, what?"

"Go home, Mackenzie."

"It was just an idea. I can find another place, and—"

Rhoda walked to the table and leaned into my face. Her hand stayed my arms. Her eyes shined with compassion, and her face filled with love. Rhoda spoke in a soft and nonthreatening tone. "Mack, God told me to tell you to go home to St. Louis."

"Rhoda, that's ridiculous. That's not the message God gave me."

She folded her arms. "Okay, what message did God give you?"

"I don't know, but that wasn't it."

It had been nearly a week, and Rhoda hadn't said another word about me leaving. *Good.* Then, to my surprise, Noel started texting me. My heart fluttered every time it buzzed, but I refused to open his messages. Everything was falling in place with Goodman, so there was no need to rock the boat. Working on the set of *The Christmas Carol* was within my reach.

One morning, on my way to work, my cell chimed as I was exiting the Metra. "Hello."

"He's back."

"Valerie? Well, good morning to you—?"

"Noel and . . . the other woman," she informed me as a dutiful secretary.

My heart dropped. When I thought about Noel, I became indignant. I wanted him to chase me, beg me to forgive him, apologize over and over again until I was satisfied. It was a juvenile game, but it was a game I wanted to win.

Three hundred miles away and Valerie was still stirring the pot with Noel ingredients. My shoulders slumped, but I recovered when I almost stumbled from my unsteady legs. A man gently lifted me and moved me to the side.

"You all right?" he asked with a smile snatched off Noel's lips. The stranger didn't wait for my answer as he continued on his way. In a delayed reaction, my head nodded. Pushing my cell phone closer to my ear, I strained to follow Valerie's rambling.

". . . and girl, let me tell you, they were all cozy, constantly nudging each other and smiling. I was watching them. It was disgusting, but I have to give it to him. He has good taste. I think she's deaf, too, and she's white. I guess he felt more comfortable sticking to his own kind."

The news left me disoriented. So Noel had found a replacement before I did, and he had the nerve to bring another woman up into my church while I was away in Chicago. *Forget convincing myself that I had gotten over him,* I fumed to myself. He had already dismissed me. Humph! I had one foot dipped into the street then I jumped back. Good thing. Chicago cabs don't brake or honk. Pedestrians entered the intersections at their own risk. "Valerie, Noel's not white."

"But he's deaf, girl. I thought you would want to know," she rushed and disconnected.

If I hadn't renewed my contract with Verizon, I would have hurled my cell phone in the street. "I can't believe this," I raised my voice, interrupting a homeless man's nap. His cup rattled before his eyes opened. I dropped two dollars in his offering plate and kept going.

CHAPTER 41

"Lord, you set me up," were the last accusatory words on my lips as I climbed into bed last night. "Why did you set me up, Lord?" was the first question I uttered as I slid out of the bed to pray this morning. What was wrong with me? If I was truly over a man, then why was this news loosening the Band-Aid on my bleeding heart?

Once again, while on my knees, I struggled to look beyond the hurt and thank God for what He had done for me already. I prayed until my face became damp. Sniffing, I said, "Amen." Commanding one leg, then the other to stand, I patted my cheeks on the way to the bathroom.

Blinking, I faced the scary sight in the mirror. Shutting my eyes, I backed away, screaming. Rhoda's bare feet scrambled up the hardwood stairs to my bedroom door. I removed unsteady hands from my face as she entered with a rolling pin. With one glance, she released the utensil, causing it to ricochet off the floor. It tagged a crystal lamp shade like a pinball before attacking my toe where it came to rest.

Rhoda screamed, "Aaaaahhhh," as I yelled to match her hollering. I hopped around on one foot squeezing my baby toe. Rhoda kept shrieking. Finally, I limped back to the bed and collapsed.

Slowly, Rhoda approached my body and examined the damage. "Whew, Mack, I forgot how bad you look in the morning when you've cried all night. You've done some major damage this time. Your hair has taken Mohawk to a whole new level."

Moaning, I massaged my foot. "Right now, I'm concerned about your rolling pin hitting my toe. My eyes and nose haven't been this swollen since college—and my lips—they look like I overdosed on collagen."

Rhoda turned to leave the room. "Where are you going?"

"To get sunglasses, cucumbers, ice packs, and a wide-tooth Afro pick."

My eyes drifted close. "God, I'm sorry I disrespected you. I repent. I know you didn't set me up, the devil did." Rhoda returned quickly and sat next to me as I mumbled.

"Mack, Mack, you're not going in and out of consciousness, are you?"

Twisting my mouth, I answered sarcastically. "No, I'm not, Nurse Rhoda." Then I felt chilled flying-saucer-slices of cucumbers on my eyes. Through a blurred slit, I couldn't believe it, Rhoda *was* wearing sunglasses. She continued, placing a plastic cold pack on my nose and a freezing cold towel on my mouth. Her method of detangling my hair was soothing and gentle.

"Mack, I'm sorry if I upset you when I said you should go home. You know I'd never say anything to hurt your feelings, don't you? I've got your back on any decisions you make. You know that don't you? Don't you—"

How was I to respond when Rhoda's arctic home remedy was numbing my face? It was the same as being reclined in a chair and the dentist making small talk while drilling in my mouth. I couldn't blame Rhoda. I was responsible for my plight. The combination of bawling my heart out, blowing my nose unmercifully, and a tormented spirit that induced lack of sleep, created a never-before-seen Halloween mask. Crying in college over a worthless athlete never had this end result.

When she removed the frigid towel from my lips, I explained. "Rhoda, it wasn't you. Valerie, from my church, told me Noel has a new girl-friend. He's moved on, Rhoda, he's moved on," I repeated only for verification to my own ears. When I took a deep breath, I began to gasp for air.

She patted my arm. "Mack, don't work yourself up into another frenzy. You've shed enough tears over that man. I'm getting mad now."

"Rhoda, I'm not getting worked up about Noel. Will you remove these ice packs from my nose? I can't breathe."

"Oh."

Rhoda patched me up to look presentable. However, she couldn't help mend me mentally or spiritually. God would have to heal that. She lent me her copy of *Daily Inspiration for Women of Color* to read on my commuter train ride. Philippians 4:8-9 urged me to meditate and consider all things good and positive.

Closing my eyes, I asked the Lord to remind me of the honest, pure, and virtuous people and things in my life. Before I knew it, I was downtown when the theme from "Star Wars" played on my cell phone. "Hi, Daddy."

"Good morning, baby, you doing okay?" Daddy cleared his throat. "He called."

"Who?"

"That Richardson boy, he's worse than a tele-marketer. He called three times. Actually, it was an interpreter. He should've been at church—at least, that time of day. You would've been."

Noel had waited more than a month to start tex-ting me. Then he returns to church with a woman in tow, and now he wants to get a hold of me. Be-fore I left for Chicago, it seemed as if I held my breath, waiting to hear from Noel. I was checking my emails even after I came to Chicago. All of a sudden, he wants to talk, which would've been fine until Valerie mentioned another woman. Then, feeling like a fool, my dignity rebuked him, be-cause apparently he had moved on before me. "I'm sorry, Dad."

Daddy continued to complain about Noel, and a few times, I almost joined in, but Noel wasn't worth elevating my blood pressure that was consis-tently normal. Once Daddy ran out of steam, we disconnected. Immediately, my cell phone chimed again—Valerie. I took a deep breath. Now what? "Hello?"

"That's two Sundays in a row, and get this, he had the nerve to introduce me to her after service." Valerie paused. "Let's see. Her name is Lana, Liza, or Leah, or something like that."

I didn't want to hear this, yet I listened anyway until I reached the theatre and gripped the door's handle. "I've got to go."

"Hey, no problem, sista. I'll keep you posted."

Yeah, I was afraid of that. Seconds away from hitting END on the call, Valerie screamed into my ear.

"Oh, Mack, wait. I'm engaged!"

"What?" *Valerie's engaged? Oh, the poor man,* I thought. Rhoda has William, Noel has his "L" woman, and now Valerie. I wasn't even eligible for admission to Noah's Ark. Every person and animal seemed paired off except me. *Lord, if the world was coming to an end, Lord, please take me first in the rapture,* I thought. "That's wonderful. Who is—"

"Nick, silly. God sent him."

I was having a bad day, and it didn't seem like it was going to get any better.

Saturday was the day of my reckoning. I needed a year of fasting to help Rhoda prepare for her upcoming nuptials. I took in a deep breath. The "I am woman, hear me roar" motto was not working. I barely had enough emotional strength for a meow.

Strapped inside Rhoda's Dodge Charger—an engagement gift, courtesy of William—Rhoda maneuvered between cars on the highway like an ice skater. Once downtown, we could've treated three people to lunch at McDonalds with what it cost to park. It wasn't that I was cheap as some have called me. I was practical, and commuting on the train downtown made more sense. Getting out of her car, we walked a few short blocks to our first destination—K & K Flowers on South La Salle Street. Rhoda showed me the bouquets in the paper, but the photos couldn't illustrate the beauty God had created.

When we walked inside, the presentation of floral arrangements and sweet fragrances fought for our attention. Rhoda gravitated toward a display of white roses, freesia, and orchid stems with stephanotis. The spray was astonishing. The others bowed to its brilliance. "Rhoda, if you don't pick these . . ." *then I would,* I thought. Of course, that was only if I was still getting married.

Rhoda rubbed my arm. "I'm sorry, Mack. I tried not to talk about mine, but I couldn't wait anymore."

The sales consultant approached us. "Miss Brownlee, the stephanotises are out of season in December. Unfortunately, it will cost you more."

Rhoda looked from the woman to me for advice. Displaying a genuine happy face for my dear friend, I shrugged. "Don't look at me. I'm just a bridesmaid, not the bride."

Exasperated, Rhoda gritted her teeth before stating, "I don't have any bridesmaids. You and William's cousin are my maid of honor and matron of honor."

"Oh, yeah. I forgot."

"I really like the stephanotises," she mumbled,

caressing the petals, "but I need to stay within my budget. Can you work with fewer flowers and still create the cascading effect?"

"Of course, Miss Brownlee."

Rhoda selected the flowers, and paid the two hundred dollar deposit. Then we jumped back in the car and drove to preview a few banquet halls. Not impressed, Rhoda's next mission was the bridal shop and I dreaded that stop.

I had my reasons for sitting in the viewing area, bawling. With each breath I sucked in, more tears fell. Rhoda had attempted to console me. Two sales women handed me tissue and a glass of water, trying to quiet me before I disturbed other clients. Folding her arms and tapping a shoe, Rhoda traded her concern for an annoyed expression. "This is a fitting, Mackenzie, not a funeral. You're embarrassing me," she hissed.

"I can't help it," I whined, sniffing. Rhoda's assistant re-appeared with a new travel-size box of Kleenex. "It just isn't fair. That dress is identical, right down to the designer that I considered for my wedding. Thank God I hadn't put down a deposit." Out of more than two thousand styles of bridal dresses, and Rhoda and I had picked the same Cynthia C designer gown. What were the odds of that?

"Go home to St. Louis, Mackenzie."

"But—"

"No, buts. Tech week is ending and you said the previews are next week. You're practically finished with the play. Pack up your stuff and go home."

CHAPTER 42

Tears blurred my eyes. After all the hard work and long tedious hours, the finished set for the play was indescribable. The music was so energetic that I hummed some of the lyrics all day. I praised God for allowing me to be part of something so magnificent.

Later that evening when I parked in Rhoda's driveway, I heard voices. They were loud and angry as I slammed the car door. Tilting my head, I strained to follow the direction of the quarrel. By the time I reached Rhoda's porch, the voices grew louder.

Alarmed, I checked the address, 256 Storm Court. I had only passed by it once, and that was a night it was so dark I thought she had moved her house. I braced myself to charge the door like at a detective on a *CSI* episode. My kickboxing skills were downplayed when I used too much force on a door that wasn't quite closed, propelling me to literally slide into the foyer and roll over like a dog. Recovering, I tried to stand, but the hem of the ankle length skirt snagged on my sandal's heel. Forget it. I sat on the floor.

William and Rhoda were arguing? William's words were accusatory and threatening. Rhoda executed rapid responses that sounded scary, too. I had never heard him raise an octave to Rhoda. What was going on? William wouldn't harm Rhoda, but why was he so mad? Maybe I did walk, or roll, into the wrong house.

"God, Rhoda, I cannot believe you did that. Here I'm working my tail off building you exactly what *you* said *you* wanted, and you go off and put a deposit on a spec house." William's fist pounded a wall or countertop. The force echoed.

Interesting, maybe Rhoda was going to sell me her townhouse, I thought, but she never mentioned anything.

"Heath, you act like I intentionally backstabbed you. You know that I've visited display homes for decorating ideas. I walked into this Sahara home model, and I didn't want to leave." Rhoda's voice shook with awe. "I just thought I was taking some pressure off you."

"Really? Well, guess what, baby? It's too late for that. I enjoy creating things with my hands, molding things to your specifications. It's an honor to have built you a simple attic getaway room. I could've added a boat house or an underground bowling alley for that matter. All you had to do was tell me."

"Humph!" She paused. "Well, excuse me for thinking I was being considerate."

"Yeah, excuse you, baby, because you weren't thinking!"

"Let me tell you something, William Wilkerson . . ."

Oooh, she's using the "W" word. If she was calling him William, Rhoda had to be hot. I made myself comfortable.

". . . if you're getting that upset about something that can easily be fixed, then maybe we aren't compatible. You need to change your attitude on how we deal with a disagreement."

"My attitude?" William shouted louder than he did when I first barged into the house. "Let me tell you something, my petite black beauty."

"Oh, so now you're calling me names," Rhoda shouted.

Whew, this argument was a good one. I became a cheerleader, pumping my fist in the air. Silently, I refereed, encouraging Rhoda to sic him.

"Name calling? You listen to me, my little Nubian princess. It's your heart and mind I desire. I love the feel of your smooth dark skin. Do you have a problem with that, because I envisioned our children with our skin, our hair, and our eyes . . . do you have a problem with that?"

"Heath, don't make me look like I'm the antagonist. You were the one who came in here, yelling and screaming at me without asking for an explanation. I know I shouldn't have used our joint account for that deposit."

"I'm leaving, because if I don't, I may say something to really make me withdraw my proposal . . . goodbye."

"Get out of my house until I can calm down," her cracked voice managed a scream.

"Fine!" William slammed his fist like a sledge hammer on her table or counter. Regardless, I was sure that something had a dent in it. His hard boots shook the ground as they moved across the kitchen floor. *Take cover*, my mind shouted as I scrambled to get up. My eyes darted around the room. The closet was the most conspicuous, providing Rhoda didn't have something crammed inside. I made a dash for it as William's heavy footsteps grew louder.

Rhoda's clicking heels that followed stopped. Quietness descended around me. I sucked in my breath. "Baby, this is stupid. We, you and I, didn't handle this right. I can't leave like this. Forgive me. If you really want that other house, I'll finish the other one and sell it."

"Ahhh," I sighed.

Rhoda waited to respond. "Maybe I didn't think it through. I'll get our money back."

"We've never had a blow up like this. Something's going on that is beyond our control. What it is? We need to ask God to keep us."

"Ahhh," I sighed softer, craving what Rhoda was getting from William—love.

"Did I mention how much I love you? Come here, girl."

I stuck my ear to the closet door, listening. Shoot! She was whispering then her voice cracked or it could've been William's knee. I heard moans. They were making up and I was in the closet about to pass out, or suffocate.

"Jesus, I thank you for Rhoda. Give me wisdom to cherish her as the lady she is and watch what I say. James says *if any man among you seems to be reli-*

gious and bridleth not his tongue, but deceiveth his own heart, and my religion is in vain. Lord, help me not to utter idle words. Give me a mind to think before speaking . . ."

Partaking in their prayer, the Anointing fell on me. I broke free from the constraints of the closet. My prayer and praise mingled with theirs. Without any inhibition, I worshipped God until tears screamed down my face. I lifted my hand one more time as the last "Hallelujah" rolled off my lips. As my lids fluttered opened, I faced William and Rhoda. Reconciled, they were wrapped in a tight embrace, watching me.

"Oh, praise God. Thank you, Jesus . . . uh, I heard shouting and became concerned when I literally rolled in. I didn't want to intrude. I kinda hid when I heard William coming . . ." I rambled.

"Out," they said in unison, pointing to the front door.

Like a dejected stray dog, I didn't question their edict. I would get mad at them later for talking to me as if I were a child. Until then, I dragged my feet and headed for the door. I got into my car. Without looking back, I knew my destination—the closest 7-Eleven. Rhoda's jubilation was feeding my depression.

I waited two hours before returning to the town-house. William's SUV was gone. I exhaled; the coast was clear. Unlocking the door, I tiptoed inside and froze. My bags were neatly packed. I even recognized ones that weren't mine, but I had used during Christmas. Rhoda was stretched across the sofa with a leg swinging as if she was posing for a photographer. She slowly watched my approach.

"What's going on?" I asked, knowing the answer, and wondering how she crammed all my stuff into my suitcases and three of hers.

Rhoda stood, negotiated around my bags, and hugged me. "I love you, Mack, but it's time for you to go. God told me, I told you, and you haven't budged, so this is a way of Heath telling you. Your disobedience is rocking the boat—my ship. I've got to throw you overboard. God will help you to swim. He won't let you sink." She paused. "Heath and I have never had an argument like that before—never."

"Figures." I squeezed my lips. "What are you saying? I'm either Jonah in the whale or Peter with Jesus in the boat?"

She shook her head as tears spilled from her eyes. "I wouldn't call you Jonah or Peter, but you do know that I've put people out after some of my gatherings. Listen, Mack," she said, reaching for my hands, "I need to have peace, and you need to find peace. I love you, and I wouldn't do anything to put you in harm's way except when you stumbled out of my closet," she joked. "I don't know what is going on with Noel, but your life goes on with or without him. Weeping endureth for the night, but your morning will come and bring joy with it. God spoke light into existence and sliced through darkness. The only thing God has to do is speak, and it's a done deal. I pray that God will speak light into your life."

"I know."

We cried, sniffed, and prayed. "Okay, sista, I release you to God."

Stepping back, I gasped as I planted my hands on my hips. "What? You're using slang. Maybe there is hope for me."

Laughing, we looped our arms and marched to the kitchen. "How about a drink before you put me out, and I need something strong."

"I got it, fresh squeezed lemonade coming up."

"Rhoda, please tell me you didn't pack my PJs?"

"Would I do that?" She laughed and slid a tall glass in front of me.

"Yeah, you would, but that's okay. You know I'll raid your stuff for a T-shirt."

Late into the night, we talked about my summer at the Goodman, laughed at my antics of hiding in the closet, and I listened as she spoke of William. She asked me about Noel more than once, but I shook my head. "Nope, tonight it's all about you."

"Yeah, it is all about me," Rhoda teased.

The next morning, I woke surprisingly well rested. Dropping to my knees, I prayed, ending with accepting my fate, forgiving my trespassers, and moving on as Noel had done. I got up, showered, dressed, and gathered my unpacked toiletries.

William and Rhoda stood at the bottom of the steps, waiting for me. Their blissful smiles had returned. As soon as my shoes touched the landing, they engulfed me in a group hug. For a moment, I thought I was about to be thrown in my car.

I couldn't control the tears. William continued to hug me as Rhoda sauntered into the kitchen and returned with a bottle of Holy Oil. She anointed our heads, including hers. Bowing, we prayed for my happiness and a safe journey back home. Afterward, William lifted my bags and packed them neatly in the backseat of my car.

I turned and faced Rhoda. "What? No breakfast?"

She pushed me toward the door. "And ruin my reputation? Nah, I put a muffin, grapes, and a cup of vanilla flavored decaf in your car."

Thanks," I mumbled teasingly as I settled behind the wheel and strapped on my seatbelt. Standing behind William, Rhoda muffled her sniffling with a tissue. William's stone expression wasn't convincing. I looked away. I didn't want to cry anymore.

"While you were still sleeping, Little Mack, I had your oil changed, added air to your tires, checked your fluids, and filled up your gas tank. If you have any problems with old Gertrude, call me. I have a friend who works for AAA. One phone call and he's on his way. When you get home, get a new car. " William bent down and kissed me on my cheek. "You know I love you."

"I know."

"If Noel doesn't work out . . ."

"He didn't work out." I sniffled.

William's eyes brightened with hope. "I've got a buddy."

We chuckled. Bumping William out of the way, Rhoda bent down to hug through the car window. "I love you, Mack. God's got something for you."

I nodded as my tears fell anyway as we hugged again. Finally, I cleared my throat. "Well, I'd better go."

Rhoda stepped back into William's waiting arm, which hinged about her tiny waist instantly. Attempting a smile, I turned the ignition, looked behind me, and backed up. Giving one final wave, I drove off. As I glanced in my rearview mirror, Rhoda and William were dancing in the street.

CHAPTER 43

It took Noel Richardson one week to knock at my door. Through the peephole, my heart fluttered, my eyes feasted at the sight, and my mind screamed forgive, girl, and forget, but—wait a minute.

As the scorned woman, it was my right to refuse his two video conference call requests, turn off the Messenger option when I logged onto my computer, delete his emails—all twelve of them—including his text messages, but not before my traitorous eyes read, "I know I proposed, maybe too soon . . ."

As far as I was concerned, it took him long enough to show up on my front steps. Briefly, I debated if I should crack the door, or swing it open. Shrugging, I opened the door as though I was expecting him. We stared at each other. "God, I missed him," I whispered to myself.

The peep hole didn't see what I saw. My eyes reacquainted themselves with Noel's hazel eyes, traceable lips, and majestically built body hidden under black precision-pleated slacks and a white polo shirt. Draped with a poker face, I repeated to myself, "God, I missed this man."

Reality refreshed my memory as I stood face-to-face with the man who had hurt me. I struggled against bellowing the accusatory remarks I had stored in my heart. I over-powered my mouth and locked it, signing, *"What are you doing here, Noel?"*

"I don't know."

I would've laughed if it was a joke. I opened my mouth, ready to hurl three months of fury. Arching a freshly waxed brow, I ignored his puppy dog expression. *"Wrong answer."*

Taking a deep breath, he shook his head. "Mackenzie, that's not what I meant. Can I come in?" Noel stepped up into my doorway uninvited. He towered over me. His closeness was hypnotic as unfamiliar cologne tickled my nose. I wasn't ready for him to gain entry into my home or my heart.

He exhaled at the same time his hand rode the waves of his hair to his neck. When I didn't budge, his hand nervously rubbed his chin. "Mackenzie, I'm here to tell you I love you, to ask you to marry me again, to ask for your forgiveness, to explain what happened—"

I lifted my hand. "Hold up. Why don't you start with the last thing and tell me how it's connected to the first thing—you loving me." Folding my arms, I leaned against the door frame. "Convince me that you ever loved me."

"Can I at least come in?" His eyes held determination. It was a battle between forgiveness and stubbornness. He rubbed his chest with his right hand, signing, *"Please."*

Arms still interlocked, I twirled around, hinting for him to follow. I concentrated on walking and focusing on the sofa. I couldn't recall a time after we started dating that Noel and I didn't touch. He would play with the curls in my hair, stroke my cheek, or play with my fingers as we signed to each other.

If Noel touched me now, I would lose my dignity and forget about our argument. Yet, my body pouted as it anticipated his touch. I sat and expected him to take a seat. He didn't.

"I don't know if you can repair my broken heart," I strained. Thank God, Noel couldn't hear how pathetic I sounded.

Water filled my eyes. Looking at the splendid specimen God had breathed into life, I saw flashbacks—Noel, the man who proposed. Noel—the man who stormed from my house and never looked back, and Noel—the man, who according to Valerie, had another woman. *"Ricky, you've got a lot of explaining to do,"* I signed and folded my arms again with as much attitude as God gave a black woman.

"Ricky, who's Ricky? I'm Noel." Concern etched across his face.

Chuckling, I waved my hand. *"Never mind, it's a line from an old 'I Love Lucy' show."*

Noel squatted in front of me. Hesitantly, he reached for my hands, steadying them with the stroke of his thumbs. "I was stubborn, proud, and arrogant—"

"Stupid," I added freely.

Nodding, he squeezed my fingers. "Okay, I'll accept that."

"Good." I squinted. "How about insensitive, in-considerate, a liar, a cheat and—"

He lifted his finger to my mouth and stilled my lips. "Whoa, baby, I've never lied to you, or cheated."

"Noel, what happened? You were enraged, yelling and shouting, and then without a goodbye, you marched out. You stopped going to church, and when you returned, you weren't alone."

"Mackenzie, the healing service left me a little upset, okay, angry—not at me—at God. That's no excuse for me to snap at you, baby. Can I use my deafness as an excuse for my outburst?"

"No, you can't."

Releasing my hands, he reached up, and with the back of his hand, rubbed my cheeks. Closing my eyes, I leaned into his hand. Sighing, I enjoyed the moment. Then my lids popped open. There were still questions I needed answered.

"Why were you mad at God?" I backed away from his contact.

Inhaling, Noel paused before exhaling. "Some-times – not all the times – when I witness God's miraculous healing power, I wonder why not me, Lord? The Spirit was so powerful. I felt that I really didn't need to be at the altar to get blessed. Just being in the crowd, I felt the anointing would spread. I was pretty arrogant, huh?"

"Yes."

"It took me a minute before I had recovered from my pity party. I'm sorry, Mackenzie. I shouldn't have taken that frustration out on you."

"Noel, it took you more than a minute, try months."

"I'm stupid, remember?"

"How could I forget?" This time I reached out and smoothed the unnoticeable fine hairs on his chin. Power and strength are sexy, but a man's vulnerability was endearing. Pulling his chin closer to my lips, I mouthed, "I love you." As I puckered for a kiss, I thought about the other woman.

Regaining the scornful woman attitude, I shoved him, causing him to lose his balance and fall back on his behind. He didn't try to get up. Instead, he drew his knees to his chest and dangled his arms from his knees.

"There was never another woman. As for our disagreement . . ."

I held up my finger to interrupt. *"Make no mistake about that day. It was a full blown argument,"* I signed slowly.

"You're right. Pride wouldn't let me admit that I was wrong and you were right for urging me to go to the evangelist. Embarrassment kept me from coming back, so I worshipped at my family's church for a while. Pierce interpreted for me when I couldn't read the preacher's lips since they still didn't have a Deaf Ministry, but it wasn't the same. Pierce wasn't you."

When he lowered his voice, he had no idea how sexy his whisper sounded to me that I could've fainted. "Okay, that explains where you've been. Now, about the other woman."

With so much emotion, he slowly signed, *"There could never be another Mackenzie. A lady visited my family's church, and when she saw Pierce signing for me, she came over and sat next to me. After a few Sundays, she said she wasn't coming back because she still didn't*

*feel a part of the worship service. That's when I invited
her to our church. I had no choice but to return and face
the lashing you would give me.*

Shrugging, I grinned and Noel's lips curled.
"Oh, you know me so well. Okay, you've apologized. You've explained. Where is my re-proposal?"

Then my dream abruptly ended. It always did
with the "proposal." Everything seemed so real
that I could reach out and touch Noel. Sighing, I
rolled over and squeezed my pillow. Moaning, I
smiled before my lids fluttered open. It was the
same fairytale that had visited me since the first
night I had returned home. The next morning, I
had cried, but I welcomed the fantasy.

Of course, I penciled in my desired answers, including Daddy appearing in the apparition and
tackling Noel. I've been tempted to pencil out that
part, but I figured Noel could use a little roughing
up.

Yawning, I wrestled with the covers. I stood and
stretched before going into the bathroom. After
coming out, I bent by my bed for my morning
prayer, ". . . whatever happens tomorrow at church,
I believe you'll give me strength to face it in Jesus;
Amen."

I showered, dressed, and was still taking curlers
out of my hair when the doorbell rang. Going
downstairs, I sucked in a deep breath before
reaching for the door handle.

"Valerie?"

"Yeah," she replied, popping her gum before
walking in without a welcome home hug or kiss to
the cheek. Squinting, she scanned my hair. "You
missed a curler. You seem disappointed. Whom

were you expecting, anyway? Remember I phoned earlier that I'd be over. You sounded drowsy, but you answered clearly, 'I can't wait to see you.'"

"Did I?" Closing the door, I led her to the kitchen. I laughed to myself. I could remember every detail about the dream, but I couldn't remember the phone ringing.

Claiming a chair at the table, Valerie rested her purse. Then my mind and nose began to play tricks on me. Valerie's perfume ridiculously smelled similar to what Noel was wearing in my dreams. I frowned. *Could a person smell in their dreams?* I wondered. She crossed her leg and folded her arms. "So . . . how was Chicago?" she asked, bored, then briefly distracted by sweets on the table.

"Go ahead, Valerie, help yourself."

"Thanks." With no shame, she reached for the cookie jar and twisted the lid free. While fighting with three headstrong sugar cookies, I noticed her ring. I had forgotten about her engagement. As she replaced the top, I took a good look at her. She wore heavier makeup and her hair was cut to feather around her face. Valerie's top was flirty with ruffles at her neck and sleeves.

To a stranger, she was beautiful and confident. To me, Valerie was pretty and never content despite the ring commanding her finger. Crumbs were still on her lips when she began fumbling with another jar tip until a few peppermints spilled on the table. I sighed and sat across from her. "Valerie, I know you didn't come over my house to eat."

She grabbed another cookie, and studied it, before nibbling. She mumbled between bites. "Got any milk?"

Lifting my brow, I became suspicious as I stood and headed for the refrigerator. After pouring her a glass, I reclaimed my seat. Even though Valerie ate a lot, she never seemed to gain weight. Always the dainty eater, it was unbelievable to see her devour cookies; gulp down a tall glass of milk before popping a peppermint into her mouth.

Tapping my finger on the table, Valerie's verbal silence was beginning to irritate me. "Uh, Valerie, is everything okay between you and Nick? What happened to make you go out with him in the first place? How did he propose? When is the wed—?"

Taking a deep breath, Valerie forced a smile as she dabbed the corners of her mouth. Looking me straight in the eye for the first time, she forced a photo-shoot smile. "Mackenzie, I'm so glad you're home. You really look good."

I rested against the back of my chair and frowned. Something wasn't right. Valerie was never this temperate. Lifting a brow, I was about to find the reason for her peculiar behavior, but she leaned toward me.

"Listen, I needed to bring you up to speed on what's going on at the church."

Always predictable, Valerie was ready to explode. *Tell me something positive,* I silently challenged her. *What about the sermons Elder Coleman had preached all summer? Why couldn't she recall the scriptures as she did the gossip?* I wanted to question her, but didn't. Planting my hands on the table, I pushed back. "I can wait, Valerie, please. I don't want to hear one word about anybody or anything.

I can't constantly chew off what you're feeding me. Noel and I broke up. Whatever he's up to doesn't concern me."

Valerie smirked, rubbed her hands together. "Oh, this concerns you—"

"No. I mean it, Valerie. If you spread anymore gossip, true or false, I'm going to fellowship at another church. Of course, Pastor Coleman will want to know why, and I'll regret informing him that I'm trying to grow spiritually and you're one of the stumbling blocks."

Valerie responded to the threat by leaping up and overturning her empty glass that left a trail of milk on the table. Valerie's mouth dropped open—I wished I had an eraser to aim at it—she was speechless. She put her hands on her hips, which had spread a little during the summer. "Then you already know. You probably haven't heard all of it. Let me tell you my . . ."

"Valerie, please. Have you ever read any of 2 Thessalonians 3? *For we hear that there are some which walk among you disorderly, working not at all, but busybodies.*

"This time," she paused, her voice cracking, "it's about me." Tears fell down Valerie's cheeks. One landed on the table, absorbed by a forgotten cookie crumb.

What had Valerie Preston done this time? Concerned, I scooted back my chair and rounded the table to hug her. I didn't know what to say. "Valerie, please tell me . . . please tell me this isn't about something you did in the dark that has come to light. With or without the father, I'll stand by you."

Valerie broke free from my embrace. "Where did you hear that from?" Her eyes widened in shock. "Someone told you that I was pregnant? How could someone spread lies about me like that?"

Stunned at the hypocrisy of her question, I stuttered, "You're not pregnant?"

"No, what made you think that?" She frowned. There was no evidence of her tears.

"Oh." Embarrassed, I covered my mouth. If it wasn't for Valerie's gossiping, I would've assumed Valerie's second indiscretion would be yielding to moments of sexual weakness, because she desperately wanted a husband. Plus, I had seen her openly flaunt her endowments to some who were married and others who could've been unsaved.

Reverting back to her old self, she waved her arm in the air before she planted it on her hip. "I may be a lot of things, including a sexy saint, but I am not a fornicator. I'll have you know that I haven't slept with a man since God redeemed me . . . the second time. Humph!"

CHAPTER 44

"Okay, Valerie . . . that was too much information even for me. To keep me from making anymore assumptions, why don't you tell me the reason behind your thirty-second breakdown."

She huffed. "Okay, since you're prying information out of me, I'll tell you. I was upset because some saints have been going behind my back blabbing to the pastor that I've been creating division among members at church. Which is not true, I only tell what I know."

Swiping her purse off the table, Valerie stormed from the kitchen, but whirled around before reaching the front door. "Can you believe some elderly mothers at the church cornered me? I thought they were about to lay hands on me. Instead, they scolded me as if I was their child. You know I only had one mother."

"They should've laid their hands on you," I mumbled. Valerie's mouth must've done some serious damage while I was away. I looked over the fact that Valerie was more interested in the business going around the sanctuary than about God's business coming from the pulpit, but who was I to point fingers?

This trial with Noel had my flesh and spirit going back and forth. Physically, I wanted to slap him—what would that accomplish? Spiritually, I wanted to pray and fast him out of my system. I needed someone to talk with, but the more I thought about William and Rhoda, I developed an attitude about them putting me out in the time of need. Although Valerie befriended me when I first visited the church four years after graduating college, she was not the one.

"Now, I was respectful and didn't tell them to mind their own business, but whew . . ." Rolling her eyes, Valerie smacked her lips. "Let's just say, I know how to outrun them in these heels after I said what I felt like saying." Stretching out her leg, she showcased her stilettos. "The icing on the cake was . . ." she sighed as her voice faded, and sadness masked her face, "Pastor Coleman called me into his office. He listed one accusation after another. Finally, he asked me if the reports were true." She shrugged with an attitude building. "Some were. Some weren't."

"Valerie," I pleaded, "saints don't operate like that." I shook my head in frustration. Valerie didn't see anything wrong with casually repeating things she overheard to anyone who would listen, and I was one of them. I sighed. "Go on."

"Pastor Coleman removed me from all of my posts, the Deaf Ministry, the Singles Ministry, and the Kitchen Helping Hands."

"Oh." I wasn't surprised. She could be grounded

from all the church auxiliaries for a long time until she matured in Christ. I probably needed a seat beside her.

"Mackenzie, didn't you hear me? He sat me down for three months." Her nostrils flared. Her expression was perplexed. "You'll be the leader in the Deaf Ministry. Plus, you'll be weighed down with all my duties as counseling interpreter, deaf training, and recruitment. It will be ruthless with your schedule."

"Girl, I can handle that." Valerie frowned as I spoke without thinking. "Oh, I'm sorry, I wasn't here for you. Nick was by your side, right? What does he say about all this?"

She relaxed the stress lines on her face. "He's been in my corner ever since he proposed. C'mon, I'm ready to go. I can tell you all about Nick while we're shopping. When Pastor called me into his office, Nick accompanied me . . ."

She didn't hear me say let me grab my purse and finish combing my hair. When I reached the top of the stairs, she was still complaining. It was going to be a long day and I wished I had stayed in bed rather than agree to go shopping with Valerie.

When I came back downstairs, she was leaning against the door. Bypassing her to the kitchen, I cleared the table and deposited Valerie's dirty glass in the sink. "While we're out, I need to stop by Kmart to get some extra school supplies for my classroom," I yelled. "I don't want to wait until the last minute and the sales are gone."

"Sure, I want to bring you up to date on Noel anyway."

"Please don't," I said, groaning. "You're supposed to be a recovering gossiper, remember?" *Lord, I need another friend,* I thought. Valerie drove, and during the spree, she talked about the virtues of Nick, how God had him for her all along, and Noel had almost tricked her. We shopped at Macy's and Dillard's before we made it to Kmart. I was in the school supply aisle when she mentioned Noel's name.

"Listen, Valerie, I can't take it anymore. I hate to become your last friend standing, but you're poisoning our friendship with this mess."

She confessed, "I really can't help it, Mack. I think I've got diarrhea of the mouth."

"Valerie, you don't need a prescription to buy Imodium AD—"

"Mackenzie."

The voice was unmistakable. My heart pumped faster. I turned like a radio-controlled robot. Noel's hazel eyes confirmed what I already knew, and this wasn't a scene from a dream. Without moving, his cologne attacked me from a distance.

Valerie poked me several times in my arm. "This is hard for me, Mackenzie, but I'm going to fight the temptation to stay and eavesdrop on this conversation so I'll see you in a minute, okay?"

Maybe I nodded, but I never answered. Noel held my attention as he quietly stepped closer. Somehow, he was more handsome, buffer, and . . . oh my, he was wearing a beard. His black shirt and pants magnified his upgraded looks. This wasn't a hallucination. "Noel."

"Mackenzie, can we talk?" he signed.

His confidence irked me. Didn't an argument divide us? Didn't time and distance widen our separation? Even though I had been back a week, I wasn't ready for this encounter. It was too sudden for me. I hadn't had a chance to rehearse my lines or build up my resistance. I still loved him, but he didn't appreciate me. I wanted to cry. I wanted to pray. I thought about screaming, yelling, or punching him. My initial shock faded. *"How did you know I was here?"* I signed then crossed my arms. I didn't blink as I started to construct my wall.

"I saw you get out of Valerie's car as I was parking my car not far away. I didn't recognize you at first because your hair is longer, but you'll never lose your curls. God, Mackenzie, you are so beautiful. I wasn't leaving Kmart until I found you." He chuckled then continued signing, *"I should've figured you'd be in the supplies aisle."*

I didn't return his humor. I had enough drama with Valerie within the past three hours. I rejected my resistance's weakened state. *"Make an appointment, Noel,"* I signed and walked away to find Valerie. The next time I came face-to-face with Mr. Romance, I wouldn't be tongue-tied.

That night, Noel didn't return in my dreams and I barely slept. Tossing for the third time in less than a minute, I reached over and hit the clock before the alarm buzzed.

The muscles in my stomach were running on a treadmill. My heart rate was climbing, and I was panting. During the night, my mind gave my body a workout. I had to shake off Noel's sudden appearance. All week, I had looked forward to seeing my pastor and fellowshipping with the saints, but all my prayers, fasting, and Bible scriptures hadn't prepared me for Noel. I was determined to stay away from close encounters with him.

After pulling back the covers, I sat on the edge of the bed with my head bowed. I actually dreaded going to church. Noel called me beautiful, but how? I may have looked good on the outside, but on the inside, I was a wreck. Getting up, I went into the bathroom.

I returned to the bedroom and got on my knees. "Lord, I feel my world is crazy right now." The Lord stirred, commanding my tongues to speak unspoken requests. As His power exploded, my troubled spirit relaxed until I whispered, "Amen."

After a shower, I donned a very feminine dress and slipped my toes into four-inch stacked heels. Wanting something different, I swept up a bunch of hair in the back, then twisted and pinned it. My only makeup was a bronzer Valerie had insisted that I purchase while we were shopping. The effect was astounding. I blinked to authenticate it was me. Turning off the bathroom light, I grabbed my Bible and shoulder bag then headed to the kitchen.

"Good morning, Daddy."

He lowered his newspaper and glanced up. "Good morning, princess. You look beautiful, just like the first day your mother smiled at me."

"Thank you." I kissed the top of his head, re-membering my childish request to be more like her when I grew up.

He lifted his *I love Daddy* mug to his lips. "I guess

you'll see that loser today." He squeezed his lips. It had nothing to do with the taste of his coffee. "I can't say I'm sorry about the two of you breaking off the engagement. It saved me a lot of money for a wedding." He squinted at the wall as if Noel's picture was posted on it. "Every time I thought about how he led you on . . ." he snapped his mouth shut. "I better keep quiet, it's Sunday, and I know God's listening."

God's listening all the time, I wanted to remind him, but didn't. "I'm all right, Daddy. I've got this under control. I love him, but I can't go through that hurt again. I'm going to church to praise the Lord." Grinning, I saluted him.

"Pray for your old man while you're at it," he stated before hiding behind his paper again.

"Always, Daddy. Always." Turning around, I opened the refrigerator door for juice and a bagel. After scanning the contents, I changed my mind and reached for a white-powdered doughnut and settled on a tall large glass of water.

Taking a seat, Daddy shared part of the Sunday's *St. Louis Post-Dispatch* newspaper with me while we quietly ate our breakfast. When I finished, I gathered my dishes, rinsed them, and stacked them in the dishwasher. Kissing him again, I strolled out of the kitchen.

"I may come with you next Sunday, princess," he yelled from his spot at the table.

"I would like that." I kept walking. The phone rang as I grabbed the doorknob.

"Mackenzie, it's for you," he shouted.

Returning to the kitchen, I took the cordless

from Daddy's hand. "Hello? Praise the Lord, Pastor Coleman." I smiled at the familiar voice.

"Welcome back home," he replied.

"It's good to be back. I can't wait to hear this morning's sermon." I clutched my Bible and winked at Daddy.

Pastor Coleman chuckled. "Great. I'll ask God to deliver one. Sister Mackenzie, please see me today in my office after service."

"Yes, sir," I confirmed and disconnected. Under my breath, I protested. Great. My first day back at church, and already I had to interpret for one of Valerie's counseling sessions, which meant it had to be either a pre-marital, or marriage session if it was on a Sunday. It was the only time Pastor Coleman scheduled them. My heart raced. Our church had only a few deaf members and none were married. That only meant one thing, an eligible person was about to be wed, and it wasn't me, or the Campbell sisters.

CHAPTER 45

The church's parking lot swelled with cars. Somehow, I managed to seize an empty spot that was camouflaged between two SUVs. My apprehension evaporated once I got out my car, and stepped foot on familiar ground. I inhaled the air as I walked, smiling at recognizable cars parked in predictable spots. Out of pure nosiness, I searched for Noel's car in its usual row. It wasn't there.

I couldn't decide if that pleased or disappointed me. I continued, feeling like Dorothy entering The Emerald City. My heart pounded with excitement, reveling in the memories. Not paying attention, I nearly tripped on Mother Velma Jones' cane.

"Chile, look a here. Welcome home," she announced with open arms, discarding her walking aid. After a death grip hug, she released me and pointed to the ground. "Get that for me, will you, Sister Norton."

Once I retrieved it, I positioned the cane to her liking. She eyeballed me from head to toe. "I've missed you."

"I missed home, too."

"Good, don't make sense to let a young man run you away, any hoot." She nodded, speaking her mind before resuming her wobble to the entrance as I escorted her.

Senior Usher Howard Lane held the door open, waiting for us. "You're lookin' awfully jazzy this morning, Mother Jones," he greeted.

Blushing, she waved her cane, causing her to tilt to one side. We quickly steadied her. Once she was securely inside, he glanced at me and grinned. "Why, Sister Norton, is that you?"

"Yes, sir. How are you?" I smiled, entering the threshold.

He gave me a lengthy, hardy handshake. "As long as I can walk and talk, Sister Norton, I've got no complaints," was his standard response.

In the lobby, others stopped to kiss my cheek or wrap me in a hug. When the choir's booming voices shook the display cabinets in the vestibule, I closed my eyes in thanksgiving. As I veered right to the hall that led to the sanctuary's side entrance, I continued to wave. I still hadn't practiced what I would say to Noel, but who cared? I was so overwhelmed with joy that nothing he said or did could spoil my exhilaration.

Valerie approached me; her face was glowing. Her fingers were intertwined with Nick's. Gone was the distraught woman who was at my house yesterday. Nick's eyes lit up when he saw me. Grinning, he left Valerie's side, and hurried toward me. Still a linebacker in size, he lifted me in a hug, causing one of my new shoes to dangle before it dropped to the floor.

He lowered me to retrieve my shoe. As I tried to balance myself on Nick's shoulder, Noel appeared and shoved Nick aside. "I got this, man."

Dazed, I held my breath as I stared into Noel's wavy black hair instead of the glare from Nick's bald one. After Noel completed the task, he leisurely stood, closing the cozy space between us. His body language dared me to blink, so I inhaled, breathing in his fresh scent that mingled with the air. "Thank you," I whispered.

As Noel nodded, backed away, and disappeared down the hall, my heart screamed, *Wait! Okay, I'm ready to talk now.* What was I suppose to do with the love I still harbored for this complex man?

"Hey," Valerie said, too cheerfully. She embraced me. "Don't think I didn't witness that, but my lips are sealed this time . . . I'm trying, Mack. Prayer does change things and Nick is showing me that. God had Nick before my eyes all this time and I never saw him." She smiled. "God knows what we need."

Walking through the door to the sanctuary felt like the first time. I scanned the pews before locating my heart's desired target. The deaf section had increased and was more culturally diverse. Former deaf student-in-training, Andrea White, sat signing. When I captured her students' interest, she glanced over her shoulder and smiled. Standing, she greeted me with a welcome hug.

We separated as the choir befittingly began their rendition of Israel and New Breed's "Rejoice." The

Campbell sisters sprung from their seats and raced to me, signing for my undivided attention. I pulled them into a group hug.

"I missed you, Sister Mackenzie," Daphne signed.

"I thought you were never coming back," Keisha signed, grinning as she proudly showed off her missing front tooth.

"I'm here just for you, too," I signed, pinching Keisha's nose. *"Now, go back to your seats, you two, so I can talk to you."*

"Okay." Obeying, they skipped their way back to their places, which so happened to be cuddled between their parents and Noel—traitors. Shaking my head, I chuckled, some things never change. Briefly, I made eye contact with Noel. Although he watched me, his expression was unreadable, but I saw a glimmer of admiration, or maybe I was dreaming again. I blinked. A new face came into focus on the other side of Noel.

Unfortunately, Valerie wasn't exaggerating this time. The woman was downright gorgeous. In church, Jealousy reared its ugly head, but I had to forcibly rebuke that spirit. This was my church homecoming not a showdown.

Lord, I thank you for peace because you know the flesh would've been climbing over the pew by now, taking off my earrings and deciding whom to smack first, I thought. I didn't want God to hear that nonsense, but He was privy to it before I thought it. This scenario was simply a trial—spiritual versus carnal; love versus I sure don't like him (since I shouldn't say hate); and you broke my heart versus I'll break your legs.

I turned around, knelt at my chair, and prayed for thanksgiving and strength. I sat as the choir finished its selection. Already at the pulpit, Pastor Coleman spoke to the music director and the choir began their rendition of "Lord, Make Me Over."

I made eye contact with each person in the group as I lifted my hands. Slowly, my fingers brushed the air. Through facial expressions, I testified that I wanted the Lord to make me over. By the time the song ended, tears were streaming down my face. While I attempted to compose myself, Andrea handed me a Kleenex and began to sign.

Emotions under control, my lids fluttered. I scanned the sanctuary, refusing to make contact with the sanctified enemy—as if there was such a thing. A sudden eerie feeling draped my body as I sensed eyes scrutinizing me. My peripheral vision confirmed that heads were tilted in my direction. I did believe many were truly glad to see me, but even more probably wanted to see how a previously engaged sister from the church would respond to her ex-fiancé replacing her with, as Valerie stated, Noel's own kind.

Valerie's eyes were glued to me, too. She may be holding her tongue, but Valerie wasn't going to miss anything. Nick, whose head was bowed in prayer, had his arm securely wrapped around her shoulders. I missed that security with Noel. I sighed to release the memories. Was Valerie right? Did Noel belong to Valerie all along? It sounded foolish, but I reached for a plausible explanation, anything would make sense to why Noel and I didn't work out.

Dismissing the distractions, I bowed my head and rested my hands in my lap, waiting for Pastor Coleman to start his sermon to sign, *"Press toward the Mark of the High Calling,"* Pastor Coleman said. *"That's not a request, but a direct order. God's given you the equipment, now go for the touchdown. Shoving, forcing, pushing, elbowing, thrusting, rushing, and whatever it takes to score that touchdown, or for you ladies, to catch that early bird special. Philippians 3:14 says, I press toward the mark for the prize of the high calling of God in Christ Jesus."*

He shook his head. *"Have you ever heard of anyone competing without a prize, church?"* He looked from one side of the sanctuary to the other. *"What's your mark today? What prize are you trying to win? We're not talking about what you find in a Cracker Jack box. It's bigger than that; it's worth more than the lottery."* Pastor Coleman stopped and pointed to his Bible. *"God's calling you today, you, He wants you. This isn't Uncle Sam calling. This is an Executive Order. It's a private party and an invitation is required."*

I continued to sign as Pastor Coleman preached until a take-no-prisoners tornado touched down and God's commanding presence rushed through the congregation. Men rejoiced as I had never witnessed before—jumping, running, and shouting their praise. Women cried as God touched their bodies and removed burdens from their hearts. No one stayed rooted in the same spot, including Noel, who danced his way into the aisle.

Through my blurred vision and hand clapping, Noel began walking toward me until he invaded the perimeter of my personal space. His arm reached out and touched my face. "It's okay, baby."

When he hugged me, I had no idea why I cried in his arms, at church, or in front of the woman who had replaced me.

CHAPTER 46

Even after I reclaimed my seat, I remained sedated from the warmth of Noel's cradle as the Holy Ghost continued to soar. Since I could no longer concentrate on the remainder of the service, I asked Andrea to continue. I didn't regain mental control until after the benediction and the congregation had scattered from the sanctuary.

Perplexed about Noel's actions earlier, and my response, I gathered my purse and Bible and joined the exodus from the sanctuary. I wanted to go home, but couldn't. "What did Noel mean? Why did I cry? Why did he hug me, and why did I let him?" The questions were producing a brain freeze, without me nursing a Slurpee. I didn't think Tylenol, Excedrin, and Bayer could thwart a catastrophic headache.

I detoured to the bathroom. After closing the door, I walked to the sink and steadied my belongings on the counter. Dabbing my face with chilled water, I prayed and relaxed. My headache lessened, but the evidence lingered. If only I could make it until I got home and could lie down. I didn't like the dazed-looking reflection in the mirror, so I opened my purse and dug through the side pockets for my beauty aids. I reapplied my bronzer and lip gloss. With a critical eye, I looked at my outfit from different angles. I twisted the dress until I had manipulated it properly on my body. Then I dabbed perfume on my neck and finger combed my curls.

The primping didn't keep my mind from reliving Noel's hug. "Maybe that was his apology," I concluded, shrugging as I left the ladies room. In the hall, I rounded the corner and my heart skipped as my feet stumbled. My eyes had not deceived me, but verified what I had already assumed. There *she* was, relaxing in a chair outside Pastor Coleman's office—the competition.

"Hi," she signed.

Oh, she wanted to talk? With as much dignity as my parents taught me, I managed a smile and nodded as I glanced at her hand. The diamond sparkling from her ring finger was bigger than the one Noel had given me. *I need more dignity,* I said only for God's ears. She tried to engage me in a conversation, but I continued on to the pastor's office.

How could Pastor Coleman ask me to sign their marital counseling? Noel cheated me out of experiencing our marital sessions, yet I was about to interpret his with another woman. *God, I can't do this,* I cried out silently.

Yes, you can, He answered.

No, I can't, I argued back.

So Noel was on the other side of the door, waiting for an interpreter. I had been nothing more than a game to toss back into the toy box. I made one last quick eye contact with Sitting Beauty. Not only did she smile, she winked. My fingers tightened their hold around my Bible. Oh, thank God, thank God, thank God, I was in church. Hold your head up, girl; don't let them—no her—see you sweat. Too, late, I'm already sweating. Taking a deep breath, I almost gagged, inhaling my own my perfume.

I stared at the door until I blinked. *Mackenzie Norton, Noel called you baby, he hugged you, he wanted to talk to you. That man is not in that room. Your mind is playing tricks on you. Go on, girl, God said you can do it.* My alter ego gave me a pep talk. Nodding, I swallowed and knocked at the same time Noel's unmistakable laugh escaped.

"Come in," Pastor Coleman's voiced boomed from the other side.

It was too late to back out. Inching the door open, I prayed that the devil was playing with my mind. Pastor Coleman stood from behind his desk. As I stepped farther into the office, Noel came into view as he stood. Refusing to allow Noel to see the hurt in my eyes, I glanced up, looking for help from God. I didn't see a bright light, instead, everything went black.

Light faded in and out until it pierced the darkness. A bearded Noel came into focus. The voice wasn't his. It wasn't strong, but strained. I relaxed, I was dreaming again. Then I heard Pastor Coleman's voice. Alarmed, I shook my head to deny the truth, I wasn't dreaming. I was awake in a nightmare. As a cold sweat covered my skin, I became fully alert. My lids fluttered open as Pastor Coleman stood over me with a bottle of Holy Oil about to pray. Noel was squatting next to me on the sofa where they must have laid me. He looked concerned as he rubbed my hand, but I ignored him.

My pastor moved his lips, but I couldn't register a word. Finally, I understood him. "Sister Norton, are you all right? You fainted. Should I get one of the church nurses?"

Noel aided me as I struggled to sit up. I managed to utter, "Pastor Coleman, is this . . . this is a pre-marital session, right?" I straightened my dress and smoothed away hairs from my face.

"Yes, it is. Brother Richardson assured me that despite the rumors, your November 27th wedding was still on. It's because of those rumors, you'll be the head interpreter for the next few months."

Rumors? I thought. "Pastor Coleman, I thought I was signing for a session. That woman . . ." I pointed to the door.

Taking a seat, he picked up a pen and tapped it on his calendar. "Sister Lana had to reschedule until her fiancé flew in this afternoon, but I do need to settle these rumors. You never contacted me for prayer so I didn't know what to think until you returned. I'm pleased you and Brother Noel worked through things."

I shook my head. There had to be something loose in my brain, because the conversation wasn't making sense. I squinted. "Excuse me?"

"I know this is your first pre-marital counseling session, but Brother Noel assured me you two could wait while Sister Lana and fiancé, Brother David, went ahead of you. He's flying in from Texas and should be here any minute. Your fiancé was keeping me company."

I closed my eyes and pinched my nose. I did need a Slurpee.

"Baby, are you okay? Pastor Coleman, can Mackenzie and I have a few minutes, alone?"

"Considering Sister Norton isn't feeling well, of course. Maybe we should reschedule Sister Lana's counseling session, too, since she won't have an interpreter." He stood and left his office.

Less than fifteen seconds after the door closed, I turned slowly to Noel who had innocence painted on his handsome bearded face. I squinted then opened my eyes to make sure I had a clear perception. My nostrils flared to suck in every drop of oxygen I needed to breathe. I twisted my mouth to exercise my lip muscles. I counted to three before using them.

"You've a lot of nerve," I said angrily, gritting my teeth. The man had never seen crazy until I jumped at him. My left hook missed his stomach. Grabbing my other hand, he foiled the special delivery slap that was making its way to his face, but my heel didn't miss his foot. He wrapped his arms around me, restraining my arms behind my back.

"Hush, woman. This is Pastor Coleman's office." Noel's attempt at whispering missed the mark.

"Let go of me, now!"

"I can't, Mackenzie."

Noel's voice, his touch, his cologne held me captive as I stared into his hazel eyes that I'd missed. When I relaxed, he released me. That's when I elbowed him. "What have you told Pastor Coleman?" I jammed my hands on my hips.

He folded his arms. "If you would've read my text messages, my emails, or taken any of my video conference calls—which you know I hate—then all of this would've made sense. Yesterday, you told me to make an appointment. Well, it's a good thing I had scheduled this meeting a month ago. "

"Don't put this on me, Noel Allen Richardson. You are the one who left me. I have a long memory. Shall I give you the date, hour and second? I can't believe I just acted a fool in my pastor's office because of you." Picking up my Bible and purse, I lifted my chin. "How presumptuous of you to act like we've reconciled when you have no idea what emotional roller coaster ride you strapped me into. I'm not feeling marriage right now." Without a further word, I opened the office door to make a dramatic exit when I bumped into Pastor Coleman who was talking to Lana and another man.

"Excuse us, Pastor. I think Mackenzie needs some fresh air," Noel said behind me, nudging me forward.

Nodding, Pastor Coleman gave me another critical look. "All right, but . . ." he held up the peace sign, "you both need two sessions." Shaking his head, Pastor Coleman invited Lana and her guy, who had arrived, into his office. "Sister Lana, I know you can lip read, so I'll try and go slow and we can use a pad if necessary."

Interlocking his fingers with mine, Noel tugged my hand. "We need to talk, sign, or write notes, but Miss Mackenzie, you will communicate with me."

Humph! He just didn't know. I was Fred Norton's daughter and I didn't have to do anything.

CHAPTER 47

As soon as we walked out of the church, I broke free and released the fury I had dreamt about. "Do you have any idea how much pain and suffering you've caused me?" I yelled and signed. Noel was causing a volcanic eruption of my emotions.

"As a matter of fact, I do." His even toned response just irritated me. Although Noel couldn't hear, he could react to my facial expressions.

I was anything, but calm. This day had become overwhelming. I squinted at his blank expression before turning and speed walking away.

"Wait." He reached out and grabbed me. "Mackenzie." He sighed in frustration. "I went to talk to Pastor Coleman about Valerie's gossiping."

Now he had my attention, so I turned around, frowning. "You what? Why? How could you?"

Stuffing his Bible under his arm pit, he readied his reply by signing, *"How could I? Let's just say I got tired of saints becoming hostile when they greeted me, thinking I'd broken your heart—"*

"You did," I said as my eyes watered.

Noel stared and exhaled before he continued, *"In prayer, God revealed to me that Valerie was feeding you mistruths. I didn't know what she was telling you, but I had to stop the lies. I explained to every mother, minister, and saint in church who would listen to me that I loved you, and you were away to fulfill a dream. Pastor informed me I wasn't the first one to complain and he would take care of it. So why did I do it? Valerie was getting in the way of the love affair I had with you."*

I tilted my head, digesting what I thought he signed. "So," I said, twisting my lips, "you're blaming Valerie for your behavior?"

"No, I'm not."

"Good. See ya." I whirled around and resumed the walk to my car. My dream was less complicated than this. Since Noel didn't call my name and I didn't hear any footsteps, I concentrated on getting to my car and away from him. I dug into my purse for my keys. Just as I retrieved them, Noel snatched them out of my hand. His arms encircled my waist with my keys in one hand and his Bible in the other, trapping me.

"Mackenzie, you don't owe me a thing except to allow me to explain. I owe you so many things, but I need your permission to give them."

I didn't blink, or even breathe until I began to feel faint, then I exhaled. In the distance I heard the rhythmic sound of heels approaching. I refused to turn away, but there was nothing wrong with my hearing.

"Ah, look honey, Brother Noel and Sister Mackenzie have made up."

I didn't recognize the voice as the footsteps faded away. Looks are so deceiving. Just because

Noel had his arms around me didn't mean we had made up.

"Mackenzie, I'm going to let you go," Noel paused, waiting for my confirmation. When I didn't give him the satisfaction, he continued. "All I ask is that we go somewhere and talk, please."

He had too much determination in his voice to be asking. Earlier, his eyes betrayed him. I didn't see one ounce of pleading, instead pure confidence winked at me. His arms tightening around me weren't helping either, because I missed him so much; still I refused to go down without a fight. Looking over my shoulder, I mouthed, "You only get one shot."

Bowing his head in relief, he released me and stepped back. Taking my hand, he massaged my fingers as he led me to his Cadillac. Slipping my keys in his pants pocket, he pulled out his keys and pointed the remote to his vehicle while watching me. Instead of unlocking it, he did the reverse.

I returned the favor and snatched his key ring. I rolled my eyes, and with one push of the button, unlocked the car. He wasn't fazed at his blunder as he opened my door and waited for me to get in. After I buckled up, he leaned in before closing the door. "Once I explain, you'll kiss me, woman, and I don't mean a tap on the lips either."

"I wouldn't pucker up just yet."

After sprinting around his car, Noel got in, buckled up, and drove off. We waved at Pastor Coleman and the first lady as they walked out of the church, holding hands. Afterward, I folded my arms and looked out of the window as we exited onto the highway.

Tired of the silence, I pushed his radio button. The station blasted the song the choir had sung this morning, "Make me Over." Twisting the knob, I lowered the volume. Everything seemed staged, but the choir couldn't be bribed, plus I didn't know how I felt about him taking his concerns about Valerie to the pastor. As a member of the body of Christ, he had every right and an obligation to do so; it was something that I probably would never have done because I tolerated Valerie.

Without an inkling, Noel strolled into my life, stormed out, and then came smashing back. Nothing made sense anymore. It seemed that I was the only one out of the loop. When he turned onto Midland, I knew he was taking me to Heman Park, where memories resurfaced again. Parking his car, he turned off the ignition and faced me. *"Let's walk."*

I wanted to sit in the car and remain stubborn, but I was tired of this mental drama. I met his eyes and almost surrendered—almost. He didn't wait for me to answer as he got out, walked around to my door, and opened it. He squatted until we were eye level.

"Noel, I can't walk through the park in these heels. I need to digest just today's events. Let's talk later this evening, so take me back to get my car."

"No, baby, we're talking now. I'm pressing toward the mark, and Mackenzie, you are my prize."

This man was making me crazy. "I don't think that's what Pastor Coleman meant."

"That's what I mean now and from the first moment I spoke to you."

He was easily dismantling the Noel-resistance I had constructed over the summer, and it was happening in less than twenty-four hours. It started with the Prince Charming slipping on Cinderella's shoe act. I was still trying to figure that scene out, and the hug in the sanctuary. While I asked God to clue me in on what was happening, Noel unbuckled my seatbelt, lifted me out of the car and carried me.

Exhausted from the mental crossword puzzle, I rested my head on his chest and enjoyed the comfort of his arms, signing. *"Your undying love and I'll make you kiss me apology had better be good."*

"Oh, it will be, but if you continue signing to me while I'm walking with you, the scene could be ugly when I trip and we both come crashing to the ground."

I smiled. This was one of the Noel and Mackenzie moments that I remembered. When he didn't put me down, I perked up. Where was the man carrying me? In the distance, I saw my answer— the park table and bench where we had our picnic. He slowed as we neared the destination.

"In the movies, this is the part where some guy dumps his woman, but you mean so much to me that I would never mistreat your heart. I love you, Mackenzie."

I faced him, acknowledging his tender expression. "I love you, too, Noel."

"Good," he said as he rested me on my feet so gently that I almost forgot I was mad at him—almost. "Plus, if I drop you, I'd have to find another woman to marry me, and that's not going to happen," he taunted and took off running for cover, laughing before I could smack him.

We were being silly again. My heels were definitely a deterrent, so I freed myself of the contraptions, unconcerned about my expensive pantyhose, recent foot massage or my self-applied pedicure. I gave chase.

Noel turned around, and started jogging backward. There were no visible signs of exertion. Shaking off his suit coat, he didn't look as it fell to the ground. He loosened his tie and whipped it from around his neck, discarding it like trash.

I couldn't believe it. The man was doing a striptease in the middle of the park, and we'd just left church. So far, I couldn't see a kiss coming out of this.

Since I wasn't an athlete, I couldn't regulate my speed as I barreled toward his chest. To make matters worse, he stood with his legs spread and his fingers wiggling with a smug expression, conveying the message: come and get me. That's exactly where I was heading in less than ten, nine, eight, seven . . . I closed my eyes before the collision.

One minute I was running, the next, firm hands gripped me around my waist, lifting me off the ground. The impact would've caused another man to at least stumble backward. Not, Noel. He didn't sway as he kissed me before planting me on the ground.

Cupping my chin, he focused on my lips. "You okay?"

I nodded, winded. "Now what was that all about?"

"I needed you to run off some steam before we talked." Noel laughed as he bent down and scooped up his jacket, then his tie. He faced me.

"Did you have to striptease, Mr. Richardson?

"I was doing no such thing. I was hot. I usually don't jog in a suit." Noel winked. *"I didn't know you could run so fast."*

"Me either," I mumbled, leaning into him. Now that recess was over, Noel owed me answers. Wrapping our arms around each other's waists, we strolled back as Noel snatched up my shoes along the way. Once we reached the bench, he laid his jacket where he wanted me to sit. Then he stepped up and made himself comfortable on the table.

My eyes feasted on him. He had rolled up his sleeves. Without his tie, Noel unbuttoned his shirt at the neck. Noel's shoes were polished, but the dusty evidence of our frolicking remained. Noel couldn't be confined to a model in *GQ*. Noel was GQ. Suddenly, I felt self-conscious. My near-ankle length dress was airy and carefree, but I was sure my pantyhose didn't survive. When Noel saw my fingers brushing back my hair, he halted the process.

"Don't, Mackenzie. Do you have any idea how exquisite you are? I like the curls you're wearing today. They are a reminder of your wild and sassy personality. It fits your energetic zeal for God. Believe me, I've missed this vision."

I bowed my head to hide the emotions that were stirring within me. That was short-lived when Noel reached out and cupped my chin, easing my face closer until my brown eyes stared into his hazel ones.

"Now you're sure you won't interrupt?"

I jutted my chin in challenge and lifted my hands. *"No, I'm not sure, but I need you to talk to me, Noel. Make me understand what happened the day you stormed out of my house, and didn't return my emails until last—"*

"Mackenzie, you're already interrupting before I have started, baby."

"Sorry."

"I was angry when I walked out of your house that day. I was mad that the devil got into the mix right after we left such an exhilarating church service. I was also devastated that you, my baby, and the woman I asked to marry, questioned my walk with God."

Noel dropped his head, lost in his thoughts. During his intermission, voices competed for my attention. Briefly, I squinted behind Noel's back, bringing into focus men who were playing football. When Noel lifted his head and hands, I snapped back and gave him my attention.

"After our fight, I drove aimlessly around and almost got myself killed a couple of times driving like you."

I rolled my eyes and teasingly punched him in the knee.

"Mackenzie, the first thing I did when I got home was fall on my knees and talk to God. By the time I opened my eyes, it was dark, my clothes were wrinkled, and my stomach muscles ached. I pleaded with God to keep you from losing faith in me, in us."

This man really loves me. I knew it months ago, but the intensity of his expressions confirmed or re-affirmed what my heart refused to doubt all summer.

"Baby, don't ever doubt my relationship with God. To

a person who has always heard, it seems like the most logical thing for a deaf person to want to hear, but that's not always God's will. I had been deaf for about a year when God's voice echoed in my mind. He said that things that happen in my life—good or bad—are for His works to be manifest. John 9 confirmed what God told me."

Reaching for my hands, Noel squeezed them. Without breaking eye contact, he guided my hands to his mouth. The hair from his mustache tickled them, sending shivers down my spine, then he placed soft pecks on each finger.

"I don't need a revival, or healing service for God to manifest His Works. God is God and will do as He pleases, sometimes with witnesses, sometimes without, but when He speaks to me, I'll hear His voice again. I'll admit, you had me doubting myself for a minute. I petitioned God, seeking confirmation that I hadn't missed my opportunity for His blessing. You were disappointed in me, I was disappointed with you, and God was disappointed."

I thought I knew Noel, but I really didn't. Before me was a man who had unshakeable faith in God until I played his hand, having him to question God.

"To regain God's favor, I went on a forty-day consecration and periodically fasted. I studied my Word like never before, and stepped up my prayer life. I ate only one meal a day. During that time, I needed to hear what God was telling me, and you would have been a big distraction, but . . ." he grinned as his eyes flashed his admiration, *". . . as soon as day forty was over, I was hungry to see you."*

What woman wouldn't have blushed, including

me? God, we need to get to the altar—quick. This man was stirring up all the gifts you gave me.

"When I asked Valerie about your whereabouts, she was tight-lipped. Of course, they were loose when it came to making assumptions, and spreading tales as if she had all the facts. I wanted to strangle her, but God led me to go talk to the pastor. By the time I met with him, he informed me I wasn't the only one who had complained. Are you upset about that?"

I shook my head.

He smiled. *"I had no idea what she told you. My text messages—all twenty-three of them—went unanswered. Desperate, I contacted your father through video conferencing. That was a disaster. Again, I sought the Lord. He instructed me to go forward with our wedding plans, according to your specifications and become more aggressive in witnessing to my friend, Lana. At the same time, she met a Christian, David, guy through the Internet, and after three months, he proposed. Since David was a Christian, she was diligent to become one. Sometimes, she had beaten me to church and was sitting in the pew waiting for me. She repented, was baptized, and experienced the fire from the Holy Ghost. Of course, Pastor Coleman wouldn't marry her without those two marital sessions with him. While she was in utopia, I was afraid I'd lost you. I had to trust what God told me. My summer was pure agony while you were vacationing in Chicago. Now, you can speak, sign, or forever hold your peace concerning my hearing."*

"I love you."

"Good answer."

Noel Richardson **ALWAYS**
gets his woman

EPILOGUE

Two days after Thanksgiving at six-thirty in the evening, I, Noel Richardson, fell in love again. It was swift and irrevocable. As I stared into the brown eyes God carefully placed into her alluring face, I had to admit she was the reason I seemed to lose common sense whenever I was in her presence. Yes, I had succumbed to Mackenzie's charm and as her new husband-to-be, I planned to savor all of our sweet moments.

Less than an hour earlier, my evening was a blur. Not because of the day's activities, but because candle lights danced throughout the sanctuary. Our flower girls, the Campbell sisters, were in sync without the sound of music as they began the processional, sprinkling their rose petals onto the runner. They wore identical smiles, purple velvet dresses, and baby's breath in their spiral curls.

Keisha and Daphne had rebelled when they discovered Mackenzie and I were really going through with our wedding. The pair refused to sit with me for three Sundays after Mackenzie returned from Chicago, yet, I think they were happier to see Valerie go. Eventually, they offered their services as flower girls in our nuptials on one condition—if they could take pictures with me on the wedding day without the bride.

I smirked at the memories that disappeared once Daphne and Keisha were parked at the altar. I frowned as I turned to my left. Women! Mackenzie had a scheme up her own sleeve, a deadly weapon—Moses. He was our ring bearer, and Moses wasn't too happy about me taking away his heart-throb.

I looked up as the center doors opened, and swallowed hard. The version of my African-American Cinderella entered the sanctuary, floating to me with a smile gleaming, a contrast to her father's blank expression. I stopped counting the number of times he slammed the door in my face when I showed up at their house. Every time he opened it, I hadn't moved.

His last words were, "I'm not welcoming you into the family, so I won't have to say goodbye when my daughter kicks you out." After that statement, he grinned so wide, I'm sure I saw his wisdom teeth. Today, I had a smile of my own. God had the final word.

The gift God gave me stopped less than a foot in front of me. Mackenzie searched my eyes, looking for the love that I would promise her. When Pierce nudged me, I remembered I was in the presence of guests. The soon-to-be Mrs. Rhoda Wilkerson freed Mackenzie's arms of her bouquet.

Eloquently, Mackenzie lifted her hands and

began to sign as Pastor Coleman asked me to recite my vows. When her hands stopped in mid-air, I knew it was my turn. Speaking, I also signed, *"Mackenzie, I love you. I'll never take my eyes off you. As I sleep, your face will fill my dreams. I will honor you, protect you, and give you my body and soul. I promise to be faithful even though you're a handful."* I chuckled as a tear escaped, blemishing Mackenzie's made-up eyes. "Mackenzie, I will always hear your words before I see them," I said proudly.

Holding my face between her hands, Mackenzie stepped closer. "Noel, you're a praying man, and you've taught me so much. I'm so blessed to know that God created you just for me. You're perfect in every way. *I'll never question that again,"* she signed to me only. "I promise to honor you as my husband, love you as my boyfriend, cherish your presence in my life, and obey you as the head God created you to be. I love you, Noel."

My own eyes misted, but I refused to be a wimp and let one drop fall. Following the pastor's instructions, she signed for the ring. Turning around, Pierce discreetly wrestled with Moses, finally plucking Mackenzie's wedding ring from the pillow.

Once I slipped Mackenzie's ring on her third finger, I couldn't release her hand. When she leaned forward to kiss me, I knew Pastor Coleman had pronounced us husband and wife. A tear revolted, and escaped anyway, once I digested the realization that Mackenzie was now mine, and I was hers.

With our fingers intertwined, we turned and

faced the audience. Instead of clapping, our guests lifted their hands and wiggled their fingers in applause.

Now hours after our reception, sequestered in our plush honeymoon suite, I gazed at my wife. She was a titillating vision adorned in a shear white robe. Underneath, a satin and lace getup beckoned to me. Standing less than a foot away with her arms stretched, the temptress was issuing her invitation. She wasn't fazed about the grotesque scar across my chest. She said she would kiss and make it better. Hmmm, I think it did hurt a little.

"This is our moment, Noel."

God, help me to live through it, I reminded myself to breathe without responding to her. This is what Mackenzie had promised me—our dance. I used all the restraint within me not to ravish her. Instead, I had recalled all the songs I heard prior to my deafness, but at sixteen, what would I consider a romantic slow song?

Becoming impatient, Mackenzie folded her arms and lifted that brow of hers. "Noel, I'm waiting." She eyed me expectantly, teasing.

Accepting my wife's invitation, I moved closer. "I love you, Mackenzie, but right now, looking at you I can't think straight, and I'm trying. There's only one song that keeps coming to mind."

"Let's hear it." Reaching up, her sweet smelling hands dragged my face to hers. I forced myself to look at her lips that fascinated me. "Noel, I'll dance to whatever tune you hear. Go for it."

With permission granted, I did as she instructed. Stepping back, I flexed my biceps before lifting my fist in the air. She wasn't the only tease.

As my muscles shook my black-satin boxers that covered hips, I rubbed my thumb against my finger in a snapping motion.

Mackenzie stepped back, bewildered.

I opened my mouth, and let the words spill, "Ah, ah, ah, ah, staying alive, staying alive. Ah ah ah ah, staying alive." Mackenzie's eyes sparkled with amusement. Mimicking my pose, we danced around our bridal suite. It might have been John Travolta's song, but God gave me the dance and the testimony that I was indeed alive. Plus, I rejoiced because I knew I was going to get my woman. After all, this was my story, and I believe in happy endings. Oh, one other thing, we did dance the night away. That's all you need to know!

BOOK CLUB DISCUSSION QUESTIONS

1. How would you feel if your church started a Deaf Ministry?
2. What do you think about Noel's opinion that he wouldn't be healed unless God spoke the word and it had nothing to do with his faith?
3. Noel didn't seem to be jealous of other persons' healings. Can you say the same when God does something for one person, but not others?
4. Do you know any Valeries in your church? What was her main problem?
5. Would you befriend someone like Valerie?
6. Should Valerie have been reported to the pastor for stirring up confusion?
7. How would you have handled the situation if God told you to pack your friend's bags and ask her to leave?
8. God gave Noel instruction concerning Valerie. Why did he wait?
9. Why did it seem that Noel and Mackenzie argued before or right after church?
10. Can you relate to the discord in your household on Sundays?

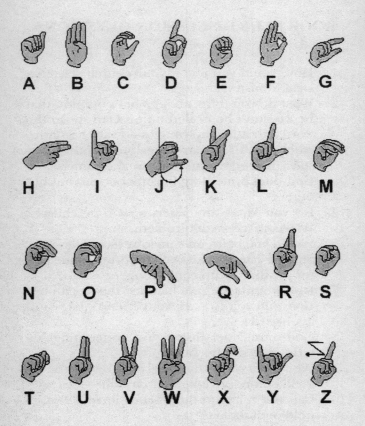

About the author . . .

Pat Simmons is a Jesus baptized believer, and has worked for various media outlets for more than twenty years. She holds a B.S. in Mass Communications from Emerson College in Boston, MA. She is married and has a daughter and son attending college. Her hobbies/interests include getting carried away uncovering dead people whether it is her own genealogy or other families.

She is nosy by nature. She's known for making friends wherever she goes, and being the life of the party—only if there's four guests or less. Pat praises God for the inspiration to write, and the "village people" for helping her get the job done. Her novels include *Guilty of Love, Talk To Me,* and *Not Guilty of Love* (September 2009).

About my characters . . .

Rhoda Brownlee and William Wilkerson actually lived in Mississippi during the mid-1800s. They were my great-grandparents. William's brother, Sam, did actually change his race and move up "north."

Although I haven't been able to verify Rhoda's parents, signs point to Ned and Priscilla Brownlee as her grandfather. Martin Brownlee, b. 1866, was possibly her brother.

Read more about them and take a look at their pictures on my website *www.patsimmons.net.*

Your comments are encouraging and a blessing. Please drop me a note:

pat@patsimmons.net

patsimmons.blog.com

Or 3831 Vaile Ave Box 58, Florissant, MO 63034

Coming Soon

CROWNING GLORY

By Pat Simmons

CHAPTER 1

Without a test, there can be no testimony. Karyn Wallace reminded herself five minutes after she agreed to a date with Levi Tolliver. She wasn't Cinderella, and Karyn doubted the widower would be her Prince Charming.

Yes, she was affected by the most beautiful dark chocolate eyes she had seen in her lifetime. They were hypnotic, even camouflaged behind designer glasses, which were angled perfectly on his chiseled nose. Levi's skin was a blend of chocolates: dark, milk, and white, which created a creamy undefined tone. His thick, black wavy hair and thin mustache were nice touches, but it was Levi's dimples that seemed to be on standby, waiting for his lips' command to smile. Buffed at—she guessed about—five feet, eleven inches, Karyn wasn't intimidated by Levi's height as he towered over her petite stature.

"You might as well surrender to what God has stirred between us," Levi stated as if he had sealed a business deal after his seventh visit, and counting, in a month to Bookshelves Unlimited where Karyn worked as a kid specialist bookseller.

Suspicion set in. *What does he know about God in my life?* At twenty-seven, Karyn was too old to play games. Sometimes the devil injected the word God into conversations as bait to Christians so they would believe they'd found a kindred spirit. Where was Levi's spiritual allegiance? She didn't have time to test the waters to see if she could survive another relationship gone awry. The memories of one bad relationship had a way of lasting a lifetime.

When he moved intimately closer, his lashes mesmerized her, catching Karyn off guard. "Deny the attraction, Karyn."

She hated dares. Bluffs got people into trouble, hurt, or sometimes killed. Karyn blinked. Now, she was getting carried away. Anchoring her elbows on the table in the store's café, Karyn nestled her chin in her hands. She took pleasure in delaying her response. After all, he was interrupting her dinner break.

"I'm attracted to flashy cars, white kittens, black-eyed peas, and—"

"Me," he interjected as a fact.

Karyn refused to confirm or deny his assumption, but she silently admitted she was enjoying their banter. There was something intoxicating about a person who oozed confidence. Despite her outward boasting, building her self-assurance was—at times—an inner struggle. Shrugging, she continued as if she didn't hear him. "Although I don't own a flashy car or a white kitten, I can put away some black-eyed peas."

"Your preferences are noted." Levi lifted a brow and held it in place to make sure he had Karyn's attention. Only after she became impatient did he soften his features and smile, offering his sidekick dimples for her pleasure.

"My Buick LaCrosse is new, but not flashy. My daughter is allergic to cats, and my mother can throw down on any beans, peas, or greens." A dimple winked as he stretched his lips into a lazy grin. "For the past four years, my spirit has laid dormant, waiting on a word from God. Now, all of a sudden, with no warning, I got a message plain enough that even a caveman could read it." He snickered.

Karyn smirked. "I've seen those GEICO commercials, and I'm not impressed."

"I couldn't resist saying that."

"Maybe in the future . . ." She paused and lifted a finger. "But not any time soon." Her refusals were solely based on experience with one man, which she knew wasn't fair.

"Hmmm." He nodded. "At least it's not no again." Snickering, Levi's dimple performed an encore. "After all, with God all things are possible."

She nodded. Karyn knew the scripture—Mark 10:27. That was the first thing she uttered every morning when she prayed after waking up. Levi had been relentless in his pursuit. Why? Her appearance was simplistic: tan pants, a white polo shirt bearing the store's logo, and tennis shoes. A French braid, dipping inches beyond her shoulders, was her trademark hairdo. To some customers, she resembled a teenager, and the pay seemed to fit the description.

Whenever Levi strolled through the door, he received more than a passing glance, whether modeling a tailored dark suit or dressed in business-casual clothes: his pants creased, shirts starched, and shoes polished. When Karyn first noticed him and the wedding ring, she envied the woman who had a wonderful blessing from God: an adorable little girl and a father who doted on his child, calling her sweetheart or darling. He exhibited more patience than the average man.

After that initial distraction, Karyn had sobered during the subsequent visits. She reminded herself that God was an equal-opportunity blessing giver. She referenced Matthew 5:45, where God provided the sun to rise on the good and evildoers while He allowed the rain to fall on the just and unjust.

Tonight, Levi had entered the bookstore with a suspicious, determined stride. His presence was too bold to ignore. Even mall security officers went on alert, but backed off when it was apparent that Levi's intentions were harmless. Strangely, Karyn's busybody coworker, Patrice Lucas, who saw everything and everyone, didn't seem to notice him. She was the poster child for the O'Jays's old song, "Back Stabber." Patrice was the type to be a good friend one day and the worst enemy the next. Karyn was still trying to figure out where she placed on Patrice's list.

What is he up to? she wondered. He never came to the bookstore alone. From day one, Levi's precious four-year-old daughter, Dori, enchanted Karyn. The child had a readymade smile, minus the dimples. Her skin was a few shades darker than

her father's. Her hair was thick, long, and sometimes wild. One and two ponytails seemed to be
the only doable option for the widower.

With the recent chilly temperatures in the last
days of October, Dori was always dressed with
matching multicolored hats and gloves. As Bookshelves Unlimited's kid specialist, Karyn enjoyed
interacting with the little ones, helping them
choose games and books that were age appropriate. In Dori's absence, Levi clutched the handle of
a large gift bag as he roamed the aisles. Confident
she was his target, Karyn waited patiently until
they made eye contact, then he kept approaching.

"Do you have a moment?" He didn't wait for an
answer to his summons as he turned and headed
to the elevated platform that claimed to be the
café's territory near the entrance. It was the only
spacious area in the cluttered bookstore. Already,
Karyn's fist was fishing for a comfortable resting
spot on her hip as she formed an attitude. *If I do,
am I supposed to jump?*

Marking his spot at a white round parlor table,
he laid his bag in a black wood chair with a black
vinyl cushioned seat. The buzz in the coffee shop
didn't miss a beat as he unbuttoned his black suit
coat and claimed an adjacent seat. If he wore a
coat, he must have left it in the car. Levi crossed
his ankle over one knee and leaned back. His demeanor was relaxed and carefree as if it was his
designated VIP seating.

She hadn't planned to follow, but curious as a
feline, Karyn set aside the new shipment of stuffed
animals that recited bedtime stories when
squeezed. She strolled to where Levi was camped

out as if he was royalty. He met her eyes with tenderness. Levi's simmering smile was ammunition to detonate a romantic explosive in some poor woman's life.

For a fleeing moment, Karyn felt unworthy in his presence with her red canvas apron smeared with dust from opening boxes that had been sitting in warehouses. "What's going on?"

"It's a late birthday gift—Happy Birthday—or an early Christmas present—Merry Christmas; whichever works in my favor," he explained, patting the bag with a Macy's logo.

Speechless, Karyn fretted with her braid as her heart pounded wildly. She indulged in a secret moment of excitement. The contents represented anything but a birthday or Christmas present. It was a bribe gift. Karyn knew it and was flattered—confused but thrilled.

"But I . . ." She grasped for an excuse not to accept it, although her birthday and Christmas were ideal reasons.

Levi remained focused as he stood and pulled out another chair as if she was adorned in a ball gown. Karyn scanned the store. Besides the few pockets of café customers, it was a slow night, easily manageable by the supervisor and two other employees. Patrice could stretch any small task into an eight-hour shift.

"Let me go clock out first."

Suddenly, Patrice appeared, arms folded and eyes suspicious as Karyn signed out for a ten-minute break. Patrice didn't smile or frown, but her eyes hinted she was waiting for juicy tidbits to spread—true or false. Karyn always felt uneasy around the unkempt woman. Patrice spoke her mind without fear of censure. Fellow employees called Patrice harmless, but Karyn was wary of the woman's best intentions. Beware was written on her forehead. Since jobs were hard to find, and Karyn didn't want any rumors floating back to her boss to find fault with her, Karyn gave an unobligated explanation, "It's quiet, so I'm taking my last break."

"Sure, go ahead. I've got your back," Patrice encouraged with a wink, then added over her shoulder as she walked away, "Watch it. That guy is way out of your league."

Karyn knew that, but Patrice didn't have to bluntly voice it. Ignoring the small stab to her heart, Karyn headed for the café.

Levi waited at his post in a military stance. She stole a deep brave breath as she obliged his invitation at the table and rested. Levi retook his seat, inching his face closer to hers.

"Do you remember the first time I asked you to go out with me?" he asked.

"Yes."

"Me too." He grunted, amused, and shook his head. "How about the second?" After she nodded, Levi recounted word for word each instance she had turned him down. "To an ordinary man, you would've crushed his ego. I'm not one of them. I'm calling your bluff after your last textbook recital of 'I don't have anything to wear.'" He presented his offering. "Problem solved. I happened to be in the mall this weekend, and you weren't working." Disappointment briefly brushed his face as his words mildly scolded her. "Dori and I made a special trip to buy a book from Miss Karyn. When you weren't here, I thought I was going home empty-handed. My little girl had other ideas for my wallet, so we shopped until I practically dropped."

Karyn laughed. Levi possessed a wonderful sense of humor. He often appeared serious—until he smiled. He was a handsome man.

"When I saw it on a mannequin, I imagined you in that the outfit. I don't know why," he teased with a shrug. "Here's the deal. Since we're both Christians, I know honesty wouldn't be an issue. When you get home, try it on. If it fits, then you've just agreed to dinner with me on Friday night."

This time Levi didn't ask for a date. He already had one orchestrated as he gathered his car keys. Levi shook his head as if he could hear her formulate another ridiculous excuse. "I'll pick you up at seven, and I'm always on time."

Not only had Levi outwitted her, he had removed his wedding band. Karyn wondered at the meaning. On his first visit, thanks to his chatty daughter, Karyn learned his status.

"Daddy's a wido'. Sometimes he's sad. I think he needs someone to play with," Dori babbled on and on as Levi stood nearby, seemingly unfazed by his daughter's assessment. A few visits later, he confirmed his daughter's biography with his ring finger still bearing signs of his bond to his deceased wife.

Karyn looked away, hoping for a customer who needed her attention despite the fact she was on break. When there were no diversions, she swallowed. Accepting whatever was in that bag meant more than a simple dinner. He was challenging her. Again, she hated dares.

Once Karyn found her voice, she shoved doubt aside. She never gambled, but she hoped she was wearing a poker face. She couldn't wait to tear open her present. She knew his taste in men's clothes and little girls' outfits, but what did he envision for her? She beamed anyway. "I agree with your terms."

"I'll cherish your smile until Friday." He winked then adjusted his glasses.

"Don't you need my address?"

"Nope. I followed your bus home awhile back," Levi said, unashamed, then exited the store more conceited than when he first entered.

She didn't register his last remark as she peeked into the bag, but the gift was protected with an army of colored tissue. "Yep. This is definitely some kind of test," she whispered to herself. She had mapped out a schedule for school, work, and church. How was she going to make room for a man?